The Hamilton Conspiracy

by

Andrew Segal

Bloomington, IN authorHOUSE™ Milton Keynes, UK

AuthorHouse™
1663 Liberty Drive, Suite 200
Bloomington, IN 47403
www.authorhouse.com
Phone: 1-800-839-8640

AuthorHouse™ UK Ltd.
500 Avebury Boulevard
Central Milton Keynes, MK9 2BE
www.authorhouse.co.uk
Phone: 08001974150

This book is a work of non-fiction. Unless otherwise noted, the author and the publisher make no explicit guarantees as to the accuracy of the information contained in this book and in some cases, names of people and places have been altered to protect their privacy.

First published by AuthorHouse 3/2/2006

ISBN: 1-4259-0664-8 (sc)

Printed in the United States of America
Bloomington, Indiana

This book is printed on acid-free paper.

My acknowledgements to Aliske Web and Matthew Bell of Bell IT 2000 for their invaluable assistance.

Also, a special thank you to my wife Roberta and daughter Charlotte for their unfailing encouragement and support.

Prologue
Hamilton, Bermuda

January 19, Tuesday. Current Year.

12.00 noon. The elderly gentleman sat back in his armchair, he looked ill at ease and kept running his fingers through the fluffy white hair behind his ears and sipping nervously at his drink. His face and head were brown and wrinkled from years of reclining in the sun, and his hands, similarly bronzed, were gnarled and showed signs of twisting with arthritis.

"They want me to have him arrested." He sounded hesitant, and his speech quavered occasionally punctuating what remained of a once powerful baritone. "One man in particular keeps calling; talks to me in a curiously nasal American accent.

"I know." The young man seated opposite was an Oriental. He wore a pale blue tropical lightweight suit whose jacket sat immaculately on his broad shoulders; the trousers were pressed to a knife-edge. The two-piece looked expensive, as did the white shantung shirt and navy blue silk tie.

A gentle breeze blew in from the open windows of the fourth floor luxury flat bringing with it the sounds of the harbour, the clacking of cables against masts and the shouted instructions to crews involved in maintenance work on the streamlined yachts of their millionaire masters.

"What do you mean you know?" The old man undid another button at the neck of his faded khaki shirt as though it might make some difference in the heat. He sounded perplexed and kept crossing and re-crossing his legs, the knees, bony as his knuckles, protruding from baggy shorts looking like a throw-back to the days of "the Empire".

"I make it my business to know, Judge. That is why my clients never argue my fees." The young man's English was perfect, almost over-precise, and spoken with a soft Chinese accent. He smiled and downed the last of his drink at a single draught, the ice clinking in the heavy cut glass tumbler.

"They've been making threatening noises. Of course, you know it's happened before, though I confess they perturb me this time. But I will not be bullied or bought. If the Chief Justice can be coerced by these thugs, why good heavens, whatever next?"

"Do not be afraid Judge. I shall be watching very closely. After all," the young man smiled again, "that is my profession."

"Yes, yes of course. I'm not really worried, merely, shall we say, concerned. Still I'm glad you're here, my dear. I always feel so much more secure when I know you're in Bermuda, and not sailing that monstrosity of yours around the world."

"I am here for a month, my friend. Then I have to fry another fish."

"You mean you have other fish to fry. I'm afraid our proverbs seem to lose something in the translation." The Judge was quietly amused. He glanced at the young man's empty glass and levered his fragile frame out of the easy chair. "Let me get you another. Won't you have something a little stronger this time?"

"Later perhaps. For now, the papaya juice is very refreshing."

He handed his tumbler to the Judge who took it, and his own which needed replenishing, to the drinks cabinet behind the young man where he threw a handful of ice cubes into his glass first, giving himself a generous measure of whisky. Then he picked up a jug of juice and started to pour for the young man. "How long have I known you now, Kim? Four years? Five? And I wish you wouldn't call me Judge all the time."

"Seven years, Osbert." The same soft tone.

"Seven years. My God! Where's the time gone? Where has it gone? We shall all be old before we know it." He chuckled to himself in an undertone as the heavy lead crystal ashtray smashed into the back of his skull splitting it wide open, his brains ballooning out into the nape of his neck. He fell to the floor without a murmur, his lifeless eyes gazing up at the young man who stood over him.

The young man laughed, a high pitched staccato that seemed to reverberate and hang in the air. "Yes," he said glancing thoughtfully at his watch as he turned to make his way out of the apartment, "It is late, and I have to fry another fish."

* * *

The mid morning sunshine blazed through the large picture windows bathing the furnishings in it's light. From the kitchen came the pop and bubble of coffee percolating, its aroma wafting into the living room occupied by the woman. In the modern apartment the only other sound was the soft hum of the air conditioning, its rhythm broken momentarily by the click of the front door as her visitor made his departure.

The woman was in her mid to late thirties, her square features could have been described as handsome rather than beautiful. Her stylish spectacles were snapped in two. One thick lens forced from its frame had rolled along the floor leaving a straight red line in its wake, before finally coming to rest standing improbably on its edge like a solitary wagon wheel. From where she lay, her arms outstretched, her legs bent slightly to one side, the woman's unseeing focus was fixed on the chandelier.

Her suntan contrasted starkly with her white clothing, a sleeveless blouse, and pleated skirt now in disarray about her muscled thighs. On the white marble floor her hair spread around her head like a fan, a fan that seemed to move and change in shape and hue from its natural mousy colour to something glowing, something radiant, as sticky red spaghetti streaks oozed through its strands making a fluid halo that burgeoned quickly until it circumscribed her from top to toe in a giant crimson lake.

As death confirmed its hold on her and the bloom of life drained from her cheeks her expression became transformed into the smooth tranquility of a sleeping child.

From somewhere distant came the sound of something like a hysterical peal of laughter, or perhaps it was just the high pitched yapping of someone's dog.

Chapter 1
Hamilton: Bermuda

November 10th Tuesday, Previous year

A dazzling yellow sun nosed its way over the horizon casting shimmering silver on the navy blue surface of the sea. Dancing and looping over the water, a yellow-breasted kiskadee screamed its name over and over again.

Dotting the promenade, a handful of early morning joggers breathed the clean fresh air of a new day while a few floors above them, cocooned in five star luxury, one professional gentleman thrashed about in a restless half-slumber.

In his hotel room Jack Gregory rubbed the sleep from his eyes, dragged the silky sheets from his body and stumbled towards the marble tiled bathroom where he subjected himself to a barrage of lancing icicles under the shower. They stabbed at his chest and back hammering him into a shivering and reluctant wakefulness. Roll on lunchtime, he thought.

* * *

With a series of small splashes the two men slipped into the water and swam for the shore leaving barely a ripple behind them. Ammonium Nitrate Fuel Oil, AMFO, to demolition experts, had been planted strategically. The bang, when it happened, would be a big one.

* * *

Jack Gregory had arrived at the conference centre, nervous and uncertain. A tall man, he was vastly overweight, and despite an immense natural physical strength, he was panting and perspiring by the time he entered the building.

The modern concrete block was as forbidding as a prison, the sun reflecting off the pairs of windows in the glass frontage like sets of laughing eyes. If he'd hoped that few people would show up this morning, Jack was disappointed; when he entered the starkly modern foyer with its dull grey, square-backed easy chairs, square coffee tables and square, hanging light fittings, he found the place a seething mass of grey and navy suits.

An announcement was soon made over the speakers, and like a moving tide the throng ebbed and flowed towards the double doors leading into the conference chamber. People found their places in seats that had been arranged theatre style, facing a top table upon which had been laid out tumblers, jugs of water and a stack of copies of the statement of the company's affairs and report that would be issued to them all shortly.

Now, as the hum of conversation receded like water slipping from a bath Jack knew that the time had come. He scratched the back of his bull neck and sighing apprehensively, indicated to his colleague with a slight hand movement that he was ready. The other man scraped back his chair and rose to his feet. The day was only starting, and with it the fight of Jack's life, a fight worth $40 million to the winners.

Let battle commence, thought Jack. There was an instant of complete silence in the room broken by the confident tones of the chairman's voice.

"Good morning, ladies and gentlemen, this is a formal meeting of the creditors of Central Reinsurance Ltd. convened under Section 216 of the Companies Act 1981 for the purposes of appointing a Liquidator and a Committee of Inspection." The distinguished Mr. Anthony Trent, chartered accountant and licensed insolvency practitioner smiled expansively at those facing him, his distinctive aftershave a halo of expensive fragrance. The man's confidence was a public signature of one who had trodden this path many times before.

Seated next to him at the top table, and facing a gathering of some eighty or more angry looking business and professional people was Jack Gregory, principal director of the company, and like Trent, a licensed insolvency practitioner.

With eyebrows meshing into a black frown, Jack felt anything but distinguished this morning. "Vermin," he reflected savagely. "Out for the kill." He hunched his broad shoulders forward, his anxiety giving way to belligerence. If it's a fight they wanted, they'd get one. No way Jack

Gregory was going to simply hand over a decade of his labour like a charity donating alms to the poor.

As Anthony Trent continued his satin smooth preamble, Jack sat clenching and unclenching his fists as he contemplated in a trembling rage the unfolding of the series of events he could not have anticipated in his worst nightmare. Not two months ago, comfortable and self-assured with his lot, he'd enjoyed the status of self-made multi-millionaire. Life was good, very good.

Now, today, facing his creditors, Jack made sporadic attempts to ignore the fact that his world might shortly crumble into ruins. That he was facing the plunder of his empire by ruthless corporate bandits, so called 'respectable' directors of an American based international group of insurance companies bent on nothing less than Jack's total financial destruction.

Occasionally the noises of the harbour permeated the claustrophobic atmosphere of the conference room sounding like murmured promises of freedom to Jack and, unconsciously, he sighed at the prospect.

Whatever happened, Jack still had a slim hold on the principal source of his wealth, his company, Central Reinsurance. His colleague, Anthony Trent, would shortly be voted, by the majority of the creditors present, into the post of liquidator of Central, and matters would be brought under their joint control once more. The sharks cruising around waiting for tasty morsels of Jack's company to tear at could go to hell.

A school of half a dozen of them in dark, designer suits was ranged at the front of the conference room taking copious notes and conversing in conspicuous undertones. Jack saw the flash of gold pens, and the flicking and turning of the pages of the financial statements issued to the meeting. Occasionally, one of them would cast a glance in Jack's direction. They looked irritated, and amused; mixed signals which might have been difficult for the casual observer to interpret but to the seasoned professional, there would be only one conclusion -- that the group were here for someone's head: Jack Gregory's, on a plate.

Jack was certain of one thing -- this was the US contingent. Milling about in the anteroom prior to the start, Jack had overheard a muttered but clear Southern States American drawl: "Gregory's a fool. Shoulda sold out when he had the chance. Sure has left a lotta cash lyin' around for us to take over and invest for him." Someone sniggered, and at that moment Jack had felt the first tremor of uncertainty. Had Tony and he thought of everything in preparing for this morning? Did these people know something they did not?

The sun poured through the plate glass windows like molten lava so that despite the humming air conditioning the overcrowded room was oppressively hot and Jack constantly pulled at the front of his shirt collar to prevent it from sticking to his neck. In the background, Tony's ongoing soft delivery went some way towards soothing Jack's ragged nerves and he breathed deeply to further subdue his heaving chest.

As long as Tony could persuade this gathering of creditors to vote him in to the post of liquidator everything would be alright. That was the key. The alternative, which hardly bore contemplation, was the complete loss of Jack's and Tony's control over Central Reinsurance's millions.

* * *

Now ashore, the two men nodded briefly at one another before making for their parked car, their wet footprints quickly evaporating in the mid morning heat. Safe within its hiding place the consignment of AMFO moved about uneasily with the swell.

* * *

Jack thought briefly of his wife, Phyllida. She would be in their Paris flat right now, mid-afternoon in France. He pictured her flawless alabaster skin, the thick auburn hair, always immaculately groomed, her slightly breathless way of speaking that he found so devastatingly attractive. He had insisted she wait for him there. "Everything will be fine," he had promised her. "The creditors can blow hot and cold if they want. I'll tell them we're just looking at a temporary hitch before they get their money back."

A temporary hitch?

Maybe. But then.... who could tell? There was no way this morning's events could be predicted with any degree of certainty.

Jack's mood shifted erratically. He'd been up till nearly four a.m. in his hotel room drinking whisky and coffee in alternate sessions and his eyeballs felt as though they were plastered to the insides of their sockets. He'd finally fallen into a troubled sleep and then woken, briefly, in a cold sweat an hour later having dreamt he was trying to hitch a lift on some lonely US highway, his wife having left him taking the baby with her.

What if the vote went against Tony? Jack pondered. With a fortune up for grabs? Jack ground his teeth and ran his hands over his receding black hair. Anything was possible.

Jack's company, Central Reinsurance had assets amounting to a colossal $40 million, most of it in recently liquidated cash reserves nestling snugly on interest bearing accounts in a cluster of US banks. The company's debts were barely half that sum. The business was totally solvent, able to pay all its debts in full, this morning's confrontation was a farce that should never have happened.

It had been a two or three year build up of events that had culminated in Jack finally deciding to quit the reinsurance game nine months earlier. It was clear that his foray into the fabulous money making whirl of Bermuda based US insurance companies was coming to an end. Now that the international giants had entered the game, he was faced with a simple choice. Amalgamate, or withdraw. For Jack, ever the maverick, there could only be one choice -- as he put it to Phyllida - and that was to take his accumulated millions and retire gracefully.

Time, at forty-four years of age, to cut back on eighteen-hour days and endless jetting around the world.

Time to settle permanently in the UK, and spend his evenings in front of the television, or playing with Harriette, their eighteen month old daughter he hardly knew.

Maybe even find the time to reintroduce himself to Phyllida, his beautiful and ever patient wife of just three years. Ever patient? Jack smiled grimly to himself. Would she want to stay with him if this all went wrong? Phyllida had lost her father when he was still a comparatively young man. Then, not long after, her first husband had been killed shortly after they'd married. Even now, Jack wasn't sure that she'd ever really got over the shock.

And there was something else in Phyllida's past. Jack was sure of it. But whatever it was she kept it to herself, unwilling to be drawn out, or to confide in him. She would go into periods of silence where she'd gaze vacantly into space. She worried. About everything. Despite Jack's wealth, the sight of an unpaid household bill could send her into a panic.

Just as well Phyllida wasn't here to watch this ritualized torture. Jack was sure he made her happy though, brought her some measure of tranquility. He closed his eyes and sensed the perfume of her body, the delicious scent of her when she was aroused. Her eyes fluttering with desire and that come-on look she gave him when they both knew there was no turning back.

God, I should be concentrating, he thought. His financial life was hanging in the balance, but his head was still leaden from last night and he found it hard to focus. He looked up. The company's history was being detailed by his friend. Anthony Trent's concerned gaze caught his eye, "You okay, Jack?

"Fine, fine." Jack nodded back at him reassuringly.

How many times, he wondered, had he been in Trent's position addressing the creditors of a failed company before tying up the appointment as its liquidator, gaining full control of its assets.

Insolvency was Jack's life. He'd built his practice nursing it lovingly through bends and straights like a Formula 1 driver. It was the one profession that could give reign to his combined genius with both figures and legal matters, together with his instinct for making fast commercial decisions and getting them right first time. And of course, it had earned him big bucks.

Jack gulped some iced water from the glass in front of him. It tasted crisp and cooled him, briefly. Trent's voice murmured on but Jack was still miles away. Again, Trent caught Jack's eye. He looked increasingly worried, "Jack?" he muttered under his breath. But Jack merely inclined his head encouragingly as before.

On the human relations front, Jack would have been the first to admit he was no angel. Bigger and heavier than most of his peers at school, he'd established a reputation for being an arrogant bastard by the time he was fourteen years old and a lot of the other boys longed to see him cut down to size. He never gave them that satisfaction.

In business Jack was used to employing the same tactics, shouldering his way in to a situation and then barging aside those who stood in his way. If he wanted something he got it and the attitude coloured everything about his life. Obsessive about physical strength and what it represented to him in terms of his own driving ambition, he'd pursued a regime of weight training in his teens that would have done credit to an Olympic athlete.

Later, when work commitments made it impossible to find the time to exercise he'd found himself abating some of his relentless energy in food. Eating when entertaining clients or when on the hoof. Eating when he was hungry, and when he was not. There were never any half measures. Jack also drank too much, usually a cocktail of whisky chased with Drambuie, a `rusty nail', by the double and in quantities not for the faint hearted. Over the years the physical strength had remained but the physique was now hugely overloaded. Jack looked like a clipper in full sail, a tethered hot air balloon, a waddling Humpty Dumpty of a man.

It was morbidly fascinating for one as overbearing as Jack to find himself on the receiving end of events. There'd be no bully-boy tactics from Jack Gregory today. More like Horatio holding the bridge.

Two of the American crowd were looking in Jack's direction and openly grinning.

Jack's stomach felt as though a worm was slithering around its walls. Could he count on Phyllida keeping her nerve if he faced defeat today? And if not? He acknowledged the dreaded prospect, what would his life be without her, and Harriette?

* * *

The telephone rang on Karl Mallett's desk and he grabbed it eagerly from its cradle, his long bony fingers squeezing it as though it might at any moment escape his grasp. "Karl Mallett," his voice was hoarse, impatient.

"The meeting started on time, Mr. Mallett. Everything is under way. Everything is under control." The speaker had a gentle Chinese accent whose polite, almost whispered, tones bore no more than the hint of jeopardy.

"Luke get in okay?"

"Of course. I made sure Mr. Hepton's proxy was in order. There was no reason for him to be excluded."

"Good. AUIG's people with him?"

"Yes, Mr. Mallett, representatives from American Union Insurance Group are with him. They are well equipped with details of their claim against Central, in case they're needed. And Mr. Hepton is carrying copies of English insolvency legislation with him."

"What about this guy taking the meeting, Trent? You said he's good, got real balls. We really gonna steal this job from under his nose?"

"I should think so."

"That the best you can do? You should think so? We got a lotta money hanging on this, baby. According to Luke there's forty million in US banks just begging for us to go in and collect."

"He's correct. Don't worry, Mr. Mallett."

"I don't know. I've had a bad feeling about this one from the start; and Clay's with me on this." Mallett nodded at a pudgy, pale-faced man sitting on the opposite side of his desk who signalled his agreement. "I mean what the hell do we know about English insolvency law that says we can take on a seasoned pro like Trent and beat him at his own game? And what about the AUIG claim? It's about as straight as a corkscrew. I know Luke's got big ideas, but, Christ, Hepton Mallett Dixon's supposed to be a respectable law firm."

"As you said, Mr. Mallett; forty million dollars. You and Mr. Dixon think about that and trust me. If Mr. Hepton remembers my briefing, you'll see, Mr. Trent will shortly be consigned to oblivion; together with his associate, Mr. Jack Gregory."

There was a long pause. Then, "Okay, my friend. We'll wait for Luke's call. It all sounds cool. Let's make sure Trent and his pal don't know what's hit them."

"I assure you, Mr. Mallett, we're as good as there already. It really is all too amusing." The sound of a high pitched, long drawn out giggle floated from the telephone receiver, and the line went dead.

* * *

The two men shook the water from their clothes before climbing into the silver, 7 series BMW that had been parked a few paces away. The inside of the car was like a kiln, still the air conditioning would soon have them in a delicious cocoon of cool air.

* * *

At the meeting, Trent had moved on to the Statement of Affairs, explaining the financial details of the company. Time was passing quickly though Jack continued to be largely oblivious to it.

From the increasing blue-grey fog, a swirl of cigarette smoke wafted around Trent's head, and he waved it away with a casual flap of his hand, continuing his presentation in the calm tones of a professional with twenty years of dealing with hostile creditors on occasions like this.

People were showing signs of becoming restive in the stale atmosphere, with a shifting of feet and shuffling of papers.

Trent had been on his feet for fifty minutes and was at last drawing to a close. Jack straightened up and forced himself to think clearly. The back of his neck prickled with anticipation. In a moment he would face a bout of questioning that would require intelligent and specific answers from him. He breathed deeply and pressed his damp hands into his lap. He had no satisfactory answers for them because he was almost as ignorant as they were about the events that had precipitated the gathering.

"That completes the company history and Statement of Affairs." With a rustling of papers, Anthony Trent stacked his documents together and cast his eyes about the room. "All creditors' claims," he continued, "with the exception of those submitted by American Union Insurance Group are agreed.

Reaching into his inside jacket pocket, Jack extracted a Dunhill panatella and was about to light it when he paused. Best not to look too relaxed, he decided, and put the cigar away.

"Let me be absolutely clear, ladies and gentlemen," Trent gazed intently at the bank of staring faces, "had it not been for the receipt, two months ago, of the stupendous claim from AUIG, that item detailed on your list in the sum of twenty-two million dollars, a one hundred percent payout to you all would have been a matter of days away."

That fact should put some of them on my side, Jack thought, grimly. Now, Tony just needs to tell everybody; one, that the AUIG claim is pure fiction; two, that he and I are not associated professionally; and, three, allow a few questions from the floor before he wraps up the vote so we can all go home happy.

Trent paused for a moment to let the significance of his last comment sink in before continuing, "The AUIG claim changes all that, as I have explained." He stared straight at the group of six seated at the front. Sitting inelegantly sprawled back, a tall gangling individual with thin reddish brown hair stuck to his tiny skull, smirked insolently at Trent who pointedly ignored the man's gaze.

"The claim is disputed," Trent raised his voice as if to counter the obvious contempt of the tall man. "But as it suggests that Central might be unable to pay its debts within the twelve months stipulated in legislation, Mr. Jack Gregory, director and until now liquidator of the company, has convened this meeting for the purposes of confirming a new and independent nominee."

Trent inclined his head courteously and continued, "Today's appointee will of course investigate the AUIG claim and report back to creditors in due course."

Well; that's item number `one', out of the way, Jack thought. Now let's talk about professional relationships.

Anthony Trent slipped a hand casually into the jacket pocket of his lightweight Armani suit and smiled reassuringly at the assembly. "Let me at once declare my own position. Jack Gregory is a valued professional colleague of many years standing. However, I must emphasize that I have had no dealings whatsoever with Central or Mr. Gregory acting as its director and feel there would be no conflict of interest in my taking the appointment, should creditors choose to confirm it today."

Jack breathed again. And that's `number two', taken care of. Jack allowed himself a fleeting thought of his lovely Phyllida and grinned inwardly.

All cards were on the table. It would have been unethical, indeed disingenuous for Tony to deny their friendship. Better to be open and spike the opposition's guns at the outset. Despite his trepidation, Jack had to admit to himself, it was looking good. Tony was clearly on top form. Best, of course, not to count your chickens... but still, he smiled to himself, there was definitely room for cautious optimism.

Now for the big one, question time, he breathed, followed by item number `three' on the agenda, the vote.

Jack glanced at Tony, waiting for his friend's next announcement, and out of the corner of his eye, he noticed the tall American speaking animatedly to one of his colleagues. He was pointing to something on the statement of affairs. Had Jack and Tony forgotten anything?

* * *

Phyllida had paced the flat nervously all afternoon. Now, moving from the elegant rosewood drinks cabinet in the drawing room, she wandered into the kitchen with her glass. Checking and rechecking her watch she took a sip from her sherry. It spread a lovely warm sensation down her throat and into her stomach but didn't take away the feeling that all was not as it should be. Jack should have let her go to Bermuda to be with him. How could she be a loving and supporting wife thousands of miles from her husband. Not that a man like Jack actually needed any support. Without him, she felt isolated in Paris, becalmed and in the dark. She wanted him to call, to have him tell her everything was alright, to hear the reassuring tone of his voice.

She caught sight of her reflection in the glass of the new Neff oven door. Her skin looked blotchy pink and her mane of reddish brown hair stuck out untidily in all directions. She self-consciously dragged her fingers through it, realizing guiltily that she would never have neglected her appearance for a whole day if Jack had been with her. She really should get out of her housecoat and into some clothes as well. Tightening her belt into the tiny waist that accentuated her overlarge bosom, she shoved her hands deep into her pockets. Maybe in a minute.

It was now five fifteen p.m., the shadows on the streets below grew longer. Sounds of the evening traffic floated up to the apartment.

The meeting must have been going on for over an hour. Jack insisted the whole thing would be over quickly. Just a formality, he said. But his voice had been a growl when he said it and his forehead was criss-crossed with lines of tension. If only he would talk to her.

They couldn't simply take away ten years of Jack's life. Who were `they' anyway? These AUIG people with their crazy twenty-two million dollar claim.

Phyllida climbed onto a stool at the breakfast bar in the oak and pine panelled kitchen, a copy of Le Monde in front of her. Draining the last of the sherry, she idly turned some of the magazine's pages, her eyes skating over pictures of French politicians and members of the British Royal family.

Harriette was playing quietly with her toys in the bedroom; occasional sounds of happy gurgling caressing Phyllida's consciousness. Something would have to be done about dinner soon, at least for the babe, though Phyllida wouldn't touch a thing herself until she heard from Jack.

Another cup of tea perhaps. No, she'd drunk so much today it was positively oozing from the pores of her skin. One more Harvey's Bristol then. Or perhaps not. A fourth wasn't a good idea. Three was her absolute limit. Any more would go to her head and Jack would be furious if he thought she'd been drinking again.

Dear Jack, she thought. A man who made things happen. Though they were temperamentally opposites, Jack was like Daddy had been. A man only interested in carving his own furrow. Except Daddy was no longer around. Poor Daddy. All those years building up the print business; the battles with the trade unions, boardroom politics and deadlines. Then just as everything was coming together, and a purchaser of the company had been found in a sum that would guarantee his comfortable retirement, wham! A massive heart attack and he was gone within hours. It hadn't seemed possible.

She always felt safe with her father, despite the early financial struggles. Maybe it was because of those initial setbacks that she'd become so insecure.

After Daddy there'd been her first husband, Tom, to look out for her, at least until the accident. A drunk driver on New Year's Eve. Tom had been beautiful; taller than Jack, with a physique like a Greek god. Thick dark hair and black flashing eyes which always carried the spark of mischief. Sex with Tom had been a voyage into the unknown. A practical joker in things outside the bedroom, when it came to matters inside the boudoir, he was a visionary who knew how to tease a woman until she was screaming for it and then to liberate her in a drawn out ecstasy of release.

With Jack, sex was a more tentative affair, despite his obvious experience and the considerate way he pleased her. It was as though he were touching a china doll, afraid she might shatter against his enormous bulk. He needn't have worried, but Phyllida didn't know how to put it to him without offending him.

Tom had just been starting out, when they first married. Beginning to build an architectural practice. Her memories of their time together were mainly of laughter. Money had been tight, and Tom would never have been wealthy like Jack. Nor even as well set up as Dad. But she adored him, and they'd have been happy.

She had hoped to pursue a career in music. She had real promise, but with marriage she put everything on hold. As a young widow, she finally realised she was neither trained nor qualified to do anything. Too late to consider taking up music again, and loath to be a burden to her mother, the future looked bleak until she met Jack. Her man of iron. Jack was a risk taker, he told her early on in their relationship. You had to speculate to accumulate, he said. Phyllida found that life with Jack was like the thrill of a helter-skelter. With Jack anything was possible, and most things he set his sights on became probable. It was power -- that absolute assurance in self.

The phone rang out and Phyllida jumped up and snatched the receiver off the wall-mounted cradle. "Jack!" she exclaimed excitedly.

"*Comment*?" came the reply.

It was a wrong number and Phyllida sat down again, depressed.

Five thirty. She frowned. Meetings could last as long as two hours, Jack had told her.

Pointless worrying really, Jack was certain to have everything under control. She calmed herself, sighed and then climbed off the barstool and made her way to the drinks cabinet to replenish her glass. It couldn't hurt. Maybe a tumbler this time, so she wouldn't need to go back for a refill later.

Wandering back to the kitchen, Phyllida took a gulp of her sherry. They had a superb home in Burchetts Park just outside West London, and this luxurious flat here in Paris. As she thought about them, she found herself becoming agitated yet again. Might they have to forfeit either of them? Both of them?

She closed her eyes and considered the lavishness of their lifestyle. She knew she was being selfish and shallow. She was agitating about nothing. There were more important things in the world than stylish homes. She and Jack were both still comparatively young and healthy. Jack had other businesses and many talents. Realizing how foolish she was being about everything gave her a new sense of optimism. She took another swallow of her sherry. But then again, she thought, what if things didn't go as expected? What if Jack were wrong after all? Or worse, what if he was just humoring her? She shuddered as an acid wave of nausea welled up inside her like a tide of dirty water. Resting her forehead in her palms she realised she was crying. Five forty-five. How much longer before he called?

Tears ran down her face and she wiped them away with the heel of her hand. The vote would have to go Jack and Tony's way, she rubbed her eyes with bunched fists. It would simply have to.

She took a dainty sip of her drink. She must be calm. Breath in slowly. One, two. One, two.

But where was he? Throwing back the last half of the tumbler of sherry in one gulp, she thought, Jack, darling! In God's name, how much longer?

* * *

Having discreetly struggled into dry jeans and tee shirts within the confines of the vehicle, one of the two men slipped behind the wheel, gunned the engine of the big BMW into life and then pointed it towards the centre of Hamilton. The roof of the car burned hot in the midday sun and the tires made a sticky hum on the surface of the road.

* * *

"Are there any questions at this stage?" Trent resumed his seat and glanced to left and right. Jack shook his head as if to clear the cobwebs, folded his hands together interlocking the fingers and thought, okay people, if you're going to shoot me down, now's your chance.

For a bare instant nobody spoke. For Jack, it was the time to feel a thrill of anticipation, it was all going to go through on the nod. A formality. Like waking from a bad dream. Brilliant.

Trent looked up from his notes and glanced around the room. The formal business was the next item on the agenda and with it the all-important vote that would determine Jack's future.

Next to him, Jack heard the slight rustle of Tony's jacket as he straightened one sleeve. The slow casual movement was reassuring. The quiet held. He was there. All that money saved. Company intact. Control maintained.

Then, like a toe in the door, a small but articulate voice close to the front of the conference room cut into the silence.

She was in her late twenties and dressed in a yellow sleeveless blouse and sensible brown skirt. A short boyish haircut gave her an elfin appearance. Her brief-case sat across her lap like a desktop with papers strewn over it. She held a ballpoint pen in one hand and, with one extended forefinger, settled her heavy horn rimmed spectacles on a nose seemingly too small to support them.

Jack recognised the type immediately and groaned inwardly.

She was a professional, `meetings person'. One who worked the circuit on behalf of client creditors, ostensibly for the purpose of reporting the proceedings, but with the real object of diverting the vote from the top table ideally in favour of her own employer.

In short, a harbinger of trouble, in this case big trouble. Her only likely competition would be from others with the same idea in mind.

The gentle rise and fall of Tony's breathing emphasised the man's absolute calm. Jack felt taut, though not yet unduly alarmed. He generally preferred being questioned by the women professionals whom he always found competent and well prepared and, unlike their macho brothers, polite.

"My name is Jennifer Clark, of accountants Jackson Tullogh in the UK. I represent Mid-West Insurance which is owed just $20,000. We're not the largest creditor here." Settling her spectacles on the bridge of her nose with the point of her forefinger, she sounded almost apologetic.

Get on with it then, Jack thought.

"I have just one question." She waved her ballpoint in the air as though she were shaking a thermometer.

"Yes, Ms Clark." Trent was smiling, leaning forward on his hands, encouraging, avuncular. "Please go ahead."

Ms. Clark then proceeded to engage in a recap of the whole of Tony Trent's company history, hammering him with questions on every detail of its life from inception to date. She took copious notes, and suffered no interruptions. The ballpoint pen was continually waved about in the same innocent and childlike gesture. It was as if that toe in the door was forcing it wider every moment and Jack began having visions of the meeting drifting from the control of himself and Tony.

* * *

A couple of hundred yards away, the cache of Ammonium Nitrate Fuel Oil surged slightly as though echoing the unease at the creditors meeting. It wouldn't do if the bang happened too soon.

* * *

Trent, who looked perfectly composed, fielded most of the enquiries himself, only occasionally looking to Jack for assistance.

"And what about this claim from American Union Insurance Group?" Ms. Clark's pushed up her horn-rimmed spectacles. Her voice was curious.

The group of six representing AUIG continued to whisper among themselves, shuffling papers and turning pages of the financial statement, apparently taking little notice of anything going on.

A long blast from the hooter of a yacht knifed into the room and Jack thought about his own boat, the "Phyllida" and wished he was on it, wished he was in Paris with his family, wished he was out of this damn place.

Anthony Trent answered, "The claim landed on Mr. Gregory's desk out of the blue a few weeks ago. When he saw it...."

"Mr. Trent," she interrupted him curtly, "I wonder if we could have some replies from Mr. Gregory. You seem to be doing a great deal of talking on his behalf." She had had the floor exclusively for nearly three-quarters of an hour.

The entire room was staring at him and Jack felt a *frisson* of doubt, a feeling that something unexpected was starting to happen.

* * *

In a bar in the centre of Hamilton two sun-tanned young men in jeans and tee shirts sipped ice-cold lagers. Neither man spoke to the other. One of them glanced at his watch from time to time.

* * *

Trent was totally unperturbed, "Of course, Ms. Clark." He flashed a smile at her. "Mr. Gregory, perhaps you'd like to come in here."

"Certainly," said Jack. "I received the claim from AUIG about two months ago."

"Can you be more precise, Mr. Gregory?" Ms. Clark's pen was poised expectantly.

"Well, no. I don't remember the exact date." Jack had heard this approach from the floor at least a hundred times before. Work some trivial line on the director until you make him a nervous wreck. Then home in for the kill. Nominate your own choice of liquidator and bludgeon the chairman into surrendering his position.

"Mr. Gregory," Ms. Clark was smirking. Crossing her legs she resettled the case across her lap and adjusted her horn rimmed spectacles with the point of her forefinger. "Do you expect us to believe that you've forgotten the precise date you received a twenty-two million dollar claim? You'll have to do better than that."

Insolent cow, thought Jack, stifling his temper. "I'm afraid I really don't remember. I just know that when the claim arrived, I was staggered. It made absolutely no sense."

"What did you do next?"

"I consulted with my solicitor, David Purdoe."

"Mr. Gregory, I believe you are a licensed insolvency practitioner?"

Jack frowned. She knew damn well he was a practitioner. Swallowing it, he replied evenly, "That is correct."

"How long was it before Mr. Purdoe granted you the benefit of his expert opinion, Mr. Gregory?"

"I'm not certain. About three to four weeks I'd say."

"Three to four weeks Mr. Gregory? You were the liquidator?"

"That's what I said." Jack could feel his blood beginning to boil over but still he held himself in check.

"And then?"

"Why then creditors were informed of the position and this meeting was called."

"Mr. Gregory, as a licensed practitioner, will you please tell us why it took you three or four weeks before you decided to call a halt to your clearly inadequate administration, granting creditors the courtesy of a chance to replace you?"

"The claim is a nonsense." Jack was becoming increasingly uneasy, he was allowing himself to be cornered by a pathetic line of enquiry.

"Oh, really?" Ms Clark lunged. "Aren't you impugning the integrity of AUIG with that last remark." The room was filled with a babble of sound as creditors argued the point among themselves.

"Dammit, Madam," Jack smashed the side of his fist onto the table. "Aren't you impugning mine?" Then, his jaw set, Jack sat back in his chair and folded his arms defiantly and gazed at a point behind Ms Clark's head. "I'm not prepared to pursue this line of questioning any further." An embarrassed silence closed over the room.

The meeting had been going on for over two hours, and now Anthony Trent used the opportunity created by Jack's outburst to move in discreetly, diverting attention from Ms. Clark, while drawing others into the debate which dragged on for a further three quarters of an hour.

Reaching into his inside pocket again, Jack extracted a cigar, too bad if it gave the wrong impression. His lighter flamed at the tip and Jack tasted the savory tobacco on his tongue.

Looking around at the sea of mainly male faces Jack spotted a figure close to the side of the conference room he'd not noticed before the meeting had commenced. She might have been Asian, or of mixed race. Dressed in a satiny turquoise coloured dress, her straight black hair cascaded down to bare olive-skinned shoulders. From Jack's position he could see the girl's split skirt revealing one shapely thigh almost as far as her hip. She was quite startlingly exquisite.

Several creditors were business associates of Jack's in Bermuda. One of them, a large red-faced man in a rumpled light grey suit announced himself as Howard B. Charlesworth, President of General Life and Pensions Inc. of Illinois, owed two million dollars. Jack blew smoke into the air, adding to the fog already in the room and smiled to himself as he listened to the tributes to his honesty paid by the man and others after him. Jack studied the glowing end of the panatella and drew on it again. This is more like it, he grinned inwardly. Even the pretty Asian lady looked impressed.

Thankfully, Ms. Clark had shot her bolt too early. The tiny woman with the elfin hair cut regarded him with smouldering fury from behind her heavy spectacles.

* * *

In the harbour, the hoard of explosives again shifted uncertainly.

* * *

Still, the six men at the front said nothing. Obviously they were there to just observe. Despite the excruciatingly slow gains he'd made, Jack's head was splitting.

At last, a gap opened in the questioning. The room seemed to echo with the silence. Trent raised his head from the minutes he was taking, and, putting his pen down, gazed around to see if there were any further points anybody wished to make. There were none.

Now! Jack thought, anxiously looking at Tony; seize the advantage to close. Grab it man, while we're ahead.

"If there's nothing more?" Trent said enquiringly, "I'll move on to the formal business of this meeting which is the appointment of a liquidator, and a committee of inspection."

The group of six suddenly straightened as one and faced the front like a bunch of skittles that had just been reset. Ms. Clark fiddled with her glasses, but still said nothing.

Jack shifted his bulk to face front and held his breath. Come on, Tony. Don't bugger around. Say the magic words, "I am the duly appointed liquidator..."

"I can advise creditors," Trent continued, speaking slowly and deliberately, "that at a meeting of the shareholders of Central Reinsurance earlier today, my appointment was confirmed as liquidator of the company."

That's it, my friend. Finish it now, finish it. Jack clamped his jaw shut; any more pregnant pauses from Tony, and Jack would make the closing bloody announcement himself.

"I have fifteen million dollars in proxies in my favour." Trent waved a sheaf of papers in front of him. "As a matter of form I'm asking, are there any other nominations for the post?"

Finally, after three and a half hours of digging and delving, the moment it had all been leading up to. Jack's palms were soaking again, and he unobtrusively detached his shirt from where it had become stuck to his chest. He felt tight inside, his guts knotting like a steel cable.

Tony would allow only a second before announcing himself as the duly appointed liquidator; then there could be no going back. They'd have it, Jack and Tony, in the bag. Then let those bastards from AUIG squeal, their claim would be unceremoniously slung out. Jack would sue them for fraud and Ms. Clark could take a running jump.

But why was Tony delaying? It should have been wrapped up by now. All it took was a second. A second? It seemed more like a year. Jack's head was throbbing like a steam hammer and his vision was blurred. He could hear Tony's voice from afar, dulcet, reassuring. He must concentrate. Focus man. For Chrissake, focus.

Ms. Clark had asked a question. Oh really? How amusing. Question time is over, madam. Jack was thrashing about in the dark.

* * *

In the crowded central Hamilton bar, the two young men in tee shirts had been joined by a third. Their glasses of lager were empty. The new arrival was of Oriental extraction and immaculately groomed. Despite the heat he looked cool in his expensive navy linen suit. He glanced briefly at the other two, and, appearing satisfied, slipped each man a fat brown envelope before taking his leave.

* * *

"As I explained at the start of this meeting, I have known Mr. Gregory for a number of years in a professional capacity," Trent was replying to Ms. Clark's late enquiry. His tone was like silk, and he adjusted his cuff links with casual deliberation as he spoke, a ploy designed to momentarily distract, and one that Jack recognised well. "I have however had no dealings with Mr. Gregory in the matter of Central Reinsurance, and can assure creditors that my independence is in no way compromised."

"Compromised, Hell!" The tall American from AUIG was on his feet. He stood with legs spread, one arm extended towards the chairman, his index finger pointing accusingly. Jack felt as though he had been stabbed through the chest with a red-hot poker. He involuntarily reeled backwards in his chair as the man went on, "You known this guy for years, and you expect us to believe you're gonna be independent?"

"I can assure you..." Trent began.

"Assure nuthin! I ain't been impressed by what ah seen here today. My name's Luke Hepton of Hepton Mallett Dixon. I'm a US lawyer specialising in what you people call insolvency." He made the word sound like a peculiarly British crime. "I been sittin' here for nigh on four hours listenin' to you two twistin' an' turnin'. I ain't heard a single straight answer to a single straight question yet. Ah reckon it's time you heard from a representative of the largest creditor in this room, the American Union Insurance Group, owed twenty-two million dollars by your company Mr. Gregory."

Jack half rose to answer, but Tony's hand on his forearm restrained him. Hepton turned his back on the table and addressed the assembly as though he were chairing it, "Seems to me that what we need here is a truly independent liquidator." In his fervor, Hepton sounded more like an evangelist than a lawyer. "And ah would be proud and honoured to be voted into that position."

Trent stood up, he was over six feet three inches tall, and his sun-tanned face framed by a head of fair hair made him an impressive figure. He grasped one impeccably tailored lapel, his arm against his chest in the manner of a barrister cross-examining a witness, and adopted his most forceful tone. Jack had never known his colleague to come unstuck before, and, despite his nerves, he was absolutely certain he wouldn't now.

"I'm afraid, Mr. Hepton, that your client's claim is contested. It cannot be allowed for voting purposes." Jack smiled grimly to himself. Trent was stretching a point, relying on Hepton's ignorance of English insolvency law and its applicability in Bermuda. It made no difference, AUIG's claim would be rejected in due course anyway. But at this moment, it was crucial.

Hepton's next remark turned Jack into a shivering block of ice. "Oh, but you're wrong, sir. Ah've been reading your Companies Act 1981, and your Insolvency Act and Rules 1986." He smiled in a lopsided sneer and waved copies of the Acts and Regulations aloft in each hand. "Hepton Mallett Dixon don't charge their clients a thousand dollars an hour just to sit in meetings like this taking notes."

"I'm not aware of any provisions in any of the Acts you're holding that permit the appointment of an American lawyer as liquidator of a British company, Mr. Hepton," Trent smiled calmly.

"And I ain't aware of any provisions that don't. Anyway, we ain't talkin' 'bout a UK company, Mr Trent. What we're talkin' 'bout sir, is a Bermuda based and registered company. UK law has persuasive effect, but it don't rule here, Mr. Trent, sir. It don't rule here."

"Very well, Mr. Hepton, I hear what you say," Trent seemed entirely unconcerned with the outburst, but Jack was in a living nightmare. "Even if what you say were true, and I'm not prepared to admit that it is, there is still the question of your claim. It is disputed in its entirety."

"Then why's it on this here Statement of Affairs, sir?"

"The claim is contingent. It is shown in the interests of prudence." Trent was bluffing, Jack knew it. But if attitudes and confidence were anything to go by no one else would have guessed it. Trent spoke with the authority of a High Court judge.

"It don't say contingent right here, Mr. Trent."

"It doesn't have to. The nature of, and controversy attaching to the claim have been made abundantly clear to creditors."

Hepton paused for a moment and turned around to face his audience once again. He cupped his chin in one hand, resting his elbow in the other and closed his eyes as though he were deep in thought. Jack had no idea what to expect, but it felt as though the explosion had already taken place in the way that explosions do. The sound and blast were about to follow that micro second of silence that always preceded them.

"Ah'm afraid to have to tell you you're wrong, young man. You're gonna have to read you're own Act and Rules a bit more carefully, Mr. Trent, sir. Because as I recall, it says right here," he waved the documents about once again. "It says right here," he repeated, "that if a claim is disputed, the chairman of the meeting shall mark the claim as objected to, but allow it for voting purposes. Did you know that Regulation, Mr. Trent? Or did you want me to quote you the reference?" Hepton was grinning hugely, his hands loosely on his hips, the Acts and Rules on the seat behind him.

Before Trent could respond, Ms. Clark cut in tersely, "I nominate Mr Luke Hepton of Hepton Mallett Dixon as liquidator of Central Reinsurance." Trent raised a hand in a gesture of reply. He had a twinkle in his eye and was clearly not about to relinquish control of the meeting that easily.

"Seconded," the voice came from one of the group of five.

"That's it, fellah," said Hepton as he walked over to Trent flapping a hand at him dismissively. "I am the duly appointed liquidator of Central Reinsurance, and that's my chair you're sittin' in, sir.

Jack slumped back in his seat exhausted, a vision of Phyllida's gentle smile floating behind his eyes. He vaguely heard the uproar in the room, but it meant nothing to him. We've lost it, was all he could think, forty million dollars and we've lost it all.

Chapter 2

November 10, afternoon

Jack lay back on his hotel bed, the palm of his hand supporting the back of his neck. His other arm hung lazily over the side of the divan, the long, downward stretching index and middle fingers gripping a slender Dunhill panatella from who's glowing tip a blue grey thread wended it's way in a disciplined line up his arm before evaporating in a flourish of curlicues high above his head.

His body was without feeling, it was as though it had died, decomposed and returned to the elements, leaving behind only his head. His skull felt as though someone was administering a battery of dull pickaxe blows from inside it, and he wondered whether he shouldn't get himself a very large Scotch and Drambuie. Then he remembered, he'd taken several aspirin in the last few hours, and he didn't feel like having his brain start to spin as well.

Phyllida had called forty-five minutes ago; she wanted to know why he hadn't been in touch. How had everything gone? Was he okay? Her worried voice showed that she immediately saw through the screen of inconsequential rejoinders with which he had tried cheerfully to reassure her. He could almost hear her thinking, 'absolute hooey', her favoured expression when she was irritated, and as close as she ever came to swearing.

He closed his eyes; she would have to know eventually, but how was he to explain it to her? For all of her husband's success, Phyllida was as desperately insecure as if she had spent her life in squalor.

The room was deathly quiet. Usually Jack liked the silence, it helped him to think; but today, it felt oppressive, like an unseen buffer cutting him off from the rest of the world. He closed his eyes and the telephone suddenly shrieked at him and his body jolted with the shock. Taking his hand reluctantly from behind his neck he reached for the receiver. He waited for a couple of seconds, then said, "Hello?"

There was nothing; no reply, no discernible sound. Jack tried again, "Hello?" Then with a growing sense of annoyance, "Look, who the hell is this?" He was tempted to put the phone back, but hung on for another moment, just long enough to hear something that reminded him of the lapping of the sea against the hull of a boat at anchor, before the line went dead.

Jack shook his head and said aloud, "Some silly bugger playing games." Then the scene at the meeting earlier in the day, flashed across his mind, and he experienced a moment of disquiet. It was nothing he could put a fix on; something else, something beyond the pandemonium that accompanied the loss of his company. Just a sense of something being not quite right.

He drew deeply on the cigar tasting the smooth sweetness of the tobacco, and let his arm flop again at his side. Absent-mindedly blowing a series of smoke rings in the air, Jack decided it was time to cut through the tangle of thoughts, fears and emotions that assailed him.

When you know before a fight, he thought, that you have to win at all costs you get scared. When it looks as though you've lost because of your opponent's duplicity, you get angry. Frightened too perhaps, but mainly angry. Jack was angry now, he was raging and his mind began to clear.

They, the enemy, in the form of AUIG, had gained control of the mass of his wealth, but there was still the considerable earnings from the UK insolvency practice to be reckoned with, and those from the string of petrol stations he owned. There would be more than enough money to take them on, in Bermuda, in Britain, and in the US if need be. They'd had him on the ropes in round one, now he'd start the long haul back. He was far from finished, and shortly they'd know it.

Jack sat up and swung his legs over the side of the bed. There were people to call and things to do. All of a sudden he felt like a man in a hurry. He stubbed out the cigar and reached for the phone.

He called Tony Trent first. Trent was staying at the Miramar hotel in another part of Hamilton, having agreed to wait in his room until Jack felt like talking. Jack felt like talking. Trent's voice answered the line almost before it rang. His voice was the same as ever, solid, reassuring, "Hi, Jack!" he said. "How're you feeling?"

"I'm okay, Tony. Just trying to put myself back together again. There's a lot to do. First, tell me what happened after Hepton got himself appointed. I remember the noise, but not much else. I don't even recall how I got back here."

"Well, Hepton took the Chair, and, after grinning like a prize ape for a few moments, he made a charming little speech about how he was going to act in the best interests of all the creditors. He was going to see to it that they got a maximum payout as soon as possible. Someone pointed out that if he hadn't come along when he had, the creditors would be looking at a one hundred percent payout right now. That threw him for a second, and then he sidestepped it neatly by going on to another question.

"I could see that he was lost, didn't have a clue how to finish things off, so I edged myself in. I pointed out that he'd probably want to appoint a liquidation committee in the usual way. He was obviously floundering again. Seems he'd read all he needed to in the Insolvency Act about getting himself appointed, but little else.

"He thanked me kindly, and said that he'd just been about to suggest the same thing. So while he was preening himself again, I quickly addressed everyone on Hepton's behalf, as though I were acknowledging his genius, and lending a bit of ready assistance.

"Before anyone realized what I was up to, I had Howard Charlesworth of General Life and Pensions, agree to sit on the committee. Hepton looked a bit unsure of himself at that stage, but I went on talking as though I were his nominated mouthpiece. Then I got James Fulman in for Etheridge Lock."

"You mean?" Jack said.

"That's right, your solicitors. As you know, they're down on the Statement of Affairs at twenty-five thousand." Trent paused for a moment, then said anxiously, "Jack! Are you still there?"

"Yes! Yes! Of course, I'm here. I'm just listening to the boy wonder. I'd just like to know, where was I while all this was going on, asleep?"

"Jack, you looked totally knocked off your feet. You just stared glassily ahead. I though you were going to pass out, you were so white."

Jack shook his head, and making a fist, extended his thumb and absent-mindedly clicked the back of the nail up and down against his teeth, "I don't remember any of it. I think I must have been unconscious with shock. Just as well I didn't fall over. Might have interrupted your shenanigans. So you got two people on our side. How many on the committee? Three?"

"No, five?"

"Pity. With two out of three on our side we'd have had the majority to stop Hepton milking the estate for fees. Okay, what about the rest?"

"Ms. Clark, inevitably recovered herself quickly enough to volunteer her services, and then she started hustling around for support. A man called Ed Pasteur, Senior Vice President of Fleetwood Assurance was the fourth member elected. He's owed one point eight million. I think you'd better take it he'll be against us. Finally, we got a volunteer. Guy called Vernon Walters of Hermes Equitable. In for three hundred and forty thousand. An unknown quantity. So, we're split two each way, with one to try and convince."

"You did well, Tony."

"I only wish I'd done better. Let's face it the circumstances are unusual, if not unique."

"No need to apologise. No one could have predicted any of this. We've just got to try and think ahead. Stop this bastard from helping himself to everything I've earned. In the meantime, I'll fly back to England to see whether I can contest any of it. I'll talk to my partners and David Purdoe. Let me know if you come up with anything, Tony. If need be, I'll go to leading counsel. Whatever it takes. Whatever it costs."

"You're sounding better again, Jack."

"I'm disappointed of course, and I'm down. But I'm far from out. The fight back starts here, Anthony." Jack always addressed Tony as Anthony in moments of levity between them. He cradled the phone between his shoulder and chin, reached out to the bedside table and, extracted another panatella from its box, lit it, and blew a jet of smoke towards the ceiling.

He could feel the adrenalin beginning to pump through his veins as the prospect of upending Hepton, the interloper, sparked his sense of resistance and retaliation. 'Hepton the Interloper', the idea made him grin to himself.

Jack started to talk fast as the ideas came to him.

"I'll see to it that Hepton is tied up in as many legal knots as David and I can devise for him.

"Then, I'll see about having the committee of inspection, or the courts, examine this so called twenty-two million claim, and having him removed as liquidator.

"Then, I'll have him and his partners in Hepton Mallett Dixon indicted for aiding and abetting a fraud.

"After that, or better still before that, I'll have every piece of paper in the offices of American Union Insurance Group scrutinised. I'll have their directors locked up, and see to it the authorities throw away the key."

"Hey! Hey! Hey! Slow down, Jack. You sound like a man with a train to catch," Trent laughed.

"Too right, my friend. It'll take more than the Luke Heptons of this world to stop Jack Gregory."

"What was that? Are you still there, Jack?"

"I'm here. I'm here."

"Ah! I see. Good. Right." Trent pondered, then said quietly, "Jack, did you just click the line or something?"

"No, why? I didn't hear anything." Some of Jack's effervescence bubbled down, and the faintest shadow of doubt crossed his mind.

"Hmm. Just me being paranoid. Still, it's probably more sensible to say as little as possible over the phone."

"You're right." Jack flicked some ash into the ashtray and rubbed smoke from one eye with the heel of his hand.

"I'm in Bermuda for a few more days, then back to dear old Blighty. Call me if you need me."

"Bless you, Tony. And thanks for all you've done." Jack hung up and sat for a while on the edge of the bed gazing at the wall of his room. The cigar had lost its flavour, and he stubbed it out. The moment had passed and he felt weary. There were other calls to make, but they would have to wait. There would be little he could do before seeing David Purdoe so he might just as well restrain his impatience.

* * *

He must have fallen asleep, or maybe just dozed. Minutes? Hours? Sighing deeply, Jack stretched, feeling the knotted muscles in his arms and legs loosen slightly from the tension of the day. He walked over to the balcony and slid the heavy glass doors aside and stepped outside leaving the refrigerated cool of his room behind him. Immediately, he was enveloped in a cushion of warm evening air.

He still had on his tie, and he dragged at it impatiently, pulling it away from his neck, and undoing his top two shirt buttons. It would be dark soon, and quickly, in the way that it happened in this part of the world. No late sunny evenings here, lights would all be on by six thirty p.m.

Out in the harbour, moving almost imperceptibly in the swell was the Phyllida. She was all graceful lines and streamlined bodywork. Thank God, Jack mused, I had the sense to buy her in my own name, and not the company's. That's one asset friend Hepton won't be able to get his sticky fingers on.

Then a thought occurred to him, I wonder if I'll have to sell her to cover the legal fees I'll be racking up. He immediately banished the prospect from his mind.

Anchored far out in the harbour was another super-luxury yacht even more magnificent than the Phyllida. Jack recognised the lines of an Oceanco he'd not noticed her before. He squinted now against the sequined glitter of the sun on the waves and tried to make out her name. All he could discern was an image near the prow resembling a hunched silhouette. From his vantage point on the balcony it looked to Jack like an old man with a sailor's cap. After it were two words neither of which were discernible.

He decided he had waited long enough, the aspirins would have worked their way into his system by now. It was time to enjoy a large Scotch. As he turned away from the front, there was a gentle knocking at the bedroom door, and Jack went back into the room sliding the glass doors shut behind him once again. For a moment he wondered whether he was mistaken. He could see no one through the peephole in the door, and there was no reply when he asked who was there. "Odd," he said aloud, and threw open the door.

The woman was very tall, on her high-heeled sling-backs she must have been six feet. She looked about twenty-four or twenty-five. Her complexion was pale olive and faultless, but her eyes were Western. Then again her nose was aquiline, but the long straight black hair that tumbled elegantly to her shoulders was Far Eastern. Jack frowned, hadn't he seen her, or someone very like her at the meeting this morning?

She wore a knee length, sleeveless, close fitting wrap over garment, tied at the waist by a slender gold belt. The beige and coffee colors of the outfit complemented the color of her skin in an effect so startlingly beautiful it took Jack's breath away. She was more stunning than anything he had ever seen in any magazine and, for a second, Jack stood with his mouth half open. Then realizing how stupid he must look he asked, "Yes?" and self-consciously ran a hand through his sparse hair.

"Mr. Gregory?" The woman's accent suggested nothing beyond the fact that she was educated. She sounded confident. It seemed to help Jack and he recovered his composure. "That's right," he replied. "Can I help you?"

"My name is Tamu Yeung, I represent the Manhattan Group of Hotels. We make it a point of policy to enquire into the welfare of all our new guests. May I come in?"

Jack stood aside to let her past him. Slipping a hand nonchalantly into his trouser pocket he said, "I'm afraid your people have got it wrong. I've been staying at this very hotel for the last ten years." He watched her as she paced ahead of him, noticing idly as she did so, the imprint of her shoes in the pastel grey carpet.

Spinning round to face Jack she smiled, "We are an autonomous company within the group whose sole aim is to maximise the welfare of our clientele. The hotels don't contact us, we contact them and go over all of the guest lists they supply us with. There's no record of you're ever having been approached by one of our staff before. May I take a seat?"

She was standing next to Jack's bed and looking down at it. He noticed that the counterpane was ruffled and wondered whether he shouldn't straighten it for her. But he had no chance to move because she immediately sat on the edge of the divan and crossed her legs.

Jack was about to move to the drinks cabinet to offer her a drink, when he noticed that the woman's dress had parted as she seated herself. She was leaning back on the bed supported by straight arms propped behind her back, her crossed legs extended.

For an instant Jack thought, what goes on? And he walked towards her, puzzled, noticing as he did, the tiny black triangle of the briefs she was wearing. Then he realised what he was seeing; she wasn't wearing briefs. He was dumbfounded for less time than it takes to draw breath, and then he was bombarded by a profusion of images; Hepton laughing, hidden cameras, blackmail, divorce, Phyllida's face, shocked, devastated. He walked to the door in a fury and opened it beckoning the girl towards it. He said just one word, "Out!"

She got up slowly and straightened her dress before walking calmly past Jack. She smiled politely and without looking at him said softly, "I'm sorry we haven't been able to be of assistance to you on this occasion, Mr. Gregory. Perhaps next time." And she was gone.

It was several seconds before Jack moved. Someone's playing some very funny games, he thought, and poured the stiff whisky he had promised himself earlier. Then, reaching for the bottle of Drambuie, he added a generous dash. It tasted good, the rough edged sweetness at the back of his throat having an immediately calming effect. Jack idly twisted the glass tumbler between his palms and gazed around the room.

He took another draught of his drink and decided to watch the sun go down. Leaning against edge of the balcony he gazed down at the street and observed the shadows as they lengthened almost perceptibly. In another ten minutes or so it would be dark. He listened to the sounds of the evening. Lights were shining from office and hotel buildings, and along the front. Vehicle headlamps like bright batons probed this way and that. The boats moored by the quay took on a cosy toy town appearance.

Looking out at the Phyllida Jack saw its lights blazing on the quarter deck and winking from portholes, the beams from the latter, broken occasionally by the movement of someone within. Something was different. Then it dawned on him. The Oceanco was no longer in sight. Something in the distance, and moving away, might have been the other boat but in the advancing dusk, and from his vantage point, Jack could not be sure. He frowned and shrugged, and thought about his own yacht.

Smiling, Jack briskly rubbed his shoulders as a slight breeze made goose-bumps on his skin. Next time he was in Bermuda, he would bring Phyllida and Harriette with him.

Time for a refill he thought, surveying his empty glass. Another glance at his beloved Phyllida anchored in the harbour before going in. She was riding high in the water he noticed.

The Phyllida was then suddenly higher, and rising gracefully, majestically out of the water. She broke amidships and folded down at the stem and stern making a steeple thirty metres high, before she shattered in billowing clouds of flame into a million fragments of steel and glass.

The ear-splitting roar of the explosion followed an instant later, but served in no way to enlighten Jack's semi-conscious bewilderment. A phone was ringing.

In his head?

In the hotel?

Jack staggered into the room and put the receiver to his ear. He could hear what sounded like the throb of engines and the lapping of water against a hull.

There was a brief moment before a man spoke. The voice was precise, Oriental. "Mr. Gregory?"

"Yes", he whispered in reply.

"This is the Ancient Mariner."

"Ancient Mariner? Ancient Mariner?" Jack straightened up and frowned. "What the hell is this crap, and who the fuck are you?" he bellowed.

"You didn't like the girl?" The soft-spoken voice sounded concerned. "She was there to maximize your welfare, Mr. Gregory. Still, maybe you prefer the fireworks display I put on for you." He giggled. "You got insurance? You got to have insurance, don't you?" Or better still, `reinsurance.' That should be, `central', to your thinking; don't you agree?"

Jack closed his eyes and ran a hand over his scalp. It was greasy with his horror and smeared his palm. He was shivering, the cold perspiration on his body making his shirt cling to him.

The man's laughter was high pitched; it came in a long staccato burst that seemed to jump out of the telephone and hang reverberating in the air.

Chapter 3

November 13, Friday

The tone of the throbbing jets changed imperceptibly as the massive Lockheed Tristar gradually lost height. The blaze of sunshine that illuminated the club class cabin gave way to an increasing gloom as the aircraft began bumping through the heavy cloud that blanketed the south east of England. Rain spattered the portholes, and, despite the ambience of the pressurized interior, Jack instinctively pulled his jacket closer around his neck.

The flight had been comfortable and relaxing. The cabin crew on the British Airways flight had been as courteous and attentive as always. At thirty thousand feet Jack's problems had seemed a long way off and he had been able to start thinking about what he had described to Tony Trent three days ago as, `the long fight back'. The first stop would be David Purdoe, his lawyer; but not until Jack had had a good night's sleep and rid himself of his jet lag.

Phyllida knew that things had gone drastically wrong. The last time Jack had spoken to her in Paris she had sounded worried, notwithstanding his best efforts to reassure her. She had returned to England the previous day and would be waiting for him at the airport with the Range Rover. Whatever happened, he must appear his usual breezy, optimistic self.

As Jack came into the airport arrivals lounge she was waiting for him. She wore a long fawn coat and knee length boots. Her pale brown polo neck jumper and matching skirt were separated by a wide beige colour belt which revealed her tiny waist. Her thick reddish brown hair was blow waved and hung softly into the nape of her neck. She stood slightly apart from the rest of the crowd, and as he approached her she smiled and threw her arms wide to greet him.

God in heaven, he prayed as he hurried towards her dragging his case behind him, give me the strength to protect her from whatever's in store for me. But even as the hope crossed his mind, the memory of the explosion, the thought of the dead crew members, and the recollection of the continuing police investigation in Bermuda, made stark the simple reality of the situation and he involuntarily shook his head.

If she perceived the disguised worry, she ignored it, "Hi, darling." She hugged him tight. "Good flight?"

"Fine, fine. I could use some uninterrupted sleep though."

"I heard about the boat, Jack. There was a small article in the papers. They described it as a tragic accident. And as Tony got back yesterday, I asked him." There was a slight tremor in her voice.

Jack smiled grimly and started to guide her towards the exit, "What did he say?"

"Nothing really. Just that the police were looking into it, and that foul play wasn't suspected. Something about gas canisters on board going up and taking the fuel tank with them."

"So far that's all I know."

"But Jack, the whole crew was on board. That's how many...?"

He put the case down, and turning to face her put his hands on her shoulders, "Don't, Phyl. It can't do any good."

"But the captain, Jack. He was your friend."

Jack tried to cut the recollections that crowded his mind, the men's faces, each and every one of them, the laughs they'd shared, the rough and familiar language when there were no women present. "They were all my friends, Phyl," he said quietly.

She looked down at the ground and whispered, "Do you think it had anything to do with what happened at the creditors meeting? I mean..."

He interrupted her, heard himself in a hollow expression of amusement as he flung his arms comfortingly around her neck, "Darling, darling; you've finally guessed, I'm really James Bond, Tony is 'M' in disguise, and you, of course, are Moneypenny." It's so easy to lie, Jack thought, when you have to.

She brushed a tear away from her cheek with the back of her hand and smiled faintly, "Oh, Jack... I was so worried for a while, so frightened."

"Well don't be. Okay? I've got my work cut out on the business front without adding my beloved wife's fantasies to the agenda." He saw her sigh with relief as he took her by the arm and ushered her towards the short stay car park.

From Heathrow they picked up the M4 motorway and made for the A423 leading to Burchett's Park just east of Henley on Thames. She drove the Range Rover and he dozed intermittently, lulled by the action of the windscreen wipers as the vehicle ploughed through the driving rain.

As the first familiar houses came into view, the post office and the local school, Jack sat up and rubbed his eyes. Past the Lion's Head and up the hill, they would soon be home. Jack put his hand affectionately on the back of Phyllida's neck feeling the downy hair under his fingers. "I've missed you both."

"I thought you'd never say it," she replied in a tone of mock petulance.

"How's the bubs? I can't wait to see her."

"She's a little imp. Into everything. When I bore you a daughter, sir, I expected her to be as reserved and demure as her mother. Not a holy terror." Phyllida glanced at Jack coyly, "As I imagine her father must have been at the same age. It seems I was to be mistaken."

Jack grinned. But as they drove through the open wrought iron gates that bore the legend 'Highview', and approached the house a hundred yards further on through an avenue of mature silver birch, Jack's excitement at the prospect of seeing his daughter was tempered with a continuing if inexplicable unease. It was the same sensation he sometimes experienced before an important meeting of creditors if he felt that something ghastly and unexpected would spring from the woodwork and take them all by surprise.

He'd had that same feeling before the meeting of Central Reinsurance, despite his outward bravado and Tony's complete confidence in the outcome. And he had been right. He'd learned over the years to trust his intuition more and more.

They climbed out of the Range Rover, and as the car doors clunked shut, the housekeeper, Mrs. Llewellyn, appeared at the entrance to the house with her arm around the baby who sat comfortably on her hip. A dumpy little lady with rosy cheeks and a no nonsense manner about her, she looked up at the rain, and, remaining under the shelter of the porch, smiled broadly, "Well now, Mr. Gregory," she spoke with a thick Welsh accent, "It's good to 'ave you back safe and sound isnet?"

The baby flung her arms open, her eyes wide with excitement and squealed, "Dada 'ome, dada 'ome."

Mrs. Llewellyn handed Harriette to Jack who nuzzled the little one's cheek as he carried her indoors. She smelled of talcum powder and baby freshness. "And what have you been up to, you little monster?" Jack asked sternly. Harriette just giggled and went on squeaking, "Dada 'ome, dada 'ome."

"You must be starvin', Mr. Gregory, I'll get you a tea and something to go with it in a jiff."

"Thank you, Mrs. Llewellyn," Jack called back, as Phyllida accompanied him and the baby into the sitting room.

Harriette struggled to get free, and Jack set her down and watched her as she alternately waddled and crawled about the place. Then with a groan of relief he flopped back in one of the chintz covered easy chairs. Phyllida came and sat on the arm of it and gently massaged the back of his neck.

"Mmm," he murmured. "It was worth coming back just for that alone." It was always worth coming back to Highview; its thirty acres of ground, part covered by woodland; its oak beams and antique furnishings; its ancient kitchen lovingly restored by Phyllida to its original state of flagstones and copper.

Outside, the storm spattered against the French windows. Inside it was warm and secure and a long way from his recent traumas. Jack looked up at Phyllida as she bent to kiss him and his lips met hers full on. She made a little murmuring noise at the back of her throat and he started to say, "I've been away far too long this time. I think perhaps we might..." He was interrupted by the jangling of the telephone on the side table at his elbow. He grimaced and reached for it, saying, "No peace for the wicked." Then he winked at her, and, raising one eyebrow, murmured conspiratorially, "This'll only take a moment. Then we'll take up where we left off."

She grinned back as Jack put the receiver to his ear. There was a silence, then, straining to hear, Jack said, "Hello!" At first there was nothing. Then he heard once again what sounded like the lapping of water against the hull of a boat, and a soft voice with an Oriental lilt to it spoke, "You had a good flight home, Mr. Gregory? British Airways give their clients a good service, as I do mine." The man sounded as if he were smiling as he spoke. Jack sat up straight. His heart was beating against his ribs and he felt a dead weight settle in the pit of his stomach. Then realizing Phyllida was looking at him with an expression of concern, he forced himself to lean back again and smile at her.

The voice went on, the tone serious now, "It will be difficult for you to wave goodbye to all those hard earned dollars, Mr. Gregory, I know. But listen to some advice, my friend, you have been a first division player, and that is most impressive." He paused. "However, my clients are premier league, and that is a different ball game altogether, if you take my meaning." He laughed shortly, the same high-pitched note that Jack had heard so recently in Bermuda. "It will be better for you not to take on a match you cannot hope to win. Let us insure," he emphasized the pronunciation of the word insure, "that we keep our priorities central in our minds."

The man paused as if to let the significance of the tasteless play on words sink in. Then he continued like one delivering a lecture. "As your Bertrand Russell once said, a young man needs good health and an adequate income. My clients are not philosophers, Mr. Gregory but I suggest that you be philosophical about this whole matter. You understand?" Another pause, then, "The Ancient Mariner wishes you good day." He laughed again, a machine gun burst that felt like bullets ricochetting around inside Jack's skull, and the phone went dead.

"Who was it, Jack?" asked Phyllida. "You've gone as white as a sheet."

"Oh, nothing," he dismissed it with a shake of the head, but he felt nauseous, and it was a struggle to appear calm. "Just something to do with business. Not important." He smiled at her, his face and hands cold as ice, his heart hammering, as he wondered, what the hell happens next?

Chapter 4

November 16, Monday

The last time the public was treated to a hanging in connection with a bankruptcy offence was in London's Spitalfields Market in the year 1711. A great cheer rent the air as the condemned man dropped through the trap door, his head twisting sickeningly to one side as the rope twanged taut.

Such was the stigma once attaching to personal insolvency that in Victorian times references to bankruptcy were frequently delineated in print by the letter 'b', followed by a series of dots.

Charles Dickens graphically described the traumas associated with bankruptcy in his depiction, in his book, Little Dorritt, of the Marshalsea, a village like prison on the river Thames where the heroine's father spent some twenty years until his debts were eventually paid in full.

Other debtors were not so fortunate and languished in jail until they died. Insolvency, then, was poorly regulated and run mainly by lawyers. The Insolvency Act 1986, the definitive insolvency legislation in the UK in the twentieth century, heralded a change of attitude as the Country moved towards the new, `Rescue Culture.' Stringent professional standards were required, and for the first time the need for the insolvency practitioner to be licensed was introduced. The days of the insolvency 'cowboy' such as the infamous Hissing Sid Caplan, were numbered. At least in the UK.

As Jack Gregory approached the London offices of his solicitors, Etheridge Lock, he ruminated on how insolvency had changed over the past few years; changed mainly for the better, he decided. Unfortunately the improvements did not stretch much beyond these shores. There was a provision to extend part or all of English law to the Channel Islands or Colonies the power was as yet unexercised. And that was part of the problem.

Jack could see no way in which Luke Hepton's appointment as liquidator of Central Reinsurance could be attacked, let alone overturned. Hanging, were it reintroduced, would be too good for that bastard.

"Sit down, Jack, sit down." David Purdoe was a little man with a pear-shaped figure. His rosy cheeks looked as if they had been rouged, and his skin was as smooth as a baby's. It was doubtful he had ever had to waste time in the morning with shaving. He extended a small feminine hand, which Jack took in his own enormous paw. David smiled a lot, a feature of the man, which taken with his appearance, might have given the impression of one who was girlish to an extent, and harmless in the extreme.

The effect was utterly misleading. When it came to women, David was relentless and unwaveringly successful. When it came to the law, David Purdoe was deadly. When it came to defending his friends, the man was ruthless. An individual who'd been picked on at school because of his lack of height, he learned that with brains you could achieve anything, with wit you could reduce your less intelligent opponents to jelly and with perseverance and charm, you could impress anyone, particularly the ladies.

Jack sat in the cramped, ill-lit office and surveyed briefly the orderly piles of working papers that littered the floor like random mole-hills. "I suppose you've heard?"

"Quite right, quite right," David enthused. Adversity could usually be counted on to bring out the fight in him. "Before we start, your usual?"

"Please," said Jack.

David reached for the intercom, "Celia my dear, can you bring me a tea, and also one coffee for our guest. Make it strong black, and add four teaspoonfuls of sugar." David grimaced at the thought and turned back to Jack. "I gather it was one helluva meeting. Wish I could've been out there with you." He sounded as sorry as one who's missed a great dinner party, rather than one sympathizing with a client who has just been publicly carved up. "Tony Trent has already called me with an update on what happened. He was very concerned about you, Jack."

"I'm okay now, David. Don't worry about me."

"And it seems this man Hepton is going to be a force to be reckoned with."

Jack nodded, "You know your man Fulman's on the Committee of Inspection."

"Of course, he called me right after the meeting. He won't need any prompting from me to fight your corner during Committee meetings. But I'll discuss strategy with him before each one."

"We've got at least two out of five on our side on the Committee, and one unknown. That was smart manoeuvring by Tony. Thank God he kept his head."

"No matter, dear boy, no matter. We've things to consider."

There was a soft knock at the door, and a tall woman in her late thirties walked in bearing a silver tray with a pot of tea and a steaming cup of coffee. She wore stylish designer spectacles, a navy blouse and an absurdly short matching skirt which rode up at the back, revealing shapely thighs, as she stooped to leave the tray on David's desk. When she had gone, Jack gazed at David, and sighed, "Honestly, David..."

But the solicitor held his hand up interrupting his friend, "Don't be fooled by appearances, Jack. She types over a hundred words a minute, and has a better memory for detail than I do. I told her she should study law in the evenings and she took my advice. She's brilliant, dear boy, quite brilliant. I shall be gaining a lawyer shortly and losing a secretary."

"All right, David, I believe you. But I can see now why you never married."

"Speaking of marriage, how is your dear wife taking all of this. Charming lady, charming lady."

"Phyllida's okay for the moment. Bit shell-shocked, but otherwise fine." Jack shifted his bulk in the small armchair in an attempt to find a more comfortable position and reached for his coffee. "Talking about Phyllida, something's happened that wasn't reported in the Bermuda press." He hesitated as though collecting his thoughts, and then absent-mindedly took out a long panatella from the top pocket of his jacket.

The gold Dunhill lighter flared at the tip of the cigar and Jack slowly inhaled letting the strong flavour circulate around his tongue as the smoke drifted from his nose and mouth. He tapped the back of his teeth with a thumbnail as he pondered. Even now he could hardly believe what he was about to tell his lawyer, and the memory chilled him to the bone. "The yacht's blown up, David."

"What? What happened? Gas cylinders? Fuel tank?"

"Try explosive. Enough to lift forty metres of boat out of the water like a toy and blow it apart."

David took a sip from his cup of tea, for once he wasn't smiling. "You're telling me they wanted to kill you?"

"No. That's not what they wanted. If they'd really intended to do that they could've killed me at any time, couldn't they. But that would have looked far too obvious. No, all they wanted was to be able to milk the funds of Central, without me in Bermuda getting in their hair. So they decided to scare me off by wiping out the boat and my crew. What's murder after all when you're looking at that sort of loot?"

Jack blew a stream of smoke up at the ceiling and continued, "On a job like this the liquidation fees will be fabulous. Hepton will milk it for all he can, probably divide the cash surreptitiously with American Union Insurance Group. I should think that working out some form of mutual commission would be well within the scope of their combined intellects.

"Then there'll be the final dividend to be distributed from whatever balances remain at the end of the liquidation. It'll bother Hepton having to share what's left with the other non-preferential creditors but when you remember, AUIG's claim represents fifty percent of total unsecured claims, so that he'll be handing back half of all the cash that's left to them, I doubt that Hepton or his clients will cry too much, other than all the way to the bank."

Jack thought about his crew, the vision of them was returning to him now with increasing frequency; the skipper and mate, both burly six footers from Hull. The two locals, the engineer, a man with three young children and the cook, forever cracking ghastly jokes, and two brothers, the steward and the deck hand. Six men murdered. Jack closed his eyes and drummed his fingers on the desk in front of him and breathed in deeply.

He gulped at the scalding sugary drink and looked up at David again, "I suppose they also intended to get rid of one useful source of finance to me. The Phyllida's worth a couple of million of anybody's money."

"Isn't it insured though, Jack?"

"Of course, it is. But I don't know whether I'm covered for this sort of thing. I've started making enquiries already but I'm getting odd replies from the insurers. The Phyllida was insured with Lloyds, of course, but through agents in Bermuda. They're talking about exclusion clauses if the boat was maliciously damaged. Or the possibility that poor maintenance could have resulted in something like the gas cooker blowing up."

"Could a cooker go up like that? Surely not."

"You'd be surprised. In a confined space, a small explosion could be devastating. But I doubt it was that. I could smell diesel when I went down to the quay afterwards. The area stank of it."

"So? What does that mean?"

"Ammonium nitrate fertilizer mixed with diesel fuel oil, otherwise known as AMFO, makes a highly potent bomb."

David stared at Jack, incredulous, "How on earth do you know that?"

"I'm in the insurance business, remember. It's something I picked up from a bomb disposal expert, years ago. It would have been easy to get hold of the small amount of fertilizer needed and to smuggle it aboard; and the boat ran on diesel. You get the picture?"

"But you've got other assets and sources of income in this country, haven't you?"

"Certainly. There's the insolvency practice; very lucrative. And the string of petrol stations, together with sundry other odds and sods. But after what happened to the yacht, I just don't know." Jack hesitated a moment, and then gazing straight at David Purdoe, said, "Remember, the whole crew died, David. Every bloody one of them."

"Good heaven's above, Jack." David shook his head slowly as though the realisation of what had happened was just sinking in. "Does Phyllida know any of this?"

"Only that the boat exploded and the crew was killed. Not how. Or perhaps why." Jack leaned forward as though to add something, but David raised a hand as if on cue, "I know, Jack. I won't say a word to her."

"Thanks, David. I don't know how she'd cope if she found out. She worries."

"Hardly surprising, Jack. Who wouldn't?" Then David shifted excitedly in his seat, "But that doesn't change a thing, you know. We've still got to fight it every inch of the way. For a start, what about this claim AUIG put in?"

"Twenty-two million dollars."

"Right. They couldn't have just made it up could they? How do you falsify a thing like that?"

"Unfortunately," said Jack, "it's all too possible. The insurance industry operates on the basis of, `Utmost good faith', but every field attracts its own detractors. Take AUIG; they operated what's known as a 'Quota Share' with a number of reinsurance companies, Central included. It's common in the business."

"That's where they lay off a proportion of their risk with another company?"

"Exactly. It's usually something of the order of ninety percent and with a company that specializes in reinsurance."

"Like Central."

"Precisely." Jack leaned forward and flicked the end of his cigar over the ashtray. "Say the insurers take on some new business, maybe a spot of 'Kidnap and Ransom'. Policies of this nature are highly specialized, and, absolutely secret. They're usually taken out by international corporations in respect of their most senior executives. Those covered in this way won't want to see their names in lights; they'd become immediate targets for kidnappers. So, when there's a claim, the dictum of "Utmost good faith," comes into play."

David nodded enthusiastically. "Is that where the question of duplicity might arise?"

"It shouldn't, but it might. Before the reinsurance company pays out the ninety percent it has contracted to, it will want sight of the original policy document issued by the insurance company to its client, the international corporation or whatever. Then the reinsurance company, in this case Central, would want evidence that the premiums on that policy had been both paid, for example, by AUIG, and received by itself i.e. Central."

David put the tips of his fingers together and looked contemplatively at Jack, "Surely that would be simple to prove. There would be copy invoices, policy documents and proofs of payment to show. Central must know if it's received premiums, mustn't it?"

Jack smiled grimly, "Not necessarily. Where a great deal of inter-company business is transacted in this way, auditing of fees paid and received, particularly in 'Kidnap and Ransom," can get complicated."

"So, what happened here?"

"Nothing. That's the point. When AUIG banged in their claim, months after Central had been put into Members Voluntary Liquidation, they supplied a copy claims advice and the usual letter advising that they were anticipating making a claim up to the limit of their exposure. They also enclosed a copy of the policy document and the invoice ostensibly submitted at the time the claim was settled by them with their own client. The curious thing is, both documents pre-date the original liquidation of Central by three months." Jack finished his coffee and put the cup and saucer back on the desk.

"Wow!"

"That's right. Wow! We are all expected to believe that AUIG sat on a twenty-two million dollar claim for almost a year doing absolutely nothing before deciding to chase it up with us."

David whistled, "I see precisely what you mean."

"Of course, it stinks. The claims advice is probably a back dated sham; though it would be well nigh impossible to prove it. Their invoice to us is interesting though. It's one of a group with numbers on them suggesting something totally out of sequence with other claims invoices they submitted to Central Reinsurance at about the same time. A group of smaller contrived claims to camouflage the real fake."

"How do you prove any of this, Jack? Unless you propose calling into question the probity of AUIG."

"Quite. And who would take seriously the complaints of the now `insolvent' Central Reinsurance Limited? It would look like a case of sour grapes. I'm afraid that short of breaking into the premises of AUIG, there's not a lot left to us."

"Nil desperandum, dear boy, nil desperandum. There's plenty for me to start working on with what you've just given me."

"There is?" Jack sounded surprised.

"Oh, yes. I've had some experience of negotiating in kidnap and ransom."

"Well, I'll be damned, David. You are a dark horse. Who were you acting for?"

"A number of large insurance companies. I dealt on behalf of the insurers with the negotiators, often they were ex-SAS boys. AUIG will be asked by me to come up with evidence of their negotiations, proofs of payment to insureds and so on. I'll also take up the question of the out of sequence invoice numbers. You won't have to break in anywhere, Jack."

"I'm relieved to hear it," Jack grinned, "I don't see myself shinning up and down drainpipes, at least not with my weight."

The solicitor rubbed his hands together gleefully, "No Jack, we fight on, but on our terms not theirs. Then there's the question of the validity of Hepton's appointment to be investigated. I'll check the position from the point of view of UK and Bermudian insolvency law.

"We'll hit them on all fronts, Jack, all fronts. We go through the courts. Understand? Everything straight down the line. We do not deviate one jot. We'll take it to the House of Lords if we have to. But we will not play their game. Do you understand me, Jack? Do you? If we try to do it their way, we are lost."

"Okay. I see what you're saying," Jack smiled. "I wasn't going to suggest we do otherwise. But I have to admit I'm very uneasy. I don't know for certain whether this thing with the yacht is tied in with Central or not, though frankly it must be. And the police hadn't come up with anything by the time I'd left Bermuda. Although, believe it or not, they seemed to be dropping some sideways hints about my possible involvement.

"If that's not bad enough, I got an odd call after the explosion by some lunatic calling himself The Ancient Mariner, and then again after I got home. I was being warned off." Jack leaned forward again in his chair, astonished.

"David! What is it?"

The other man had sat back, the color drained from his face. "I've come across him, Jack."

"You have? When?"

"Years ago when I was working on a kidnap and ransom case."

"Go on."

"Several negotiators, top men -- and I mean the best -- died in an abortive attempt to locate and free the young daughter of an Italian industrialist. The negotiator on behalf of the kidnappers, a quiet-spoken man with a Chinese accent calling himself The Ancient Mariner, found it all very amusing. He had a most peculiar screaming laugh, I was told afterwards."

"That's him, isn't it, David? That's the same man."

"He's very dangerous, Jack. I doubt there's a more accomplished killer on the planet. He's also multi-lingual, and extremely rich. He goes to the highest bidder. And in this game the stakes are pretty high."

Jack felt his hand tremble slightly as he took the dying cigar from his mouth. He licked his dry lips, "Okay, David. They've frightened me, but we're still going to keep my end of things on the level. They don't want the sort of enquiries that would stem from my murder. So we keep it legal, too. Legal all the way."

There was a moment of silence as the two men stared at each other contemplatively, then the telephone rang on David's desk. He grinned, back to normal, picked it up and went on talking to Jack as he put the receiver to his ear. "Of course, let's not get paranoid. We'll keep this thing in proportion. You'll be fine, dear boy, just fine." Then he turned his attention to the caller, "Who is it, Celia? I said there was to be no interruptions."

Jack watched as David listened, the solicitor's face adopting first a look of concentration, and then a furrowing of his normally smooth brow. "I see," he said. "Yes, he is with me now. Did you want to speak with him? Very well, I'll let him know what you've said. Thank you. Goodbye."

"What was all that about?" Jack could feel that sense of foreboding again. He moistened his dry mouth again.

"Do you operate one of your JG Petrol Stations in Liverpool, Jack?"

"Yes, I do. I bought it a couple of years before you and I first met. Why? Is something wrong?"

"Is it on Nathan Road?"

"That's right. It's one of my three most profitable sites. David! What the hell is going on?"

"It's burning."

"What?" Jack exploded.

"That was the Liverpool fire brigade. I didn't stop to ask how they knew you were with me. But the place is ablaze; flames thirty feet high. They've got eight fire-trucks there. There was a small explosion. Apparently two of the staff are being treated for minor burns."

"Jesus Christ Almighty, I've got to get up there," Jack said, and ran from David's office without another word.

* * *

By the time he reached the Jaguar in the underground car park off Kingsway, Jack was gasping for breath. He stopped and looked at his watch in the half-light, it was twelve-noon. What the hell am I hurrying for? Whatever's happened has happened; running around like a madman won't change anything.

He stood still for a moment, collecting his thoughts and unwinding. He stared at the car, all 4.2 litres of it in its glossy racing green. A step up from the fifteen year old VW Beetle he'd started out with years ago.

Putting the brief case on the ground, Jack fished the car keys out of his trouser pocket and opened the car door. No, he thought as he gradually got his breath back, I'm not wasting valuable time driving up to Liverpool, I'll make calls from David's offices where I won't be disturbed.

* * *

Back in David's building Jack found himself ensconced in a cubbyhole even smaller and darker than that occupied by the little lawyer. Celia had instructions to keep Jack topped up with coffee and he was making calls.

First off, Jack got in touch with the local Divisional Fire Officer for Liverpool, "My name's Gregory, and I'm the owner of the Nathan Road site," Jack said. "Can you bring me up to date."

"Certainly, sir." The voice was calm and authoritative. "I can tell you that the main building is a charred wreck. On the forecourt, the manager's car's been reduced to a hulk. And the garage's protective canopy has collapsed. It's all a heap of bent and buckled metal."

"God in heaven," said Jack

The Fire Officer went on, "You'll want to speak to the police as well. I suggest you call them, sir. No doubt they'll want a word with you, too."

"Police?" said Jack, an uncomfortable feeling working up inside him.

"I can't speak for them, and I'm not saying anything either, sir. At least not at this stage. Our own Fire Investigation Unit will be moving in as soon as the area is clear." He paused, "If you'd care to telephone the station later I'll let you have a more detailed opinion." The Divisional Fire Officer added politely, "And now, sir, if you'll excuse me, I really have a great deal to do."

Jack got through to the local constabulary, immediately. The Sergeant's tone was guarded, "It's too soon to say, sir. I have my suspicions though."

"What suspicions?" Jack's lips were dry, and he moistened them and wondered, what next?

"Well, sir, a filling station doesn't simply go up like this on its own." He stopped for a moment, then added cryptically, "It would need a little help."

"Are you saying this was deliberate?" Jack cradled the phone in the crook of his neck and shoved his hands into his jacket pockets; suddenly, despite the stuffiness of the office, he was feeling cold. "Sergeant, can you tell me anything of what's been going on here? For a start, where are my staff?"

"Your manager, Ranjit Singh?"

Jack nodded, expectant, and the Sergeant continued, "He's over at the hospital with one of the two youngsters."

"Hospital! What hospital? I was told, minor burns. Who's been hurt, and how badly?"

"Well, sir, it seems that just before the explosion..."

"Explosion?" Jack asked quietly. He began to experience a sense of having been this route before. In his mind's eye he could see forty metres of yacht rise from the harbour in Hamilton Bermuda, and shatter into a million fragments.

"Yes, sir, I'm afraid so," the Sergeant sounded sympathetic and concerned. "It seems a car stopped briefly to fill up, an old Ford Capri. Then the driver, a Chinese gentleman, hopped back into his vehicle slamming the door, gave a parting wave from out the car window, and moved off without paying. The two lads ran onto the forecourt to stop him driving away. They were at the edge of the site when everything went up. Apparently away from the pumps and close to the pavement. The manager saved himself by running into the garage shop, but he was still thrown by the blast and injured.

"He immediately summoned the fire brigade, ambulance and ourselves. If the other two lads had been closer to the pumps than they were," the Sergeant paused, "putting it crudely, sir, they'd be charcoal by now. As it is, they missed the worst of the explosion. Do you have any idea who might have wanted to carry out such an act, sir?"

Jack pictured the devastation, the burnt and buckled steel and charred timbers of the perimeter fencing. Jack thought, Hepton again. This is no isolated act of vandalism. A Chinese non-paying customer the Sergeant said. He gave a wry smile and said under his breath, "I sincerely hope not."

"What was that, sir?"

"No, nothing, Sergeant. Look I'd better get in touch with the hospital. See how Ranjit and Chris are getting on." He gave the officer his various phone numbers. "Call me if you need me. Or if you find out anything I should know."

Just how badly burnt were they both? Did they know anything he should know? Within seconds he was through to the Royal Liverpool Hospital and on to the ward where Ranjit and Chris were apparently in adjoining beds. Neither man had suffered broken bones, despite being thrown by the force of the explosion. But both had sustained burns and lacerations.

"What happened, Ranjit?" Jack asked. "Are you hurt?"

The manager's tone was uncompomisingly angry. He spoke loudly and quickly, "This is an absolute bleddy disgrace, Mr. Gregory. I am paid to manage your petrol station not to get blown up."

"Ranjit, for God's sake man, don't you see that..." But Jack stopped himself. Feeling at a loss to know what to say or do, he asked, "Look, can you tell me anything at all about what happened? Is there anything I can do to help? Anything."

"I'm not talking to you any more," Ranjit's tone was lower now, his voice registering disgust. "Chris is here. He can talk."

Jack heard the phone being handed over to another and Chris came on the line. "Mr Gregory?

"You okay, Chris?"

The voice was sullen. The lad was as angry as his manager, "Nothing serious. Some burns and cuts."

"What happened, Chris?"

"Last night," the boy faltered. "It was very late. The telephone rang."

Jack stopped breathing and stared ahead. Don't tell me, he thought. Let me guess.

"When I picked it up," Chris went on, "At first I could not hear anything. I said, 'Hello? Who is there?' But there was no answer, just a silence. I was about to hang up," he added, "when a voice said, `Georgy Porgy pudding and pie, lit a fire and waved goodbye'. Then there came a very long laugh. It was piercing, like an animal in distress."

Closing his eyes, Jack sighed deeply. It's him. I might have known it. He's over here. The bastard's playing his games over here. And now the man's a bloody poet. Jack pondered remembering the cynically polite tones with which he had been addressed over the telephone in Bermuda just after the yacht had blown up.

But what in heaven's name for? Hepton and his crew had taken over the Bermuda set up and that's where the real money was. So why send their expensive thug to the UK? They couldn't take over the filling stations. Jack nodded to himself slowly finally understanding. Ruining the sites meant ruining the business and thereby stemming a source of income that could have been used to finance legal proceedings to fight them. All very simple really, he decided. "Is that it, Chris?" Jack asked.

"Yes," he replied. "Except for one thing."

"Tell me."

"Paul got the same call last night. At home."

"Shit!" Jack said, and immediately felt embarrassed. "Sorry, Chris. I... I'm not thinking clearly."

In the background Jack could hear a nurse saying, "I've allowed you fifteen minutes. Now you both need rest."

Jack said, in closing, "Look, Chris, if you, Paul or Ranjit need anything..."

Profoundly disturbed, Jack next contacted the Hursthall Street site on the North West outskirts of Liverpool. Thank God, no bombs. No panic. No sign of any problems.

The site was a superb one. It had been redecorated recently in the company's colours of green and blue, and equipped with new state of the art Gilbarco pumps which had cost a fortune. Still, Jack had thought, they'd pay for themselves pretty quickly. They'd need to; this site, along with several of the others had been mortgaged and re-mortgaged as Jack had updated their plant and equipment.

The manager of several years standing at Hursthall Street was Ashok Shama. About the same age as Jack, he was a man given to smiling a lot and one upon whom Jack could rely with total confidence. He was assisted by Prakesh Gupta and Raj Lali.

Ashok sounded more subdued than usual, "Good evening, Mr. Gregory,"

"Hello, Ashok. You sound worried. I suppose you've heard the news about Nathan Road."

A customer came in to pay at that moment and Ashok called through to one of the back storerooms to Prakesh to come and serve him. Then the manager returned his attention to Jack.

"Mr. Gregory, I have something to tell you. I found a foolish message had been left on the answering machine when I opened up this morning. I intended to wipe it, but forgot. Then I heard about the fire at Nathan Road and the peculiar telephone calls that Chris and Paul received. I decided to keep the tape for you to hear. I will play it for you over the phone."

Jack took a deep breath and folded his hands together in his lap. They felt moist and uncomfortable. Ashok flipped a button and Jack heard the cassette whirring inside the machine. Then there was a series of clicks, followed by several short beeps, and a long one. After that there was a pause, then the silence was broken by a soft voice with the suggestion of an Eastern accent which said:

"Hickory dickory dock,

A bomb blew up Ashok,
He was struck down,
That laughing clown,
And burned with his gasoline stock.

Cupping his chin in one hand, his elbow propped on the desk, Jack said nothing. The tape wound on for several seconds, then there came the now all too familiar sound of a long drawn out cackle. "Ha ha ha ha ha hee hee hee hee hee," The cassette fell silent, save for the turning of the spool. Jack shivered, and involuntarily shook his head. They're closing me down in Liverpool, he thought. I can't risk peoples' lives there keeping this site open if that's what they're up to.

"Ashok, you're to put the barriers up, and shut up shop as of now."

"But, Mr. Gregory?"

"No `buts', Ashok."

"Really, Mr. Gregory. It is frightening of course, but one must not permit oneself to be intimidated by this nonsense."

"I'm sorry, Ashok, but this person means business. I'm not prepared to jeopardise your safety, or the safety of the lads there." Jack folded his arms, leaned back on the chair and stared at the ceiling. Now what? Ashok had a wife and two kids.

A wife, God! The thought struck home with such force that Jack felt as though he'd been hit on the chest with a hammer. How many others among his managers had wives? How many other sites had received threats as of now; or would do in the immediate future?

A horrific scenario began developing in Jack's mind. How long could he rely on this source of income if he were forced to close down more of the petrol stations? How would loans against the freeholds be funded, and staff paid while...? While what? He reached a dead end. While he put the sites up for sale? And anyway what would they fetch if he tried to dispose of them other than as going concerns? As dormant businesses, they'd fetch a fraction of their trading value.

Thinking intently about the man at the other end of the telephone line, Jack asked, "Ashok, have you had any contact from any of the other managers today? Or recently?"

Ashok murmured, "No," and Jack sighed to himself. Maybe his friend the Ancient Mariner only intended to intimidate Jack for the time being. The prospect gave Jack scant comfort; but it was time to move on and see what was happening at some of the other sites before the night shifts started to come on duty.

Ending the call, Jack started to dial the number of a site on the North West side of Manchester.

The manager, Michael Warner, a short stocky Midlander was assisted at the site by one Sean Overton. Both keen gardners, the filling station with its flower bordered lawns looked more like a garden centre than a garage. Warner picked up the receiver, "JG Petroleum."

"Evening, Michael."

"Evening, Boss," Warner was handling a piece of correspondence when Jack called and Jack could hear the envelope being torn open.

A long low whistle came down the line and Jack said, "What is it, Michael?"

"Listen to this, boss."

Jack felt his insides begin to churn. Not bloody Manchester as well, he thought. Even before Michael started to read it out loud, Jack knew where it came from, and it made him shudder.

It read:

> Little Mike Warner, I'll blow up your lawn,
> You'll weep midst the bedlam and pieces of Sean,
> But where is the hero of this tale of dread?
> He's under the rubble: Asleep?
> No. Stone dead.
> The Ancient Mariner.

"What's this all about, Boss? And who the hell is The Ancient Mariner?" Warner waited for a reply, then said, "You don't seem surprised. Is this some kind of joke?"

"Believe me," Jack said softly, "this is no joke. Evidently word hasn't reached you, Michael."

"What word's that?"

"I'm being threatened, Michael. Whoever this man is, he's blown up the Nathan Road site in Liverpool injuring two of the lads there, and he's promising to repeat the performance elsewhere."

Warner breathed in sharply.

"How long have you had this letter, Michael, and how was it delivered to you?"

"I found it on the counter here after a bloke came in to pay for his petrol. He was Chinese. I remember him because he looked really expensively kitted out -- you know high class suit, silk shirt, the works. Funny thing though, he was driving a really ancient Ford Capri. I thought at the time, odd, you'd expect to see a man like that driving a better motor."

"I don't know how many similar letters have been or are about to be delivered to the other garages, Michael, but I've made a decision," Jack said emphatically. "I'm closing down the whole operation, whatever it costs me."

Taking his digital organiser from his inside jacket pocket Jack punched the keys bringing up the telephone numbers of eight of the garage sites and read them out to Warner, "Phone them all and instruct them to shut up shop immediately. Tell them I'll explain everything in due course."

Jack thought quickly again, calculating plans, snapping out instructions.

It was dark when Jack finally found himself approaching the M4 motorway heading West towards the A423 to Henley on Thames and Burchetts Park. Home.

Every site had received some threatening letter that day. Every last one of them. Most thought it was just a joke. Others who had heard about Nathan Road were more circumspect. The Divisional Fire Officer confirmed Jack's worst fears. It had been a bomb.

Jack glanced at his watch and thought of Phyllida. It would be after two a.m. before he got back, and he realised he'd not spoken to her since midday. He composed his thoughts before calling to let her know he was on his way home, it wouldn't help to let her see or hear the turmoil he was in.

Reaching the roundabout leading on to the motorway moments later, Jack sighed and keyed in his home telephone number and was about to press the `send' button when his attention was taken by the glare of headlamps being flashed in his rear view mirror. Someone's in an awful hurry, Jack frowned in irritation and looked up as a battered Ford Capri hurtled past him on the outside lane in a roar of tuned up power.

The driver's window must have been open, because an arm appeared from it waving appreciatively as the car cut across Jack's path. Jack slammed on the anchors and slewed the Jag out of the path of the Capri whose wheels spun in a cloud of burning rubber and exhaust fumes as it accelerated for the exit toward the Southbound route.

Damn fool driver, Jack thought as he steered onto the motorway. Someone's spent a bundle souping up that old jalopy.

It was hard to tell what the motorist looked like in the dark, but there had been a suggestion in the man's profile revealed in the instant he had leveled his car with the Jag, of Far Eastern origin.

"Oh, Christ!" Jack said aloud, and hit his forehead with the palm of his hand "I must be losing it. A bomb. A Chinese driver. How clever. How very clever. And I just missed the bastard."

Chapter 5

November 17, Tuesday

It was two forty when Jack's two brilliant double beams of quartz halogen illuminated the trees and front of the house accompanied by the sound of gravel being crunched on the drive.

Jack's home, Phyllida thought excitedly. She put her book on the bedside table and, dragging the covers aside, reached for her dressing gown. Jack had only called twice that day. The first time at noon. He sounded slightly out of breath and beneath the usual sheen of confidence she had detected a note of concern in his voice. It worried her. Jack called again much later when he was on his way home. This time, his tone had a faraway sound to it, as though he were preoccupied with something.

Phyllida hurried into her dressing gown, straightening the folds at the front as she did so. Jack seldom, if ever, confided his business worries to her.

All that had changed dramatically. From the fragments of information he had imparted, Phyllida understood that her husband had become a moving target. Jack was not faced with the usual sort of combative commercial happenings that any entrepreneur would accept as part of the normal cut-and-thrust of business. There was an element of menace in this that was affecting Jack profoundly, and Phyllida had no clear idea what it could be.

She wondered about the telephone call Jack had taken shortly after his return from Bermuda. At the time, he had made light of it. But she had seen the troubled look on his face, recognized the ill-disguised frown, noted the hasty reassurances he'd proffered. None of it had convinced her that Jack was in anything but the direst trouble.

Phyllida sighed. Jack must not suspect that she was in any way worried or concerned about the events surrounding him. She would be his rock. And home would be his haven, as far as she could make it for him.

Glancing quickly in the dressing table mirror she tugged a comb through her mane of hair and primped it back over her ears with her fingers. She had not removed her makeup from the day, and now she quickly inspected it for smudges. She tightened the sash about her tiny waist and hurried downstairs.

Slamming the car door shut, Jack gazed up at the house. There were lights on everywhere as though it was early evening rather than the dead of night. The building always had a welcoming feel to it. Home. There really was no place like it.

Dwelling again -- despite his better judgement -- on the past few hours, Jack had visions of smoke filled horizons and injured staff, and was tempted, briefly, to start going over the whole Bermuda horror in his mind once more. He started towards the front door, the sharp gravel lumpy underfoot. For a moment his legs were leaden and his broad shoulders felt bowed under the weight. Then, straightening his back he smiled grimly. He'd never been afraid of anyone or anything in his life. The buggers had a long way to go before they beat Jack Gregory into submission. And anyway, he resolved, he couldn't let Phyllida see him looking worn out and worried.

She'd be asleep, Jack had just decided, when the front door was thrown open and Phyllida ran out to meet him. She looked gorgeous in her dark velvet housecoat. How ever did she do it? Even her makeup was impeccable.

"Darling," Phyllida flung her arms round Jack's neck practically toppling him over. "I'm glad you're home. You must be exhausted. I'll bet you've had nothing to eat all day."

Jack dropped his brief case on the drive, and laughing at his wife's enthusiasm, hugged her back. "You're right, I'm starved. But I need to get some sleep if I'm to get into the office early tomorrow."

"Why not take the day off, Jack? You were going to take things easier when you'd run down Central. Surely everything will wait for a day or so. We can wander around the woodland together. Everything's gloriously fresh and clear. You've always said how therapeutic it is just walking the estate."

With his arm across Phyllida's shoulder, Jack led her back into the house, "I know, I know," he agreed. "Well, maybe I'll have a bit of a lie in. Get to the office at around eleven. I can't take a whole day off though. There's too much needs seeing to right now."

With the door closed behind them Phyllida said, "You go and take a peep at Harriette while I make something for you to eat. What would you like?"

Jack pondered for an instant and then smiled. His mouth watered and he said quickly, "Toasted egg and bacon sandwich." Then he looked at Phyllida slightly guiltily and explained, "Sorry, darling. It's my blue collar roots."

Grinning back at her husband Phyllida announced, "Right, sir. One toasted egg and bacon sandwich it shall be."

From where they were in the hallway, Jack could just make out the door to Harriette's bedroom on the floor above; it stood slightly ajar. Kissing Phyllida on the cheek he said, "Back in two shakes," and, taking them two and three at a time he bounded up the stairs to the top landing. Then he tiptoed towards his daughter's darkened room and peered in, pausing to let his eyes become accustomed to the darkness.

Harriette's cot stood in a far corner by the window, and as Jack softly approached it he could hear her breathing gentle as a breeze. She was lying on her stomach, her head to the side, one peach-down cheek uppermost. Jack stared at her, unmoving, but she sensed his presence and opened her eyes. Instantly she was awake. "Hayo, Dada," she bubbled happily, and turned on to her back, extending her arms for him.

God, he loved this baby. Loved her till it hurt. Phyllida had wanted more children, he had wanted more children. At least two, she had said, maybe three. But it wasn't to be. There had been complications during the pregnancy. For a time, the doctors had expressed concern about Phyllida's condition. The pregnancy might have to be terminated if the mother's life was not to be put at risk. Phyllida would not hear of it. This was her child, and no one was going to take it from her. She would not lose her baby whatever the cost. Jack had gone along with it - it had to be Phyllida's decision - in dread of losing his wife.

Harriette had been premature; at three and a half pounds she had seemed a tiny helpless little thing. Tiny she may have been, but helpless she was not. She screamed and raged her defiance at the world, and hanging on to life tenaciously, gained weight more quickly than the hospital predicted she might. Mother had survived, and baby had flourished. But there would be no more children. The risks were too great.

The little one circled her arms around Jack's neck, and giggled, "Hayo, Dada. Dada home." She smelled of sweetness and warmth and freshness and life. She exuded that indescribable fragrance of all babies, and Jack inhaled it as though he were inhaling a part of his daughter, acknowledging as he did that Harriette was as much of his essence as if he had carried her nine months within his own body.

"And what have you been up to today?"

"Toto," she giggled.

"Toto?" Oh yes, Jack remembered, the baby's teddy bear. When she tried to say teddy, it came out as Toto. Harriette's head rested on Jack's shoulder and he felt her breath against his neck. She was drifting off to sleep again. "Toto," the baby yawned contentedly.

"Bed for you, young lady," Jack said as he gently lowered his daughter into her cot and pulled the blankets up to her chin.

She turned on to her side and yawned again making little swallowing noises. Muttering something about Toto under her breath, Harriette's breathing became deeper, more regular.

"What did Toto do today, darling?" Jack murmured as he stared down at her. But he realised she was already asleep.

Downstairs in the kitchen Phyllida had a plate piled with egg and bacon sandwiches waiting, and Jack joined her, wolfing them down hungrily. Phyllida ate more slowly, chewing deliberately, and looking at him as though trying to glean what was really going on behind all his expressions of sanguinity. As if by staring at her husband she might read his mind. She finally asked, "What's happening, Jack?"

Jack looked across at her. The question had taken him by surprise. He hadn't intended to confide in her yet. If at all. Phyllida dried her hands on a serviette and raked her hair back through her fingers before purposefully flicking her head from side to side to discipline her unruly tresses into some sort of order. There was no point in keeping up the pretence he realized. She would guess eventually, if she hadn't already.

He explained everything. Talking through mouthfuls of food, as if to give the impression that it was all of little consequence. He tried to look, to sound, casual. Jack told her that the man Hepton was using to intimidate him signed himself off as The Ancient Mariner. She would be amused by the pseudonym.

Phyllida was not amused, and Jack realized it had been unwise to try and make light of the situation.

"It's like something out of a comic, Jack. The Ancient Mariner? Why, it's absurd. Has he really been responsible for all that's been happening?"

"It looks that way. And it's anything but absurd. When the Mafia first made their presence felt in the United States in the 1920's, they signed themselves off as La Mane Nera."

"What's that?" Phyllida said as she sipped her mug of tea.

"It means The Black Hand. The authorities thought it was very funny in the beginning. Then the killings started and nobody laughed any more. I haven't been laughing too much recently. I wasn't going to say anything to you."

"Why ever not?"

"I was afraid of worrying you."

"Nonsense, Jack." Phyllida got up and walked around the back of Jack's chair and gently massaged his neck and shoulders. "Anything that affects you affects me. Don't you dare not confide in me again."

The tea was hot; it scalded the back of Jack's throat and burned its way satisfyingly into his stomach. So now she knew. Perhaps it was for the best after all. Certainly he felt less isolated than he had up to now. He twisted around and smiled at Phyllida and got up, linking his arm through hers, "I need some shuteye, darling."

"You go on ahead," she whispered back. "I'll clear away for Mrs. Llewellyn.

Walking towards the stairs Jack was tempted to ask, but what do I pay Mrs. Llewellyn for then? But he let it ride.

After drifting off to sleep quickly, Jack twisted and turned restlessly, Phyllida cuddled up against him. In the early hours he found himself checking the illuminated time by the bedside clock every hour and was tempted to get up and make himself a hot drink. But he decided against it, realizing he would probably only awaken and possibly worry Phyllida. It wasn't just the financial problems that nagged at him now. There was something else. Something potentially far more alarming.

They could have it all, he thought. They'd got most of what he owned anyway. He would give notice, through David Purdoe that there would be no contesting the claim of American Union Insurance Group in the liquidation of Central Reinsurance.

Phyllida stirred, opened her eyes and stared at her husband. "What is it, Jack? You haven't slept in hours."

"I didn't mean to disturb you, darling. I was just thinking, maybe I shouldn't try to fight this thing. I mean, if anything happened to you or the baby."

"Tommy rot. Nobody has threatened us. We're not the targets. It's Central's cash they're after. And stopping you from fighting them by trying to throw out their spurious claims." Phyllida punched him playfully in the ribs, "And anyway when did Jack Gregory ever run away from a fight."

The comments were reassuring. Phyllida's attitude helped him to relax and Jack felt himself calm down as he concentrated on rest. But still, there was the germ of something else pressuring him, like a tiny pickaxe tapping away on the inside of his skull.

* * *

November 18, Wednesday

At eleven thirty the next day, having parked the car in the partners' garage in a nearby mews, Jack approached his offices in Queen Anne Street in the West End of London. The imposing, five-storey period building with its high-arched windows and wrought iron balconies had been more spacious than required when the four partners and thirty odd staff had moved in five years ago. Now, it could barely accommodate its six partners and fifty-four employees.

Nodding at Geraldine, the young receptionist, Jack bypassed the lift and raced up the stairs to the third floor and then plodded up the next two to his fifth floor office. He reached the top landing and stood for a moment before continuing towards his own office breathing heavily in the stark realization that with his weight and current level of stress the exercise would more likely kill him than render him fit.

The office's interior, like the rest of the block, had been decorated in pastel shades and soft natural wood finishes. Mirrors and furnishings had Art Deco curves and swirls to them, both conducive to work and at the same time to introducing an aura of tranquility.

Jack had barely sat down at his desk, when June Graham, his secretary of the past ten years, hurried in carrying a wire tray bearing what looked like a one foot high mountain of mail. She was an attractive woman with a pale complexion and bright blue eyes, both of which features starkly contrasted with her black hair which she kept short and combed straight back off her face. In her early forties, if she had ever had a soft spot for her employer, she had kept it hidden under a camouflage of terse efficiency. She was the only person in the firm ever allowed to put Jack in his place; a privilege he felt she exercised with far too great a frequency.

"Welcome back, Mr. Gregory." June had refused, despite Jack's many exhortations, to call him by his first name. She sat down opposite Jack and crossed her legs, adjusting the collar of her white blouse and straightening a crease in the otherwise immaculate skirt of her perennial dark two-piece suit.

"What have you got for me, June?"

"As usual, I've just left you the urgent things."

"Well, that's a relief," Jack smiled as he surveyed the correspondence awaiting his attention.

June ignored her employer's attempt at levity and went on, "Of course, you've advised the partners about the problems Mr. Gregory. They want a meeting with you at one p.m. today. I haven't been able to find out what's on the agenda. But I do know they're extremely worried."

Great news, Jack thought. All he needed was to lose the confidence of the partners he'd brought into the business, and he'd be on the street, in a manner of speaking, without any source of income. Hepton couldn't have planned things better.

"I've arranged for sandwiches to be brought in." June stood up, and reaching forward she placed the letters on Jack's desk where he could reach them as the plop and bubble of coffee percolating filled the room with its deep brown aroma. A moment later she poured from the large chrome dispenser and presented Jack with a mug of the steaming black liquid.

"Okay, what's next?"

June sat down again, "I've allowed an hour for the partners' meeting. Then, you're seeing Mr. George Taylor and his son at two o'clock. They're directors of a family owned business. Goes back over fifty years."

"Liquidation?" Jack drank from the mug.

"That's right. The creditors' meeting's booked for three weeks time."

"Bank Overdraft?"

"Half a million."

"Debenture?"

"Unsecured." June smoothed her skirt again. So far she hadn't needed to refer to her notes.

Jack gulped back some more of his coffee, "I wonder how the directors managed that? Still, at least the bank won't be able to bang in a Receiver over our heads. How's the voting going?"

"A small surplus of proxies for the chairman. You've got support from all the major creditors, it should be all right on the day, I see no reason why you shouldn't get the appointment."

"Hmm, many a slip, June," Jack muttered, as he recalled the Bermuda meeting. "What else?"

"At four, you're seeing Maria Curzon. Self employed. Designs and makes jewellery. Used to employ up to half a dozen staff. Times are not good. She's run up debts to the Inland Revenue. Doesn't want to go bankrupt."

"You've suggested an Individual Voluntary Arrangement to her?"

"Yes. She's amenable to the idea."

"Good." Jack drained the mug. "Any more?"

"A small company liquidation. Nettlefold Ltd., furniture manufacturers. The three directors will be in at six to see you. I've quoted five thousand up front. They're happy with that."

"That it?" He smiled, the office was buzzing just the way he liked it.

"Yes. Until tomorrow. You've got a Section 98 meeting at eleven, Albany Motors Ltd., and then meetings every two hours, until nine p.m. They're all in your desk diary." She glanced in the direction of the big maroon colour book on Jack's desk.

"Day after?"

"Meetings from eight till eight. I'll brief you on the morning."

"Thanks, June. Okay; I'll start on the correspondence now." Jack reached forward and began leafing through the pile June left in front of him. He had not got as far as completing the first letter when his phone went. "Who is it Susan?"

"Mr. Simkin, Inland Revenue about the investigation on the Northmount case, Mr. Gregory."

"Put him through."

The conversation lasted fifteen minutes during which time the Revenue discussed the possibility of proceedings being instituted by Jack to disbar the directors of the company from holding any further directorships for the foreseeable future.

Before Jack hung up, one of his senior managers, Colin Kervil, a tall, pale complexioned young man, came into the office and was waiting for him. "We've got problems with the Eric Methven IVA." Colin sat down in one of the easy chairs opposite Jack's desk.

"Methven? That's the electrical contractor."

"Right," said Colin.

The telephone sounded on Jack's desk, and at the same time one of the junior secretaries came in with a pile of telephone messages for him. He took the call quickly, then turned back to Kervil, but the phone rang again.

As Jack dealt with the matter, the receiver cradled between his shoulder and chin, June returned with some legal documents which she placed before him. Clamping his hand over the mouthpiece, he looked up at her, and she said as though prompted, "Formal disclaimer of the Sopworth lease. We're almost out of time.

Looking surprised Jack exclaimed, "It's a year old and nothing's happened?"

"I'll talk to you about it later. In the meantime, can you sign here?" June indicated a spot between penciled crosses on the document, and Jack signed before returning to his caller.

Kervil got up and whispered, "Shall I come back later?" Jack nodded in reply.

Finishing his conversation, Jack paused to draw breath - office was like a madhouse, it was good to be back - then turned his attention again to the pile of correspondence. Picking the first letter off the top, he glanced at the time on his desk clock. It was one ten. His colleagues would be waiting impatiently for him in the fourth floor conference room, and he was late already.

They were worried, and had not given June their agenda. Deliberately? he wondered. In preparation for the meeting, Jack had June send a memo to the partners briefing them on what had transpired in Bermuda, including the unknown caller with the Oriental voice. Of course, it looked lousy. Who was Jack to argue? Were they concerned Jack was now a liability to the practice? In the competitive world of the insolvency practitioner there was simply no place for losers. Time to face the music, though somehow Jack had the feeling his partners wouldn't be playing his song today. Lighting a panatella, Jack strode purposefully from the room. We'll see, gentlemen, he thought. We'll see.

* * *

The partners of J. Gregory Associates were waiting for him, ranged down both sides of the oval boardroom table.

Jack seated himself at their head and surveyed the talent arrayed before him. All of them licensed insolvency practitioners. All of them used to dealing on a daily basis with the sort of crises that would reduce most people, over a short period, to nervous wrecks. Jack had never seen any one of them truly panicked. It would take an earthquake, he thought, to stampede these men, all of whom seemed to greet their professional lives with a sense of hungry optimism.

Despite Jack's appraisal of them, right now none of the partners were smiling. Most of them looked pale and anxious. To Jack's right, Jeremy Downham, the bluff Yorkshireman in the team, was looking serious. Next to Jeremy was Clive Whitmore, thin faced, ever intense, looked drawn and tired, his eyes sunk deep into their sockets. Bryan Threadgold, big man, broad shouldered, healthy complexion, the extrovert, was not offering any of his usual jokes.

To Jack's left Charles Goldman, stocky and greying, and at fifty-one, the firm's elder statesman, regarded Jack with apparent concern. Finally, Leonard Gorman, with copies of the Insolvency Act and several other pieces of legislation on the boardroom table in front of him, was busy making notes and shuffling papers. Was he imagining it, or was Leonard studiously avoiding Jack's gaze?

Jack drew on his cigar, and gazed over the heads of the partners. Do they want me retired from the practice, he wondered. There was certainly that feeling in the air. Well, he'd soon find out. Breathing in deeply, he braced himself and spoke, "Good morning, gentlemen."

He got no further before the telephone on the boardroom table rang out its high-pitched bleep. Jack leaned forward, irritated, and pressed the conference button, "Didn't June tell you we weren't to be interrupted except for emergencies, Sue?"

"Yes, Jack. But the man was most insistent. He said he wanted to speak to all the partners while you were in debate."

Jack frowned. Who the hell knew they were in conference outside the firm? Then, as if he had known all along, he nodded to himself, and said, "Okay, Sue. Put him on."

Then a soft-spoken voice with an accent spoke, "Thank you for giving me your time, gentlemen. So very kind. I have composed a little piece of poetry for you. Your English nursery rhymes are so charming don't, you think?"

"It's him, gentlemen," muttered Jack. "Obviously." It was nightmarish and Jack bunched his fists and thought, if I could only get my hands on the bastard. He could feel his temperature rising up his neck and head and wondered if his face looked as flushed as it felt. The others were staring at him waiting for his reaction. With an immense effort he brought his fury under control. No point letting them see him lose his cool.

Concentrating his attention on his hands, Jack slowly unclenched the fingers, and giving his colleagues a knowing smile, picked up his cigar and drew on it with forced nonchalance as the voice on the telephone went on. It recited,

"Twinkle twinkle dark inflection
You'll soon have a big inspection
Questions asked and details sought
And six practitioners brought to naught."

Nobody around the table moved a muscle. The sun streamed into the room glaring off the teak surface of the conference table, while outside the distant hum of traffic droned on.

Someone murmured, “The man’s bloody insane. What does he think this is, a kindergarten?”

“Surreal,” said another.

Again Jack fought an impulse to reach forward and take the telephone receiver and snap it in two.

The voice went on, “I hope the impending visit from the Insolvency Monitoring Unit of the Department of Trade and Industry doesn’t cause you too much embarrassment. Like me, gentlemen, you would really benefit from having friends in the right circles. The Ancient Mariner bids you all `good day’”.

Once again there was silence on the line, then followed a high-pitched scream of laughter, “HA HA HAA HEE HEEE HEEEE HEE HEEEEE!!!” and the telephone went dead.

Everyone was speaking at once. All Jack could think was that if the partners had wanted him out before, now they would not need to cover their embarrassment with clever excuses. He raised his hand and the meeting quietened down. They all looked grim and uncomfortable.

Jack couldn’t stand slow executions. If you were going to chop someone down, for crying out loud make it quick.

“Well?” Jack’s voice was loud; it sounded bellicose. “So now you’ve all heard him. I assume none of you had heard him before.” There was a general shaking of heads.

“Sounded like Batman’s ‘Joker’ if you ask me,” muttered Leonard Gorman.

“You’ll find he’s not given much to jokes,” Jack observed dryly. “Except at other peoples’ expense.”

Charles Goldman leaned forward and looked annoyed. Clearly he was about to speak for the others. As the senior partner present he’d been elected spokesman. Jack waited in anticipation for the words that would end his stewardship of the practice he had spent nineteen years building. He breathed in deeply. From the street below the sound of traffic filtered into the conference room while the second hand on the wall clock clicked loudly in the silence.

Finally Goldman spoke, “Jack, you know I speak for all the partners here,” Goldman gazed from left to right and Jack thought, for God’s sake throw the bloody switch if you’re going to. Goldman hesitated, sighed, and continued, “when I say that you can count on our absolute loyalty. We are backing you one hundred percent. We are not simply a partnership. Heaven help the world of business if all it concentrated on was business. We are all trusted friends.”

There were murmurs of “Hear, hear!”

The realization that he had been wrong, that he had completely misjudged the loyalty of his partners washed over Jack like a cold shower. He wanted to thank them – in fact, to hug them, Lord help. All he could see were heads nodding in agreement and smiling faces. Worried frowns maybe, but smiling faces just the same. Instead, he retained his composure, and grinning back at them, said quietly, “Thank you.” He breathed deeply with emotion. “Nice to know we’re all still on board together, gentlemen.”

Chapter 6

November 18, Wednesday

"What's happenin', Kim?" Luke Hepton stood barefoot in the luxury kitchen of his New York penthouse, telephone in one hand, a percolator in the other, about to pour a coffee. From the direction of the bedroom he could hear the sounds of a stirring body. It had been a good night with the girl. Said she was eighteen. More like, fourteen. Still, real tasty. If only he could remember her name.

The almost delicate Oriental tones assailed him, "I am in a block opposite the offices of J. Gregory Associates. The partners are presently in conference, Mr. Hepton."

"What're they saying, son?"

"I'm afraid I am not a lip reader."

"I thought you had the place bugged?"

"It is regularly swept for devices."

"You still in control of things or not?" There was an edge to Hepton's voice.

"Very much so. Mr. David Purdoe is on his way to speak with the partners. He is a competent lawyer, but there are no options available to him. I know. They will be disappointed.

"Also, a visit from our friends at the Department of Trade and Industry is imminent. It would have been useful if it could have been arranged for today, but regrettably it could not be guaranteed. Still, I am hopeful they'll find the time."

"Thought you could guarantee anything."

"I am not God, Mr. Hepton."

"Sure charge like him, boy," Hepton said, and laughed uproariously.

"That reminds me, my latest account has been with you for some time."

"Yeah, yeah," Hepton replied. "Cheque's in the post. Keep in touch," he said, and slammed down the receiver.

* * *

Charles Goldman sighed heavily and scratched the back of his head, "Jack, I must tell you, an odd series of taps and clicks have been picked up by staff here over the past few weeks. I've got a security firm regularly sweeping the offices for bugs. We've been clear so far. The phones may be being tapped from time to time from outside. You don't need access to the offices for that."

The telephone on the boardroom table rang again. Charles Goldman, glancing at his watch broke the silence, "That's probably David Purdoe arriving now." He picked up the receiver and listened, then nodded to the others, "He's on his way up."

A few moments later the door to the boardroom was thrown open and the diminutive lawyer swept in. His black hair looked as though he had just run his fingers through it backwards, and his tie was askew. Depositing his ancient Gladstone bag on the far side of the boardroom table with a bang, he came over to Jack and clasped Jack's brawny right hand between his two diminutive ones, "You're looking well, dear boy, you're looking well." He made the usual pleasantries among the others present, and then opened his bag and extracted several files and notebooks that he deposited on the table.

There was a tap at the door, and June appeared bearing a large tray with cups of tea that she proceeded to distribute among the partners and their guest.

David sat facing Jack, rubbing his tiny white hands together; he looked pleased with himself. The others sipped their tea and waited expectantly for the solicitor to begin.

"Well gentlemen," he proceeded, after a theatrical pause, "I'm pleased to say all is far from lost. We're talking about Central Reinsurance today and our campaign to wrest the liquidation from the hands of Mr. Hepton before bringing it home. There's also the question of the David Purdoe registered secret weapon." He winked at the partners like a mischievous elf. "But more of that later.

"First, I am going to suggest that we issue concurrent petitions in Bermuda and the UK to have the liquidation of Central put in the hands of the courts. I know," he said, holding up a hand before Leonard Gorman could protest. "Hepton could use the strength of his claim to oppose it. If he does, I'll use a section 130 application to get a provisional liquidator appointed."

Clasping his hands together, Clive Whitmore said softly, "Sounds good, David. But I think the problem of Central's millions deposited in US banks needs to be addressed. If fast action isn't taken, Hepton will dissipate those funds before we can move."

Without pause, David continued, his eyes blazing with missionary fervour, "At the same time as legal moves in this country are taking place, I am going to have proceedings issued in America under Section 304 of the United States Bankruptcy Code to recover the forty million dollars of Central Reinsurance's funds held by American banks."

It was Jack's turn to smile. Listening to the irrepressible little man was a joy, and for the first time since the meeting of creditors in Bermuda he felt a flash of real optimism, "How will US courts view our application, David?"

"They will view it with sympathy, Jack. Section 304 grants a sophisticated legal forum to foreign representatives seeking to recover assets in the United States. Yes? Do you see? Foreign representatives, Jack. That's us."

Charles Goldman shook his head. "Apart from opposing us, David, is there any other way that Hepton could gain the initiative and get in ahead of us?"

David drank from his now cold tea, and grimaced before replacing the cup on its saucer. He shook his head when Jack motioned towards the telephone to call for more. "Nothing we need concern ourselves with today, gentlemen."

Gorman drummed his fingers on the table contemplatively; he still looked unconvinced. "Until we get an order of some sort in either a Bermuda or UK court, as I see it, we're still a long way from succeeding."

Still beaming, David said, "Ever the cautious one, Leonard, ever the cautious one. Of course, there's a long way to go and there are no sure fire resolutions. But we have a mass of ammunition at our disposal. And that is what I am getting at today. I'm going to blitz the man with everything I can. And yes, we shall all need to temper optimism with prudence, and prudence with optimism. But we must continue to think positively all the time."

Jack frowned as he glanced at some of his notes. The brief easing of his concern had given way once more to the realization of just how uphill the task facing him was, and he slumped slightly in his seat.

"Remember," David's voice cut into Jack's thoughts, "there's still the question of AUIG's claim. Do you see? It has never been properly verified. I remember what you said about `out of sequence' invoice numbers, Jack. I'll suggest they tender a sworn proof of debt. They'll either refuse, and arouse suspicion, or else accept, and perjure themselves.

"Finally, gentlemen," David said, slowing down at last, "and before we adjourn -- the David Purdoe patented secret weapon." David surveyed the gathering, his cheeks shining like rosy red apples.

All eyes turned towards him. Even Leonard Gorman looked up from his note taking to cast a wry smile in David's direction.

"Come on, David," said Jack. "Just put us out of our misery will you?"

Placing his palms together as if in prayer, David began, "Some years ago, I met a barrister, brilliant man, at an international lawyers' convention. A much older man than me, he had never married. We kept in touch over the years; I often called, or wrote to him if I needed someone to bounce ideas off in matters of international law. He always had the right answer. Never let me down.

"His brother, a Chartered Surveyor, was based in the Caribbean, still is as far as I know. The brother has a grandson, Timothy, aged about thirteen."

"Same age as Gerald, your nephew," Jack interrupted.

David held up one finger, "Precisely. And, as chance would have it, presently attending the same boarding school, Saint Christopher's in Letchworth, Hertfordshire."

Jack was intrigued, "Go on."

"The two boys are in the same class -- both very bright, and both football crazy -- they get on like a house on fire. Well, I met my friend, at a school Open Day last year. He'd flown in especially for it. He's terribly proud of Timothy, spent hours telling me about the youngster's achievements at school. I'd not seen the old boy for some years, and it was nice to chat with him face to face again.

"Of course he was delighted that Gerald and Timothy were friends. In fact he's invited Gerald to his place next summer, so his great nephew can have a chum from England to stay with him for part of the long holiday."

"David, where, in the name of all that is holy, is this leading?" Jack asked.

"The barrister gentlemen, is no longer a barrister. In fact he has not practised at the bar for some years." David surveyed the room with an air of triumph, "The former barrister is Osbert Standish. He is now a judge. In fact he is the Chief Justice in Bermuda."

Jack gave a low whistle, and there were murmurs around the table. "You took long enough to tell us, David. Why didn't you let us in on the secret sooner?"

"Two reasons, dear boy, two reasons. Firstly, I wanted to confirm our options and proposed legal attack on Hepton. Secondly, I wanted to get a purely impartial view of our likelihood of success in the Bermuda Court. Standish is incorruptible. But there's nothing wrong with my sounding him out. And that's what I've done."

David Purdoe hesitated again and beamed, his cheeks glowing.

Adjusting his position to avoid a ray of sunlight that had caught his eye, Bryan Threadgold grinned, "Jack looks as if he's about to throttle you, David, if you give us any more of these pregnant pauses."

"Very well. Very well," David held up his hands in mock defeat. "Standish is on our side. If we petition in Bermuda, he'll give us the winding up order we want. If we petition over here, he'll see to it that the Bermuda courts give us co-operation as far as he is able.

"He doesn't trust Hepton any more than we do. Seems he's come across the type before and would like to see him cut down to size. Hinted that Hepton had been badgering him recently. There's a lot needs to be done in Bermuda, and I'm sending one of my staff out ahead to start getting things organized almost immediately."

This was better, much better. Shoving his chair back, Jack stood up and made for the drinks cabinet at the back of the conference room, "David, that's the best news I've heard in some time. I think we can afford to indulge ourselves in a little celebration. What can I get you?"

The telephone rang again and Jack felt mildly irked. Then he dismissed his impatience. What did it matter? There was time for everything and everyone right now. Nothing was going to interfere with his new mood of optimism.

"Who is it, Sue?" Jack pressed the conference button.

She sounded confused, nonplussed. "I've got an international call waiting for you. He says he wants to speak to the partners."

The room became darker as the sky suddenly clouded over, and Jack went over to switch on the wall lights. The euphoria was dead.

"And, sir..."

"Go on, Sue, what else is there?" Jack asked quietly.

"I...I've got three gentlemen here from the Department of Trade and Industry, Mr. Gregory. They say they've instructions to investigate the firm immediately, following allegations of malpractice. They say they can close you down right now if they find anything untoward." Sue could be heard saying something to someone in the background, and then she went on, "They... they're on their way up now, sir. And... they're running."

Speaking through clenched teeth, Jack said, "Okay Sue, don't get upset. Just put the call through, and ask June to come in, will you."

They all knew who it was going to be. Even before the Southern drawl started. Of course, Jack was the only one who'd heard it before but they all knew just the same.

"You folks all there?" the voice boomed.

There was complete silence.

"Ah said, you all there? Or maybe you all dead."

"We're here," said Jack. "Just get on with it, will you."

"You had a call from my protégé, little while ago. He's a good boy. Charges a high fee, but gives one hundred percent service." Hepton's tone changed abruptly from the jocular to the menacing. "You all little men, you know that? You all outta your league. Gonna have a visit soon from your own DTI. When we finish with you guys, y'aint gonna have a practice. You gonna regret the day you crossed Luke Hepton."

All Jack could see was a blur of faces, mouths moving in animated conversation. He wasn't concentrating, wasn't seeing things clearly. How in God's name had the man managed to... The door burst open and three men carrying brief-cases charged into the conference room trailed by two secretaries who tried ineffectually to stop them. Two of them were average height, and the third, a little man with grey hair combed back off his face approached Jack.

"Sir, my name is Cuthbertson, Reginald Cuthbertson of the Department of Trade and Industry Insolvency Monitoring Unit." He held up his ID with one hand for Jack to inspect whilst making no attempt to shake Jack's hand with the other. Jack just stared at him in disbelief.

"I have to warn you," Cuthbertson said, "there have been allegations of corruption made against this firm. We have the power to investigate every book and record you hold, and to require you to give us sight of all those not kept on the premises."

Jack felt his heart hammering in his chest. It was Bermuda all over again, except that it was more than Bermuda. At the back of his mind he saw a developing scenario involving the loss of all his assets and income from every source and the resulting inability to fight AUIG. They were going to walk off with everything. One by one, each of his lifelines was being attacked. Cut off. He felt adrift on a raft that was taking water and rapidly sinking.

Cuthbertson had his palm extended, his two associates were dealing with the other partners, but Jack had not heard what he'd been saying. He was repeating it. "I must ask you to be good enough to let me have your keys to the premises, Mr. Gregory. Neither you nor your colleagues will be allowed access to these offices until our investigations are complete."

June came into the conference room. She stood with her mouth agape in shocked silence.

"I would suggest you seek the advice of an independent solicitor," Cuthbertson gave David Purdoe an odd look. "In the meantime, I have to tell you that it would be inadvisable for you to say anything in the presence of myself, or my officers, without first considering your position. And then any comment you may have to make should only be made through your lawyer."

Jack looked across at David Purdoe and what he saw filled him with dismay. The little man's face was completely drained of color and he seemed to have aged ten years. Then, David recovered himself, and swiftly going over to Jack's side he whispered, "Give them your keys, Jack. There's no reason why you shouldn't co-operate with them."

"Then what, David? Then what?" Jack muttered. "For Christ's sake? They're taking my bloody practice away; Hepton and his cronies and his Oriental protégé. Can't you do something? We can't just stand here like dummies."

"*Festina lente*, Jack. *Festina lente.* We don't just stand here like dummies." David sounded better, some of the color began to return to his cheeks. He had his hand on Jack's arm, and beckoning the others to follow with an inclination of his head, was gently propelling Jack towards the door. "We go to my offices. Right now. The Department of Trade will clear up here. June will explain matters to the staff. We regroup our forces, dear boy, we regroup our forces."

As Jack left the offices accompanied by his partners, stepping into an overcast Queen Anne street, the sound of an Oriental voice kept ringing in his head, "Questions asked and details sought/ And six practitioners brought to nought..."

"Bloody hell!"

Chapter 7

December 16, Wednesday

It was five a.m. and Jack couldn't sleep. He'd been twisting and turning restlessly for hours, and had eventually stolen quietly from the bedroom, careful not to wake Phyllida. Now he lay back in the steaming jacuzzi, the bubbles popping all around him; in his hand, his favourite drink, a large Scotch laced with a generous dash of Drambuie. Breakfast. Whisky helped him think, made him more alert, kept him awake into the small hours if necessary. It also soothed; the blandishment and the balm.

Four weeks. It had been four God forsaken weeks since the DTI Insolvency Monitoring Unit had stepped in without warning and closed the practice subject to a satisfactory conclusion to their investigations being reached.

Four weeks, during which time the partners continued to finance wages, rents, rates and all the other running costs of the business while receiving not a *sou* in fees.

Twenty-eight days since the garage sites had to be closed after one of them had been sabotaged, several more threatened and two of the staff had ended up in hospital. A month of meeting wages and interest out of personal resources on some three million in loans, and all without banking a penny in takings.

Jack downed the glass in one go and replaced it on the side of the tub. The alcohol tasted like stale tea and the sweat that stood out on his forehead was cold. He was freezing despite the boiling water. This morning the booze was neither spur nor fillip. And as for giving comfort he might just as well have been on some medieval rack. His body ached from stress and felt as though he'd been beaten up.

Jack was a planner and a doer. A man not used to waiting upon anyone or anything. For two fortnights, Jack had broken his inactivity by endless pacing of his study carpet, between endless cups of coffee and cigars and endless calls to David Purdoe. Calls which David fielded patiently while reassuring Jack that proceedings were all underway and telling Jack he had to realize that if he wanted things to happen yesterday, he would still have to wait until tomorrow.

But nothing had happened. Nothing was happening, except that Jack was going slowly and steadily insane. The yacht's insurers held out little hope of any reimbursement. The circumstances were suspicious; the insurance didn't cover malicious acts, etc. etc. He could try employing the services of a loss assessor if he wanted, but it was unlikely he would have any greater success. They were very sorry. Sorry be damned. But they were probably correct: this was Hepton's sabotage.

Hepton, bloody Hepton. Jack could still see the rangy man with the thinning ginger hair plastered to his tiny skull waving his copy of the Insolvency Act and Rules, pointing at Jack and gloating, while addressing Jack's friend Tony, "Mr. Trent, sir. It says right here."

Money draining away like water and nothing coming in.

"Mr. Trent, sir. It says right here."

Going slowly deranged. Bloody inactivity. Week after week after week. Did Hepton have his hands on the US deposits? Forty million dollars. Ten years work. Would David Purdoe's overtures to the US Courts be in time? Would he be able to produce a UK representative, as required, with an interest in the money? Jack knew the answer before he even considered the question.

For all of David's optimism, he would never be able to present the petitions to the relevant US courts in time, the courts having jurisdiction in the areas of the banks holding the company's monies. And even if he did there was every likelihood that he would either be opposed by Hepton, or otherwise simply turned down on any number of grounds Jack could think of.

The initial overtures to the High Courts in both England and Bermuda to have Central Reinsurance placed into compulsory liquidation, thereby taking the administration -- at least temporarily -- out of Heptons hands, had already met with the man's vehement opposition, and further hearings were awaited. Even if any one of them were finally successful, Hepton would have long since grabbed the cash.

Despite David's cheerful bluster at the partners' meeting a month ago, the position looked hopeless nonetheless. Lost. There would be nothing left in the end. Nothing except the prospect of years of legal battles to try and retrieve some of the money and Jack's good name. Legal battles that

Jack had little chance of financing. Only the garages held out some hope and even that was fast diminishing.

Sighing softly, Jack reached over the side of the jacuzzi and poured himself another drink. He would be meeting Danny Jacobovits the auctioneer the next morning. Dynamo Danny. Within a week of Jack's first instruction to him, Danny had completed a recce of all the petrol sites and produced a printed brochure to assist in marketing them.

It had been a Herculean effort. If anyone could do a deal that would fetch what the petrol stations were worth it was Danny. But Danny would need to work fast, damn fast. On the basis of recent history, the combined equity in those assets, a million plus, looked about as safe as snowball in hell.

Climbing out of the jacuzzi, Jack draped a towel around his waist and stood briefly surveying himself in the bathroom mirror. What he saw shocked him. Had he been too preoccupied in recent weeks to notice the change in himself? His already thinning hair was thinner still. Running his hands over his head he noticed how easily the flimsy strands came away and stuck to his palms. He shrugged, baldness was no big problem. What worried him was how quickly his jet-black curls had become flecked with grey. His face was grey. The eyes, heavy lidded and tired, were underlined by prominent blue veined shadows. And he'd lost at least thirty pounds in weight. Ah well, he mused, at least his doctor would be pleased.

"Jack Gregory, you look a bloody mess," he said aloud. And in that moment resolved to stop torturing himself with either the quest for revenge, or else the imperative to recover his money. The attack would be maintained anyway on Jack's behalf, by David Purdoe. Jack would concentrate his energies on assisting Danny and direct his concerns to nothing less than the happiness and well being of Phyllida and the baby. In the end, that was all that mattered.

The businesses could always be re-established, there was time, he was only forty-four. There would be other investments, other projects he could take up. The insolvency practice could be regenerated once the DTI was through with it. Assuming of course that he kept his license to practice.

Unless! A thought suddenly crossed his mind. If the DTI's investigating team was Hepton's work, either directly, or indirectly through his `helper', what else might the man have planted? The knowledge of the humiliation that would ensue from the loss of his professional status hit him, and Jack felt a shudder in the pit of his stomach at the prospect.

Shrugging off the feelings of frustration and futility that weighed on him like a leaden blanket, he threw aside the towel and dragged on a robe and strode from the bathroom. He made straight for the study at the end of the corridor.

The room was all warm browns, with an antique desk and swivel chair and an Edwardian reading lamp juxtaposed with a mass of high-tech machinery.

Sitting at the desk gave Jack the sense that he was in control of events again. It took away the feeling that he was being manipulated by people and events beyond his control. His personal correspondence was being redirected via the post office from Queen Anne Street to his home address and he was faced with a mountain of it; most having accumulated since the offices had been summarily closed. He would dictate some replies for June to pick up and type at home, before returning them to Jack for signature. The rest, Jack would dictate straight into the voice-activated computer and print up himself.

At eight a.m. Jack went down to breakfast. It had been a productive two and a half hours work and he felt much better. His mood improved still further when he was greeted by the sight of his wife and daughter waiting for him in the kitchen. Harriette was in her high chair and waving a spoon in the air. "More," she giggled. "More..."

Phyllida put some pegs of orange on a plate in front of Harriette. "Say please, Harriette."

"Meeze," she chortled happily picking up a piece in her fingers and forcing it sideways into her mouth.

Then Phyllida turned her attention to Jack. Putting her hand on his shoulder she looked him straight in the eye, concerned. "You slept badly," she said softly.

Jack shrugged and looked non-committal, "A bit restless I suppose. Still, I did some catching up this morning. There's a ton of correspondence still needs attention, but I'm on the way. I'm also seeing Danny tomorrow morning."

"The auctioneer?"

"The same. He has high hopes for the petrol stations. But with everything closed down I'm not expecting too much from him. If he can produce a miracle, that'll be quite sufficient." Jack smiled and Phyllida noticed it.

Phyllida came up behind Jack. She put her arms around his neck, and pressed her breasts and hips against him, nuzzling his cheek, "You should smile a bit more often, my handsome fellah. It suits you."

Jack stretched his arms up and hugged her back, "Hasn't been too much to smile about lately. Still, I'm taking it as it comes from now. Hepton's got practically everything anyway, there's not much more he can take, is there?"

"How do you mean?" Phyllida released her hold of Jack and went over to the pot to pour some tea.

"I mean the petrol stations are nothing to do with Central Reinsurance. Whatever I clear from those is mine. Subject, of course, to the usual tax constraints when I take the money out of the business."

"I probably shouldn't ask, Jack."

"Go on, darling, ask. If there's something worrying you..."

"I was wondering about this house. Could Hepton...?"

"Nope." Jack smiled again. "Maybe I should've gone into things in more detail before. But I never really wanted to involve you. The house is in trust in the baby's name. Has been since she was born. It protects her. It protects you. There are tax advantages, and it puts it pretty well beyond the reach of the likes of our US attorney. Not that he could ever put himself in a position to have any claim against the house in any event."

Phyllida sighed deeply, "Well, that's a relief. I should've realized you'd have everything taken care of."

"It'll take more than the likes of Hepton and his mob to put the old maverick out to pasture. Were you that worried, darling?"

"Just a bit," she lied.

Mrs. LLewellyn came into the kitchen bearing a handful of mail, "Good morning, Mr. Gregory. It's a lovely sunny day now isnet? Will I put the post on the sideboard here now before I start on the beds?"

"Thank you, Mrs. Llewellyn," said Jack. "That'll be fine." The housekeeper paused on her way out to tickle the baby under the chin, and the little one waved her arms about and squealed with delight.

While drinking from the cup of tea Phyllida had handed him, he idly flicked through the letters. Something about one of the postmarks attracted Jack's attention. The franking indicated it had been mailed three days earlier from the Bermuda offices of AUIG.

Jack's brow furrowed as he ran his finger under the sealed flap of the large brown envelope and slid out its contents. "Bugger it," he mouthed silently as he riffled through it. But Phyllida had seen him.

"What is it, Jack? Tell me?"

Jack pursed his lips to one side speculatively and bit the inside of his cheek. "Could be a slight problem."

"What sort of problem?" There was a silence. "Jack, if I'm going to help you, you must confide in me. Even if it means I worry as much as you do. Nothing matters, darling, don't you see that? As long as I have you and the baby."

"It's a writ," he said simply, and sat down at the kitchen table.

Phyllida sat opposite him, and then reached down to retrieve a piece of the orange Harriette had dropped on the floor. Absent-mindedly tossing it towards the sink with the waste disposal unit she turned back to Jack. "What kind of writ?

Turning over the pages of the document, Jack glanced up at Phyllida, "It's addressed to me by a Mr. Luke Hepton, liquidator of Central Reinsurance. In essence what it says, is that in my capacity as Director and majority shareholder of Central, I transferred out some ten million dollars of the company's money, with the object, he believes, of financing some of my other business commitments. Principally, the garages. Although it does go on to detail further so called financial interests."

"Jack, I don't understand; but surely, if Central was your own company, you could do whatever you wanted with it?"

"That's right. At least up to a point that's so. I could do as I wanted as long as my company remained solvent. At the moment the company is, for all practical purposes, insolvent. Thus the so called creditors, of whom AUIG just happens to be one, have a vested interest in seeking evidence of whether or not all transfers of cash I made from the company were legitimate, approved by the board, minuted, and so on."

"And were they?"

"Legitimate? Absolutely. Minuted, etc? God knows. Moving, as one frequently has to, at a thousand miles an hour, and making on-the-spot decisions involving large sums of money, often resulted in the finer points of detail being left to be cleared up at the same time as the year end accounts were prepared. It's likely that all sorts of transactions will have been carried out which Hepton in his infinite wisdom is now going to question or seek to overturn."

"What does he want then?"

"Oh, nothing much," Jack smiled wryly and concentrated his attention on Harriette for an instant before turning back to face Phyllida. "Only his ten million dollars back," he murmured. "That's all. Still want me to tell you everything, Phyllida?"

"Absolutely," she said fiercely and banged her cup down on the table. "Every damn thing."

* * *

December 17, Thursday

Jack was ready and waiting, already impatient to be started. He had crept out of bed at five o'clock leaving Phyllida sleeping peacefully, and, having showered quickly, dressed in casual grey sweat-shirt and slacks. He stared out the bedroom window through the early morning mist that curled down the long drive and wondered whether Danny would be on time. Danny was never late. If he said he'd be somewhere by a certain time, he would be there. Come hell, traffic or high water. It was now five fifty-eight and Danny was due at six, and, Jack mused, the man was about to spoil his hitherto unblemished record.

As Jack checked the time again, he grinned broadly at the sound of a motor coming up from the main road. Danny brought the Mercedes crunching to a halt on the gravel outside Jack and Phyllida's front door. Even from his vantage point, high above Danny's car, Jack could barely see his friend's head over the steering wheel. Why did he have to drive such enormous cars, Jack asked himself.

Dynamo Danny. Of indeterminate age, though probably in his mid sixties, Daniel Jacobovits was a man of curious contradictions. His apparent tendency to quiet self-deprecation was coupled with frequent displays of brash self-confidence, which bordered on vanity. The son of Polish immigrants, he came to the UK at the age of two, and remembered nothing of the country in which he had been born.

Mr. Jacobovits senior had been a tailor running a small business in the East End of London making bespoke suits for a wide range of clients. Working seven days a week for years on end, he had managed to finance his son's education at a small private school in Hampstead. He hoped his boy would have better things to look forward to than working round the clock like his father.

Daniel had been consummately disinterested in things academic, despite being possessed of a prodigious memory, and a phenomenal talent for mathematics. At the age of nineteen Danny set up on his own. Concentrating on doing deals, buying and selling job lots, making bargains here and there, perceiving and anticipating customers' requirements -- he never looked back. Keeping his permanent staff to a maximum of three, a secretary and two helpers, Danny made some spectacular killings and became established as a bonded auctioneer living in some style in a luxury flat in North West London.

Jack greeted Danny at the front door. The older man was dressed as usual in an immaculate two-piece suit. "Morning, Danny," Jack whispered, as though his voice might carry upstairs and wake his wife and daughter. He extended his hand. "How're you?"

"I'm lovely," came the reply.

Jack smiled and shook his head, "Danny, you're always lovely."

"Course, I am. You want I should be a pessimist?"

"No, but don't you ever worry? In ten years I've never known you to get upset about anything. Not even that wayward son of yours."

"Jack, you got to think positively. Most things that keep us awake at night turn out okay in the end."

"I know. But that doesn't stop them from being a source of worry on the way." Jack closed the front door behind him, and accompanied Danny out onto the gravel, their feet crunching on the pebbles.

"Look, I know you've got big problems right now. But keep your eye on the positive side. You've got your health and strength, a beautiful wife and a gorgeous baby. I know you're trying to get back the fortune that bastard Hepton's got his sticky fingers on. But he can't have spent it already. Things'll work out, mark my words. They always do."

Danny twirled his car keys in his hand as they walked. "The practice is being given a hard time by the DTI, I know. But they won't find anything that'll let them close you down. Trust Danny, he knows. And then there's the garage sites. You're looking at a million plus equity there. You're not broke yet Jack not by a long chalk." Danny was ushering Jack into the Mercedes, "We can take mine," he said as he held the door open.

"Danny, you're a tonic."

"Course, I am. I see things clearly that you're too close to get a perspective on."

Peering intently over the steering wheel, Danny directed the vehicle down Jack's drive and onto the main road.

Just before his friend turned the car into the mainstream, Jack glanced over his shoulder out the rear window in time to see Phyllida waving at him from their bedroom window. She must have woken at the sound of Danny's car starting up. Or perhaps the baby. She was holding Harriette propped on one hip, her arm about their daughter's waist. The little one was waving in her funny way, opening and closing the fingers of one chubby little hand, and apparently giggling all the while.

Jack then leaned forward, and, resting one hand on the dash, turned his attention to Danny, "All right, Danny, what's this all about? You said you wanted to show me something urgent. Fine. But why on earth did we have to make such an early start?"

Danny took his eyes from the road for a moment and glanced at Jack, "I think we may have a slight problem, my friend." He spoke in uncharacteristically measured tones. "Nothing that can't be handled, but something that needs to be dealt with quickly.

"Don't tell me," Jack said wearily cynical. "Someone's stolen the garage sites."

"Hmm! I wish it was that funny. But it isn't. I'm afraid someone is dumping used tyres on some of the sites. I noticed it was happening when

I started going around to prepare the catalogue I've had printed for the sale of everything.

"I know, you spoke to me about it a couple of days ago."

"Yes, well, at first it didn't seem like much, a few old tires here and there. But I've revisited some of the petrol stations, and the number of tires at each address is increasing, and increasing fast. Someone is really taking advantage of the situation and saving themselves a fortune in dumping charges."

Shrugging, Jack said, "So, what's the problem? Someone's chucked a few worn tires off a lorry at some of the garages. I understand they're expensive to get rid of, so the empty sites are a gift. We'll make it harder for them. We'll make the garages more secure. And, if the dumping persists I'll get David Purdoe to start issuing proceedings." Jack was frowning, "Is that all of it then? Is that why you've dragged me out at six in the morning Danny?"

"Hang on, Jack, hang on. It's not that simple. For one thing, who're you going to get David to issue proceedings against? We don't know who we're dealing with. And, making sites secure involves laying out money."

"How much? Do you have any idea?"

"I can give you a rough outline. You'd need two men to be *in situ* twenty four hours a day; that means a caravan to accommodate them."

"Terrific! Anything else?"

"A dog."

"A dog?"

"Yes. The two men would need a dog for added protection."

"Okay, Danny," Jack sighed. "I'm beginning to get the picture.

What's all this likely to cost? Dare I ask?"

"It's not a difficult exercise. If each man is on somewhere between say five and ten pounds per hour, make it eight pounds for the sake of argument."

"All right, eight pounds an hour. Then what?"

"That tots up to three hundred and eighty-four pounds a day. Add the dog and caravan, say another sixty or seventy quid. Call that the round sum of three point two grand a week. And that's per site. Remember, we're talking six addresses here, so far." Danny raised his eyebrows speculatively. "We, or to put it bluntly, you Jack, could be facing a monthly bill amounting to as much as seventy-six thousand Pounds for security. I was doing some figures before today." Danny turned to face Jack again, "It's not good, I'm afraid."

Jack shifted his broad shoulders uncomfortably in his seat, a familiar sense of foreboding dragging his spirits down. "You realize, if we find substantial numbers of tires at the sites today; if this is not a random thing, I could be staring at the prospect of having to secure all seventeen sites."

"I wasn't going to mention it right away, but yes, Jack, you might."

Breathing in deeply, Jack fished out a calculator from his sweatshirt pocket and held it in the palm of his hand, "God in heaven, Danny. I'd rather not contemplate what I'm faced with right now. This has got to be the work of Hepton and the Chinaman again, hasn't it?

"Who else?"

"What do we do?"

"For a start, we don't panic. We clear the sites of tires where we need to before the costs of that exercise start running away with us, we get the security organized, and then get every last garage sold double quick."

"And if they won't sell quickly?"

"Jack, they're all in prime locations. I've got the catalogues prepared already with descriptions of each individual petrol station, its tank capacity, number of pumps, number of cars calling every day, turnover, profitability. You name it. I've even included the Liverpool site damaged in the explosion, with an adjustment to cover costs of reinstatement if the insurance doesn't pay out."

"I'm impressed. How did you manage to get everything together so quickly?"

"My life, Jack. Course, you're impressed. You don't employ me for my good looks. Have you forgotten? I found nearly all the garages for you in the first place."

"True."

"I've simply kept all the info on them. I knew you might want to sell some of them one day. I used to be a boy scout, I like to be prepared."

Jack raised his eyebrows, "You're fantastic, Danny."

"I'm lovely."

"You're lovely," Jack shook his head and smiled. "Where to first, Captain."

"I thought we'd take a look at Sheffield to kick off, then go on to Manchester. If we've got time, we'll do Birmingham and Liverpool. London seems to have been left alone, at least," he added cryptically, "up to now."

"Seventy-six thousand Pounds a month for security for six sites, eh, Danny?"

"You said it."

"That's two hundred and seventeen thousand for all the sites," said Jack as he tapped out the figures. "That's unreal," Jack sat back and reached into his pocket for a cigar, "Mind if a smoke?"

"Be my guest," Danny said, and reaching forward, pressed the cigar lighter to activate it.

"At that rate the equity would be wiped out in well under a year."

"Yup."

"And there's still borrowing charges accruing on the loans on dormant sites to take into consideration." Jack paused and stared into the distance, "Danny, I could be confronting imminent, total disaster."

Danny scratched the crown of his head contemplatively, "Could be even worse than that."

"What! How?"

"You haven't included the costs involved in clearing away the tires."

"Wonderful."

"Sorry, Jack."

Jack felt a trickle of perspiration at the back of his neck, and he tugged at his shirt collar, "So what's that going to cost? Go on, surprise me."

"About a grand a vehicle."

"But that's a fortune."

"I know, but we're looking at thirty ton trucks to hire, with added labor to load and unload. Then there's the charges we'll have to pay for dumping the stuff."

"Are we really going to need vehicles that size?"

Danny rubbed the back of his hand against the point of his nose, "Could be."

"Who arranges everything? I mean vehicles and labor and so on?"

"I do."

"Everything?"

"Everything."

"That's a relief."

"Course, it's a relief."

"Christ, Danny, I wish I could be as bullish about everything as you." Then, as though he were unwilling to waive his caution, Jack asked, "How many lorries, Danny?

"That's what we're about to find out today."

Easing himself against the car's padded backrest with his eyes closed, Jack hauled on the cigar dragging the smoke deep into his lungs, "And you said I should be an optimist?"

"Why not?" Danny smiled confidently. "I've got three interested parties going the rounds this week, and I haven't even advertised the garages in the *Financial Times* yet. When I do; then you can sit back and watch the sparks fly."

"How are you going to arrange a sale? On an individual basis, or all in one?"

"Any way I can, Jack my boy. Any way I can."

"How long could it take?"

"You know the answer to that one as well as I do."

"Sure I do. How long is a piece of string? But give me something, anything to go on."

"Reasonably?"

"Reasonably."

While he considered the question, Danny grimaced and wrinkled his nose as if he had something sour on his tongue. He rocked his head from side to side for a few moments, then shrugged, "Could be three, four months; maybe longer. If one buyer takes the lot, we could see it all cleared up in less time than that. If we need to break things up into several parcels, possible overlapping offers, people needing to tie up finance..." Danny paused, "Could be anything from a month to a year; even longer. Who knows."

"Christ Almighty, Danny," Jack massaged his palms against his thighs and muttered under his breath, "What a bloody mess."

The two men continued in silence until Danny took the lead off the motorway signposted for Sheffield. Propping one elbow in the palm of his other hand, Jack absentmindedly tapped his front teeth with the back of a thumbnail, "I know it's crazy, but I keep hoping that this isn't going to be Hepton's work."

"Pigs should fly, Jack."

"You realize, of course, that if this is Hepton, he won't simply sit back and let us sell the sites unhindered."

"The thought had occurred to me. But let's cross that bridge when we get there."

"But Danny, I need this money. All of it, and fast. Else there's no way I can fight the man. Legal fees will cost a fortune, and I've already had a writ issued against me by Mr. Luke Hepton for ten million."

"You never mentioned that before."

"It's the latest episode in this exciting saga. I didn't mention it, because talking about it means thinking about it, and I don't have any answers right now. Except to fight on."

"I think I could use one of those cigars, Jack."

"You mean it?"

"Almost. Look, if need be, I'll work on this seven days a week. Okay, it looks black right now. But the equity is still intact; if I can set up sales quickly, we can start to haul in the cash, and keep security and interest charges to a minimum. You've been looking at a worst case scenario which might never happen. We're well ahead of the game right now, Jack my boy. Just trust Daniel Jacobovits, and all will be well."

Jack grinned, "Danny, you're lovely."

"I'm lovely. Course, I'm lovely."

The car approached the first of the Sheffield petrol stations on the Hills Road junction with Mutrix Road, when Jack, touching Danny lightly on the shoulder with one hand, pointed forward with the other, "What's that up ahead?"

Danny squinted, and shook his head noncommittally.

"Something's spilling out into the road." Jack's throat caught as the car got nearer and he couldn't speak. For a moment he could hardly breathe.

Danny had said nothing right up to the moment when Jack roared at the top of his voice, "Tires, Danny, on the forecourt, round the pumps, in the street, everywhere. For the sake of Jesus Christ, a whole bloody sea of them. And this is only the first of seventeen sites."

Chapter 8

December 17, Thursday

Phyllida closed the curtains and sat down on the bed with Harriette on her lap. Jack would be gone all day with Danny and she shouldn't wait up for him. He'd promised that he would tell her everything that was happening, but had he? Was he? Or was there more? Was he still trying to protect her? How could she possibly give her husband her support if he kept things from her?

If they lost everything they could start again, Jack had said. Jack wasn't even worried about the money Hepton had taken, would take. God she was so confused. She ran a hand over her brow and pushed the hair back off her forehead.

Harriette hugged her, and her tiny voice insistently broke into Phyllida's thoughts, "Dwink Mummy, dwink."

"Yes, darling," Phyllida blinked away the demons in her head and concentrated on her daughter, reaching out as she did so to the bedside table for the plastic topped baby mug of water.

"Tanku, Mummy." Phyllida watched her daughter's small rounded cheeks pumping up and down as they moved in time with her drawing on the drink and felt flooded with love for the sweet smelling bundle of vulnerability. She hugged Harriette to her, feeling her daughter's minute heartbeat pattering against her own. Please God help us through this, she thought, if anything were to happen to Jack...

If Jack suspected for one moment how afraid for the future Phyllida really was; if he ever guessed that the support she had promised him depended absolutely upon the strength that she in turn drew from him... She wanted to close her eyes; it was early morning and she was terribly tired. Her eyelids felt heavy. She needed to sleep, to try and stop worrying.

Jack would be home later, that slight smile playing at the corner of his mouth, a sweet smell of cigar all about him. Darling Jack. Phyllida lay back on the bed with the baby, still sucking at the drink, snuggling up next to her and found herself blessedly drifting off to sleep.

Suddenly starting with a jolt, Phyllida sat up. Something was wrong. Her head was heavy, temples throbbing; she'd been wrenched from a deep sleep. All she could hear was the bell of a police car, no an ambulance, a fire engine. It couldn't be, they didn't have bells any more. Glancing at the bedside clock, she saw it was coming up to six thirty. She'd been asleep for less than half an hour.

The phone rang with the insistence of a petulant child. Phyllida put the receiver to her ear. Her voice sounded cracked and unreal to her, "Hello?"

There was a moment of silence, and then an American voice said, "Would this be the Gregory household?"

She knew who it was before he'd said another word and felt a rush of fury jumbled up with blind terror. Swallowing back the lump of fear in her throat she tried to sound as calm as she could, speaking through a jaw juddering as though it were freezing, "That is correct."

"My name is Hepton, Luke Hepton. Ah'm the liquidator of what was your husband's company. He may have mentioned my name to you?" The southern American drawl sneered at her with open contempt.

Phyllida clenched her fists; she wanted to yell at him to leave them alone. Her fear of the man could not blank out a rage the like of which she had never experienced. She paused until she felt calmer. "What do you want?" was all she said.

"I thought you'n me'd have a little talk. Nice'n cosy like. Leastways, just while your husband's away inspecting his gas stations."

"How do you know what my husband's doing today?"

"Lady, they's a whole lot we know 'bout you and your old man. Wouldn't do to go into too much detail though."

"You mean you've bugged our phone?"

"Let's just say we're keeping an eye on things," Hepton sniggered. "Need to ensure that Mr. Gregory don't do nuthin' to jeopardize the interests of the unsecured creditors of Central Reinsurance."

"Hah!" Phyllida exploded. "Don't make me laugh. Jack's already told me that before you sharks forced your way in, all of the creditors were expected to receive one hundred pence on the pound."

"I think you mean one hundert cents on the dollar, lady."

"Don't be facetious with me, Mr. Hepton. You and your type are nothing more than vermin."

"Lady, you got a sharp tongue. Gonna get you into a whole lotta trouble one day."

"Are you threatening me?"

"Heavens no, ma'am. Just making an observation. Professional people don't make threats now, do they?"

"Why did you call, Mr. Hepton? What do you want?"

"Well, ma'am, like I say, it is incumbent upon me in my capacity as liquidator of Central Reinsurance to act in the best interests of the unsecured creditors. Your husband's constant opposition to my appointment is beginning to give me cause for concern. I mean I'm having to spend creditors' money in meeting legal fees to fight Mr. Gregory."

"How very inconvenient for you. And were you forced to spend creditors' money in paying the Chinaman a fee to blow up one of my husband's petrol stations?"

"That's a lotta talk for one little lady."

"Don't patronize me." Phyllida's voice rose several notes. "If you don't have anything sensible to say, I'm going to hang up this telephone."

"No don't do that, Mrs. Gregory, I really would entreat you most respectfully to listen to what I have to say."

Phyllida said nothing.

"Okay, lady, you don't have to answer me if'n you don't want to. But you hear this and you hear it good, 'cos I'm gonna say it just one time. You haul your old man off my case. I get any more obstruction from him in carrying out my legal obligations and I'm gonna start being a lot less polite than I been up to now. He's almost outta funds anyway, I know that. But I'm gettin kinda tired of havin' him pickin' away at my side. He's bitin' off a lot more'n he can chew. Take my word for it, I can and will get really short tempered if'n he don't call a halt on this. You hear me?"

"Go to hell," Phyllida screamed, "Jack will never give up. Never." She slammed down the receiver disturbing Harriette with the noise.

For several minutes Phyllida stared ahead into space, her chest heaving, her neck and forehead bathed in sweat. Then she slipped out of bed, leaving Harriette resettled, and, stepping into the en suite bathroom, turned on the shower and stepped under its boiling torrent letting the steamy heat calm her nerves.

* * *

December 18, Friday

It was two a.m. before Jack got back home. Immediately she saw him, Phyllida knew things were bad. His shoulders were bowed and he was drawn, his stubble of a beard showing dark on his chin after nearly twenty-four hours without a shave.

Phyllida's heart went out to him. Taking Jack by the arm, she led him into the kitchen and sat him down while she put the kettle on, "I'm making you a mug of hot camomile tea, Jack. No, not coffee," she said anticipating his next remark. "You need to rest and unwind, and then I want to hear all about what's happened. "She contemplated telling Jack about the call from Hepton, but decided to delay it for the time being; he looked as though he had quite enough to occupy his attention.

Sitting at the kitchen table opposite Jack, warming her hands on a mug of hot chocolate, Phyllida waited for him to speak.

Jack closed his eyes and sipped the searing liquid, the camomile slowly relaxing his muscles and bringing with it a sense of peace. Nothing felt real to him any longer. Danny's enthusiasm, as ebullient as ever, had failed to convince Jack that he was anywhere but on a roller coaster to financial oblivion.

The familiar feeling that he should keep all this to himself nagged at him. Phyllida demanded he tell her everything. She would have to know one day, whichever way it eventually went.

"I might have only three months at best," Jack said finally, and watched to see if Phyllida's expression changed.

Placing the mug on the table, Phyllida matched her husband's gaze with her own, "Three months 'til what, Jack?"

"Three months for me to sell all the petrol stations before the liquidation of JG Petroleum Holdings becomes an insolvent one. Three months before I run the risk of losing control of it. If that happens, I lose all the equity I was hoping would help finance us for the immediate future, and me in my fight against Hepton." Jack smiled grimly, "The odds against succeeding are about a thousand to one."

Phyllida was looking at Jack quizzically, her head slightly to one side, "I didn't know JG Petroleum was in liquidation."

"It's not. At least not yet. I'm swearing a Declaration of Solvency at David Purdoe's in the morning and passing the necessary resolution at the same time appointing myself as liquidator."

"Do you mean in the same way you did with Central?"

"That's right," Jack said, and took a gulp of camomile. "I've no choice; the business is solvent, at least on paper, although the sites aren't operational. I could sit back and do nothing while Danny starts selling them, but if things go awry quickly then I'd be compelled to call a meeting of creditors to appoint an independent liquidator."

"Not you."

"Not me. If the liquidation looks as though it's going to go insolvent in say three months or more from now, the law requires me to go through that procedure."

"As you did in Bermuda?"

"Right. I can only remain liquidator of my own company as long as it's in a position to pay out everyone in full. Once that changes and there's a shortfall, the liquidation has to be conducted by a practitioner who has had nothing to do with the running of the business."

"I'm not sure I understand. What difference does it make who winds up a company; as long as they're a licensed practitioner?"

"It's the principal of conflict of interest. If a company has been badly run -- and if a director has been guilty of malpractice or simple incompetence and his creditors have suffered as a result -- it may be necessary for the liquidator to submit an adverse director's conduct report. Such a document might well recommend that the director be disbarred from holding directorships for a given period."

Getting up to wash out her mug, Phyllida nodded in the direction of Jack's, which was empty of camomile, but he shook his head, "I see, if the director just happens to be the liquidator as well, he's hardly likely to recommend his own disbarment," she said.

"Exactly."

"I still don't understand why you need to wind up the company right now. What's the point? What are you going to gain from it?" Phyllida said, glancing at Jack over her shoulder.

"I gain time. A lot of the creditors, both the unsecured, and those who are secured with loans charged against sites, for example the oil companies, will be wanting to know why their debts aren't being paid on time, or their loans serviced. If I put the company into what is known as Members Voluntary Liquidation, I've got a year or more before I need to pay them out."

"But you didn't get that year with Central?"

"No, because within that time, a claim, albeit a spurious one, was lodged with me. The claim was so large that it turned a solvent situation into an insolvent one, and I was compelled to give the creditors -- who were now ostensibly facing a shortfall in their claims -- the opportunity of selecting an independent liquidator of their own choice."

Sitting down at the table again, Phyllida took Jack's hands in her own, she looked perplexed, "But, darling, it all went wrong at the meeting in Bermuda."

"Yes, it did, because of Hepton. But Hepton doesn't have a licence to practice in this country. I think we're pretty safe from him and his influence here." Jack took his hands from Phyllida's and resting his elbows on the table rubbed his temples wearily.

"But that's not all," Jack sighed and told Phyllida about the massive costs of clearing the tires from the petrol sites he and Danny had visited.

"Jack, that's incredible."

"You can say that again. So, to summarize," Jack rocked back on his chair folding his arms across his chest and glanced up at the ceiling speculatively and muttered details under his breath. Phyllida vaguely heard him refer to security charges, costs of site clearance and interest on loans both old and new.

Eventually he turned back to her, "Assuming all sites are protected from the outset, I'll need to find almost a million within three months, as I said. By that time we're practically into deficit."

Phyllida pondered for several moments, "Of course, there's always the chance you won't have to secure all sites from day one."

"True. And Danny might negotiate better deals on the lorries. He might also secure quick sales of some, or all of the garages. But for once I don't think it would help to be too hopeful, no matter what Danny says. I've got to accept that this could be a worst case scenario."

"What's the best case scenario darling? If I'm not being naively optimistic."

Sighing, Jack said, "Quick disposal, probably to an oil or property company. Completion in a month. Security on only six sites. Minimal interest charges. Split the cost of clearance with the buyer to speed things up. We might still see a half to three quarters of a million surplus."

"Well, that's the ticket that gets my vote."

Jack smiled and stretched, "I've had it for one day. `To sleep, perchance to dream', my love, is what I need." He stood up, absent-mindedly spotting some unopened mail on one of the kitchen counters. "I'm starting to sound as theatrical as David Purdoe. Must be close association."

"Silly," Phyllida came round the table and pushed Jack playfully in the chest. Then slipping her arms around his neck, she looked at him coyly, "Just how tired is Mr. Gregory at the moment?"

"Well, now," he mused kissing her ear, "we might possibly see if we can muster a modicum of early morning energy."

"Come, Tarzan," said Phyllida cocking her head to one side. And turning on her heel, she took Jack by the hand to lead him from the kitchen.

But something played at the back of Jack's mind and he delayed for a moment, "Phyl, what are all those letters on the sideboard?"

"Leave them, Jack," Phyllida murmured. "Come to bed. They're just statements. They'll wait till the morning."

"Okay," he replied. "You go on up, I'll bring the water." Opening the door to the cupboard over the sink, Jack extracted two glasses, and started to fill them from the fresh water filter, glancing at the mail as he did so. He had intended to leave it untouched as Phyllida had suggested, and, in no more than idle curiosity spread the letters in a fan with one hand while the second glass was filling.

As Phyllida had said, there were statements in the familiar envelopes from Amex and Barclaycard. There were also monthly accounts from John Lewis and Selfridges, and what looked like a couple of circulars. That was it, and with the second glass full Jack was about to follow Phyllida when he spotted a brown envelope under the rest of the pile.

Deciding he should leave it until the morning, Jack then sighed, and, putting down the two full glasses slid the letter out from under the others. Instantly he did so he recognised the familiar DTI logo and again debated whether to open it now or leave it. Telling himself that curiosity killed the cat, Jack slid his finger along the inside of the flap and extracted the letter. Be optimistic for a change, he decided. Follow Danny's advice and Phyllida's example.

From the top of the stairs, Jack could hear Phyllida's whispered entreaties to hurry up, and he skimmed through the letter as fast as he could. It was high time they gave him back his practice anyway, and it would be wonderful to end an exhausting day with a bit of good news for a change.

The correspondence stated that the DTI inspectors had examined some sixty of his practice cases in all. Some in depth, others superficially. The inspectors had no quarrel with the way the practice was being run by all but one of the partners. Evidently something minor, Jack concluded, judging by the general tone adopted. Indeed, it went on to say, there was no reason why the firm of J. Gregory Associates should not reopen for business forthwith. "About bloody time, too", Jack said aloud.

Sighing with relief, Jack skipped the last couple of paragraphs, and then read them again more carefully. A complaint had been levelled by a creditor about the way in which one of the firm's cases was being handled. The creditor was concerned at what appeared to be a classic `phoenix situation'. The directors of a window glazing company had recommenced business immediately after their company had been put into liquidation. They were trading with the same staff, and from the same premises and with the same stock as previously. What was more, the creditor had reason to believe that the directors had taken over the goodwill of the old business without paying a penny for it.

Running his hand over his head, Jack considered the final few sentences of the DTI's correspondence. They viewed the matter with the utmost gravity. Jack was wanted for questioning at DTI premises in London in approximately five weeks time, the date to be agreed. He should allow at least two days for the interview. Until then, he was to take no part whatsoever in the running of his business. His other partners were free to return to Queen Anne Street as of now. Failure to comply with DTI instructions would leave Jack open to immediate prosecution, and summary withdrawal of his insolvency practitioner's license.

It was going to be a great Christmas.

Chapter 9

January 18, Monday. Current Year.

"Fire risk?" Jack shouted into the telephone. "What the hell do you mean fire risk? And why the devil didn't you tell me about this before, Danny?"

At the other end of the line Danny's voice sounded aggrieved, "Jack, I'm a dealer in merchandise not a fireman. My life, you want I should sell the sites for you. The idea's just been put to me, I thought I should talk to you about it."

Jack fiddled with the Newton's Cradle on the desk in his study at Highview. The idea of making essential calls from the office in Queen Anne Street -- even if he avoided having anything to do with any of his cases either directly or indirectly -- had crossed Jack's mind, and been immediately dismissed in the light of the DTI's warning to him. There seemed little point in taking the slightest risk of jeopardizing his license before the interview he was now scheduled to have with the DTI in a week's time. The festive season had been anything but festive, although to be fair, Phyllida, ably assisted by the LLewellyns had done her best. Little seemed to be improving.

Trying to assess the implications of Danny's revelation, Jack meditatively pulled back one of the chromium ball bearings and let it drop against the others hanging in line. With an emphatic click it made a connection setting up a series of clicks as the line swayed back and forth under the consecutive impact of the two end ball bearings as they jumped in turn, out and back, out and back.

"You still there, Jack?"

"Yes, Danny, I'm still here."

"Well?"

"It's taken you more than four weeks to come up with this little gem."

"I didn't come up with it, Jack. A fire officer from the local brigade collared me at the Hills Road garage in Sheffield while I was showing a customer around. He read me the Riot Act, said I'd better get in touch with all the other local brigades and let them know what was happening."

Sliding a cigar from the pack on the desktop, Jack flicked the Dunhill lighter and watched the flame as it caught at the end of the panatella. He inhaled and blew smoke towards the ceiling idly watching the swirling patterns it made. "Okay, what's the damage this time?"

"Did you ever hear about that fire in Canada?"

"What fire?"

"There was this massive blaze of tyres a few years back, covered the whole local area with a black fog of fumes. They couldn't put it out."

"How many days did it last?"

"Not days Jack."

"Go on surprise me; weeks?"

"Get this! It lasted for years. Years, Jack! It just smouldered on, sending black clouds into the atmosphere until there was nothing left to burn."

Leaning forward, his elbows on the desk, Jack buried his face in his hands for an instant. Then he retrieved the telephone, "I suppose I should blame myself as much as anything for not realizing it sooner. Too preoccupied with other things, although, that's no excuse." It was at that moment that the full import of the situation hit him, and Jack sat bolt upright, "My God, Danny, the petrol tanks; they're as near as full, dammit all."

"Yes," Danny's voice sounded far away.

"We, that is I, am responsible for half a dozen time bombs."

"That's right, Jack."

"All it would need would be single a match, a random act of vandalism."

"That's all it would need."

"Hang on a minute." Jack pushed his chair back from the desk and went over to where the percolator was starting to bubble. Turning it off, he poured himself a thick black cup, and added four spoonfuls of sugar before returning to his place. "Okay, Danny, listen carefully, I want to know the following: What do the local fire officers require of me, as of right now? Is there any reason why their instructions can't be carried out to the letter? I'm not prepared to risk lives under any circumstances.

"Next, has the advertizement for the garages been published yet? You said it was expected to go in a few days ago. You've had weeks to organize that since we last did the rounds of all the stations."

"Hey, Jack! You're forgetting we've had the usual two-week Christmas lull. And yes, the ad went earlier this month."

"Any response? If so, what and from whom? I want names, addresses and contacts. You had three potential buyers prior to the ad. You've already told me they've seen everything. Has anything materialized? Have offers been made?"

"Jack!"

"Have there been any tyres dumped at any of the other sites? On your advice, Danny, I've only secured the first six. I know I'm saving on the costs involved but am I risking other people's lives in other areas? Could I be faced with further removal costs greater than the costs of guarding the sites?"

"Jack, Jack, slow down already. My life, he's like a bull in a china shop." There was a pause, and Danny went on, "Right. Are you listening?"

Taking a deep breath, Jack said, "I'm listening."

"Good. First off, the local fire officers require that all petrol tanks be emptied, and that they be sealed off entirely with concrete."

"Can we do that?"

"Not till we clear the tyres out of the way."

"God! Talk about Catch 22. This is horrendous. All right go on."

"The ad drew over one hundred responses."

Jack picked his cigar from the ashtray and drew on it, "Well done, Danny. For once a bit of good news."

"I've got more. When the three original buyers finished viewing I started dropping hints about them getting bids in before each other, and also before the FT ad went in. They wanted to know what I expected the petrol stations to go for, so I upped the ante."

"Make me smile."

"I re-valued everything, and without going too far, I guess you could be looking at a gross of around four and a half mil. And that's taking into account the state of the burned out site at Nathan Road, Liverpool.

"Say again, Danny."

"Four and a half million pounds."

"Whew!" Jack breathed. "That would give me a good one point five million clear of borrowings."

"Right."

"And a lot more time to play with before the question of insolvency and a possible creditors' meeting might arise."

"Correct."

"It might not arise."

"Agreed. If I make a quick sale you'll be in the clear, with lots of equity to finance the campaign against Hepton."

"What about the other sites? Anything happening? Any tyres appearing?"

"Not so far. Please God, it should stay that way. I should be in a position to accept a quote in the next two to three days, and then to start the clear up operation shortly after that."

"Will the time taken to clear away the tires slow up the sale?"

"It shouldn't. As long as we can promise vacant possession. If I sell quickly enough, there won't even be the time for you to empty the tanks or do the concreting. The new owner or owners will be responsible for their own security. It won't be your problem any more."

"That just leaves me to find the two hundred and fifty thousand I reckon I'll need for haulage charges. The bank has agreed a facility in principal. I'm seeing them later today to sign up mortgages against some of the petrol stations. Daniel, my boy, it's looking better."

"It's looking better."

Looking grim Jack said, "As long as nothing goes wrong."

"So what should go wrong?"

"Don't ask. God, Danny, I'm starting to sound like you."

"So what's wrong with that?" "

Despite himself, Jack grinned, "You're lovely."

"I'm lovely."

"I'll talk to you, Danny," Jack said, and hung up.

* * *

January 19, Tuesday

There was a knock and Mrs. Llewellyn poked her head around the door, "Will I be after doing this room, Mr. Gregory?"

"Not just yet, Mrs. Llewellyn. Give me an hour and it's all yours."

"You're awful stuffy now in yer, isnet? Shall I open a window and let in some fresh air before you incinerate yourself with all those cigars?" Mrs. Llewellyn looked disapprovingly at the ashtray with Jack's now burned down panatellas. "And Mrs. Gregory wants to know if you're coming down for lunch."

"Tell her `yes' for me please, Mrs. Llewellyn. And by all means open a window, and clear away the ashtray. Then I need an hour of hush," Jack said, wagging a finger at her in mock remonstration.

When Mrs. Llewellyn finished bustling around, and Jack had a fresh drink in front of him, he telephoned David Purdoe, "Morning, David. How're you?"

"I'm fine, dear boy. I'm fine."

"You know the DTI have partially hauled off? I've been too much up to my eyes in it to call you."

"Charles Goldman just informed me. Isn't that excellent news? I think it demonstrates conclusively that Mr. Hepton and his agent from the Far East are not invincible." It sounded as though David were smiling as he talked, "Six practitioners brought to naught indeed."

"Well, there's still one of them out of commission, David."

"Yes, yes, yes. But we're dealing here with Her Majesty's Government. The Department of Trade and Industry may occasionally be brusque, but they are not corrupt."

"I've got an interview coming up with them, David. I must say I'm not looking forward to it."

"But, Jack, you've got nothing to hide."

"Of course, I haven't. What worries me is not what I have to hide, but what they do."

"Why, whatever do you mean?"

"Any investigating body may have a vested interest in keeping the real purpose of their enquiry to themselves."

"You're losing me, Jack."

"There may be all sorts of reasons for it. It's a regrettable weakness of human nature to form conclusions based on impressions, and then to seek only to verify those conclusions. The, `no smoke without fire' syndrome."

David sounded thoughtful, "I suppose."

"Then again, they may wish to protect their sources of information."

"Point taken, Jack. Presumably Hepton has been enlisting some help in the UK. But in the end, whatever it is the DTI think they're after, unless they can prove a case based on incontrovertible evidence, they will have to let you return to your practice. All that Hepton has done is to embarrass you, cost you money and to a minor extent impede the progress of your defence against him "

"Isn't that enough for starters?" Jack laughed.

"Yes, Jack it is, But it doesn't close you down. And your partners are already back at work, presumably mending a lot of fences. I think you're worrying unduly. I really do, dear boy."

"David, I'll tell you what worries me. It's the unknown factor. Maybe it was simply the tenor of the letter I received from the Department requesting an interview. It was so curt; it suggested to me that they know something that I don't. Maybe in the end what concerns me most is the possibility of some miscarriage of justice happening in the future. Things happen, you know."

"Yes, of course, they do. But they are a genuine rarity." David's voice was soft, professional and reassuring. "I think you're so overwrought with what's been happening in the last few months, you're beginning to expect to find the enemy under every stone."

"I suppose, you're right," Jack breathed. "Very well then, you'd better update me on what's been happening since we last spoke."

"Well Jack, apart from your problems with the DTI, we may as well face it, this whole episode is going to be a very uphill task."

"How far have things progressed?"

"The first petition was presented in Bermuda yesterday. I arranged for it to be issued there on behalf of Pristine Print Limited, the creditor you suggested"

"Only yesterday? But David, it's over two months since Hepton took over the liquidation of Central. Two months, for heaven's sake."

"I know, Jack. But these things take time to present to Court."

"Okay," Jack sighed. "I should've realized. What happened?"

"Mr. Hepton turned up at the court and opposed the making of the winding up order."

"God in heaven," Jack groaned. "I thought you said the Chief Justice was a friend of yours."

"He is, but it seems that Mr. Hepton has a silver tongue when the occasion demands it. He put forward a very strong case. I'll let you see a transcript of the hearing when I get hold of it.

"Well, all is not lost dear boy. Osbert decided that he wasn't going to be rushed into anything, and adjourned the hearing for forty-eight hours. I've spoken to him briefly over the telephone, off the record. I've faxed my assistant in Bermuda the information required to have the learned judge see things our way."

"Is all this legal, David?"

"Perfectly. All I'm doing is ensuring that friend Osbert gets a proper look at all the cards that are being dealt. I would add, that although Hepton's legal arguments were impeccable, Osbert was not impressed by the man's manner. Called him a Confederate cut throat. Told me he was not about to be bullied or browbeaten by the likes of him."

"Strong stuff. Okay David, you're the expert. But wouldn't it have been better if you'd been in Bermuda yourself?"

"Hard to say, Jack. I'm really needed here to coordinate the rest of the campaign against Hepton. I think we'll be alright next time. In fact I'll give you odds on it."

"And the rest?"

"Petition in London, due to be heard next Monday. Section 130 petition ready to be presented immediately after I know the outcome. Section 304 application in US courts prepared and ready to be lodged as soon as we can show them we have a legitimate representative of an estate in a foreign proceeding."

"Good work, David, good work. What about AUIG's sworn proof of debt?"

"Requested, but not yet forthcoming. I think they're finding a problem with it, Jack. And I don't wonder. We're going to be home and dry on that front as well."

"Excellent." Jack paused; there was something else. "My God, I nearly forgot. How could I forget? Have you lodged a defence against Hepton's claim against me for the ten million?"

"Of course. The defence went in mere days after the writ was received. I told you it would. You see why I'm needed here don't you?"

"Of course, you're quite right. I must say, I feel much better David. Thanks a million. Keep in touch. Let me know the minute the next hearing in Bermuda has taken place." Putting his hands behind his head, Jack leaned back and stretched. Then he lit another cigar and contemplated the percolator before turning his attention to a scratching and the sound of a whispered voice outside the study door.

Pushing the door open, Phyllida popped her head around, much as Mrs. LLewellyn had earlier, "Just a minute, Harriette," she said, restraining the baby, who in the next instant had wriggled free of her mother's grasp and was waddling towards Jack. "I'm sorry, darling, she followed me up and insisted."

Leaning forward with arms outstretched Jack scooped up his daughter, and hugged her before planting her on his lap. "One of the benefits of losing forty million, my love," he said to Phyllida, "is that a man gets to see his wife and daughter rather more often. And that really can't be a bad thing now, can it?"

Sitting on the edge of the desk, Phyllida looked down at Jack. She was wearing a white blouse and denim jeans; something Jack had hardly ever seen her in, "I brought the mail," she said, dropping a couple of letters in front of Jack. "And I came to tell you that lunch is served, sir; if you would like to join us."

"Can't wait," Jack grinned. "I'm starved."

"You look better."

"I feel better."

"Have you spoken with David?"

"I have. And that's why I feel so much better. A couple of hitches, but basically things are going well, very well indeed."

"Darling, I'm so glad. Come now, before everything gets cold."

"On my way." Getting to his feet, and putting the baby on the floor, Jack glanced down at the correspondence, "Hello! This one's got a Bermuda stamp and postmark. Probably friend Hepton offering to throw in the towel before we throw everything we've got at him."

Snapping up the envelope, Jack slit it with a letter opener and extracted the contents, "I was right. It is from the partnership of Hepton Mallet Dixon." Scanning the correspondence, Jack felt his chest tighten and a vein in his neck begin to pulsate. "I don't believe this."

"What is it, Jack?"

"I just do not believe this." He was bellowing at the top of his voice and Harriette started to cry.

"Jack, please, tell me darling. For heaven's sake; what has happened?"

"I'll tell you what's happened," Jack raged as he flapped the pages about in his hand. "On an expedited hearing, Mr. Luke Hepton, liquidator and interloper extraordinaire, has secured judgement against me in the sum ten million dollars. Yes," he shouted, as he saw Phyllida's jaw drop open, "That's right, ten million, dollars. What the bloody hell David Purdoe has been doing I cannot imagine! He was supposed to have lodged a defence. I can tell you this, when I get hold of my solicitor, I shall have his guts for garters."

* * *

"David? What is it? Come on man, spit it out." Jack eased himself forward in his armchair and shrugged uncomprehendingly in response to Phyllida's whispered, "What's the matter?"

"David, what is so important that you need to call me at this hour. It's ten p.m." Jack pressed his forefinger and thumb to his temples and grimaced in concentration. "I can't hear you. What is that noise?" Suddenly, an ice cold feeling in his gut, Jack recognised the sounds he was hearing at the other end of the telephone.

"You're crying, David. What in the name of God has happened? Tell me. Where are you? Yes, I'll be there in half an hour. I'm bringing Phyllida with me. Just sit tight and do nothing," Jack said and hung up.

"How soon can you be ready?" Jack asked Phyllida.

"Give me five minutes to dress and tell Mrs. Llewellyn what's happening." Phyllida had already opened the wardrobe and grabbed a pair of black slacks which she quickly slipped into before struggling into a white cashmere sweater and then running downstairs.

In the hall, Phyllida and Jack shrugged into coats and walking shoes, and stepped into the crisp night air. It was snowing, and their feet crunched on the white powder that settled on the gravel. "I should've garaged the car," Jack muttered as he hurriedly swept the windscreen clear of the white blanket forming on it.

The roads were thick white and with little traffic. The snow had begun to drift. Jack took the drive more slowly than he otherwise might, and didn't arrive at David's home until around past eleven. The five bedroom thatched cottage was occupied by David alone. He had a daily help but otherwise he favoured his own company except when he had a lady to stay. An event which occurred more often than not.

Opening the oak front door to Jack and Phyllida, David appeared unkempt and dishevelled; his hair stuck out in all directions and his shirt was crumpled and was hastily shoved in the waistband of his equally creased trousers. His complexion was ashen and damp, as though he had recently washed his face, or been crying. He rubbed his hands together nervously, clasping and unclasping them as he spoke.

"Come in, Jack, Phyllida." David's voice had none of its usual verve or vitality; it was hollow and empty, quavering slightly as if he were trying to keep himself under control.

He led them down a corridor into his living room, all chintzes and mahogany. On his walls were what appeared to be signed drawings, or possibly lithographs, by a number of Impressionists. Jack noted Renoir and Degas among those on display. Curled up in a corner of the settee was David's blue Persian, Bounty. The cat looked up when Jack and Phyllida walked in, and promptly went off to sleep.

David motioned them both to armchairs, and sat himself next to Bounty on the settee, "Can I get you anything, hot drink, something stronger?"

"No David," Jack said. "Let's get on with this. You look absolutely terrible, whatever has happened?"

David rested his elbows on his knees and let his hands hang limply between his thighs, "You remember I said I'd sent one of my staff to Bermuda to make contact with Osbert Standish?"

Jack was leaning forward looking at David intently, "Yes, I remember. What happened? Was contact made?"

"Oh yes, contact was made. In fact Osbert called me to say that whilst not committing himself to anything over the telephone, he was well nigh certain to make a decision in our favour."

"You mean the compulsory winding up order we were seeking for Central?" Jack asked.

"That's right."

"But David, that's great news."

"Yes. Yes it is." David was again appearing to have difficulty controlling his feelings and covered his eyes with his hands for a moment. Then, looking up as if something else had just occurred to him, he said, "You know, there was another matter Osbert alluded to. Something about that $10 million dollar claim that Hepton's lodged against you Jack. And in particular the judgement the man's managed to secure on the expedited hearing. Something about an injunction."

Gazing straight at Jack, David was emphatic, "Let us be quite clear on one thing, a defence was entered by me, and entered in good time. There was no question in my mind but that judgement should never have been granted. The whole episode was and is most peculiar. Osbert was however not very forthcoming - talked in imprecise terms about bullying and blackmail - clearly reluctant to go into any detail. He seemed to be suggesting that after tomorrow the matter would almost certainly be redundant anyway. That the winding up order would wrap it all up.

"I wonder..." David paused, apparently lost in thought, and then went on again, "Osbert said he'd give my assistant all the particulars to bring back to England, together with instructions on how the matters of the judgement and so on should all be dealt with from this end. Just in case, you know. Whatever happened, he said there'd be no problem as long as his directions were followed." David's brow furrowed as though he were trying to recall a specific item.

Jack said nothing, he merely gave David time and space to get out whatever it was he wanted to say.

Phyllida sat back and crossed her legs, and put her hands together in her lap. She too waited unspeaking for David's next comment.

"Something odd about my call with Osbert," David was shaking his head as he spoke, as though he were trying to ascertain what it was he had found so unusual. "There was a sort of click on the telephone line during my connection with Bermuda, and when Osbert and I spoke, the words seemed to have an echo to them. Do you think the line might have been...?"

"I'm sure it was bugged," Jack cut in. "And I'm pretty sure the lines at my office are, and for all I know, those at Highview too."

"Oh dear, oh dear," David was crying now properly; his hands went to his face and mucus from his eyes and nose dribbled between his fingers falling in drops to the carpet. "Whatever shall I do? Whatever shall I do?"

Grabbing a Kleenex from her bag, Phyllida went to sit on the arm of the settee next to David. She put an arm comfortingly about his shoulder and held the tissue under his face for him. David said nothing, but grabbed the paper handkerchief and put it across his mouth and nose. He was shaking uncontrollably, as helpless as a child.

Feeling an indescribable sense of dread, Jack said, "David man, for the love of God, will you cut the preamble, and tell us what has happened."

Speaking haltingly through his tears David said, "It was all going so well." He paused. "All going according to plan." He stopped again. "We were going to get the compulsory winding up order for Central Reinsurance and rid ourselves of that monster Hepton once and for all."

Jack and Phyllida glanced at each other and shook their heads in unison as if each were signaling the other to say nothing.

Blowing his nose, David pocketed the used handkerchief and turned to Phyllida, "Thank you my dear. Thank you both so much for being patient with me." He breathed deeply and closed his eyes as if the information he had to impart was too terrible to contemplate. Then he continued, spelling it all out slowly and distinctly.

Jack heard what David had to say, but the words didn't register. It's so easy to delude ones self into believing the best. Pretending that the terrible things one knows beyond any doubt have happened, might not have happened after all. That they might have been personal misinterpretations of events.

Of course the blowing up of the Phyllida in Hamilton harbour had been the work of the Chinese man working for Luke Hepton. Jack knew it, had known it from the time of the first telephone call received in his hotel bedroom after that girl had shown up. The softly spoken voice with the Far Eastern accent; the voice that belonged to someone who seemed able to see all and hear all. The lack of police progress, the disinterest of the insurance company and the weeks and months that had elapsed since that horrific day had somehow all conspired to rob the event of some of it's edge.

None of the families of the crew had contacted Jack after he had written to them. Perhaps they too had put their own interpretation on the facts - had sought to come to terms with an incident that could not be reversed - in their own way. It was almost as if the thing had never taken place, and, increasingly, Jack had pushed it to the back of his mind.

Phyllida's mouth had dropped open, and she looked very pale. She was gazing at Jack as though he should be saying something. David had been talking, but Jack had not heard a word; or had not wanted to hear a word.

"I'm sorry David, I don't seem to be concentrating. Tell me again," Jack said.

Phyllida looked as though she wanted to say something to Jack, but she seemed to think better of it, and said nothing. Her face was drawn and she looked very ill.

Staring vacantly ahead, his tone of voice flat and lifeless, David repeated, "So you see dear boy, I shall have to ask you to be so kind as to instruct another solicitor in this matter. You appreciate, under the circumstances I shall no longer be able to act for you. For myself I don't care. But when others are involved..."

It still hadn't filtered through to Jack, and Phyllida whispered, "Darling, can't you understand what David's been trying to explain to you? Why don't you say something to him?"

Running his hands over his scalp, Jack mused, I need a haircut, probably a shampoo as well. "I'm sorry, David," he said again. "Yes of course, if you think I should instruct someone else..."

"For heavens sake, Jack," Phyllida was staring at her husband as though he were mad; then turning to David, she said, "Tell him, David. Tell him again."

Mopping his eyes with another Kleenex handed him by Phyllida, David continued in the same monotone, "All the information was there. All we needed. I'd been e-mailing and faxing stuff to and from my assistant in Bermuda all day, Monday. And there'd been conferences that had been held informally, and off the record, but on my instructions, and with my directions between my assistant and Osbert.

"You see, Osbert said he needed to have the entire picture so that when the matter was reconvened for hearing in the Supreme Court of Bermuda, he would not be sidetracked a second time by Hepton. He wanted to be certain he would be in a position to grant a winding up order, placing the liquidation of Central Reinsurance under the supervision of the Supreme Court of Bermuda.

"And when he last spoke to me, less than twenty-four hours ago, apart from a few minor details my assistant was going to brief me with, Osbert had reassured me we were there. The order would have been made on the reconvened hearing tomorrow, the twentieth of January, at 11.00 a.m. their time, 3.00 p.m. our time. Home and dry, home and dry."

"And isn't the order going to be made now? Has something happened to prevent Osbert from going ahead as promised?" The vein in Jack's neck was throbbing and his mouth had gone sticky dry.

Putting the handkerchief away from his face, David inhaled deeply and calmed himself. His cheeks were shiny, and his nose and chin were running and slimy wet, "No, Jack, that's what I've been trying to tell you. Just before I called you both this evening, I received news from Bermuda, that my secretary and assistant, Celia and my friend, Chief Justice Osbert Standish, had both been found murdered."

Chapter 10

January 21, Thursday

"Hi yah, Kim." Luke Hepton lay back on the vast circular bed in his penthouse duplex and surveyed the winking nightlights of Manhattan. He was still dressed, and his shoes, muddy from the slush outside, soiled the otherwise immaculate white lace counterpane.

"Hello, Mr. Hepton," the softly spoken voice was unmistakeably Oriental.

"Ah heck, call me Luke, son, we known each other long enough now."

There was no reply, just the gentle slapping of water against the hull of a boat.

"Okay. Have it your own way," Hepton sounded resigned. The earlier snow had given way to a heavy rain, which washed the windows of Luke Hepton's apartment. He stared at it, seeing glinting smudges of yellow from the lights of other apartments in nearby blocks reflected on the drops of water that ran down the panes of glass.

"Are you still there, Mr. Hepton?"

"Yeah, yeah. Ah'm still here. You done good, Kim," Hepton grinned. "You done real good. Gimme an update. Run the whole thing by me one time, son."

"But you know most of it already. You have enacted everything I have suggested."

"I know. But ah like to hear it from you anyway."

"Mr. Gregory is being painted into a corner. He failed in his attempt to have a winding up order made for Central Reinsurance in Bermuda. That was mostly due to your eloquence, Mr. Hepton."

"Yeah. Guess it was. Ah done pretty well that day with that old fool Standish. It really woulda helped his cause if he'da seen things our way.

"Say, Kim, I'm gettin' his successor appointed. He shouldn't be no trouble. Douglas Tandy? He'll be the new guy, the new Chief Justice of Bermuda. You know him?"

"I believe I do. I understand that like poor Osbert Standish, Mr. Tandy's predilections are, how shall I put it. Not dissimilar to my own."

There was a pause, then Hepton said, "Ah yeah. See what you mean. Even better. At last we can count on some real co-operation from the judiciary. Now talk to me some more about our Mr. Gregory."

"Mr. Gregory's campaign of survival is withering on the vine."

"Witherin' on the vine. Ah like it son, ah like it. What else?"

"His aims to apply to the US courts for relief under Section 304 of the Bankruptcy Code, are a non starter. He does not have the necessary appointee in place, either in the UK or Bermuda, through whom to apply.

"His applications in UK courts to have the Official Receiver take over as provisional liquidator, either on a petition for a compulsory winding up, or pursuant to Section 130 proceedings, have been stillborn."

"You gotta nice turn of phrase, Kim."

"We have, as of course you are aware, judgement against Mr. Gregory for $10 million in the Supreme Court of Bermuda. If he proposes applying to have judgement set aside on the grounds that his defence was not heard, we shall say that no defence was lodged. It will be hard for Mr. Gregory to fight that, or anything else, as we have also managed to have him tied up with a Mareva Injunction. His access to funds is strictly limited, as far as we know at present."

Kicking off his shoes, Hepton surveyed the hole in the toe of one of his socks, "Anything else? Ah'm mightily enjoyin' this. Seems a shame to stop right now."

"Mr. Gregory is trying to raise money by the sale of his seventeen garage sites."

"I know, I know. You stopped that yet?"

"His buyers up to now have been seeking funds through the oil companies."

"You told me. And I already spoke with them, Kim. They ain't gonna be lendin' Gregory's buyers no money."

"I too have spoken with them, Mr. Hepton," Kim sounded testy. "I thought it was agreed that I should have the sole responsibility for coordinating this cbrief-casepaign."

"Yeah, I know. But ah just couldn't resist having a little fun myself."

"We are not playing games here, Mr. Hepton. And please do not imagine that by pre-empting my plans that you will save any of the already considerable fees that have accrued."

"Okay, okay, son. Don't get touchy. Your money's on the way."

"You mean the cheque is in the post?"

"Don't get funny with me, kiddo."

"On the contrary Mr. Hepton." The voice was so soft, it was barely audible. "Don't you get funny with me."

Twisting uneasily on the bed, Hepton sat up and surveyed the half empty bottle of vodka on the side table. His mouth watered, but he resisted the temptation to reach for it. It was more important to end this conversation on a satisfactory note, "Look, a transfer's been arranged between Chemical and that Belgian bank you wanted, in Geneva."

"Thank you, Mr. Hepton. It would be appreciated if in future my bills were met on time."

"Okay, no problem. Had a slight hitch this time with the partners. But they're all on board right now. They like the look of the prospective profits in this venture. Know what ah mean?" Hepton sniggered.

The silence this time came from the other end of the line, as though the Oriental man were considering the situation in his own mind. Eventually he spoke again. He sounded brisk, as if he were summarising the position, "Gloucester Properties, a UK public company have made an offer for the garage sites. They don't need oil company funds, but they will withdraw their offer anyway. I know their chairman."

"Jeez, Kim," Hepton grinned. "How the hell do you do it? Is there anybody you don't know?"

"Quite a number of people, Mr. Hepton. Thankfully, few of them are of any consequence."

"That it then?"

"Almost. You are always in such a hurry. Mr. Gregory will be having difficulty financing the removal of tyres from his sites, while having to pay for security at the same time. He is squeezed to the limits and beyond. His wife is ill with worry, and he is starting to lose patience with everyone.

"Shortly, I feel confident, he will start quarrelling with Mrs. Gregory. His judgements, whose unpredictability brought him a fortune in the past, will now be too erratic under conditions outside his control to be of any use to him. He will start to crumble."

Stretching for the vodka, Hepton put the bottle to his lips and took a long draught. It warmed him inside. Reassured him that before long he'd have the nuisance that Jack Gregory presented out of his way. "You seem very certain of everything."

"That's what you pay me for. Finally, and with the object of helping Mr. Gregory into his financial grave, I am proposing to have a Statutory Notice presented to him in regard to the ten million dollar judgement. I am going to make him personally bankrupt. Documents will be prepared for your perusal and signature in due course."

"Neat, very neat. You got it all taped."

"If by some small chance the Department of Trade are unable, with the information I have arranged they be provided, to withdraw his insolvency practitioner's license, bankruptcy will have that effect anyway."

"Wow!" Hepton drew again on the bottle of vodka.

"Precisely, Mr. Hepton. Wow."

"Is there any chance any of this could fail, Kim?"

"Mr. Hepton, we are, as you might say, firing on all twelve cylinders."

"That's a mighty big motor."

"I also have one further little surprise for Mr. Gregory, in the unlikely event that all twelve cylinders should fail. What you would probably call my, `Ace in the hole'."

"And that is?"

"I shall tell you if the need arises."

"I need to know right now." Unused to being argued with, Hepton could feel himself becoming annoyed.

"You will have to exercise a little patience."

"Lookee here, son, who's running this operation anyway?"

"I am, Mr. Hepton. As long as you pay my fees, I am."

Hepton said nothing. He was more unsettled than he could ever remember having been. As he waited for Kim to say something, he thought he heard the faint sound of laughter in the distance. It was a long high pitched staccato. Of course he might have been mistaken, it was so soft. Then the line went dead.

Chapter 11

February 8, Monday

"Phyl, I don't think I've never suffered a greater sense of disquiet in all my life. It feels as though I've been shackled to a ball and chain before being blindfolded and then ordered to run for my life." Walking uphill through the woodland in the grounds of Highview, Phyllida's hand in his own, Jack stopped and turned to look back through a gap in the beech trees over the surrounding countryside.

It was a cloudless winter day with no more than the faintest chill in the air. The January snows had largely melted away leaving behind traces of slush here and there. Phyllida was wearing brogues and a brown woollen pullover and corduroy skirt. Her cloud of hair, flaxen shot through with streaks of russet in the bright sun, was swept back off her face and held in place with combs at either side of her head. The clean atmosphere had brightened her earlier sombre mood and brought a hint of colour to her cheeks. Jack, she realized, was becoming harder and harder to reach, often brooding in his study into the small hours of the morning.

He looked exhausted, his face was sunken and his black eyebrows knit in a permanent frown over eyes that were haunted. He'd lost weight, ordinarily no bad thing. Though he was clearly paying the price. A volatile man at the best of times, Jack was, these days, clearly having increasing difficulty keeping his temper on a leash. There had been occasions when he had come close to flying off the handle with both Mr. and Mrs. Llewellyn for the most minor matters. He'd even been short with her, Phyllida. Something she'd never seen in him.

His loss of weight had been dramatic and his suits hung on him like limp tent canvases. At any other time Phyllida would have been delighted. As it was, she wondered how long Jack could survive the terrible pressures he was under. Only Harriette seemed to take Jack out of himself, and he would spend every spare moment he had chatting and playing with the baby.

"Talk to me, Jack."

He gazed into the distance without expression as if he had not heard her, "I will, I will." His voice sounded as though he were somewhere else, and, letting go Phyllida's grip he shoved his hands roughly into the pockets of his tweed jacket.

"No, Jack. Now! I said I wanted to know everything. Don't try to protect me. I'm not a child. I want to know what's happening." She was panting as though she'd just run up a hill and was out of breath.

Turning to face her, Jack took both Phyllida's hands in his own, "I'm sorry, Phyl. But it doesn't always help me if I talk about things. In a way, by just handling what I need to on a day-to-day basis I cope better. If I look at the whole picture at any one time it just becomes too daunting."

"Yes," she whispered staring intently into Jack's brown eyes as if they might provide some insight into her husband's reasoning. "But what about me? We've had this before. I'm not living in a vacuum. I need to know what's going on. Can't you see that?"

Shrugging, Jack let go of one of Phyllida's hands, and keeping the other firmly in his grasp, resumed walking with her, "All right. Though there seems to be so much happening, and not happening, I hardly know where to start." He walked on silently for several minutes, staring at the leaves and twigs on the ground, his shoulders bowed as if he carried the weight of the world on them. Eventually he glanced at Phyllida as though to reassure himself that she was still there.

"Nothing's working out right," he sighed. "I was relying on the value in the boat providing me with a substantial financial buffer. It's gone, and the insurers are unlikely to pay out a penny. I've spoken with loss assessors, briefly, and they talk about unusual circumstances. I don't know whether they've been warned off -- there aren't that many of them in the UK -- or whether they genuinely won't take on what could turn out to be an expensive failure for them.

"Legal remedies in this country, Bermuda and the States are all at a standstill. Hepton will have taken over the US bank balances by now. Tony Trent tells me Hepton has convened a meeting of the Committee of Inspection of Central Reinsurance. He's almost certainly going to ask them to vote him a fee. That'll be the beginning of the end of the big bank balances I held in America."

"Jack, can't you do anything at all to stop him? He's like a runaway train."

"Precisely. It's doubtful. One or two of the Committee members may be on our side. If so, it might be possible to stall Hepton; but for how long? He'll keep on bringing it back to the Committee until he gets his way and they vote him what he wants. God knows how much he's already taken in expenses anyway."

"How is Tony these days? You've hardly mentioned his name for months. Can't he do anything to help?"

"Tony's fine. Keeping an eye on things for me, which is about as much as he can do at this stage. I anticipate I shall shortly be needing him for other things."

Phyllida gazed at Jack, she felt worried and knew she looked it, "That sounds ominous. What other things?"

"Danny tells me Gloucester Properties have pulled out of the garages deal."

"Oh, Jack, no!"

"He says everything was going swimmingly, when they just dropped out of the whole deal without warning. They won't even discuss it with him over the phone. As far as they're concerned the whole thing is a dead duck."

"What are you thinking?"

"You know what I'm thinking. That this isn't just another bloody coincidence."

"Has Danny got any other interested parties?"

"He says he has, but what the hell, how do I know they won't also be warned off? And anyway, the sort of offers they're making are derisory."

Wrapping her arms around herself, Phyllida said, "I'm feeling cold, darling. Shall we start back?"

Jack nodded and they turned and began to retrace their steps downhill.

"Are the petrol sites still secure?"

"No."

"What? Why not?" There was a nervous edge to Phyllida's voice and she fidgeted with the combs at the side of her hair. "I thought you said you'd laid on security."

"Yes, but only on those sites where tyres have been dumped." Breathing in deeply, Jack looked as though he was pondering whether or not to go on. Then he said, "There've been isolated incidents of tyre dumping at several other sites. It's as though I'm being handed out some sort of warning of what might lay in store if I don't leave off trying to harass Hepton."

"But you said that nothing was happening on the legal front anyway."

"That's right. That's why they're only issuing warnings."

"Is there still a fire hazard?"

"As Danny would say, `You shouldn't ask.' Only, believe me when I tell you I'm not joking. The local fire officers are all going mad and threatening me with everything in the book. Danny's been fending them off. But they're right to be worried. If our international friends, or any local vandal were to put a match to any of that rubber the outcome would be too horrendous to contemplate. I have nightmares about it."

"You told me you wouldn't do anything to risk anybody's life."

"That's right. And I won't. But don't you see, I'm in a `no win' situation here.

"Just a minute," she was angry and sounded it. "Why aren't you doing anything about it then? I thought you were clearing the tyres away."

"It's all on hold."

"On hold? But why?"

"Because there's no point in clearing everything away if I can't sell the damn petrol stations. It'll simply mean having to go on paying to keep every site secure till I do get a buyer. That could be months, years away. If I pay to have every garage made as safe as the local fire officers would like, our man from Hong Kong will simply render them unsafe again."

"I see," Phyllida paused, apparently placated. "Well while the money you raised to clear the tyres is in my account at least it's earning interest."

"It won't be for long."

Phyllida's eyes narrowed, "Why not?"

"I have plans for it."

"But how will you pay the hauliers when you need to?"

"Out of the proceeds of sale of the sites, when that event takes place, and as long as there's sufficient to cover all the borrowings. At least that's the theory of the thing."

Phyllida rubbed her hands together to try and make them warm and wrapped her arms around herself again, "And if there isn't enough to cover it?"

"I'll worry about that when the time comes. But I think there's a shortfall, at least on paper, already. That is unless Danny can negotiate better offers than he's been getting recently."

"Where does Tony Trent come in then? You said you'd be needing him shortly."

"If there is a shortfall I shall have to convene a meeting of creditors to give them a chance to appoint a liquidator of their own choice."

"Tony Trent?"

"I hope so."

"Will he take the meeting?"

"He's agreed to."

Phyllida pondered this for several moments, then she said, "Isn't this how it was with Central Reinsurance, starting out as a solvent winding up with you as liquidator, then apparently going insolvent and the creditors putting in Hepton instead of Tony."

"Yes," Jack said quietly. But AUIG put in a contrived claim which enabled them to manipulate the vote. A claim which David Purdoe had been following up. Trying to get them, that's AUIG, to provide evidence of its veracity. Another matter presently on hold," Jack muttered grimly.

"What would happen if Tony failed to get the appointment as liquidator of JG Petroleum Holdings?"

"It all depends."

"On what?"

"On whether the creditors' choice happened to be a friendly liquidator or not."

"I've a feeling I'm not going to like the answer to my next question."

"You said you wanted to know everything, Phyl. Are you sure you want to ask it?"

"I'm absolutely sure. Tell me." She was looking at the ground as they walked, absently shuffling fallen leaves with the toes of her shoes

"An unfriendly liquidator might be disposed to making a swift sale of the sites at any price just to demonstrate to creditors that he's not prepared to unduly delay matters. He might want a quick fee irrespective of the commerciality of any deal. Not all professionals are as business orientated as me. There could well be nothing left for the shareholders. That's me again." Jack smiled wryly, "There probably won't be anything anyway. Also, he might just decide to take issue with the recent bank borrowings I've secured on the sites."

"The moneys I'm holding?"

"Exactly."

"Meaning what?"

"If a hostile liquidator were to successfully contest the validity of those recently established charges, it would mean the burden of repaying the borrowings from the bank, my darling, that two hundred and fifty thousand pounds in your account towards the cost of clearing the sites, could fall to me personally." Jack sighed, "And I have no money."

"But I thought you just said you had plans for that money."

Jack made a grunt of assent.

"Come on, Jack. What is it? What are you going to do with those borrowings."

They were in sight of the house now and a fresh breeze sprang up with a bite that made Phyllida squeeze her hands together once again, and Jack roll his shoulders against the cold as though he were trying to rid himself of some invisible yolk.

"I'm going to try to get back some of what AUIG have taken from me," Jack said fiercely.

"How?"

"I don't know yet. At least not for certain, but I'm working on an idea."

"You're not going to do anything illegal are you?" Phyllida was studying the backs of her fingernails as if they might somehow provide the answer to her question.

"Possibly," he replied simply. "Do you still want me to tell you everything?"

Shaking her head, Phyllida replied slowly, "I'm not sure. You could lose everything, Jack."

"I have lost everything."

"Your professional status."

"The DTI are working on divesting me of that."

"You might go to prison."

"I'll try to avoid it."

She was irritated at this new turn, felt her face flush with annoyance. "Jack, I thought you said you'd never do anything illegal. Have you thought out the consequences of whatever it is you have in mind? And what about Harriette and me? Don't we count for anything?"

Feeling himself beginning to bubble up with rage, Jack turned to face Phyllida and took her by the shoulders, "Don't you see, Phyl? We've been through all this before. They're trying to break me. There is no escape from them. I've already told you, this is a fight to the finish. If I don't win, I really will lose everything. Very likely you and Harriette included."

"Me and Harriette? But how? Do you think Hepton is going to arrange to have us both killed too?" Phyllida's eyes were wide with fear.

"God knows." Jack shook his head, immediately relenting his rush of anger. He wanted to shout aloud, to vent his spleen at the sky, at anything. All he'd succeeded in doing was terrifying a wife already prone to panic. Retracting as best he could, he went on gently, "No, it's not what I think he wants. He knows it would be too provocative. No, it's just a crazy feeling I had for a moment."

Phyllida watched her husband as they walked on in silence. Jack looked as if he were turning things over in his mind before commenting again. When finally he spoke he sounded exasperated, "I don't know what else they've got up their sleeves, Phyl, but I can't afford to sit back and wait to find out." His voice was rising quickly as though he could no longer contain himself and he was red in the face. "I've tried doing things the nice way and it hasn't worked. Now I'll try doing it their way and we'll see what happens."

Witnessing her husband's helpless fury, Phyllida found herself fighting to hold back her tears, "But, Jack, you told me your father had always said `Don't mix it' -- that you shouldn't try to do things other people's way. These are major criminals you're thinking of taking on. You won't stand a chance against them."

She was crying now, the tears streaming down her face and he took her gently in his arms and they clung to each other.

In his mind's eye, Jack could see his father's face, pale and concerned, exhorting him to, `Always keep it straight down the line son, it's how you do things best. Box 'em, don't fight 'em. You're not an alley cat. Leave the back street scraps to the rest.'

"I wish there was some other way," Jack whispered. "I only wish there was."

Their feet were crunching the gravel as they approached the front of Highview. Reaching into her pocket for a handkerchief, Phyllida blew her nose, "I don't want Mrs. Llewellyn to see me like this."

She'd wanted to know the truth. But not this truth. There was enough for Jack to cope with without pitting himself against the law too. She breathed in deeply and closed her eyes. Just hope I don't crack, she thought. Got to be there for him whatever he does.

Inside, the front hall of the house was warm, it felt as if the whole of Highview was wrapping them in a protective blanket. Picking out the mail from the box behind the front door, Phyllida looked around the place and smiled, "At least we've got this, darling. We've got our home. No one's trying to take this away from us."

"I suppose you're right," Jack breathed. "Maybe I was over reacting a bit. Silly of me I suppose. I'm sorry, Phyl, I didn't mean to upset you. I really could do with a bit of time off though. I think I'll just ignore everything for a few days and unwind a bit. Concentrate on you and the bubs."

"Yes, and you can forget about the mail as well. I'll put it all in your in-tray, and you can start to open it again in maybe a week's time." Smiling,

Phyllida waved the fan of letters she held aloft indicating that they weren't to be touched.

But Jack's face went pale. He looked as though he'd seen an apparition.

"What is it, darling?" Phyllida came and put her arms around Jack's neck. "What's happened?"

"It's probably nothing, but you're holding correspondence from Bermuda. I recognize the grey envelopes. They always use grey envelopes."

"Leave it, Jack. Go and rest. I'll put these in your study and you can look at them in a week from now. You're driving yourself too hard. You'll make yourself ill. Whatever it is, it can't be that important." Phyllida's voice was shrill, and she stood unmoving, her hands by her sides, her face an unspoken plea to her husband not to present her with any more disasters right now, as Jack took the letters from her.

"I'm sorry, Phyl, but I won't be able to rest till I know what's in this," he said, slitting open the letter with his forefinger. "As I said, it's probably nothing but I'll have no peace knowing it's here waiting to be opened."

Watching Jack as he extracted the folded papers and flipped open the pages, Phyllida was unable to gauge his reaction to the contents. His face was expressionless, and she felt a sense of relief that nothing had provoked any angry responses. Thank God, she thought, then tried to sound cheerful, "I'll put the kettle on, darling. I don't know about you, but I'm screaming for a cup of tea."

"A cup of tea would be wonderful."

"Anything of any interest?" Phyllida enquired with a false light-hearted tone.

"A couple of things, my love." Jack held out one sheet of paper, "This is a summary judgement against me for the ten million Hepton was suing me for. David Purdoe was going to contest it, but along with everything else, it seems to have been overlooked. Seems silly really when you realize we're talking ten million dollars." Jack smiled grimly, "It is rather a lot to lose sight of, isn't it? But I've delayed finding another solicitor in the hope that David would change his mind and start working for me again. The other document is what is known as a Statutory Demand."

Standing in front of her with the letters in his hand, Jack looked so calm and at ease there clearly wasn't any cause for Phyllida to be concerned, he obviously had matters well under control.

"What's a Statutory Demand?" She felt hesitant nonetheless. A word of reassurance was all that she required. Just one single word.

"It allows me twenty-one days to pay the ten million, failing which Mr. Luke Hepton, liquidator extraordinaire, will be issuing a petition for my personal bankruptcy."

"My God, Jack. Bankruptcy! How will that affect you. Us. Will we lose the house?" Her face was breaking up and she looked and felt as though she might weep at any moment.

Jack shrugged noncommittally, "I don't know. We shouldn't. Remember, I put Highview in the baby's name for tax purposes when she was born. We could have a fight on our hands."

Closing her eyes Phyllida said, "I just can't believe it. They won't stop at anything will they?"

"That's how it would appear."

"But Highview means so much to you, Jack."

"Only while I have you and Harriette to share it with me."

She clamped her jaw tight, there would be no tears, she just felt cold and empty, drained of life and emotion. "Do what you have to do," Phyllida whispered, her mind made up.

"Very well," Jack said taking her in his arms again. "If you're sure."

"I'm sure. I don't want to know the details, Jack, not unless I have to. But if you were to go to jail," Phyllida could feel her voice begin to falter, "I'd wait. You know that?"

Jack nodded, his cheek against hers.

"If it took for ever, my love, I'd wait."

* * *

February 9, Tuesday

It was two a.m. Jack's sleep was disturbed, he thought he'd heard a baby's cry, but Phyllida -- always aware of Harriette's wakefulness or otherwise -- had not stirred. He must be dreaming. If he kept his eyes shut he would get back to sleep quickly again.

Turning on to his side Jack was aware of a beam of light in the far distance of his semi-slumber. A beam of light like the one he'd seen not so very long ago shining underneath the bedroom door. God above. He sat straight up in bed, his heart palpitating.

"What is it, darling?" Phyllida murmured, and reaching out, put a hand gently on his shoulder. Her hair, golden in the moonlight, was spread across the pillow and her face was full of sleep.

"Nothing. I thought... Nothing," Jack said and eased himself out of bed. Fumbling his way towards the door he thought, I must be going mad.

I know what I saw. But when he opened the door and looked down the corridor it was quiet and dark. Tiptoeing along to Harriette's room, he peeped in. The baby was lying on her tummy, her head turned to one side. One hand was on the pillow beside her face, and she was sucking her thumb. Jack wanted to pick her up and hold her to him, smell her baby sweetness, hear the beat of her tiny heart.

"I must be hallucinating," he told Phyllida when he got back into bed. "I could've sworn I'd seen a light on in the house."

"Lie down, Jack, and hold me," Phyllida held her arms open to him and Jack took her in his own, crushing her against him hard.

Feeling the softness of her breasts against him Jack realized they had not made love for some considerable time. Phyllida pressed her hands into the small of his back, he could feel her long elegant fingers moving against his spine and shoulder blades. Her nipples brushed hard across his chest and she put her hands behind his head and held it like that as she moved her face to his. Realizing how badly he wanted her, and she him, he kissed her long and deep, savoring the honey of her saliva. But something was wrong.

"I can't, Phyl."

"What's wrong, darling?"

"I don't know, I just can't. I feel so bloody impotent. About this. About what's been happening. About everything."

"It doesn't matter," Phyllida closed her eyes and waited for her own sense of urgency to diminish. "It doesn't matter one bit, my love. I know you're going through hell right now. Just hold me, darling, and let's sleep."

"Sleep. That knits up the ravelled sleeve of care. Sound and untroubled. Wouldn't that be wonderful?"

"You're seeing David Purdoe in the morning, aren't you? And Tony Trent?"

"That's right."

"Give them both my love, won't you?"

"Of course, I will. You know we must try and get out of the house a bit. Cinema or theatre," he murmured drowsily.

"There's a production of Macbeth in town. I'll try and get seats."

"Fine. But what made you suggest Macbeth?"

"Don't you know, darling?" she smiled. But Jack was sleeping.

* * *

February 9, Tuesday

The office was as dim lit and cluttered as always, and Jack found himself wondering how anyone could possibly work in such uncongenial surroundings. David Purdoe extended a hand, and smiled sadly, "Hello, Jack. How are you dear boy? How are you?"

Taking the other man's soft and feminine hand in his own, Jack wondered again at the apparent fascination David held for women. A former girl friend of the chubby little lawyer -- chatting to Jack at a cocktail party -- had confidentially attested to David's insatiable sexual appetite.

"I wish I could say fine, David. But I feel as if I were on a ski jump about to be launched into oblivion. I'm even waking up at night seeing imaginary lights on in the house."

"I must apologize for the way I behaved when last we met. I fear Phyllida would not have been much impressed."

"For heaven's sake, David. You'd just heard about the murder of your secretary and an old friend. You were obviously in shock."

"We were about to be married."

"What! David, no... you and Celia? Oh, my God. I am so very sorry. I just never realized; never suspected."

"It's not been easy, but I'm trying hard to drown everything in work. I've been of little use to you, I know." David ran his fingers through his tousled black hair. "Are you instructing anyone else? I've had no requests from anyone for anything from my files."

"I want you to take it all up for me again, David. I don't want to start with a new lawyer. As far as I'm concerned, you're the best there is."

"How kind of you to say so, dear boy."

"I'm not being kind," Jack leaned forward, an elbow on David's desk. "I'm stating facts. But I need someone with balls, David."

"Of course, Jack, of course," David replied hesitantly.

"Don't bloody, 'Of course Jack' me, David, in that pathetic little sorry for yourself voice," Jack roared.

"I beg your pardon?" Sitting back in his chair, David's eyes opened wide with astonishment.

"You heard me. If there's one thing I can't stand it's profligate self pity."

"She was my fiancée," David's eyes narrowed in irritation.

"Well she's not any more."

"I thought you were my friend."

"Friend? Friend?" Jack shouted. "Call yourself a friend? Call yourself a lawyer? I've got a ten million dollar judgement against me that my, `friend', is supposed to have contested."

"Now wait a minute!"

"A Statutory Demand against me threatening bankruptcy proceedings."

"I said wait a minute," David's tone sounded annoyed.

"We all suffer personal upsets, but we leave them at home when we get to the office."

"Personal upsets? This was a tragedy. A double murder. She was going to be my wife, dammit," David muttered.

"We don't just walk away from our responsibilities leaving clients and, `friends', to get on with it."

"Stop it, Jack, stop it."

"Life. Goes. On. Man."

"Stop it."

"You're behaving irresponsibly."

"I said, stop it." David's voice was rising in anger.

"You sit here on your fat backside surrounded by papers, pretending to work and bemoaning your lot, while the rest of us are left to stew. You're behaving like a petulant schoolgirl."

Slamming the flat of his hand on the desk, David glowered at Jack, "How dare you!" He was shouting now. "How dare you talk to me like that!"

"You're nothing more than an unprofessional dilettante," Jack bellowed at him.

David's normally pink complexion was now livid, and his face was shiny with perspiration, "Let me remind you," he hissed in rage, "that we are both fighting the same enemy."

Sitting back, Jack crossed his legs and smiled at David. "I'm delighted to hear you say it," he said softly.

Staring at Jack nonplussed, David suddenly displayed the ghost of a smile and muttered, "You bastard, Jack."

"Whatever it takes, my friend."

"We've a lot to do."

"You've a lot to do."

Turning sideways David rose from the swivel chair and picked up three large buff folders of correspondence from the top of a nearby filing cabinet. Balancing them precariously on his arms he transferred them to his desk. "How long can you spare me, Jack?"

Jack glanced at his watch, "I'm seeing Tony Trent in a couple of hours. We need to discuss the forthcoming meeting of creditors of JG Petroleum Holdings. An event I am not anticipating with anything but disquiet. I'm meeting him across the road at Jamies. Why don't you join us for lunch?"

"I'd like to, Jack, but I've far too much to do here, dear boy," he replied indicating the open files. "Far too much."

Chapter 12

February 11, Thursday

The bar, cloudy with cigarette smoke, was thronged with the usual early evening crowd of professionals, money market dealers and brokers. The Victorian built hotel, one of a type that could be found nearby all of London's main line terminals, was situated close to Kings Cross Station, and was a handy watering hole en route to home county mansions for those who dealt in sums of money who's immensity was incomprehensible to most ordinary persons in the street.

Ordering his usual, three parts Johnny Walker to one of Drambuie, Jack carried his tumbler to a small round unoccupied table next to a marble pillar in the centre of the saloon, lit up a Dunhill, and, as he had done for the past three evenings, settled himself comfortably to listen and observe.

Having finally determined on a course of action, Jack was once again experiencing a sense of purpose and a feeling of calm within himself he had not known for some months past. Sipping from the glass, Jack leaned back and enjoyed the sweet burn at the back of his throat as he swallowed the first mouthful.

At the adjoining table, two young men in dark suits and white shirts, discussed some of the day's transactions. They conversed in the quick-fire babble of dealers used to speaking and listening at one and the same time. The bar was full of similar types, both seated and standing, all talking animatedly at each other. But they were not what Jack was looking for.

Ensconced in one of the several nearby alcoves that ranged along the edge of the saloon, and directly in Jack's line of sight was something that looked far more promising. After two abortive evenings, it was time Jack's luck changed for the better.

Two men in their mid to late thirties were listening intently to an older man, a man of around fifty to fifty-five. He was white haired and suntanned, and wore highly polished white shoes with brown toecaps, and a pale cream suit, whose colour and quality reminded Jack of the sort of tailoring he would have expected to find in exclusive Continental or Caribbean locations.

Staring at the movement of their mouths, Jack tried to make out what was being said, the older man was facing Jack, with the two younger ones either side of him. But despite his sharpened concentration, the pitch and roll of conversation weaving its way through the crush of people and the constant movement of bodies across his field of vision, made it impossible to pick up much beyond isolated fragments of dialogue. It was these slivers of discussion that excited Jack.

Tens of millions of dollars was under consideration. Several times, Jack distinctly heard the word, 'discretion' spoken. After about an hour, the two younger men got up to leave, and shaking hands in turn with the white haired man, Jack saw the latter put one finger to his lips and mouth silently, 'We have never met.'

The older man looked as though he was preparing to follow the example of his younger associates and leave too, as Jack, glass in hand approached his table. "My name's Jack Gregory. I wonder if I might have a word."

If he was surprised or alarmed by Jack's approach, it failed to register on his face, "Pieter Van Damm." He smiled, and gestured Jack into a seat with the confidence of a doctor conducting his evening surgery. "Please, be my guest." His accent was continental, possibly Austrian or Dutch, with the suggestion of an American burr.

"Thank you." Placing his half finished drink on the table, Jack sat down and casually crossed his legs. "I couldn't help overhearing some of the conversation you were just having," he proffered, "and I wonder if perhaps I might put a proposition to you. An idea I've been turning over in my mind for some time. That is of course, assuming I've not been jumping to the wrong conclusions. You don't know me from Adam," Jack smiled. "If you're interested, we might be able to engage in a little business together. If I'm making a mistake, then let me apologize in advance for wasting your time."

"What did you have in mind, Mr. Gregory?" Van Damm toyed with his empty brandy glass.

Pausing, Jack surveyed the other man. To speak or not to speak, he thought. Was his scheme just the lunatic idea of a desperate man? The Alice in Wonderland fantasy of one who had run out of options. And if it was, why had he bothered to stake out the place for the last three nights? Why? When he knew full well that this bar, in this hotel, and the others like it, were the very places those interested in the germination of international financial deals of questionable probity met, or hoped to meet, others of a similar ilk. "I'll be blunt, Mr. Van Damm, I need to establish a considerable asset base, and for that I shall want bank guarantees. Is this your line of country? Can you do anything for me?"

"Do I deduce that you don't have the actual assets to underpin that base?"

"Not necessarily. But precisely where the base is established in actuality, where it appears to be established for all practical purposes and how it's to be used in due course will be for me to determine, and not the bank issuing the guarantees."

Drumming his fingers on the table Van Damm pondered, "What is it you are looking for from me?"

"An introduction."

"To whom?"

"Any senior bank official prepared to issue the necessary documents."

"Which country?"

Jack sipped from his drink. "Flexible," he said casually. Then as though having given it a moment's further thought, "Mauritius. Could you manage that?"

"I might. And if I were able to give you the introduction you seek, Mr. Gregory, what sort of monies would we be talking about in general terms? For example, how much do you have to invest? And what sort of procurement fee might I expect?" Holding the brandy glass by the stem, Van Damm spun it around swirling the drain of cognac that was left in the bottom so that it moistened the inside of the bowl.

The man was a total stranger. What did it matter if Jack told him what he had been contemplating? Van Damm wasn't the authorities. And if Jack had, by a million to one shot, picked the wrong man, so what? There were no witnesses to their conversation. All the same, he wasn't exactly used to this sort of trade. Breathing in deeply, Jack said, "I want eight guarantees of twenty-five million each. I'm prepared to pay forty thousand for each one. They must all be issued by the same bank."

Van Damm raised his eyebrows with interest, "A two hundred million dollar base for which you are offering three hundred and twenty thousand in commission. Evidently you have intriguing plans, Mr. Gregory?" It was more of a question than a statement, but Jack remained silent.

Staring into the brandy glass, Van Damm murmured, "And I ask you again, Mr. Gregory, my fee for making this introduction? Assuming of course that I am able to recommend the right person to you."

"Nothing."

"Nothing?" Van Damm frowned and clacked his glass down on the table, irritated. "Is this some kind of joke?"

Resting on his elbows, Jack leaned forward, "Look, can you help me, or not?"

"It might be possible. But for nothing?"

"Mr. Van Damm, we're not schoolboys. You know the way this thing works as well as I do. How you split the three hundred and twenty thousand commission that I shell out is for you and your bank official contact to decide between yourselves, not me. Now, are we in business or not?"

Sliding around the table to extricate himself from the alcove, Van Damm's face was as immobile as a slab of granite. Under the suntan, his complexion seemed to have adopted a slight pallor, and he looked as though he was in a hurry to be gone.

Bugger it! Jack thought. I've made a bloody fool of myself.

Standing well over six feet tall, and thin as a willow, Van Damm straightened his jacket and glanced down at Jack with an expression of disdain, "Tomorrow, Mr. Gregory. I shall see you here at the same time tomorrow."

Jack watched as Van Damm sidled quickly through the crowd and out of the hotel bar into the street. Very well, Mr. Van Damm, he thought. We shall see what you have to offer tomorrow.

* * *

February 15, Monday

It felt as though a damp hand had reached out and clutched the back of his neck in its chill grasp. Every time Jack drove through London he had the distinct impression he was being followed, and the sensation made his flesh crawl. But whenever he glanced over his shoulder, or in his rear view mirror, there would be nothing. At least nothing he could make a fix on. Still, the impression persisted.

Jack's expectations hadn't improved even though his mood had lightened following a second meeting with Van Damm on Friday evening. The man seemed to be making the right sort of noises and Jack was cautiously hopeful he might be able to secure the capital base he needed for what he had in mind. Onward now with plan 'A'.

Lunch with Tony Trent, the previous Tuesday, had been a most pleasant affair. Jamies, on Kingsway, with its unique blend of French and Thai cuisine, provided the most delicious fare, and Tony, perceiving Jack's haggard state, had insisted on a two hour meal break to the exclusion of all talk of business. "We'll discuss it in detail on Monday, Jack," he had insisted. "In the comfort of my office."

Tony had looked supremely untroubled. But then Tony always looked supremely untroubled. Even in the jaws of defeat, if he couldn't pluck victory, he always managed to give the impression that he'd succeeded anyway.

Even now, thinking of that ghastly creditors meeting in Bermuda, Jack found himself wondering how Tony could have appeared so utterly sanguine, both during and after events.

Jack's approach was, if somewhat less buoyant, rather more rudimentary. They'd lost. Ms. Clark had pursued a line of questioning which left Tony Trent and Jack Gregory demolished once its leads had been taken up by Hepton. It made him feel ill just recalling it. Lost, lost, lost; it was as simple as that.

God knows what Tony had in store for him today, because Jack was feeling anything but optimistic.

At the end of Kingsway, Jack turned his vehicle into the Aldwych and made for the modern office block overlooking the Thames which accommodated the firm of Armstrong Graebner.

Leaving the Jaguar in the building's underground car park, Jack took the lift to the fourteenth floor where Tony was waiting for him. The interior of the offices was all brown and gold and the board room both commodious -- the conference table could seat twenty-four -- and comfortable, furnished with an array of giant leather armchairs offering guests magnificent views of the river. Jack sank into one, feeling the soft dark brown hide of the armrests against his palms and fingertips.

Moulding his six feet three inch frame into an easychair opposite Jack, Tony smiled back at him with his customary air of self-assured poise. Tony's father had been a Chartered Accountant before him and Tony had followed him into Eton, and later Cambridge where he had attained blues in both rugby and rowing. Tony had been married for just four years, and in that time his strikingly beautiful wife Joanna, a qualified barrister specializing in criminal law, had produced two sons and a daughter for him.

"How've you been, Jack?"

"You asked me that last time we spoke," Jack said sullenly, "and the answer's the same, I've been better."

"How's Phyllida?"

"Bearing up."

Tony paused and surveyed Jack with concern. The younger man was suntanned and looked more like a film star than a professional man. He said quietly, "You're starting to go grey, Jack. I hadn't noticed when we last met. And you look as if you haven't slept in a month."

"I told you, I've been better," he spoke sharply, irritated at the irrelevancy.

Sighing in resignation, Tony changed the subject, "Help yourself to a cigar, Jack." He indicated the open box on the chrome and glass coffee table between them.

"Thanks, I'll stick to these," Jack replied and lit up a Dunhill panatella.

"Coffee?" Tony started to pour from a tall, blue and white Wedgwood pot, and filled a second cup when Jack nodded his assent.

"What's the news, Tony? You've kept me waiting for days; I assume it's not good."

"Hepton's had a meeting of the Committee of Inspection of Central Reinsurance in Bermuda, video-linked to the UK for the members over here. He asked them to let him take a fee on account."

"How much?" Jack held his breath.

"Eight million dollars."

"What!" Jack exploded. Hepton had clearly taken over the US bank balances, all forty million dollars worth, and was now starting to milk every cent from them. Even if Jack could thwart the bastard in the long run, by the time he did, there'd be precious little left. Still, why was Jack driving himself mad? In his own mind, he'd written off the monies long ago.

"If you remember, Jack, I said I'd have an advance chat with our friends on the Committee."

"Tell me."

"Howard B. Charlesworth of General Life and Pensions."

"A real gentleman in business."

"Voted against Hepton."

"Great. Though, to be expected." From the choice offered, Jack ladled four teaspoons of brown sugar into his coffee, contemplated the swirling liquid for a moment and then poured in a fifth. The burning syrup was like a balm and he gulped it back too quickly feeling it blister the roof of his mouth and tip of his tongue. Then he waited for Tony to continue. The worst was still to come and he knew it.

"James Fulman." Tony dropped a single cube of white sugar into his coffee and sat back, his legs crossed, absently stirring his coffee without appearing to need to drink it.

"Of Etheridge Lock." Jack picked up his cigar and drew on it, leaving the drink to cool on the glass table.

Tony nodded and went on stirring his coffee. He had long hands with slender fingers that moved with an almost balletic grace.

"Voted against."

"Of course."

"Go on."

"As was to be expected Ms. Clark representing General Life and Pension voted in favour, as did Ed Pasteur of Fleetwood Assurance. Apparently Mr. Pasteur was distinctly unhappy at Hepton's inability, or unwillingness to stipulate upon what basis his fees had been calculated. There is no way that Hepton could justify charging eight million on a time cost basis, even at his charging out rate. But Pasteur voted yes anyway."

"If there's one thing about the Bermuda meeting I remember very clearly, Tony, it's that Hepton announced to everyone that he was on a thousand dollars an hour. If he calculated his fees on a time cost basis he would need to justify about eight thousand hours, that's more than three years work. Absolute rubbish. Even if he had a posse of staff working on the case, which it wouldn't need, he still couldn't stack up that sort of sum in time costs."

"Right. So he went for another tack. He said he'd applied the Official Receiver's scale, and that he'd taken approximately ten percent of realizations, and ten percent of distributions -- four million each way."

"But hell, he hasn't made any distributions yet. He can't have. It's far too soon to have agreed all claims."

"Quite right, but Mr. Hepton told the Committee he was asking for fees based on anticipated future distributions"

"The man was talking gibberish"

"James Fulman said that no one on the Committee was enamoured of Hepton's logic, it seems not even the inimitable Ms. Clark was pleased."

"I'm delighted to hear it. Anyway, what was the outcome?"

"Vernon Williams of Hermes Equitable voted against. He clearly doesn't like Hepton, and he wasn't having any of it."

"Superb." Tony was right to look pleased with himself, Jack realized. Things had definitely taken a turn for the better.

"That was the good news. Now here's the bad. Hepton's applying to the Supreme Court of Bermuda for his fees. And it goes without saying, the new Chief Justice is Hepton's poodle."

"I should have known it was too good to be true. I suppose if nothing else we've slowed up the bugger."

"Exactly. Now let's get down to the other business of the day; the meeting of creditors of JG Petroleum Holdings.

Jack twisted uncomfortably in his seat, "How are things going?"

"Not well."

"God. I can't afford to lose this one Tony, I simply can't."

"You've still got the Mareva injunction in force against you?"

"That's right."

"Where are you drawing money from to live on?"

"From Phyllida's account. I transferred over two hundred thousand to it at the start of all this. It was supposed to be used for the cost of clearing the garage sites, but I've been using it for other things."

"David Purdoe's working on getting the ten million judgement against you set aside?"

"Correct. He's due to have the matter heard in court shortly."

"Bermuda?"

"'Fraid so."

"Well don't hold your breath, Jack. Hepton's poodle will be on call again.

Jack pondered Tony's last remark, but said nothing.

"Now, what about that Statutory Notice?"

Jack dragged on the cigar, then wrinkling his nose in a gesture of dissatisfaction, stubbed out the panatella and returned to his coffee. "David's opposing it on the grounds that a UK national can't be made bankrupt, a) on an overseas judgement, and, b) on the grounds that the thing is in dispute anyway."

"And the Mareva injunction?" Tony pressed him.

The constant reminders of all he faced gave Jack a feeling of butterflies trying to escape from out of his stomach via his throat and he had to breath deeply to calm his increasing nervousness at Tony's probing. "That's tied in with everything else. If David can get the ten million judgement set aside, he'll have no problems getting the Mareva reversed and the Statutory Demand killed. We'll get precious little from Bermuda, but all the applications we're making are taking place in the High Court over here."

"Okay, Jack, that brings us back to the JG Petroleum creditors' meeting. I've issued notices as you know. The meeting will be held at these offices next week on the eighteenth. You were relying on the surplus cash from that liquidation to fund some of your legal actions weren't you?"

Jack's spirits hit rock bottom at the reminder, "That's right."

"But there's a shortfall now."

"Yes."

"Well, it doesn't look good at all, Jack. All of the secured creditors have intimated that they want to attend the meeting. They can't vote of course, except on the unsecured portion of their claims; but they could make a lot of noise."

"Wonderful." For all of his years in the insolvency profession, Jack's one experience in emulating the directors he usually fronted for, sitting opposite his own creditors in Bermuda, had left him with a dread feeling every time he contemplated the prospect of a repeat performance.

He might almost have been there now, the churning of his insides told him. God, to have to go through all that again. As long as he had the votes, a majority in terms of the value of all his creditors' claims, he'd be home and dry. But would he get the votes he needed sewn up before the meeting?

"How are the proxies going?" Jack asked, hardly wanting to hear the answer."

"Badly. It's almost as though Hepton were orchestrating the voting himself. We've got nothing but professionals coming. Word is, they'll be out for your blood, Jack. It seems the world and his uncle have found out about the Mareva, the Statutory Notice and pending bankruptcy proceedings. On the basis of the, `no smoke without fire' principle, your professional colleagues are out to stop you."

"Don't you think I know that, Tony? I'm a member of that profession remember? Or at least I thought I was. Anyway, thanks for being so positive." Jack smiled, but despite the bold face he felt physically weak. "What's the damage so far?"

"We're short by over one hundred thousand pounds in votes. As you know, the ethical guidelines don't allow me to canvas for votes if it could be construed in any way as the harassing of creditors, so I've kept my approaches low key so far."

"Do you think I should be chasing up proxies then? I know a lot of the creditors. I've dealt with them for years."

"Gut feeling tells me you should keep as far from this as possible, Jack. Limit the damage. Also, I have to tell you, there've been murmurings doing the rounds." Tony paused, looking earnestly at Jack.

"Murmurings?"

"The profession's looking at this through a microscope. They won't like the fact that you've made yourself -- a director of companies both here and in Bermuda -- liquidator in both cases."

"So what?" Jack protested belligerently. "There was no conflict. Nothing in the ethical guidelines to say I couldn't. It was simply a convenient way..."

"Jack, I know it's not against the ethical guidelines, but you and I know it was always a bit iffy. Strictly speaking, I shouldn't even be taking the coming meeting. I'll claim independence of course, as I did last time; but we may be pushing our luck."

"God! Bermuda all over again. I have to be honest, Tony, I'm dreading this meeting. We can't afford another roasting. You have to win this time. Still", he said brightening a little, "at least no one who was at the Bermuda meeting will be at this one."

"Sorry, Jack, but that's the problem, there will be one person who was there."

There couldn't be. There just couldn't be. That would finish it. Outvoted, and with Tony, a man whose independence could be questioned at the meeting, both taking that meeting, and at the same time seeking the nomination as liquidator. Impossible. "Who is that one person, Tony?"

"Ms. Clark."

Chapter 13

February 16, Tuesday

She was rocking back and forth, back and forth, her shoulders jolting as though in spasm, her head thrown back, eyes tight shut. On the dressing table in front of her was a newly opened bottle of Harvey's Bristol Cream, it was three quarters empty. Reaching forward Phyllida poured more sherry into the tumbler until it overflowed spreading a golden pool of alcohol amongst the bottles of perfume and jars of face cream.

The face that stared back at her from the mirror was unrecognizable from that of a few days ago. Her forehead was a tangle of fine lines twisted into a pattern of agony that formed a knot between her brows. The hair, a dull mat of lank straw. The mascara smudged eyes were black craters set either side of a nose whose skin was stretched so taut it resembled the beak of a giant bird. Her lipstick was smeared where she'd run the back of her hand across her mouth. Her head was spinning and she felt very tired. She was also very confused.

If Jack was living in fear, how could she possibly support him? Her sponsorship of her husband relied, she knew full well, on its being collateral to his own resilience. Every day, he looked more drawn, more haggard. Now that she could see him beginning to fail, she realized she would not be able to sustain her own morale and his as well. She was letting him down, and letting him down badly.

The final straw for her had been Jack's apparent intention of taking an illegal course of action. Despite her promise to support him, the idea of her husband fencing with an international giant whilst playing experienced criminals at their own game was more than she could sustain. How could

Jack seriously contemplate taking on the might of AUIG, and the resources and the degenerate resourcefulness of Luke Hepton aided and abetted by his Chinese agent.

Lifting the glass again to her lips she gulped back some of the sweet liquid, welcoming the warm trail it cut into the pit of her stomach. Not much of a drinker at the best of times, Phyllida could now see clearly why Jack invariably poured himself a large drink at the end of the day. Jack had told her that his father had beat him as a small boy. His mother had stood by, or weakly remonstrated with her husband. Yet Jack had grown up with a curious respect for his father whom he saw as misguided but well intentioned. His mother, he dismissed as duplicitous, seeing her and all women as weak. The mixture had produced a man who was fiercely independent; one who would savagely follow his own convictions and stand by them, right or wrong. Until now he'd usually been right. Jack was stubborn and obstinate. His very strength was his greatest weakness. He wouldn't give in, wouldn't compromise. And it was destroying her. In due course, she realized, it would destroy him, too.

In contrast, Phyllida's father, whom she'd adored, was a gentle and loving man who relied on his family for emotional support during their hard times. He saw women as the stronger, more resilient sex. He took Phyllida to be in the same mould as her mother, a woman who coped efficiently with her husband's emotional needs when business was bad. Somehow, Phyllida managed to disguise the worst of her torment from her parents when she lost Tom. But her friends had not been fooled.

The baby cried out in her sleep from her own bedroom startling Phyllida. Glancing at her watch Phyllida saw it was after seven o'clock, Jack would be home at any moment. As if in response to her thoughts the lights of Jack's car briefly illuminated the room as he swung the Jag around and parked it outside the front door.

He'll be hungry, she thought. Mrs. Llewellyn left a chicken on timer roasting in the oven; it should be ready now. He would want Phyllida to greet him. He mustn't see her like this. Grabbing a Kleenex, she wiped her face clear of some of the makeup. God! What ever would he think?

Jack hated women who drank. Hauling herself to her feet, she took a deep breath and, smoothing the creases in her housecoat made her way along the landing. "Hello, darling," she said, forcing a smile. "Had a good day?" Leaning against the bannister, Phyllida began to walk carefully downstairs, placing one foot deliberately in front of the other. If she concentrated she could do it quite easily and maybe Jack wouldn't realize.

Jack closed the door behind him. It had not been a good day. He was glad just to be home. Glad to be able to kick off his shoes and settle down for the evening with his wife. Coming down the stairs towards him in a floor length nightdress was a lady he barely recognized. The hawk like nose, the sunken eyes and cheeks. She was hiding again, hiding as she used to, within a tent of a garment. The tiny waist obscured, she looked like the overweight lady Jack had encountered at that dinner party when first they'd met.

The sudden realization of what he was witnessing swept over Jack like a typhoon leaving in its wake the wreck of his emotions. Trying to retain some dignity for her husband left Phyllida looking utterly vulnerable. For the first time in more than thirty years Jack Gregory wanted to cry.

"I'm sorry, Phyl, I'm so sorry," he murmured. "I didn't know, I just didn't know."

Making it to the bottom of the stairs without falling, Phyllida swayed unsteadily towards Jack, smiling at him all the while.

"Come my, love." Jack said, "Let's go back to bed."

It wasn't working. Impossible to keep up the pretence, "I know you think I'm naive and foolish, Jack, but..." Stopping abruptly, her arms lolling by her sides, her eyes hooded with fear, she started whispering, "Help me, Jack. For God's sake help me."

As she fell sideways, Jack caught her in his arms, and lifting her bodily, carried her back up the stairs to their bedroom.

"We're going to lose everything, aren't we, Jack?" She was lying on the bed where Jack had rested her, looking up at him.

"No, we're not."

She glanced up at him and then around the room and sighed, "I never needed the wealth, you know. Just... just a bit of security." She paused, "And you. And Harriette. That's all." She shrugged and gave Jack a small smile, "I don't think I'm really the sort of woman you need, Jack. I'm simply not that gutsy."

"Phyllida, don't be bloody ridiculous." It was like being on a merry go round that was going faster and faster. He was in a rage at what was happening, staring at the increasing chaos of his own futile attempts to protect his wife from what might be the beginnings of a complete break down.

Phyllida sat up if she'd just remembered something, "Jack, if you went to prison, I... I know I said I'd wait for you. But, without you, I'd be nothing."

"Phyl, I promise I won't go to prison." Jack was sitting on the bed cradling Phyllida in his arms. "It's not going to be like that."

"How can you be so sure?"

Her skin was icy cold to his touch and she was crying out of control, her body heaving and shuddering, "I'm not used to living like this, Jack. I mean, they know everything that's going on. It's like they're in the room with us right now, watching us. You said yourself the phone's probably bugged." Her voice was becoming ever higher. "And even if you took it off, they'd simply replace it with another. She twisted around and put her arms about Jack's neck, "I'm frightened, Jack, of what you might get yourself into. And these people, I'm so afraid of these people."

Hugging her back, Jack said, "I know, my love." He sat in contemplation for several moments, then he added quietly, "I'm afraid, too."

"Oh, Jack, darling. Hold me, hold me tight." His warmth against her shivering body, the faint smell of his aftershave, the muscled power in his arms. The incongruity of his own fear bound her ever more strongly to him. As long as he was there for her... but she was shaking uncontrollably, couldn't stop.

Jack closed his eyes, clenched his jaw. He had to put a stop to it, had to haul on the anchors before they both started screaming. "It doesn't matter, Phyl. Don't you see? They can listen in to us until the cows come home. In the end, they can't stop me selling the petrol stations to a cash buyer, and Danny's found one."

"What?"

"Danny's found a cash buyer."

Rubbing her eyes, Phyllida sat up straight and faced Jack, "You wouldn't lie to me, Jack." She sounded a little clearer, a bit more in control.

"Scouts honor."

Taking a tissue from the pocket of her nightie, she blew her nose. "Don't play games with me, please."

"Danny's found a buyer, I swear it. The man deals in petrol stations. His name's Mistry, Mr. Mistry. And I'm not joking. With a name like that how could I be? He keeps maybe a score of stations for pin money, and the rest he buys and sells either within say a month, or longer, after renovations. I've never seen a man make so much money in so little time."

"Except you, sweetheart."

"Yes, angel, except me." He nuzzled her cheek feeling the oily consistency of her smeared make-up against his own face, and tasted the salty damp of her tears as they ran into his mouth."

"What about the ten million judgement against you? And that bankruptcy notice?"

"All taken care of, darling."

"David Purdoe?"

"David Purdoe."

"Isn't he clever, Jack"

"He's the best."

"He lost Celia," Phyllida looked as though she was about to start crying again.

"I know, darling. And he's doing what he can to come to terms with it through hard work. He's a dark horse, our David."

"All the girls fancy him," she sniffled.

"Don't they just." How much longer could Jack keep up this absurd pretence. He was weary and felt sick. Was he really responsible for Phyllida's state? And if he were, was there anything he could do to fix it? Of course there was, and he knew the answer. She must never be exposed to this sort of trauma again. He shrugged to himself, he'd have to go it alone, that was all.

"What about the money in the American banks?"

"Hepton can keep it."

"All of it?" she was as wide eyed as a child.

"All of it."

"Jack, you said there was over forty million on deposit." Reaching to the side of the bed, Phyllida pulled a fresh handful of pink Kleenex tissues from a box and blew her nose again, and then with more tissues started to wipe her face, intermittently kissing Jack's cheeks and forehead as she did so.

"After paying off all the creditors there would only have been twenty left for me though," he said.

"Oh, only twenty for you, darling." She shook her head, a slight movement. "Would even twenty million have been enough for you, Jack?"

He smiled, sadly. "More than enough. But I'll manage quite well without it as well."

"How?"

"Oh, the cash surplus from the petrol stations, my income from the insolvency practice."

"Have the DTI said you can go back to work?"

"Not yet, but they will. I told you, David's working on it for me."

She stared at him, full in the face, and he returned her gaze without flinching. "You're telling me the truth, aren't you?" It was a statement, put like a question. "I know it. I can see it in your face. Oh, darling, why didn't you tell me before?"

"I've only just got home. You didn't give me a chance."

"You've only just found all this out?"

"I've just come from David's office."

"Oh, Jack. I do love you."

"I love you, too."

"Everything's going to be all right then?"

"If you can call the loss of forty million dollars, all right, well then yes," he smiled.

"And we'll both be safe?"

"Of course we will."

"You won't do anything illegal?"

"I'll try not to," he smiled at her again.

"Promise?"

"Promise."

"Thank God," she said, her eyes closed. "Thank God."

Looking down at herself as if she had just noticed the state she was in, Phyllida said, embarrassed, "Just look at me. What must you think? I've made a complete fool of myself." Then, sliding from Jack's grasp she said, "Just a moment, darling."

He could hear her singing in the shower, and then the sound of her toweling herself down. The fragrance of her perfume floated into the bedroom reminding Jack of the first night they had spent together and gently intruding into his thoughts as he pondered how ever he was going to keep up the charade of his recent successes. And, what he would do if and when it became necessary to tell Phyllida that the house was going to have to be sold, or worse -- repossessed in his bankruptcy if he were unable to prove his daughter's title to it.

The bathroom door opened and Phyllida emerged wearing only a shortie nightie. Her face was shiny and clear of makeup, and her hair had been pulled from her forehead into a loose knot at the back of her head. Her complexion had regained a little of its color and she seemed in control of herself again. The nightie acted as a sort of unspoken code between them. Either she wore it, or Jack asked her to, and the meaning was always understood by them both. She stood in front of him for a moment, "I'm ugly," she said. "And I know it."

"Phyl. I love you."

She smiled sadly, "A lady needs more than just...." Her arms hung lank by her sides, she looked down at the floor and shook her head, "I'm so sorry. I let you down."

"What is it, Phyl? Tell me. There's something else isn't there. Something you should be talking about. If you won't confide in me, then who else?"

She paused, about to say something. There were things you didn't talk about. Things you didn't even want to think about. She simply said, "I love you too, Jack. So much." Then sitting next to her husband, Phyllida started to help him out of his clothes. Her movements were hurried with her own silent imperative. Then he was naked beside her, the bulk of his enormous body, the sinews of his muscles hard against her. She had the nightie pulled up above her breasts and her breathing was becoming quick and impatient, "Come Jack," she begged, "Need me too. Make love to me. It's been so long."

He moved his body, shifting his thighs away from her so that she couldn't see his flaccid state. Some kind of man you are, he thought. Looking at her tenderly he kissed her face and neck and moved his lips down to her breasts where, one after the other he took the hardened nipples into his mouth.

"Now Jack, now. Please."

He was with her, but he was somewhere else. He could look at her, but he couldn't see her, he could touch her, but could not feel her. He moved down her body, kissing her belly and flicking the tip of his tongue into her navel and then on down into the golden triangle of her pubis. "This is how you like it, isn't it?" he whispered.

"Yes, darling, yes. Don't stop."

Slipping his hands between her thighs, he spread them wide and tasted sadly the sweet salt of her wetness for him.

"That's right darling, like that," she sighed. "Just like that."

Chapter 14

February 18, Thursday

The silence in the conference room in the offices of Armstrong Graebner was almost tangible. It hovered like something not quite translucent, a cirrus cloud, or patchy fog. It was in the air and it was oppressive and menacing.

Seated next to Jack Gregory at the top table and shuffling his papers into order, was Anthony Trent. Like every meeting of creditors. Like Bermuda again. Included amongst his various documents was a copy of the statement of affairs of JG Petroleum Holdings Ltd., and a transcript of the company history, Tony would be delivering in a couple of moments to the thirty five or so creditors assembled in rows before him and Jack.

A few minutes previously as Jack had watched the various representatives of the creditors of JG Petroleum arriving he had witnessed the customary smug shaking of hands amongst the professionals he invariably received support from at the meetings he himself was used to taking.

Today was going to be a very different story. Jack had heard the comparisons being made of figures on the statement of affairs as groups of creditors leaned this way and that searching amongst themselves for permutations of total claim values that would result in the outvoting of Tony Trent and the blocking of his appointment as liquidator of JG Petroleum at this meeting.

Despite his resolve not to dwell upon it, recollections of the Hamilton debacle kept returning to Jack and he unconsciously fingered his shirt collar as though trying to pry it from his neck in the way he had in the humidity of that Hamilton meeting a few short months ago. Only the day before, Jack's doctor had told him, "If you don't ease up you're heading for a fall." Jack was never unwell, it simply didn't figure in his scheme of things. Illness was for the frail and timid.

The pains in Jack's chest had become sharper and more frequent in recent weeks, spreading in the last few days to his arms and hands. Normally he would have shrugged them off, but there was too much happening at the moment to take more risks. Death was not something that worried him, but he could no longer afford the luxury of his usual casual fatalism. He loved his wife, adored his baby. The thought of Phyllida trying to manage without him, the idea of Harriette without a father, didn't bear contemplation.

"Your blood pressure's through the stratosphere, Jack," the doctor had said. "If you don't find a way of slowing down.... well.. put crudely, you're a dead man." Then, almost as an afterthought he had added, "No wonder you're impotent."

Jack had asked for the doctor's prognosis, and insisted on the truth without frills. He hadn't expected it to be good; but equally he hadn't expected it to be this bad. Either something had to break in his favor, and pretty damn soon, or else his life was running on a short fuse. Whatever, he couldn't change anything. He could do no more than hope.

Overhead, Jack was aware of the throbbing of an aircraft's engines. It sounded like a bomber from an old war film, and the cacophony pounded in his ears and in his head. Overhead? They were in a soundproof modern building. The noise grew louder, nearer. Jesus, God, it was his own heartbeat he was listening to, he realized. At this rate he wouldn't even survive the bloody meeting. Got to get a hold. Simply got to calm down. But it was useless. Just had to pray he wouldn't peg out in front of everyone. What a pathetic farce it all was.

An hour earlier there had been the usual pre-meeting briefing session with Tony. A final check of the details to be provided to creditors at the meeting. Tony had worked on the case without the customary assistance of an administrator, "I want no slip ups this time, Jack. I'm preparing everything myself." Then he'd turned solicitously to the question of Phyllida, "Does she know about this morning's meeting?"

"No," Jack had replied bluntly. "I'm not chancing anything with her. I told you last week, Tony, she's not good. If things get much worse..." Jack had sighed, and left it at that.

"What a bloody mess, Jack"

"Possibly. On the other hand you could make sure we win today."

Tony had smiled for the first time that morning, "Listening to you, Jack, I should say, winning today is the least of your problems."

The two men put their documents in order, company histories and statements of affairs immediately to hand. Jack focused his meandering thoughts on the mass of faces, a sea of white blotches, staring at him and, breathing deeply and steadily, tried to quell the rising fears that threatened to overtake him. They had to win this time. There was a shuffling of papers as people prepared for the start, a clearing of throats and a flourishing of pens over note pads. Oddly, Ms. Clark didn't seem to be among the creditors.

"Good morning, ladies and gentlemen," Tony was addressing the meeting at last. In the instant before he had opened the proceedings, he had caught Jack's eye and winked at him with supreme confidence. From now on it was all in the lap of the gods, or perhaps more correctly, in the lap of Tony Trent.

"This is a formal meeting of the creditors of JG Petroleum Holdings Ltd., convened under Section 95 of the Insolvency Act 1986, for the purposes of appointing a liquidator and a liquidation committee." Tony's delivery was polished as a diamond and Jack loosened up a fraction, opening his fists and spreading his hands flat on the table before him. With the meeting under way at last, and his pulse finally slowing from its lunatic pace of a moment ago he began to concentrate on preparing himself mentally for the questioning that would follow Tony's presentation.

"My name is Anthony Trent and I am a licensed insolvency practitioner. Let me declare my position at once," Tony went on in almost identical terms to those used at the Bermuda meeting to explain his professional relationship with Jack Gregory, and to reassure creditors that it in no way impinged upon his independence as the potential liquidator of JG Petroleum Holdings.

Covering everything in detail, Tony explained how the business had been built up by Jack from modest beginnings to the present seventeen sites. He showed how the company had never made a loss in its ten year history, and advised creditors that the reasons for the company's apparent insolvency now were the explosion that had taken place on one site, followed by threats of further explosions, and the dumping of tyres at several other locations. The police had thus far drawn a blank; and the net result had been a serious impediment to the speedy sale of the business.

The statement of affairs indicated a comparatively modest potential shortfall of about one hundred thousand pounds, depending of course on what the garages eventually fetched. If a good price was obtained, creditors might still see a one hundred percent pay out. Tony had completed his presentation and come to the end of the first part of the proceedings.

It all seemed reasonable, and, looking at things objectively Jack could see no reason whatever for his creditors to take issue with him. Ms. Clark had still not arrived, and Jack found himself harbouring the remote hope that she might not turn up at all. Professionals attending meetings of creditors made a point of arriving early to allow time to study the documentation issued and prepare their questions prior to the start. Reaching forward, Jack took up the glass of water on the table in front of him and gulped some of it back. It was ice cold and refreshing. Maybe she wasn't coming. Perhaps one of those present was there in her place.

Maybe pigs could fly, Jack thought, as the door at the back of the conference room opened and a somewhat ill-tempered looking Ms. Clark stalked down the aisle between the rows of seats and found herself a vacant spot at the front.

Undoing her coat, she pulled her brief-case deliberately on to her lap and extracted a number of papers from it. She wore a high-neck dull grey blouse and plain black skirt the combined effect of which ensemble was ascetic to the point of funereal. She pushed her glasses up her tiny nose and pulled a ballpoint pen from her top pocket. This wasn't going to be any picnic. His lips went dry and his throat tightened with foreboding.

In deference to her late arrival, Tony offered to run over some of the details of the meeting, but Ms. Clark waved him away.

"That won't be necessary," she said curtly.

"In that case," Tony smiled at the creditors, "are there any questions either Mr. Gregory or I can assist with at this stage?"

It seemed that there were. For the next hour and a half questions were put forth, questions that covered every aspect of the business and the way it had been run. The assets and liabilities on the statement of affairs were examined with the thoroughness of a dentist checking a patient tooth by tooth. Nothing that had caused the aggravation in the Bermuda meeting was brought up, nor even alluded to. Nevertheless, at the end of ninety minutes of parrying high-powered questions, albeit with Tony's able assistance, Jack felt the effects. His head was throbbing and the back of his neck ached. A sweet black coffee would have been a blessing. Or better yet, a large whisky and Drambuie. Still, they had a long way to go yet before they were done.

During all the time creditors spent asking questions, Ms. Clark sat impassively looking at her papers and adding to the notes she made of replies given to enquiries raised. Maybe she was here simply to take a report, and hence the late arrival. Her presence on time had not been an absolute necessity. Certainly, she had hardly cast a glance in Jack's direction since she had first sat down.

"Anything further?" Tony made as if to shuffle his papers together and Jack held his breath. If they moved to the formal business of the meeting now, it would all be over and done with in seconds. As Tony had pointed out prior to the meeting, when Jack's own position as a creditor of the company was taken into account and added in with the rest, they had sufficient votes to carry the day.

Nobody said a word; there was nothing further to be covered. Tony could wrap it all up right now.

Ms. Clark glanced up from her notes, casually, "Just one point, Mr. Trent." Bugger the woman! Jack thought. Still, she was smiling pleasantly. Too soon to get paranoid.

"How long have you known Mr. Gregory, Mr. Trent?"

"I did cover that point, Ms. Clark, in my preamble."

"Yes, but as you may have noticed, I wasn't present for that." She spoke so softly, her voice was barely audible, though its cynicism shone through clear as crystal. If she were about to develop her line of questioning, Jack was well aware, on past experience, her voice would become louder and louder.

It was to be expected, some professionals ended up their bouts of interrogation positively shouting at the tops of their lungs. It could be a devastating experience for directors still trying to come to terms with the loss of their businesses, and it occasionally resulted in them being sufficiently confused to vote their proxies for a liquidator other than their own nominee.

Despite being fully conscious of what Ms. Clark was up to, Jack was no less unnerved.

Tony, nodding in polite acquiescence to Ms. Clark, repeated the remarks he had made in his introduction and waited for her reply.

Blinking in a show of astonishment, Ms. Clark said, "Do you seriously suggest that creditors present should take you at your word when you protest your independence, Mr. Trent? What ever do you take us for?" There were murmurs of assent around the room.

Quite unperturbed, Tony said, "Ms. Clark, I seem to recall this issue was raised at the meeting of creditors of Central Reinsurance in Bermuda when I demonstrated to creditors..."

"Demonstrated what, Mr. Trent? Don't you think you should be making it clear to this meeting that your appointment as liquidator was overturned on that occasion?" Ms Clark settled her spectacles high up on the bridge if her nose with the tip of her forefinger.

"It was overturned on a disputed claim," Tony sounded a shade irritated. Too experienced a practitioner to lose his temper, Jack wondered all the same just how much it would take for his friend to really go overboard.

"I think it's a blind to bring up the Central meeting. We're not in Bermuda now." Ms. Clark regarded Tony with what could only be described as open contempt.

Again, Jack was aware of the other man's impatience as Tony sucked in breath with a gasp of annoyance.

Before Tony could make any further comment on the issue, Ms. Clark had changed tack. She was waving her pen in the odd manner Jack recalled from the Bermuda meeting, as though it were a thermometer. "Have creditors present been advised of the Mareva injunction against Mr. Gregory?"

Jack sat unmoving, he was stunned. It was obvious how she'd found out, but it had never crossed his mind that it would be raised by her or anyone else at this meeting. Or had he merely been naively deluding himself? Afraid to face the fact that, armed with that little morsel of information she would lay waste to all the preparations Tony and he had made for this morning.

"We are waiting for an answer gentlemen." Her tone was perceptibly louder.

Recovering himself first, Tony replied, "The information had not been volunteered to this meeting because it was thought to be unnecessary."

"Unnecessary?" Ms. Clark surveyed the room with an expression of incredulity. "In whose opinion?"

"Mine," Tony had stood up to face the creditors and was leaning forward his palms flat on the table in front of him. His reply was a little more forceful than Jack would normally have considered necessary.

"You're telling us that with a Mareva injunction against your old friend Jack Gregory, an injunction that prevents him from dealing in any of his assets, you didn't think it was necessary, in your opinion," she sneered, "to inform this meeting?"

It sounded terrible. Tony had clearly misjudged badly when he advised Jack against all mention of the Mareva. Jack had been just as foolish to bury his head in the sand over the issue. It was bound to come up. And now it was rearing its head like a Jurassic monster.

Smiling deferentially, Tony resumed his seat. Having pulled himself together again he said, "Ms. Clark, with the greatest respect, the position is far from clear. My solicitors advise me that Mr. Gregory was dealing responsibly with the assets of a company in his charge. And I would add, in the best interests of his creditors."

"A company in liquidation."

"As you wish, a company in liquidation."

"And who is the principal shareholder of this company, Mr. Trent?"

Tony smiled broadly. "It is noted on the penultimate page of the documents you were issued with." Good old imperturbable Tony, back in command.

"I didn't ask you where I could find the information, I asked for a reply. Who is the principal shareholder of JG Petroleum Holdings Ltd? Can we get a straight answer to a straight question this afternoon, do you think?" The thermometer was still being shaken.

Quietly grinding his teeth, Tony replied, "Jack Gregory."

"Thank you, sir." Ms. Clark surveyed the room again, and then engaged in an exchange of mutual expressions of horror at the lack of information that had been provided to the meeting.

The room was becoming progressively noisier as creditors tried to be heard one above the other. Papers were flapping, people were pointing out figures and facts to each other and it was becoming increasingly difficult for Tony to make himself heard above the mounting tide of shouted protest. Control of the meeting was being lost. "With respect, Ms. Clark, that changes nothing. I still maintain..."

But she refused to let him go on, "Are you a bankrupt, Mr. Gregory?" Until now, Ms. Clark had hardly directed a single question to Jack.

"I am not," Jack's throat was clogged and he cleared it noisily.

"Isn't there a Statutory Demand pending against you?"

"Yes but it's being defen..."

"More information not imparted to the meeting." Ms. Clark paused for a long moment, then said softly, "And who said you could appoint yourself liquidator of your own company, Mr. Gregory? A company of which you were principal director and shareholder?"

"There's nothing in the ethical guidelines..." Jack protested weakly. Hells teeth, he was squirming now.

"Ethical guidelines, Mr. Gregory? ETHICAL GUIDELINES? What do you know about ethical guidelines?" Ms. Clark was practically shrieking, her face was bright red and she was pointing an accusing figure in Jack's direction. "Are we really expected to take this farce seriously? I suggest, Mr. Trent, that you set aside whatever proxies have been lodged in favor of the chairman of this meeting and let those creditors who have seen fit to attend this meeting in person have their own nominee appointed."

"I see no reason to deny those creditors who have lodged proxies in favour of the chair from securing their choice of liquidator." Tony spoke quietly, he was sounding distinctly guarded.

"But they haven't expressed a choice, Mr. Trent."

"They have entrusted that choice to me, Ms. Clark."

"They wouldn't have if they'd been party to this morning's proceedings." There was a howl of enraged laughter from the floor.

Closing his eyes for a moment, Jack tried to think rationally, told himself to get a grip. The lady was engaged in the usual bluff. She, and the whole floor could scream until the sun went black, they simply did not have enough votes to oust Tony. All Jack had to do was to convince himself of that fact and hope that the palpitations in his temples would die before he did.

When Jack looked up an instant later Ms. Clark was on her feet, "I see there's a director's loan account on the statement of affairs," she bellowed.

"Yes," Jack locked his fingers together on the table in front of him.

"In the sum of one hundred and fifty thousand Pounds." All her enquiries were directed at Jack now.

"Correct," Jack answered.

"And the overall deficiency on your statement is one hundred thousand Pounds."

"As you can see."

"If you were to waive your loan account Mr. Gregory, creditors might expect a one hundred percent payout."

And if Jack were to waive his loan account, he would also be waiving its voting rights and handing the meeting and his guts to Ms. Clark on a silver platter.

"I'm not prepared to do that."

"Why not? It's common practice for directors to waive all claims in the interests of their creditors. And you sir, being a licensed insolvency practitioner, at least for the time being," there were sniggers from all parts in response to her comment, "I should have thought that at the very least you would not need to be reminded of your duties to claimants." Her tone had softened somewhat, but that merely suggested to Jack that she was building up for her next assault. And she was backed by at least thirty or so willing troops.

"I'm sure I don't need to be reminded by you madam, or anyone else of my professional responsibilities. The money was put into the company by me. It is a legitimate claim. I will not withdraw it." It felt as though it was slipping away from them again. Jack Gregory and Tony Trent, Horatio and his brother holding the bloody bridge. They mustn't lose, if they did... If there was a repeat of Bermuda. There was a dull ache in Jack's chest and a tingling sensation in the tips of his fingers.

Walking towards himself and Tony, her arm raised, Jack was nonplussed for one moment by Ms. Clark, thinking she was about to strike him. Instead she threw a sheaf of papers in front of him and Tony.

It was two p.m. and the meeting had been going on for four hours. Jack was dead in his seat. If the lady had any other ideas, if she was leading up to something it was time she made it known. Another half hour of this, and they'd be carrying Jack Gregory out in a wooden box.

"I'd like you to take a look at those accounts, Mr. Gregory." Ms. Clark was still standing.

Glancing through the documents, Jack could see nothing untoward despite the warning bells he could hear in his head. They looked like draft accounts for JG Petroleum Holdings. Where she'd got them he could not imagine. They were signed off with a signature that resembled his own, and indicated figures of profit and solvency with which he was familiar. Then he glanced at Tony and what he saw made his intestines feel as though they were being sluiced with cold water.

Tony was ashen, it shrieked out through the suntan. Jack's cool and debonair friend, the phlegmatic and composed Anthony Trent, looked like a corpse shrouded in beads of sweat.

"I would like Mr. Gregory to answer my next question without prompting from you, Mr. Trent. I must be most emphatic about that, absolutely no prompting." Ms. Clark was standing with one hand on her hip, her legs slightly spread. She looked like a parody of Hepton at the Bermuda meeting. At any moment Jack expected her to extend an accusing finger in the same way Hepton had.

Tony's eyes were pleading with Jack, they scanned the accounts as if willing Jack to read the mind behind them, but whatever it was Tony was trying to say was lost on his friend.

"Are those a set of accounts of JG Petroleum Holdings, Mr. Gregory?"

Jack shrugged, "They might be." Best hedge his bets for as long as possible.

"Come, Mr. Gregory, we're not a bunch of children to be fobbed off with evasions." Now she pointed the finger, and with the whole room muttering it's support behind her, yelled, "Are those the accounts of JG Petroleum Holdings or are they not? We demand an unequivocal answer, and we demand it now."

The balance sheet was lying in front of Jack, its director's scrawled signature, resembling Jack's, at the bottom. As he gazed at Tony, he saw the other man's eyes open wide and seemingly focus on the figure for share capital.

"Will you answer the question? Or do we need to raise this matter in the High Court?" Ms. Clark was becoming hoarse.

Share capital. Share capital. What the hell was it? It must be staring at him. Of course it was staring at him. Shouting out to be noticed. Share capital was shown at three hundred thousand on the accounts. It had been increased to that figure from the original one hundred and fifty thousand by the further one hundred and fifty thousand cash, Jack had brought into the company in the final year of the company's life. At least that had been the intention. It had not actually happened that way in the end.

The statement of affairs presented to creditors at this meeting showed the correct position, being a split of one hundred and fifty thousand share capital and the figure of one hundred and fifty thousand on Jack's loan account that was never actually capitalized.

Jack, or Tony, could legitimately vote on his loan account of one hundred and fifty thousand and carry the day. It would give him the narrow surplus he required to outvote the rest. But if he were browbeaten into admitting the accounts were correct, he would automatically lose that element of his vote. If the accounts were accepted by him as true, it would mean that he agreed that the loan indicated on the statement of affairs had actually been swallowed up into that figure of share capital depicted on those accounts.

As a shareholder only, and hence not a creditor, Jack would have no vote at this meeting of creditors. Ms. Clark would have cooked his goose, and the penny had dropped just in time.

The meeting awaited Jack's reply. The mutter and murmur of comments being made in the room sounded loud in his ears and he had visions of further complaints being lodged with the Department of Trade. Cuthbertson's face loomed before him. Think clearly, man. Think clearly, he thought.

"No," Jack said, finally and emphatically. "The accounts are not correct. They show an anticipated position not realized. Your own company search should show that they're wrong." Idiot, idiot. It was all coming back to him, "Those drafts you brought with you were prepared with the intention of presenting them to the bank, if and when I capitalized my loans, which in the end I did not, at a time when I was seeking extra borrowings. They were never filed. They are private and confidential. I'd be interested to know how you got hold of them Ms. Clark. Perhaps you'd care to enlighten us."

But she was bawling at Jack. Ms. Clark had seen Tony's glance which had earlier drawn Jack's attention to the figure she hadn't wanted him to see, "You're lying," she shouted. "He answered for you," she said pointing at Tony. "I saw it. He showed you where to look. This is an outrage and a farce. I shall be recommending my clients take this matter to the High Court."

The conference room was disintegrating into a riot. Some people were standing and shouting, others were approaching the head table as if to grab from it the copy resolutions passed prior to the meeting, appointing Tony Trent as liquidator.

Tony Trent had not moved. He looked totally thrashed.

Amid the uproar, Jack got to his feet and glowered at the meeting, "This is an abomination." His voice thundered above the noise, and there was a brief lull. "As chairman of this meeting, I am moving to the formal business which is the appointment of a liquidator and liquidation committee."

He faintly heard Tony whisper, "We've blown it, Jack. Bow out gracefully. For God's sake man, while you still can."

Seeing Tony make the comment, Ms. Clark jumped in and wrested the initiative once again, "Your loan account is a nonsense, Mr. Gregory, and this statement of affairs isn't worth the paper it's printed on. I move that Edwin Curzon partner in accountants Jackson Tullogh be appointed liquidator of JG Petroleum Holdings."

"Seconded," came a voice from behind her.

"You're out of order, Ms. Clark," Jack roared back. "You don't have the votes, and I do. As chairman of this meeting I am confirming Anthony Trent of accountants Armstrong Graebner as liquidator of JG Petroleum Holdings."

Her eyes opening wider as she stood motionless facing the top table, her cheeks and the corners of her mouth twitching, Ms. Clark turned on her heel in a white hot rage, brief-case with papers protruding from it under her arm, and stamped out of the room, slamming the door behind her.

Without their Joan of Arc to lead them, those left in the room quickly came to order. The buzz of conversation died down to an embarrassed hush. People started to drift off. One or two came up to the top table to shake hands with Jack and Tony. "Tough one, Jack," one of them grinned. "But you know how it goes."

"Don't I just," he replied ruefully trying to disguise the tremor in his voice and the shaking in his hand.

"Anyway," the same voice offered, "at least you got away without a liquidation committee. Tony can handle the case pretty well without supervision. That should please you."

Soon after, they were gone, all of them. The room was silent again, save for the ghostly echoes of the meeting. The two men remained at the table, exhausted. "I'm wrecked," Jack said.

Tony lay back in his chair, spent. His face was shiny with perspiration and he looked ten years older, "I'm sorry, Jack, I let you down badly."

"Nonsense, Tony, you did just fine. And hey," he said brightening up, "we won didn't we?"

"You won, Jack. I was a passenger. I kept on thinking, if I lose this for Jack, he's sunk, without trace. Then I started debating what effect that would have on Phyllida. Everything just clouded over in the end."

Turning to Tony, Jack punched him affectionately on the shoulder, "Come on, Tony, I wouldn't have got through without you. And, at last things are taking a turn for the better. I needed a win, badly."

A pretty young secretary looked in through the open conference room door, "Call for Mr. Gregory. Mrs. Gregory's been trying to reach you sir."

"Thanks, I'll take it in here," Jack smiled and picked up the telephone in front of him. "I told Phyl to call me here at noon. She must be wondering what's been happening," he said glancing at his watch. "I didn't let on that this was to be a meeting of creditors. Gave her a story about updating accounts. Now, at least, I can give her some good news for a change." Jack put the receiver to his ear, "Hi darling, guess what? Great news."

Everything was wrong. Phyllida was sobbing into the phone. Jack was clenching the phone tightly in his fist, "What's happened?" The weariness he had shaken off in the euphoria following the meeting, overtook him again and it felt as though his temples had been caught in a vice.

"David Purdoe called an hour ago," she faltered, her voice trembling as if she could hardly get the words out. "He says that the defence he lodged against the Statutory Notice against you has been overturned by the High Court."

Jack was shivering, he was cold as if he were standing naked in an Arctic blizzard. "All right, darling," he spoke slowly through gritted teeth, fighting his own misgivings, trying to sound as rational as he could, "We'll fight on. I can still appeal."

"Not that easily, Jack. David says it's not that easy for a bankrupt to appeal..."

"Bankrupt? What do you mean bankrupt? The Statutory Demand hadn't even expired," Jack cut in.

"Oh no, Jack. There was something called an expedited hearing." Phyllida was laughing now, laughing and crying alternately, her voice peaking in an hysterical scream. "Bankrupt, bankrupt, bankrupt. David says you're now a bloody bankrupt."

* * *

February 19, Friday

Sunlight blazed into the bedroom of the Paris flat as Phyllida awoke to mixed feelings of guilt and relief. They'd had a row. In a big way. Their first ever real fight. For once she'd tried to consider their position objectively instead of automatically deferring to him. He was losing on every front. The latest blow being his bankruptcy. She'd ranted on at Jack, shouted that he was tilting at windmills, selfishly putting his family at risk for his own stupid ends. He'd finally lost his temper. He'd shouted, bellowed even until he was hoarse. God knows what the Llewellyns must have thought. At one moment she'd thought he was going to hit her.

"You raise a hand to me and you'll never see your daughter again," she'd screamed. She immediately regretted saying it. Hated herself for it. He'd looked at her blankly. As if he was seeing her for the first time. This wasn't the way to do things, and she knew it, Jack needed her. Or perhaps he just wanted her to be there with him. Either way, they were being ripped to shreds. They both needed time apart to reflect. Despite everything she was still angry. His temper was nothing short of terrifying.

Dragging the bed covers aside, she padded in bare feet to the open window. Seven thirty a.m. and the world was coming to life. A bustle of activity took place in and around the area. From the eighth floor she could hear the sounds and pick up the aromas of the city. Traffic began to build up along the Rue du Fauborg Saint Honore where their apartment was situated. She heard shouted voices of deliverymen. The Eiffel Tower was close by and the top of Notre Dame was visible, and further away at the top of Montmartre, Sacre Coeur.

A few doors along, the smell of new baked bread drifted up from the patisserie. In a minute she would brew a pot of Earl Grey, make herself and Harriette some hot buttered croissants and get on with the unpacking she'd been too shattered to consider the previous day.

She didn't want to think about Jack or about home, yet she felt she owed it to him to analyze her feelings. He looked so gaunt and strained these days. He was being obstinate, not strong. Obsessive, not single minded. He should back down, but `retreat' wasn't a word in Jack's vocabulary.

Phyllida stretched again and yawned. Harriette would be waking up at any moment now. Finally, Phyllida admitted to herself that they'd argued and she'd run away because she was frightened. Whether or not she was deserting Jack, unless she had some time and space to herself, she would crack up completely. She felt safe here in Paris.

The apartment's freezer was stocked up with supplies enough to last Phyllida and Harriette for days. And then when she felt less frantic, when she'd allowed time for her frayed nerves to mend, she would venture out with the baby and start to let the beautiful City become part of the healing process.

Sitting down on the edge of the bed, Phyllida caught sight of herself in the antique wall mirror. Her eyes were deeply shadowed and she looked worn, but rested all the same. Wouldn't it be nice if Jack could be here now, just the way things used to be? Crossing her legs as she leaned back on one elbow, her Janet Reger nightdress fell open along the length of her thigh and Phyllida ran her hand down it feeling the muscled smoothness. Jack liked her legs, he'd said so often enough, and her breasts, and... She sighed. What was the point? She was here alone.

Alone and safe. Safe from horrors in the mail, and from news of fresh disasters from the likes of David Purdoe. Safe from the telephone and the odd clicks it made and from threatening American accents liable to crop up on the line. But Jack was the quarry not her. She felt guilty again.

Flopping back on the bed her legs dangling over the edge, Phyllida threw her arms wide and closed her eyes. The last time she and Jack had made love, he hadn't penetrated. He hadn't been able to. It had been wonderful anyway, it was always wonderful. But lately she'd noticed...

The telephone on the bedside table rang and made her jump. It would be Jack. Picking up the receiver, she put it to her ear, "Hello, Jack?" she said tentatively.

But there was no reply. Must be a wrong number, she thought after waiting several moments and replaced the receiver, a concentrated frown on her face.

Chapter 15

February 22, Monday

Several times Jack thought he noticed a silver BMW in his rear view mirror, but each time he tried to focus on it the car seemed to dissolve into the traffic. When at last he was certain he spotted the saloon again cruising along two vehicles behind him, Jack deliberately jumped a red light in order to lose it, and was pleased to note right afterwards that the BMW was nowhere to be seen.

The advertisement in the Sunday Times had read simply, "UK and Overseas Company Agents," and had given a South London telephone number. The offices of the agents were situated in the basement of a grey brick Victorian tenement type building that appeared to be given over to both residential and business use.

It was an overcast day, and Jack, tugging the lapels of his jacket collar tight about his neck to gain what little protection it afforded from the chill drizzle, hurried from where he had parked the Jaguar, cursing himself all the while for not bringing an overcoat or umbrella. Cautiously stepping down the steep flight of worn stone steps, Jack was confronted at the bottom by a large paneled door who's painted surface was flaked and peeling. A faded handwritten sign under the bell confirmed he was at the right address, and Jack, having signaled his arrival, waited in the deteriorating weather conditions for someone to admit him.

By the time the door creaked open, three minutes and several pushes of the bell later, Jack was shivering cold, his face streaming with the rain and the shoulders of his jacket soaking. In a foul temper and ready to bawl out the first person he laid eyes on, his resolve evaporated when he was greeted by the sight of the elderly lady who ushered him in. She must have been in her late seventies. With wispy white hair, tiny and bent almost double, she peered up at Jack through pebble thick lenses, "Mr. Gregory?"

"That's right."

"I'm Mrs. Twomin," her voice crackled weakly.

Despite himself, Jack smiled inwardly. A moment later he almost laughed aloud when Mr. Twomin appeared. Wearing a frayed and shiny black jacket and tie, and creased, baggy, gray pinstripe trousers, Mr. Twomin might have been his wife's brother. He even peered through the same thick-lensed spectacles, "Mr. Gregory," Mr. Twomin extended a frail blue veined hand, which Jack took gently in his own.

On an inclination of Mr. Twomin's head, Jack followed him down the hall to his office. The carpet was threadbare all the way, and the office, which was clearly in the Twomins' home, smelled as musty as the rest of the flat. Compared with the haphazard collection of papers, company seals, memoranda and articles of association and weary buff coloured folders littering floors and shelves, with which Jack was confronted, Danny Jacobovits' premises were straight out of "The Good Office Guide."

Seating himself, at Mr. Twomin's invitation, in the antique office swivel chair opposite its twin occupied by the old gentleman on the far side of the Victorian pedestal desk, Jack realized he was no longer smiling to himself. His objective here was deadly serious, and this ancient firm in its wholly unobtrusive surroundings was exactly what he was looking for.

Smart-Alec agents, brash young men with brash young mouths -- boasting state of the art office technology and situated in plush West End offices were the last thing Jack needed.

Unlike that of his wife, the strength and clarity of Mr. Twomin's voice belied his age, "What can I do for you, Mr. Gregory?"

Crossing one leg over the other, Jack said, "I want to establish two companies, a holding company in Liechtenstein and a wholly owned subsidiary in Mauritius. The holding company, which will have a share capital of three thousand dollars is to be called LHC Ltd. It just stands for Liechtenstein Holding Company. The subsidiary will be Goldleaf Insurance Ltd. and its share capital will be ten thousand dollars."

As Jack spoke, Mr. Twomin wrote quickly, making notes with a Bic ballpoint on a lined legal pad.

"I want you to arrange for bank accounts to be opened in each country, one for each company. Make the necessary deposits in each." Reaching into the inside pocket of his jacket, Jack withdrew two brown envelopes and placed them before Mr. Twomin who nodded in understanding and slid them into the top drawer of his desk.

"The holding company will have two subscribers of convenience. You nominate them. I don't need to know who they are. The subsidiary will have as its sole director a solicitor by the name of David Purdoe." Jack gave Mr. Twomin the name of the solicitor's firm and his business address.

"You can also nominate the registered agents in Mauritius for me, Mr. Twomin, that is those who will be served with all papers and documents. Let me know who they are in due course. Any correspondence addressed to the company will be posted on by the agents to The Strand Bureau at 120, The Strand EC4."

Mr. Twomin glanced up at Jack, "An accommodation address?"

"Correct. Now tell me Mr. Twomin, how much will I owe you, and when will everything be ready?"

"All of the papers, memoranda and articles of association together with certificates of incorporation and statutory books will be delivered by courier to The Strand Bureau, for the attention of Mr. David Purdoe, in seventy-two hours."

"That's excellent. And the cost?"

"Five hundred pounds for each company."

"That's all?"

"That is all."

"But that's positively antediluvian. How can you possibly make a living if you charge out at that rate?" Jack shook his head in perplexity. Then, noting again the state of the apartment, he shrugged, "I'm sorry. It's really none of my business, I know."

Opening his wallet, Jack counted out fifty, twenty pound notes, "Twenties okay?"

"Twenty pound notes are perfectly acceptable." Mr. Twomin took off his glasses and extracted a large white handkerchief from his jacket pocket with which he proceeded to polish the lenses vigorously.

Placing the notes on Mr. Twomin's desk, Jack stood up to leave, casting his eyes about the room once more. Ordered chaos, he thought, surveying the mountains of paper everywhere. And, straight out of a museum, he decided as he spotted the ancient Imperial typewriter perched peremptorily on a small mahogany table at the side of the room. Even the photographs which adorned the walls and Mr. Twomin's desk were sepia prints in antique frames.

Replacing the tiny round spectacles carefully on the bridge of his nose, Mr. Twomin pushed back the swivel chair and got to his feet. Again the fragile hand was proffered courteously and taken, as delicately as before, in Jack's own giant palm.

"I'm sure I've no need to remind you to be discreet," Jack said as Mr. Twomin accompanied him to the door.

"Of course not, Mr. Purdoe," Mr. Twomin replied, with what could only be described as a twinkle in his eye.

Just before Jack left, Mrs. Twomin reappeared, shuffling towards Jack and her husband. She must have heard the end of the conversation, because she smiled up at Jack and said in her thin, quavery voice, "Good day to you, Mr. Purdoe."

Old-fashioned service, Jack smiled to himself as he dashed through the rain to his car. It was hard to believe people like that still existed. What a sweet couple.

Driving north over Southwark Bridge before making for West London and the M4, Jack spied a silver BMW streaming past him in the opposite direction. Wondering why the sight of the car made him feel uneasy, Jack recalled it was the same type and colour of vehicle he had managed to lose on his way to the Twomins' place earlier on.

He shrugged it off. On a positive note, at least he could call Phyllida in Paris and give her some good news that he had plans under way. Better not to discuss things in detail over the phone, but he'd try to get out and see her as soon as possible. If she'd consent to see him. God, he'd lost his temper. She was probably better off away from home for the time being anyway.

Five minutes later, Jack saw something that made his mouth go dry. The BMW was there again. This time it was in his rear view mirror and by the way it was swerving around it looked as though its occupants wanted to get in front of him. He was in the City, a maze of one-way streets and `no entry' signs. He had to think fast.

Pushing his foot down hard, Jack felt the car accelerate smoothly away from the BMW and he overtook three cars before becoming aware that the other car was still on his tail. A flurry of nerves rippled in his solar plexus as Jack jumped another set of lights at a crossroads, swinging right as he did so in a squeal of rubber. There was a lot of traffic for the time of day and Jack had already incurred the ire of a number of other drivers who'd sounded their horns at him. He ignored them.

For an instant, Jack thought he'd lost the BMW, but he was wrong. It had jumped the lights with him and was there by his side overtaking him as he slowed to pull out around a line of parked cars. Another hundred yards and, skidding in a zigzag path the BMW hauled up ahead with a screech of brakes. Slamming on the anchors, Jack careened to a halt some twenty yards or so behind it.

Immediately the BMW's front and rear offside doors opened up like bat wings and two men emerged. Jack took in the executive cut navy suits, white shirts and dark ties. He saw the shiny thick black hair, smarmed back from sallow complexions that looked as though they seldom saw the light of day. They were both big, very big, and their intent expressions and the way they smoothed the fronts of their jackets and straightened their ties as if they were going into a board meeting made Jack catch his breath.

The next thing Jack saw made his eyes open wide, for one of the men carried what looked like a short black truncheon. "Bugger," Jack breathed. "A bloody cattle prod." A vision of his side window being smashed and ten thousand volts being impressed into his flesh hit Jack with the force of a bunched fist. Swing around, he thought, get away from them. No good, the traffic was moving too slowly in the opposite direction. Overtake then, they're stationery, there's time. Impossible without mowing the two of them down, and anyway with their vehicle broadside on and almost at the brow of the road there wasn't room to get past them and the oncoming traffic.

To the left of the BMW was a narrow ribbon of road between the car and the kerb.

Too narrow for the Jag to get through without mounting the pavement. Too tight even if he did, there was a tree blocking his way.

He had no choice, the men were running towards him, their attention firmly focused on his face. Gritting his teeth, Jack swung the steering wheel under the palm of his right hand in a leftward windmill touching the accelerator at the same time. The Jag nosed left and Jack, mounting the car's fat nearside tyres on the edge of the kerb, shot forward towards the narrow gap that presented itself. He had a fleeting view of the two men watching him with looks of astonishment as he swept past. Then, waiting for the inevitable tearing of metal as he pushed the vehicle hard on, he was through without a touch on either side. In the rear view mirror he could see the men dash back to their car.

What now, he thought. Turn around? They'd catch him again. Drive on and he'd eventually have to stop at lights. Nothing to do but to start snaking through side streets. He swung left, they weren't in his mirror. Swung right and left. Damn it to hell. He was in a cul-de-sac. Roaring down to the end of the short road, Jack stamped on the footbrake steering right and put the car into a skid turning it halfway round. Dragging the selector lever into reverse, Jack screamed the vehicle backwards completing the turn in a cloud of blue rubber. If they came into the street now he'd be facing them full on.

Maybe he'd lost them, he thought. Maybe pigs could fly. They'd nosed almost casually into his street and were squaring to him with insolent defiance.

"Christ!" Jack muttered as he switched on the car's two pairs of twin halogen quartz headlamps. "Well if I'm going, I'll take you bastards with me." Pressing his foot flat on the boards, Jack felt the big car jump forward in a shriek of spinning tyres and a cloud of burning rubber, the engine bellowing its accompaniment to the harmony of trumpets under its bonnet as he kept one hand firmly on the horn.

He could see their eyes open in a daze of disbelief as he charged them. Straight on, you scum, he thought. In another moment... Jack braced himself for the impact as they steered wildly past him the two cars' wing mirrors clashing angrily.

It was over. Still angry, Jack raced through the same roundabout route as before, switching left and right and doubling back on himself once and again before he felt it was clear to head for home.

They're only trying to intimidate me, he thought as he sat for a moment outside his own front door at Highview. Else why not come straight here where I'm an easy target? Well, it takes more than that to frighten Jack Gregory, he said to himself grimly. There's life in the old buccaneer yet. Then he noticed it. His hands and arms were shaking uncontrollably.

* * *

February 25, Thursday

Three days later, Jack was in the Strand heading for the offices of The Strand Bureau. The warmth of the mid-morning sun was deliciously countered by a fresh breeze, and Jack's spirits were improved. Passing through the glass swing doors set in the elegant stone arch of the ancient building the interior presented a picture of unfussy industry. The reception area was all burgundy and blue, with thick pile carpet, and dark leather upholstered furniture.

Nodding at the blonde receptionist, Jack made his way past her desk and down a corridor to her right leading to the postal collection area. A sign over the open door indicated that Jack was in the right office, and he announced himself to the assistant behind the counter, a brisk middle-aged woman who glanced at him severely from over the top of her spectacles.

If Jack had had any doubts about Mr. Twomin's capabilities they were immediately dispelled when, with a thud on the counter, he was presented with a heavy brown paper packet. Slipping his fingers through the string binding the parcel, Jack hefted it, and, letting it swing by his side, strode jauntily from the building. At last things were beginning to happen. The approach might be unorthodox, perhaps even of questionable legality -- hell, it was totally illegal -- but when it looks as if you've lost everything...

It was eleven a.m., and time for something strong and hot. Stopping for a moment at a newspaper vendor, Jack picked up an early edition of the Evening Standard and then made for a nearby cafe. The tables, accommodating four, were all orange Formica with brown borders with individual fixed seats ranged in pairs on both sides of them. Not perhaps the last word in elegance. Still, the place was brand new, cheery and its glass frontage allowed the sun to stream in.

The waitress, a pretty redhead in her early twenties, wore a pinafore whose orange and brown lines were clearly designed to fit in with the rest of the decor. Jack had ordered a tea and when the girl smiled shyly as she placed a hot mug in front of him, Jack ran a hand self-consciously over his scalp.

Pull yourself together man, he remonstrated with himself. The girl was just being polite. This is no time to start deluding yourself you're twenty-four again. And Phyllida would most certainly not be impressed. Still, Jack had to admit that young girl's grin was good for his ego. It had also reminded him how much he missed his wife.

Turned back to matters at hand and tearing open the brown paper packet, Jack extracted a brief note from Mr. Twomin. Attached, it confirmed, were statutory books, memoranda and articles of association. Details of bank accounts, together with cheque and paying in books, would be forwarded per his instructions.

Finishing the tea, Jack beckoned the same waitress as before to fetch him another, and moving the parcel and letter to one side, spread the newspaper across the table.

Something struck Jack a massive blow in the small of the back throwing him forward against the edge of the table.

The second mug of tea fell from Jack's grasp, splashing his jacket and trousers in burning hot liquid as he read:

"The article referred to cigarette burns on the man's arms and legs and other signs of torture. Papers were scattered throughout the place, and filing cabinets ransacked, but family members claim nothing of any value was taken. Police suspected foul play and were pursuing enquiries."

The redheaded waitress looked concerned, she carried a cloth to mop up the mess. Was everything all right, sir? Would he like another drink?

Unaware that he had left a ten-pound note on the table, and oblivious to the entreaties of the waitress that he wait for his change, Jack stumbled from the restaurant. He had to get into the fresh air before he threw up. The place was stifling, closing in on him. He was sweating, freezing, dazed, semi-conscious.

The Twomins must have arranged all his paperwork in less than seventy-two hours, Jack kept thinking stupidly. Only hours before... Yet there it was -- that horrific headline, accompanied by a family photograph and emblazoned in mile high black type on the front page of the Evening Standard:

Elderly South London Couple
Tortured and Murdered.

Chapter 16

March 1, Tuesday

From his hotel bedroom, Jack could make out the sea and part of the harbour of Port Louis, the capital of Mauritius. The heat and humidity were reminiscent of New York in a heat-wave, although there the similarities abruptly ended. For Mauritius was imbued with an almost mystical air of serenity. Due, some said, to the Hindu doctrine of peace and tolerance that prevailed on the island. Others, perhaps more pragmatic, insisted that the dynamics of a multicultural country with an expanding economy and low unemployment contributed vastly to the country's magical qualities.

Whatever, it seemed a crime to Jack to touch this idyllic island with his own plans based as they were on sordid origins. Jack's second meeting with Van Damm had proved fruitful and the plan was rolling. Van Damm had come up with a contact name. No time for conscience now.

The flight had taken some thirteen hours and Jack was tired. He'd hardly given a moment's thought to the approach he would adopt when he met Bertrand Arnaud, manager of The Mauritius International Bank, the following morning. Van Damm had set up the appointment, so Jack would not need to beat about the bush. Equally, he could hardly walk in and demand to be given eight certified deposits amounting to two hundred million dollars on the spot in return for cash either over or under the counter.

Touching the breast pocket of his jacket, Jack felt the lump of his wallet. Walking around with twenty-five thousand pounds in large denomination travelers cheques was safer than carrying notes, but very much more foolish than arranging simple bank transfers. Still, the object of the exercise was to gain the manager's confidence. A display of this nature might be a useful start, as long as it wasn't correctly construed for the show of financial naivety it really was.

Opening up the mini-bar in the spacious hotel room, Jack was pleased to note it contained both Johnnie Walker and Drambuie. Within minutes he was reclining in a tub in the en-suite bathroom, a Rusty Nail perched in one hand on the edge of the bath, a Dunhill panatella smouldering in the other lazily draped over its rim. The cigar had a relaxing effect and the drink made him feel drowsy. He tried rehearsing what he would say to Arnaud the next day, but found himself nodding off with weariness.

He awoke with a start not realizing how long he had been asleep. It was dark and the now tepid bathwater felt chill in the air-conditioned confines of Jack's suite. He felt depressed. For all of his self-assurance, Jack was becoming increasingly aware of his own vulnerability, both legal and physical. The murders of his crew, and the Twomins, and the near misses at the petrol stations figured increasingly in his troubled mind. The early determination to hit back, to win at all costs, to demonstrate in the interests of his own and his family's safety that he could not, would not be beaten was beginning to look like an ill judged pipe dream. Yet, he asked himself still, what alternatives did he have?

The future stretched out in a series of `ifs'.

If, he could get the certificates of deposit he needed from Arnaud. If, Tony Trent would go out on a limb, risking his professional reputation, future income and possibly his liberty by preparing an entirely fictitious, but nonetheless certified, balance sheet showing Goldleaf Insurance to have a net worth of two hundred million dollars. If, Jack could get an agency rating and convince American Union Insurance Group to do business with him. And the final big `if'; if Jack Gregory could then take in AUIG with a spurious kidnap and ransom claim for twelve million dollars.

If, if, if. God help him `if' he got it wrong. All questions, no answers. Except one, the knowledge that after all he had come too far now, at least in his own mind, to turn back. Whatever efforts he made to cover his tracks, Hepton would realize that Jack was up to something. There was no option but to carry on. And, there were debts that needed repaying, a whole lot of them. Jack climbed out of the bath and toweled himself down, then without even checking the time, slipped between the sheets of the vast single bed and was asleep in seconds.

The alarm call in his room woke him early, and Jack dressed in a lightweight beige Versace tropical suit. You never get a second chance to make a first impression, he mused -- remembering a sales talk he had attended some years previously -- and made sure the knot in his Gucci tie made a perfect diamond with the bottom edges of his shirt collar.

During the short walk to the bank in the mid morning sunshine, Jack felt his misgivings of the previous evening evaporating. Think positive, he intoned, and if you can't think positive, at least act positive. More sales talk, he smiled to himself.

The bank, when Jack reached it, resembled a thousand others, and announcing himself at the enquiries desk to a young man who spoke English with a French accent, it occurred to Jack that he had still given no thought to what his approach with the manager should be. As he debated the problem a door opened and the same young man beckoned Jack inside and then showed him through a second door to Arnaud's office.

The room was ill lit, with yellowing Venetian blinds drawn against the sun, and while the rest of the bank was as cold as all banks in the tropics seem to be, Arnaud's office was sticky hot. The man was slightly shorter than Jack, and, considering the climate of the country, astonishingly pale. Jack found himself staring into the hollow eyes and sickly grey complexion of a man who looked at best underfed, or at worst, dying of some dread disease.

Arnaud extended one skeletal hand, displaying curiously manicured and buffed nails and Jack took it reluctantly in his own, noting as he did so the stringy array of veins and tendons on the back of it. "Good morning, Mr. Arnaud."

"Monsieur."

"I beg your pardon," Jack was nonplussed for a moment.

"I am Monsieur Arnaud." He spoke with a pronounced French accent.

Somehow, Jack thought, this didn't look as though it was going to be easy, "Of course, of course, Monsieur Arnaud. I believe you are expecting me." Jack paused expectantly, but getting no response he enquired, "Mr Van Damm?"

Arnaud stared back at Jack without changing his expression, "What about Mr. Van Damm?"

"Didn't he make this appointment? I assume you were expecting me. You've seen me immediately after all." It was getting worse.

"I know of nobody by the name of Mr. Van Damm. And I see many people without appointment if I am not too busy. Now, Mr. Gregory, what can I do for you? I do not have all day."

This was going to be infinitely more difficult than first anticipated. To spell it out or not to spell it out that was the question. "Do you mind if I sit down?" Jack sat down without waiting to be invited further, and Arnaud joined him, one hand resting on the desktop his fingers tapping a rhythm like a novice practising piano scales.

"Well, Mr. Gregory, I am waiting."

"I am a businessman, I run a conglomerate of companies with connections in Europe and America."

"Do you have a card?"

Again, Jack could feel himself disconcerted. What the hell had Van Damm been up to? "No Monsieur, I don't have a card." Let's try the open approach, he decided, get somewhere closer to the truth. "Amongst other things, I deal in the world of insurance, and in particular that of kidnap and ransom."

Pondering a moment longer, Jack debated, there was absolutely no reason why he should not be carrying a calling card, with the one exception -- from his own point of view -- that if he did it would need to be in the name of David Purdoe, another potential complication. But he was relying on the likely ignorance of the bank manager in matters pertaining to kidnap and ransom insurance, an ignorance that Arnaud would probably cover up with a vain show of pretended knowledge. "It is necessary for me to keep my dealings discreet. I'm sure you understand."

Arnaud said nothing, he merely kept up the tapping on the desk while staring at Jack from the black hollows of his eyes. The incessant drumming was the only sound in the room, the street outside offering no comforting noises whatever.

The whole episode was becoming eerie and Jack found himself wondering whether he shouldn't simply get up and leave. He began to have visions that he'd been set up by the Chinese man. Shaking off the notion that was so unlikely as to be absurd, he continued, "I've opened a small account on the island at Barclays, just a few thousand pounds. I'm proposing to negotiate an overdraft facility with them in due course."

"In that case, Mr. Gregory, what are you doing at my bank? You already have a banking facility." Arnaud looked obviously bored, and Jack could feel the patience he'd displayed up to now wearing thin. Sarcastic bastard, he thought.

"In matters of K&R," Jack continued, keeping his tone even, "it's a good idea to use several banks for the purposes of moving funds around. You know, keep things fluid, just out of reach of prying eyes." Arnaud's face remained impassive. This was utterly hopeless, and Jack was running out of ideas. What the hell was the man playing at?

Reaching into his inside jacket pocket, Jack extracted the wad of dollar travelers cheques and dropped them onto the desk with an air of indifference, "I thought I might start an account with that." Arnaud's eyes betrayed a flicker of interest as he picked up the batch and flipped through it. Money evidently did talk, Jack thought. Apparently much louder than words. Whatever business Van Damm had conducted with this man before, he was clearly taking no chances with his prospective new customer.

Suddenly, Arnaud appeared to come to life. He picked up his telephone and started issuing orders, confirming with Jack as he did so the style and title of the account the latter wished to hold. Jack said nothing about the certificates of deposit he wanted, which were the whole purpose of his visit. Deciding it was time to broach the subject, he finally raised the issue with Arnaud, explaining precisely what it was he wanted, but without giving any reasons for his wishing to secure the false documents. He was brief and to the point and Arnaud concentrated with the air of one used to dealing in matters of that nature.

"How much are these certificates to amount to, Mr. Gregory?" Arnaud became more animated by the moment. There was even the hint of a smile about the corner of his mouth.

"Two hundred million dollars," said Jack. It seemed like a stupendous sum of money when stated that simply. It was a stupendous sum, when based on a pure fiction. If Arnaud refused there would be little further Jack could do short of seeking out Van Damm again, if that were possible, to find another contact. And if the contact turned out to be anything like this one... Jack waited for an answer watching Arnaud's face register at first surprise, then incredulity and finally a sort of obstinate disbelief. End of the road, Jack thought. Back to the drawing board.

Arnaud was tapping the table nervously again, "Mon dieu! You leave me astonished, Monsieur."

Arnaud sat silent for several moments. His hand stilled from practising on its imaginary keyboard. Eventually he glanced at Jack, staring him full in the face, "I presume you would be willing to pay a considerable sum for these certificates."

"Oh, a considerable sum," Jack smiled. What a loud voice money had when once it started a dialogue.

"How much?" The question was put with an air of ingenuousness as if Arnaud really had no idea what he should be demanding in return for his little fraud. Maybe he'd dealt on a smaller scale before. Maybe Van Damm had made a mistake.

"Just to show I'm not playing games Monsieur Arnaud, I'm prepared to make transfers to a bank account you nominate for the next four days in sums of twenty-five thousand dollars each. I'll drop by each day to touch base with you, make sure there are no problems. On the fifth day, by which time you will have accumulated one hundred thousand from me, I will come in to the branch and you will hand me eight certificates of deposit in sums of twenty five million dollars each in return for a further and final two hundred and twenty thousand from me."

"You will give me three hundred and twenty thousand dollars and in return I will give you certificates amounting to two hundred million, correct?"

"Excellent, Monsieur Arnaud. You know with all those technical skills at your fingertips you really should be a bank manager."

"Comment? I mean pardon?"

"Nothing," replied Jack, dryly, and he got up to leave. "I'll see you tomorrow."

From Arnaud's sweltering office, Jack saw himself out through the main area of the bank whose air-conditioned atmosphere hit him like a refrigerator. Outside on the street the heat caught Jack once again like a blast furnace and he decided to make his way back to the hotel and enjoy the next few days as far as he felt able, starting with a swim in the hotel pool. If the whole thing went badly wrong, Jack would have risked, and perhaps lost, one hundred thousand dollars. But it wouldn't go wrong, it couldn't.

There were brief meetings with Arnaud on each of the following mornings until the fifth working day in the following week. On the fifth day, Jack entered the bank at eleven a.m. as usual, only to find himself being kept waiting for the first time for over half an hour. The manager had been looking increasingly confident with each passing day in a manner that left Jack feeling slightly perturbed. There was nothing Jack could put his finger on, beyond a sense that Arnaud was getting cheeky. Something about his demeanour was suggestive of a player with the upper hand.

In his office finally, Arnaud looked relaxed, he sounded almost expansive as he waved Jack into a chair, the bony hand flapping like a pterodactyl's talon, "Sit down please, Mr. Gregory."

"Are you ready, Monsieur, for our final transaction today?"

"Let me put something to you, Mr. Gregory." Arnaud's tone carried a smirk that Jack did not like the sound of. "How would it be," he went on, "if I did not recall ever having met you before?"

Jack felt his chest go tight, "I beg your pardon."

"I mean, Monsieur, we do not really know each other, do we? Let me ask you, monies transferred to private numbered accounts cannot be traced or recalled by those making such generous gifts, can they?"

"Let me answer you," Jack said rising to his feet, his face a mask of fury. "Necks broken in the course of a bank manager's day can't usually be repaired that quickly or easily can they?"

Arnaud sat back with an expression of alarm and raised his hands as though in surrender, "Please, please, Monsieur; I was joking, the question was, how do you say, purely rhetorical."

"So was the reply," Jack said grimly, resuming his seat. "Now, I believe we have some business to complete."

Arnaud, smiling nervously, reached into the top drawer of his desk and produced eight immaculate certificates of deposit, each one for twenty-five million dollars; a total of two hundred million altogether, and pushed them towards Jack.

"I believe this is what you came to Mauritius for, Monsieur."

Jack felt a rush of adrenalin. He sat looking at the certificates for a long time, turning them over and over in his hands, feeling the texture of the documents between his fingers. He was interrupted by the manager, "And now I think you have something for me as well."

Jack nodded, and using the details he had been given earlier in the week, he issued instructions over the telephone for the transfer, and two hundred thousand dollars was duly made over to the account of Arnaud's choice. Arnaud had now collected a total of three hundred and twenty thousand as agreed. "Tell me, Mr. Gregory," Arnaud said, when the transfer had been effected, "What made you choose this bank and me in particular?"

"Oh, come now, you can stop the play acting. Van Damm set up the meeting as you know bloody well."

"But who is this Van Damm you keep talking about?" Arnaud had his hands extended from his sides, palms upward in a gesture of puzzlement.

"You mean you've never heard of Van Damm, the financial fixer?"

"But never, Monsieur."

"You are Monsieur Bertrand Arnaud? And this is the Mauritius International Bank?" As Jack asked it, he suddenly realized something and slapped his forehead. "Of course, this isn't the Mauritius International Bank at all, is it?" he grinned.

"No, Mr. Gregory, we are the Mauritius Home and Overseas Bank."

One bank looks so much like another. Mauritius and bank in the title, so easy for a jet-lagged traveler to fail to take notice of. "But who are you then? You are Bertrand Arnaud aren't you?"

"Now I understand," Arnaud smiled as broadly as he was ever likely to, "I am Henri Arnaud. Bertrand Arnaud is my cousin, and by coincidence he is also a bank manager, but of the Mauritius International Bank which is a few metres down on the opposite side of the road."

As he left the bank for the last time the thought crossed Jack's mind, Van Damm will not be a happy man if he learns of this. Come to think of it, neither will Monsieur Bertrand Arnaud.

Chapter 17

March 12, Friday

Hepton watched as the girl came out of the en suite bathroom and into his bedroom. She was five feet ten, over six feet in her high heels, and in her mid twenties. Flicking her straight blonde hair over one shoulder and rolling her hips suggestively, she walked to where Hepton lay on the large circular bed. It had been a long day and his head and the back of his neck ached.

Sitting on the edge of the bed, she turned to face Hepton bending one knee towards him. Hepton slid a hand along the smooth inside of one alabaster thigh and looped his fingers under the string side of her white thong. He felt himself begin to get an erection and he groped at the front of his trousers pulling them to one side to allow himself room to get hard. The girl reached forward and, placing her hands inside his open shirt collar, started to massage his neck.

Reaching for the telephone that lay next to him, he pushed her away brusquely, "Not yet. Ah got things to think 'bout." He needed to shower.

The whole day had been a pain in the ass. His partners had yammered on for hours about his involvement with Central Reinsurance and what he was supposed to be up to, or not supposed to be up to. Shit! Hadn't he delivered the goods? Hadn't he got rid of that old fool, Standish. And hadn't he had his own man overrule those Goddamn donkeys on the Committee of Inspection allowing him eight million in fees and another couple of million in expenses. Hepton closed his fist around one of the girl's small breasts and clenched it in anger. Despite his unexpected promotion Tandy had started to go slow on the fees asked for, at least until he'd been reminded about his predecessor's early retirement from the bench.

"Hey!" She squealed tugging at his wrist. "You're hurting me."

Glancing up at her disinterestedly, Hepton loosened his grasp, dropping his hand again to the fragment of cloth between her legs. Rubbing his fingers along the bulge of material at her crotch he noticed she was dry, "Thought you was gettin' turned on, honey. Y'know, in the mood? Luke Hepton don't like to be kep' waitin' when the time's right."

"Don't worry, darling. No one's going to keep you waiting." She pouted and smiled resting her hand on the lump in his trousers, but he pushed her away again, "I said when I'm ready." Then he thought again about the partners' meeting earlier that day and grinned to himself. If Mallet and Dixon didn't like it they could take a hike.

Holding the telephone in his lap, Hepton pressed the speed-dial and within seconds the overseas number he wanted started to ring.

It was two a.m. in New York, nine p.m. at Highview, a residence in Burchett's Park, just east of Henley on Thames in the United Kingdom, when Hepton heard a familiar voice come on to the line.

"Good evening, Jack Gregory."

"Why, Mr. Gregory, good evenin' to you, sir."

"Who is this?"

"Why sir, you insult me. This is Luke Hepton, the liquidator of your very own company, Central Reinsurance, calling you with a progress report."

"What the hell do you want?" Jack growled in barely contained fury.

"It occurred to me you might be worried I wasn't gettin' my due fees."

"Your due fees? Don't make me laugh. The Committee of Inspection voted against..."

"Now I hate to interrupt you, but that's precisely why ah called. I just knew you'd be worried, so I'm 'phonin' to let you know that Chief Justice Douglas Tandy of the Supreme Court of Bermuda has today confirmed, pursuant to my application, that the decision of the Committee of Inspection be overruled so ah can get my hands on the eight million I worked so hard for."

Motioning the girl to massage his shoulders, Hepton went on, "The good judge also allowed me two million in expenses. I fear sir, that my commitment to the cause of the unsecured creditors of Central Reinsurance is takin' up so much of my professional time that there may well be a serious erosion of their dividend prospects. A sad irony, don't you think? Of course there'll be nuthin' whatever left for the shareholders of the company."

"You bastard!" Jack whispered.

Replacing the receiver, Hepton smirked at the girl, “He din’t seem as satisfied as I thought he might be. Still, you cain’t please all the people all the time. I’m ready now honey, let’s mess around, huh?”

She removed the thong and faced him, smiling, naked. Pulling at his belt and the zip of his trousers, she eased them down over his bony hips, dragging his boxer shorts with them at the same time. “You want a blow job, darling?”

“Nah. I’m in a hurry. C’mere.”

Twisting onto the bed to lay on top of him, she could smell the sweat from under his arms and between his legs; rank and pungent and she turned away, curling her nostrils in disgust. Hepton’s ribs stuck out like the struts of a boat and dug into her uncomfortably, and as his pelvis moved it felt as though she was being elbowed in the kidneys. This shouldn’t take too long. Two minutes should do it, she thought. She sighed and thought about her boyfriend as Hepton shoved into her impatiently.

Bugger it, she’d forgotten how big he was, and how fat. Anyway, two minutes at most. The smell of him, she could feel the bile rising in her throat as he dug into her. Two minutes seemed more like two hours. Any longer and she’d need a brown paper bag. His hands were on her buttocks and he was moving her around on him, this was taking forever, when would he finish? Christ, he was screwing the hell out of her.

She thought about her boyfriend again, as long as she didn’t come, it wasn’t like being unfaithful, but she was only human.

She gritted her teeth, mustn’t come, mustn’t come, she was thinking it in time with his thrusts. Mustn’t come, mustn’t come, not with this stinking filthy... He was moving faster now, moving round and round, up and down, in and out, in and out.

Fuck, it felt good. Fuck the bastard, fuck the bastard, breath in his stench, kiss his greasy skull. Going to come, got to come, got to come. Coming now, coming now, God it’s good, God it’s good. Rub hard on his cock, hard on his cock, harder, harder. She jerked convulsively, whimpering like a dog. Her back arched and her knees bent up tight splaying either side of him like a flattened frog as she flopped against him, exhausted.

He was laughing, “Fucked you good that time, din’t I, honey. Fucked you real good.”

Less than a minute later Hepton was snoring open mouthed still on his back. The girl slid silently from the bed and ran to the bathroom where she vomited for several minutes before retrieving her clothes and slipping quietly from the penthouse.

Chapter 18

March 15, Monday

It was ten a.m. and Jack, occupying a comfortable easy chair, waited, his arms folded defensively. He had stated his case.

Across the wide expanse of his desk, Tony Trent faced his friend, "It sounds crazy, Jack. You're asking me to accept a sixteen million dollar payment from a company of yours called Goldleaf Insurance into the account of one of our overseas audits, and then hand the same sum back to you personally, putting it into a numbered Liechtenstein account?" Trent sat back in his black leather, executive swivel chair, easing his tall frame into a comfortable position and crossed his legs, absent-mindedly straightening the knife-edge crease in the trousers of his Saville Row suit.

"Correct," Jack smiled.

Closing his eyes, Trent squeezed the point of his chin in a contemplative gesture with the finger and thumb of one hand, "Even if I could promise to effect the transaction, if anything went wrong..." Trent paused, then whispered earnestly, "Jack, may I remind you, you're an undischarged bankrupt. You are subject to a Mareva injunction freezing all assets and bank accounts not already caught up under the Bankruptcy Order. And you're asking me to be a party to a transfer of funds on a grand scale. Where are these monies coming from in heaven's name?"

"They're borrowed."

"But you're prohibited from borrowing money."

"The loans aren't in my name."

"In whose then?"

"Goldleaf Insurance."

"But aren't you a director of that company?"

"No."

Trent swung his head from side to side as though in an agony of indecision, "Well who is then?"

"David Purdoe."

"God, no!" Trent stopped dead for a moment, then went on, "I should have realized you two would be up to something. Of course the man's completely mad. Jack, I'm warning you, they'll throw the key away, and it'll be both of you, you know."

"Don't try to make me change my mind, Tony."

"Would it make any difference if I did?"

"No."

The telephone rang on Tony Trent's desk and he reached forward to pick it up, "I said no calls, Tessa." Jack could hear a small voice at the other end of the line, then Trent looked up at Jack, "Does anyone know you're here?"

"Not a soul." Jack could feel a knot beginning to form in the pit of his stomach, but he ignored it. Whoever was asking for him would have to wait, it was more important that Jack secure Tony Trent's agreement, at least in principal, to what he had in mind.

"Take a message, Tessa," Trent said, taking Jack's wagging forefinger as a sign that he was not willing to take the call.

"Are we agreed then?" Jack sounded confident and business-like, as though the whole thing was a formality waiting to be put to bed.

Trent sighed but said nothing, and Jack pressed on consolidating his flimsy advantage, "There will be just one more thing."

"I wasn't aware we'd agreed to the first," Trent observed dryly.

"I shall need an audit of the balance sheet of Goldleaf Insurance."

"When?"

"Right now," Jack said and extracted a sheaf of papers from his brief-case, throwing them casually onto Trent's desk where they scattered like a fan of playing cards.

"What're those?"

"Bank statements for accounts of Goldleaf Insurance in London, Mauritius and Liechtenstein and details of agency rating for the company. Also a Certificate of Deposit from the Liechtenstein bank and an agreed working capital facility from them based upon the net worth of the company."

"Which is?"

"Two hundred million dollars."

Trent's eyes opened wide and his jaw fell open, "How much?"

"Two hundred million."

"But, Jack that's impossible. How could you? For God's sake, you're a bankrupt."

"It's all there, Tony, in David Purdoe's name of course." Jack sat back and waited for his friend to reply.

Leaning his elbows on the table, his head in his hands, Trent muttered, "Jack, I'm stunned. This is absolute folly. It could finish my career. And that would only be for starters, I daren't think what might follow."

"I wouldn't ask you if I weren't desperate. You know what I'm up against."

Tony Trent looked older and more tired than he had when Jack had entered his office a few minutes before. He raked his fingers over and over through his forest of fair hair and Jack could hear the breath hissing steadily in and out of the man's nostrils as he wrestled with the dilemma he was faced with. Almost inaudibly, Trent muttered under his breath, "We're all getting sucked into this thing, it's becoming a cursed bloody maelstrom."

Over and over, Jack had reassured Phyllida his only chance of survival lay in the beating of Luke Hepton at his own game. Gazing at Trent now in the torment of his indecision, Jack realised he was asking too much. It simply wasn't on. With Tony Trent's assistance, the plan might, just might, have had some tiny chance of success; but it meant expecting his friend to put his profession, possibly his freedom on the line.

Of course, without Tony Trent's assistance the entire plan was stillborn, as simple as that. Jack mentally attuned himself to the notion of a burial. The whole thing had been an absurd daydream from the start, Don Quixote tilting at windmills. Time to come down to earth and try to pick up the pieces of his life.

It was the end. Feeling confused, bewildered and disappointed, Jack got to his feet and extended his hand to Trent, "I'd better make a move, Tony. I've taken up more than enough of your time."

"Yes, yes, of course," Trent appeared to be still deep in thought as he took Jack's hand in his own. "How are you expecting to transfer the funds?"

"What funds?" Jack asked cautiously.

"Why the sixteen million, of course."

Jack stared at Trent for several seconds as though he was unsure of what he had heard, and yet unwilling to ask him to repeat it thereby risking a retraction. "Tony, you are a brick," he breathed at last.

"Some people might call it that," Tony said ruefully. "Others might call it something else. How were you proposing to make the transfer?"

"Electronic frequency transfer. It's the quickest way."

"No doubt you have all the necessary details with you here."

"No doubt," Jack smiled.

"I'll need a while to check overseas company files and make a choice. We'll have to get this right first time. Then I'll have to extract bank account details." Trent leaned forward and, pressing a button on the intercom, got through to one of his managers to whom he rattled off a list of instructions.

Over the next three hours file after file was brought in for Trent's appraisal by a fresh complexioned shirtsleeved young man. Sandwiches appeared at mid-day without Tony having to call for them, and coffee was replenished at regular intervals. Eventually satisfied, Trent said, "Will an Italian industrial company suit you?"

Rubbing his chin as he thought about it, Jack said, "Company's fine. Country may present a problem for what I have in mind, but I'll deal with that as I go along. Who are the directors?"

"Does it matter? Armstrong Graebner have the necessary powers of attorney to effect the transactions you want. It'll be cash in and out in one. When it's picked up by the Italians, as it's bound to be, I'll explain that an error occurred at this end and was immediately spotted and rectified."

"Sounds good," Jack said. "Ready?"

"As I'll ever be."

Instructions were issued over the telephone by the two men, and sixteen million dollars transferred on the authority of a Mr. David Purdoe from the overdraft facility of Goldleaf Insurance Ltd. to an obscure Italian industrial company, thence to the private numbered account in a Liechtenstein bank, of a Mr, Jack Gregory.

It was done, and the next step could now be considered, planned and, barring hitches, put into effect. Jack involuntarily glanced over his shoulder like a hunted animal. Try as he might he could not rid himself of the notion that everything he said and everything he did was being watched. Again he shook off the feeling. Just keep thinking positively, he told himself, and it'll all turn out fine. Getting to his feet, Jack stretched his aching limbs, "Thanks, Tony. It sounds so utterly inadequate, but thanks."

"Don't thank me, Jack," Tony replied buzzing for Tessa on the intercom, "Just remember me in your prayers. I may need them."

* * *

March 22, Monday

Jack was ready to go, feeling like a jockey waiting impatiently at the tapes. Except that nothing seemed to be happening. The accommodation address in the Strand was up and running, telephones and fax lines were laid on and headed paper was printed. The adjoining office had been taken on to accommodate two staff, the number Jack reckoned he would need if the plan were to succeed. Both rooms were furnished sparsely with smart modern desks and filing cabinets finished in coffee and cream colors, and filled with computer equipment. A couple of brown upholstered easy chairs and extra tables to accommodate files taken from cabinets and tea and coffee making facilities, and that was it. Jack wished he could have brought June, his secretary, with him. But it was better she shouldn't know any of what was going on.

Jack gazed vacantly out of his fourth floor window at the reflection of the sun in the glass panes of the building opposite. It had all seemed so obvious: set up a reinsurance company, just like Central Reinsurance, and start up in business again. Then engineer a scam. Take American Union Insurance Group for twelve million in the same way they had taken him. Although they weren't about to go into liquidation, and he wasn't a giant American insurance company on the point of delivering a fraudulent claim to their prospective liquidator in the hope of taking the lion's share of any eventual dividend payout.

"Good morning," he said to himself aloud. "The name's Gregory, Jack Gregory; one time insolvency practitioner, recent reinsurance whiz kid, and at present, total failure." What was the point? The great and fearless Jack Gregory had finally hit the bottom; no family, no company, no right to practice insolvency and now a bankrupt facing the possible loss of his home whilst remaining trapped within the steel walls of a Mareva injunction.

He was drinking too much, and smoking too much. It was ten a.m., and his mouth felt gummy with the taste of stale tobacco. The only thing he wasn't over-indulging in was food. These days he looked trim, if the loss of sixty pounds could be described as leaving a man trim. Glancing down at the smouldering cigar stuck between his index and middle fingers he wondered how it had got there. He couldn't remember lighting it.

Come to think of it there wasn't a great deal he could remember giving any clear thought to, apart from the impending scam. He was operating on automatic pilot most of the time; one day slipping into another almost unnoticed. The chest pains were less insistent more sporadic; but still, they troubled him, waking him from time to time in the early hours from what was at best fitful sleep.

The one thing he had been thinking clearly about was the plan he had for AUIG. It had born him along these last few weeks on a wave of clear-sighted optimism that had run parallel to that of his foggy pessimism.

And so, Mr. Gregory, we embark upon our life of crime.' What a joke he thought ruefully. But what else was there?

He sighed, and drank from the burning cup of treacly coffee on the desk in front of him. No wonder he couldn't sleep at night, he thought, looking first at the jet-black liquid, then back at his cigar.

Staring at the cheap Casio digital watch on his wrist, Jack thought painfully about how ingenuous he had been with the Official Receiver. The Patek Phillipe that Phyl had given him was gone for good. And hadn't the other man smirked as Jack had fallen into it. "Are you aware you're ten minutes late, Mr. Gregory?" he asked and Jack had glanced, surprised, at his watch and suddenly realized what a fool he'd been. "Nice watch, Mr. Gregory. I might as well relieve you of it now, mightn't I? Wouldn't want it getting lost before your trustee is appointed, now would we?" Oldest trick in the book and he'd fallen for it. What a fool he'd been. How would he ever tell Phyllida? Jack's pulse increased in line with his anger, and he frowned in annoyance.

How long did he still have before the meeting of creditors that would be convened to appoint an outside trustee; a man to handle the administration of Jack Gregory's bankruptcy in place of the Official Receiver? How long before he decided to try and wrest the house from him? How long before the bank called in the loan guaranteed by Phyllida, and then threatened her with bankruptcy proceedings? She'd never survive it. He shuddered.

Don't fight, son, he heard his father's voice. Box. Keep it legal, keep it elegant. Do what you do best.

Screw it dad, he thought in reply. Fighting fair and being a gentleman doesn't work. I know; I tried it. Time to play the scum at their own game. Go for broke. There's nothing left to lose.

The vision of Phyllida smiling, the baby in her arms, came to him and he wanted to rage aloud, God I want them home.

Picking up the telephone, he started to dial.

First of all concentrate on picking up all the old contacts. Ten years in the business made him a lot of friends. Establishing a trading reinsurance company would be no problem. All he needed was to actually start trading, and then to start banking some desperately needed money. Build it up, and lay off all the insurance with American Union Insurance Group. Meet them on their home ground in the States, not in Bermuda where he might be known. They hadn't come to the meeting of creditors of Central; hopefully they wouldn't know what he looked like. They certainly wouldn't expect him to have the gall to pull such a stunt.

Good, the phone was ringing, his old pal, Joe Renwick's private line in Geneva. Jack felt a surge of adrenalin.

"Hello?" It was Joe's voice. Great, for once Jack had got him first shot.

"Joe, it's Jack Gregory. How're things in the old insurance world." There was a silence. "Joe? Are you there?"

"I'm here, Jack. And things are fine for me. Not so fine for you. I suppose you know your name stinks everywhere. I don't know why you're calling or what you've got in mind, my friend. But if you've any notion of trying to set up in business again, I'd say forget it."

The phone went dead and Jack stared stupidly at the receiver in his hand.

Chapter 19

March 24, Wednesday

"How are you, Phyllida?"

"I'm fine, Jack. Paris is always lovely at this time of year."

"And the bubs?"

"She's okay as well, talking a lot more, saying lots of new words." Phyllida hesitated, then added, "She misses her Daddy."

He ached at the thought of his daughter and the mispronounced words so eagerly and intensely spoken. "I miss her. And you, Phyl. How long is this going to be?"

"As long as it takes. I....I just need some time to myself, Jack. We both need time to think."

"Yes," Jack replied resolutely.

"How long have I got, Jack?"

He was puzzled, "What do you mean?"

"This flat. Won't your trustee in bankruptcy be demanding you hand over the keys?" Phyllida's tone of enquiry was a remonstrance.

"Not for a while yet. Like Highview, I put it in trust for Harriette shortly after she was born. Anyway, a Trustee hasn't been appointed so far. I've only had a preliminary meeting with the Receiver. He may try to unravel the details first, but I don't think he knows for sure where he stands on the issue. Harriette's just two years old and the chances of the Receiver or an outside trustee getting hold of either property are questionable. I'll be fighting him, whichever one it is, all the way if David can't get the bankruptcy overturned."

"I'm glad to hear it. I should hate to find myself evicted. Imagine being down and out in London, and Paris." She laughed, but the show of amusement had a hollow, angry edge to it.

"Stop it, Phyl, for God's sake let's not start that all over again."

She sighed and seemed to relent for a moment, "Is Mrs. Llewellyn looking after you?"

"Yes," Jack replied, absently going back in his mind to Mr. Coles's half sneering, "Are you aware, you're ten minutes late, Mr. Gregory?" And he berated himself yet again. He should've left the damn thing at home and put on any cheap digital. Phyllida would go mad when she learned the Patek Phillipe was gone?

"Jack, are you there?"

"Yes, of course."

"Well, it doesn't seem like it."

"Look, you've really no idea what this is doing to me, Phyl. I need you here."

"And you've no idea what this is doing to me. Anyway, what's the point of coming home, you don't seem to be more than half there anyway."

"What the hell's that supposed to mean?"

"Exactly what it sounds like," her voice rose in anger. "Call me when you can spare me the time of day."

"Don't be ridiculous, Phil. Phil... Phil?" But he was calling into a void. She'd hung up.

Highview felt cold and empty, and the study - usually a place of refuge when he needed time and space to think - was uninviting. Jack sat for several moments staring at the telephone as if doing so might bring back Phyllida's voice. He missed her and the baby so much; he hurt for them. A pity David had told her about the bankruptcy and the near impossibility of overturning it.

Finally, Jack replaced the receiver onto its cradle and then started when the phone rang out immediately. Snatching it up again Jack called, "Phyllida?"

"No, Jack, it's me." Down the line, Danny's cheery voice was a boost and Jack's gloom lifted slightly.

"Hi, Danny. What's news?"

"You tell me. Mr. Mistry is in a hurry to go ahead. He wants to know when you're going to clear the sites."

"I'm sorry I've been dragging my feet on this Danny, but I've had one or two problems."

"Tell your Uncle Danny all about it, Jack."

"Well, apart from the Bankruptcy Order."

"Which I already know about."

"Phyllida's gone to Paris with the baby."

"Hmm. Not good timing for you."

"I miss them both. I'm afraid of losing Phyl."

"You won't lose her, I promise you."

"How can you be so sure?"

"Take Uncle Danny's word for it, Jack. Phyllida's a lovely girl, but she's a worrier. She adores you. Give her time to herself; don't push her or hurry her, and she'll be back."

"You think so?"

"I guarantee it."

"Thanks, Danny."

"Don't thank me already. Now what about the sites; when are they going to be cleared? Tony said I should talk to you about it, so I'm talking."

"Not yet."

"Not yet? Why not? You said you had the funds."

"They're committed elsewhere."

"What? Jack, for God's sake, we'll lose this deal. Mistry's the original man in a hurry. If we don't give him his garages quickly he'll find others somewhere else."

Jack closed his eyes and rubbed the palm of his hand across his scalp, smoothing down the hair at the back of his head, "I can't help it, Danny. I've got to go abroad and I need those funds. Just keep stalling Mistry for as long as you can."

"You're going abroad? Why at this time of year?"

"I'm working on an idea."

"Don't tell me. You're writing a book."

"Come on, Danny. You know it's best I don't talk over the phone."

"Okay, okay. So can Uncle Danny do anything to help?"

"I doubt it. But I may need the assistance of a private investigator in the not too distant future. I don't suppose you know..."

"He doesn't suppose I know. Jack, I'll let you into a little secret; I know the best agent in town.

"You do?"

"I do. The man's a total maniac. Ex SAS, MI5, MI6 and MI7, or so he says. If you want it done, he'll do it. If it's impossible, he'll like it all the more. His name's..."

"No wait. I'll come round later and you can give it to me then. Danny, you're a gem."

"I'm a gem. Tell me something, Jack, I'm getting an odd echo on your phone line."

The depression that had lifted ever so slightly, settled heavily on Jack's shoulders again. "That's what I meant, Danny. Listen, take care of yourself, I wouldn't want anything to happen to you."

"Don't worry about me, Jack. You take care of yourself, and Phyllida, when she gets back."

God yes, Jack thought, hanging up the telephone and pressing his fist to his lips. She's alone in Paris; anything could happen to her. Or Harriette.

Chapter 20

March 25, Thursday

The man was middle height and older than Jack, probably in his early fifties. He had shiny black hair parted on one side with a hint of grey at the temples, and wore a light grey two-piece suit. With an enquiring nod, he sat down on the same park bench as Phyllida and took out a small parcel of sandwiches from his brief case. On the little finger of his left hand Phyllida noticed a gold signet ring. It was designed like a square of interlocking latticework and matched his cuff links.

Harriette was playing happily with a group of children. Although Jack called frequently on the phone, she often asked about her Daddy. Phyllida missed Jack as well, but the thought of whatever it was he was up to wasted her courage whenever she considered returning to England. And, she was angry with him. Paris might seem a long way from London, but despite Jack's reassurances about the flat and Highview being held in trust for Harriette, Phyllida couldn't help feeling that at any moment Jack's trustee in bankruptcy might arrive and demand possession. She knew Jack was keeping things from her; yet too much knowledge terrified her. Perhaps it was just reassurance she was after, and he couldn't give her that.

The day was sultry hot and the Tuilleries scattered with people engaged in as many pursuits as in a Breughel painting. It was good just to sit and watch as the world played on or hurried by. The man finished eating. Phyllida watched, fascinated, out of the corner of her eye, as with long graceful fingers he folded the paper that had held his sandwiches and replaced it in his brief-case. He made a work of art out of it. Such debonair grace, Phyllida thought, wondering briefly what he did for a living. Before leaving, the man nodded at Phyllida again and said gravely, "Bonjour, Madame."

A couple of days later, Phyllida spotted the man at the Tuilleries again, but he didn't see her. Sitting on another bench close by, he finished his sandwiches, folding the paper with the same care as before, and then became engrossed in a number of catalogues he carried in his brief-case.

A week went by before Phyllida saw him next and when she did she noticed the signet ring he wore had an S-shape pattern of what she took to be diamonds, once again with matching cufflinks. Sitting on the same bench as Phyllida, he ate his sandwiches, idly watching the children play, and went through the same routine with the wrapping paper. Everything about him was ordered and precise and yet there was a flair about the way he dressed, the matching gold accessories, the expensive looking ties and pastel shade suits he favoured, that suggested a man with an inclination to the aesthetic. Certainly not a lawyer, nor an accountant, Phyllida thought, although he looked like a professional. Perhaps he's an architect, she wondered.

The ball the children were running after scudded towards the man, and he extended an elegantly shod foot trapping it neatly beneath the point of his toe. Even in so innocuous a gesture there was something questionable about him that Phyllida recognized yet couldn't identify. His beautiful olive complexion took on a darker hue when he frowned in concentration, his eyes narrowing beneath flat black brows.

A little boy of about four or five ran up to retrieve the ball and, stopping abruptly in front of him, looked uncertainly at the man. Clearly, Phyllida wasn't the only one to regard him with a measure of curiosity. She found herself waiting with intrigue to see what his reaction would be. On another bench nearby a mother had got to her feet and started to approach; was she also worried? Even Harriette, who had been jumping up and down and waving her arms at Phyllida, suddenly stood still as though in anticipation of something about to happen.

For an instant everything seemed to go absolutely quiet; then, just as quickly, the hubbub of daily noise reasserted itself as the man, with a gentle tap, sent the ball rolling towards the small boy who gathered it between his feet and spun round before toeing it back towards the others.

Harriette waved once at her mother, and then concentrated on kicking at the ball. Turning towards Phyllida the man's attention fixed on her as though for the first time and she thought she sensed a malevolence in the set of his dark brown eyes. What she saw disturbed her, and she involuntarily sat back as though to gain distance from him. Thus she was startled when his face broke into a broad smile with a display of dazzling white teeth against his swarthy complexion leaving Phyllida unexpectedly at a loss.

"Is she your daughter?" The man's voice had a velvet resonance, which was as unexpected as his smile.

"Yes, she is." Now she was stammering and blushing. Quite absurd.

"I'm sorry," he extended his hand. "You must think me very rude. I am Jean-Claude de Riviere."

"Phyllida Gregory," she replied, noticing the restrained strength in his grip.

He gazed towards where Harriette was playing, "She is easy to recognise. Already she has her mother's hair, like the mane of a lion. I think she will one day be as beautiful as the mother." He made the comment without taking his eyes off Harriette, as though it were an objective appraisal and no more. Reassured by both the complement and the manner of its delivery, Phyllida felt no obligation to reply.

"Excuse me, you are on holiday?"

"No. We have an apartment here. My husband is tied up in his work at the moment. I come to Paris from time to time to give him a break." She felt a shadow of guilt, which she immediately put behind her. It was at least partially true.

"Your husband, he is a businessman?"

"No. Well yes and no. He's really an accountant. He specialises; he used to specialise. Oh, I don't know."

"There is a problem?"

Phyllida sighed, "You might say that. It's complicated at the moment."

"I understand. It was wrong of me to pry." He smiled at her, concerned.

"And you, Monsieur? Are you a businessman?" Phyllida leaned against the back of the bench and crossed her legs casually.

"I am an independent dealer. I buy and sell pictures for myself and for collectors in Europe and America." Opening his brief-case he extracted a number of catalogues of forthcoming auctions in Paris and London and showed them to Phyllida. "For my wealthier clients I buy Impressionists, for the more adventurous I find something else, perhaps from among the Post-Impressionists. You have a number of English painters in this category who are becoming most collectable."

He started talking about his work describing various artists some of whom Phyllida recognised, others about whom she knew nothing. He spoke quickly explaining why he thought some painters were overrated others underrated. Describing pictures that were his particular favorites he seemed able to reproduce their images and colors in the air and then to infuse Phyllida with his own enthusiasm for them. As he spoke Phyllida noticed he frequently adjusted his shirt cuffs to allow the gold links to show beneath the sleeves of his jacket.

Relating details of auctions he'd attended, he told her about finds he'd made and bargains he'd struck. At one moment he sounded like an auctioneer, in the next, a bidder. His language was forceful, then restrained, his tone loud, and then whispered. He was musician and conductor, actor and director. Phyllida could imagine him bidding for items that came under the hammer and stealing them from under the noses of the others simply by the force of his personality. Exuding a *frisson* that was almost tangible, he seemed to have the drive of an eighteen year old and the presence of a man absolutely at peace with himself.

Jack had struck her the same way when first she'd met him. She'd wondered then, shyly, what he would be like as a lover. A broad immensely powerful figure, Jack had surprised her by his gentleness and sensitivity. Now she looked discreetly at Monsieur de Riviere, a speculative glance he didn't notice, and pondered the same thing. It wasn't what she wanted. It was not what she would seek or sanction. She loved Jack and would never risk her marriage with a casual affair. But she was lonely and afraid; his conversation helped her forget, and complements made her feel accepted as a woman once more, something she had begun to doubt.

Monsieur de Riviere's penetrating eyes held her own again like twin beams of light illuminating her private thoughts and she felt her cheeks flush pink. He was speaking to her and she'd not been concentrating. He asked again, "Perhaps you would like to see an auction. I am away from Paris for a couple of months and when I return you might find it amusing to accompany me to a sale?"

Phyllida started to say no, she was going to remind the gentleman she was a married woman, but he sat back in an attitude of pretended defeat, his palms held up in supplication. "Oh please, you have a husband. I have offended your English sense of propriety. It would not be right to watch antique pictures being sold in the presence of a strange man. Or," he added softly, "strange pictures being sold in the presence of an antique man." Phyllida looked up at him, puzzled for a moment. Then as his face opened up into a huge grin she burst out laughing.

As Monsieur de Riviere stared back at her nodding as though in recognition of something he had long suspected, Phyllida heard him say, "Mon dieu, you should laugh more often, Madame Gregory. For when you do, you are no longer beautiful, you are breathtaking."

Chapter 21

March 29, Monday

"Mistry's pulled out of the deal." For once Danny's voice sounded sombre.

"Bugger it! When?" Jack asked.

"Half an hour ago. I've been trying to get hold of you but your line was tied up."

"That's all I need, Danny. The bank knows the situation; they've been plaguing Tony Trent. He's stalled them up to now, saying completion was imminent. If it's all fallen through, the bank might just take it upon themselves to put in a receiver to J G Petroleum; and I'd not put it past the oil companies to let it happen.

"A receiver will only be concerned with banging out a quick sale and pulling out an even quicker fee. If he doesn't realise enough to get out all the lenders, the oil companies would write off their losses, but it could leave Phyllida on the hook with a bank guarantee she knows nothing about."

"You mean you still haven't told Phyllida about that guarantee? Jack, how could you not?"

"Danny," Jack said quietly, "How could I? She's run off as it is. If she were threatened with bankruptcy, I don't know what she'd do." The telephone line went quiet, and Jack drummed his fingers on the desk. "Is there any chance you could put this deal back together again?"

"It's a long shot."

"You've got to try."

"I know that, Jack. The trouble is, Mistry wants to see all the tyres cleared, and they're not. On top of that the local fire officers are all going nuts. I'm running out of ideas. Some of them are talking to the police. They want to sue you, put you in prison. They say you're a menace to the community. When are you going to finish the job?"

"When I've got the money."

"What's happened about the money?"

"I've had to use it elsewhere."

"You already told me. I hope you know what you're doing, Jack."

"So do I my friend. Keep in touch."

"I'll keep in touch," said Danny, and hung up.

Gazing at the telephone, Jack reached into his pocket for a cigar; then recognising what he was doing, he resisted the temptation, and, stepping over to the table by the wall, poured himself a coffee instead.

The receiver back in his hand, Jack resolutely dialled Tony Trent's number and was put through immediately. It was time to edge a little further out on the limb with the object of achieving something positive before the bloody thing broke completely.

"Tony."

"How are you, Jack?"

"Fighting."

"Who are you fighting?"

"The whole world, it seems; barring a few exceptions."

"I'm glad to hear you say it. What can I do for you?"

"I've had an idea."

"I'm listening."

"We may have lost Mistry."

"I know."

"I want to try and get Mistry back again; but he wants vacant possession of all the garages."

"What do you have in mind?"

"Simple, in theory. Mistry's offer left us with a narrow margin of equity on the sale after the lenders were paid out. If the bank gets edgy and puts in a receiver he'll give the whole lot away and Phyllida's neck'll be on the block.

"Up to now, I believe, Hepton's been sabotaging prospective buyers by persuading the oil companies not to help this deal through by lending money to them. I guess he's also reminded the oil companies of the sort of earnings they could make by operating the sites themselves; after all, they could take them back in lieu of repayment. Remember this is a lucrative business, and the oil companies are getting involved increasingly in running their own garages. And I suspect that if there were nominal losses, Hepton would simply make it up to the oil companies out of what he milked from Central in fees. Either way, the oil companies won't lose."

"I hear you, Jack. So?"

"On the other hand, as this thing drags on the oil companies can see interest stacking up against their loan, with nothing happening yet on the repayment front."

"You think they might be interested in seeing some sort of resolution to the current situation."

"That's exactly what I think, Tony. They may well be getting impatient with Hepton. If we can only offer them something. What I have in mind is you approaching the largest of the oil company lenders for a further loan to cover the cost of removing the tyres. Remind them we've got a buyer. If they bite, I could complete the sale to Mistry very quickly, assuming Danny can get him back on board again."

There was a pause, then Tony came back sounding doubtful, "I'm not sure they'd be interested, Jack. If they've scotched every deal so far, they're hardly likely to promote one now."

"I disagree. Look, they're in the oil business, not banking. They won't want to see their money tied up and idle indefinitely. Try it, Tony. See if they'll lend us the money. I think they will. Get back to me." Jack hung up.

Studying the cigar that had found its way into his hand, Jack shook his head ruefully and blew out the bitter tasting smoke he had drawn into his lungs. Then he turned his attention to chasing up his old insurance company contacts. He'd been on the phone now for six days pretty solidly, and despite the brush-off he received from Joe Renwick, he had some success with his other friends in the industry. A few more days and he'd be ready to start taking business and thinking about laying it off with AUIG.

The phone rang and Jack snatched it from its cradle, "Jack Gregory."

It was Danny's voice at the other end. "Okay, Jack."

"Okay what, Danny?"

"I may have Mistry back on line again."

"Good man."

"He wants to see some action. I've promised him he'll see results, like yesterday. Can you produce?"

"Possibly."

"Jack, do me a favour. What's possibly?"

"It's what I say Danny," Jack snapped. "I'll get back to you." And he hung up.

At five p.m. Tony Trent called, "I've made progress, Jack."

"I'm all ears, Tony." It had been a long day, and Jack felt both weary and ill at ease.

"I approached the largest of the oil company lenders, Saudi Petroleum, and they turned the whole thing down flat."

"You call that progress?" Jack's voice was raised in irritation.

"Hang on a moment."

Jack said nothing.

"I've spent the whole day trying to get hold of the right people at the right companies," Tony went on, "and I finally succeeded."

"Well?" Jack felt and sounded disgruntled.

"The smallest of your lenders, Malaysia Oil have agreed to help."

"They'll put up the two hundred and sixty-five thousand?"

"Half."

"What?"

"They'll put up a hundred and thirty-three maximum. They say they want a commitment from you."

"Commitment? Commitment? For God's sake, Tony, don't they know I'm Mareva'd, bankrupt, emasculated, crucified?"

Tony sounded embarrassed, "I'm sorry, Jack. It's the best I could do."

"Forget it, Tony. I shouldn't have lost my rag. It's my fault. You've done well. Brilliantly, all things considered. I'll get on to Danny." Jack hung up. It was five forty-five p.m.. The ashtray on the desk overflowed with cigar butts, and his cup displayed the dregs of cold stale coffee. Jack had eaten nothing all day and his stomach was giving him shooting pains. Whether with worry, or with hunger he couldn't be sure.

Thank God for Mrs. Llewellyn. At least there'd be a meal waiting for him this evening. The way things were going he wasn't sure how much longer he'd be able to retain her and her husband. The last of his meagre cash reserves, hidden carefully in Highview, was fast running out. He wanted his family back home. He hadn't had a word from Phyllida in how long? He put the thought out of his head and dialled Danny's number. He was still in his office.

"Danny, how long will it take to empty every garage of used tyres?"

"Apart from the original six petrol stations that were loaded up, there's been odds and sods of dumping here and there as you know. We were looking at two hundred and sixty-five lorries, at a grand a time, once."

"Once? Once, we were looking at two hundred and fifty lorries. You mean it could be even more now?"

"I've been keeping an eye on everything. We might just manage with the original quote."

"How long will the whole operation take, Danny?"

"About three months."

"Can you keep Mistry on a leash that long?"

"Truth?"

"Truth."

Danny sighed, "I don't know."

"Sorry, Danny. `I don't know,' won't do. I want the sites cleared in two months. Max."

"Impossible."

"Don't tell me, `impossible,' Danny. I employ you to do the impossible. Can you keep Mistry hungry for two months?"

"Jack, for God's sake."

"Can you?"

"I think so. If we can show him something positive happening.

"Okay," Jack breathed. "Get the lorries rolling."

"Have you got the money to pay them?"

"I've got half."

"Come on, Jack, you're joking."

"I'm serious," Jack snapped back. "It's the best Tony could squeeze out of the oil companies."

"But the hauliers in Midland want guarantees on staff costs. They've given the best quote we could get on the basis that they get paid up front."

"Balls!"

"Jack, what do want from me already? You've had the blood, I still need the flesh."

"Tell 'em they can have half up front, the balance on completion. Take it or leave it."

"They'll never accept."

"Take my word for it for once, Danny. Everyone needs the work; them particularly. That's why they gave us the best quote. Offer them what I said. I guarantee they'll accept."

"If you say so. You're the boss. But what about the rest? How're you going to find the other £132,000 in time?"

"By completing the sale to Mistry, with the receipt of his cash into the liquidation, to coincide with the cheque that Tony Trent will be drawing on the liquidation account to cover it. The Midlands hauliers will get all their money that way."

"But, Jack; my life. What if something goes wrong and Mistry fails to complete? How will you meet that final payment?"

"But he will complete, won't he, Danny? You'll see to it won't you, Danny?"

"Will I, Jack?"

"Too bloody right you will Mr. Jacobovits," Jack roared. "Else I'll have your guts for garters."

* * *

April 5, Monday

It was happening at last. Jack surveyed the correspondence in front of him and held his breath. The first business was being placed his way and he would be in a position to make his initial formal approaches to AUIG. There may not be time to lay off these new contracts with the American insurers, but that didn't matter. The idea was to get trade started so that when he presented his credentials to AUIG the event wouldn't be followed by a lag that would leave them wondering what was happening.

Permitting himself a moment of optimism, Jack thought about Phyl and the baby. His wife was calling him two or three times a week now. She seemed calmer, more collected. He wanted her home, desperately, but demurred from trying to persuade her to return immediately. If the sale of the sites could be completed, at least Phyllida would be safely out of the financial picture.

Goldleaf Insurance was up and running. Right now that was the main thing. The first earnings would be pulled in shortly, and Jack would be able to start paying off some of the bills he had been sitting on. The moneys would be small at first; but things should start to advance rapidly once he was established fully.

The consequences of the dual crimes of trading contrary to the Mareva injunction while at the same time being an undischarged bankrupt, entered Jack's consciousness from time to time. What would the Official Receiver's response be if he found out what Jack was up to? The first time this concern hit Jack he immediately buried the idea. Recently, however, the prospects of what he faced began to stare at him with increasing menace. He knew his defences, his resources of positive energy, were more and more deeply tapped. His health suffered, and, despite the rush of adrenalin at the anticipation of what he planned for AUIG, he was aware that at each stage of the game he felt increasingly drained.

Without his family around his gloom deepened and his moods became blacker. He became ever more impatient with those close to him, tearing into them for what he saw as the slightest misdemeanour. At night he would awaken cold and sweating imagining himself to be in a grey stone prison cell furnished with only a wood slatted bunk bed and a rusty bucket for a toilet. How long could he go on like this? he asked himself. The same answer came back at him every time. Until either he or his persecutors were destroyed.

Pushing the swivel chair back from his desk, Jack stood up and, taking two paces, slid open a drawer of the filing cabinet and extracted a slim buff dossier marked, AUIG. Back at his desk, Jack opened the file and examined the contents. They comprised a series of letters that had passed between himself and the executives of AUIG at the time that Jack had been operating Central Reinsurance. The American based company had sought confirmation of the bona fides and proof of the net worth of Central before it would consent to its Bermuda office doing business with Jack's company.

Although all the business was conducted from Bermuda, the initial exchange of correspondence had been with the head office of the American company in New York. Central had a seven year track record at the time, and was able to produce accounts detailing its profits, and at the time its massively solvent position. Jack hadn't needed to visit the head office to introduce himself to AUIG's executives. They would almost certainly want to meet the managing director of a new company in the field, particularly one boasting a capital base of some $200 million.

The brief letter of introduction had been typed and printed; it was ready to be faxed through to New York, to be followed up by a telephone call from the managing director of Goldleaf Insurance seeking a meeting at the offices of AUIG. Rubbing his sweating palms together, Jack slid the letter into the fax and typed the telephone number of the US company. The fax machine made a whining noise, and, looking up, Jack saw that his letter had passed through the feeder and been transmitted to New York. Irrevocably committed? Not yet. There was still time to change his mind, Jack thought as he dialled the New York number.

"Good morning, American Union Insurance Group," the woman's voice came through sounding disjointed as though she were a million miles away.

"Good morning," said Jack. "My name's David Purdoe. I've just faxed a letter to your Managing Director and I'd like to speak to him, or his secretary if that's possible."

Fifteen minutes later Jack replaced the receiver. Mr. Walter Schumacher had been extremely interested, had given Jack a cordial reception and suggested they meet in New York in one week's time.

* * *

April 12, Monday

Even before Jack heard the squeal of the Virgin Airlines flight VS3's tyres on the tarmac, the buzz he had whenever he contemplated a visit to New York began inside his head. The city throbbed with life and its effect on Jack was to induce an almost intoxicating sense of promise. Smiling to himself, Jack settled into his taxi and revelled in the sense of freedom. The joy would be shortlived, he knew. Tomorrow he would be back in the midst of his nightmare. The meeting with AUIG was critical. If they weren't impressed with him, the whole thing would have to be called off. His plans would all have come to nothing. But for now, the universe held only a glorious feeling of promise and the anticipation of a comfortable night in a luxury hotel. Whatever the state of his finances, Jack couldn't risk having the directors of AUIG finding him in anything but a prestigious hotel. The Waldorf, with its mixture of opulent yet subtle elegance suited his purposes. Carrying sufficient cash for a one-night stay, and having previously requested a specific room on the third floor, Jack registered using his own name.

His shoes kicked off, Jack had hardly lain back for more than a moment on the vast bed when there was a gentle tapping at the door. He sprang up and opened it to find a smiling David Purdoe facing him. His suit was rumpled as though he had been sitting in it for some time, and his black hair was, as always, tousled, "Come in, David. Good flight?"

"Excellent, dear boy, excellent." David settled himself in an armchair. "But then you should know, you were only four rows in front of me."

"It was good of you to come with me."

"Nonsense, Jack. You forget, I am the managing director of Goldleaf Insurance. The least I can do is to be on hand while negotiations are afoot."

"How will you spend your day tomorrow?" Jack sounded concerned. "I've dragged you all this way on what might be a wild goose chase."

"I shall spend it reacquainting myself with the most exciting city in the world. In other words I shall walk and shop until it's time to get back to the airport for the return flight."

"In the meantime," Jack grinned, "what can I offer you to drink?"

David made a steeple of his fingers and gazed at Jack with an intent expression on his face. "The drink can wait for a moment, Jack. While

I've no wish to upset your excellent mood, I should tell you that before we left England I was contacted by a Mr. Bertrand Ffolkes of accountants Lacklan Fleet."

Jack was undecided whether or not to get himself a drink, and stood hovering over David while trying to make up his mind. "And who is he?"

"Mr. Bertrand Ffolkes, dear boy, is your recently appointed trustee in bankruptcy, and he's been pressing me, your solicitor, to get you to contact him. It seems his missives to your home address have gone unanswered."

Of course Jack knew. Who was he fooling? He'd seen the mail arriving, noted the embossed headed paper and recognised the references to his bankruptcy at the start of every letter before promptly tossing it in the bin. He'd never glanced further than the first few lines of each piece of correspondence, so he'd never known whom had been appointed as his trustee. Now he knew and he groaned aloud.

"You'll have to see him, Jack. You can't run away for ever."

"But you know I can't see him right now. If he finds out what I'm doing he'll hang me from the nearest yardarm. I've no choice; I've got to stall him for as long as possible."

Chapter 22

April 13, Tuesday

Jack slept well; probably his best night's sleep in months.

The telephone at the side of his bed rang and Jack leaned over lazily and picked up the receiver. "Yes," he said, cautiously avoiding announcing his name.

"Morning, Jack, morning," David's voice was ebullient. "Are you all set?"

"Almost."

"Excellent, Jack, excellent," then David's tone changed. He sounded worried, concerned, "Jack, I know we've been over this before, but are you sure you weren't followed to America? Are you certain that the Twomins' murderer didn't discover what you are planning?"

"I can't say. Nothing is certain. Gut feeling tells me that the Twomins, knowing how intent I was on discretion, had already formed the companies and covered their tracks before they were killed. I just don't get the sense that I'm being followed. If I'm wrong, then I shall either find out this morning, or else have the FBI hot on my tail after the event."

"On our tail, Jack. Not just yours. I suppose you realise that we could spend the rest of our lives looking over our shoulders."

"I hadn't forgotten, David. And, don't think I'm not grateful. I am fully aware of the risks you're taking as well."

"I never thought I should react to anything in my life in the way I have over this," David whispered. "But they took Celia from me; and I'll do anything I can to get even."

"I'd better go, David," Jack cut in.

"Good luck, dear boy, good luck."

Sitting in the back seat of the cab, his brief-case on his lap, Jack felt relaxed and comfortable. New York hummed with activity on all sides. It was hot and humid, and the air was filled with petrol fumes. Cars blared their horns, people ignored the pedestrian signs and rushed across the road in front of them, and everywhere there was the same sense of urgency and purpose. At times it seemed to Jack that he was in the midst of a sublime anarchy where anything and everything was possible. He loved it.

The taxi drew up outside the skyscraper that housed the offices of American Union Insurance Group, and Jack's pulse began to pound.

The entrance, paved in a shiny pattern of white and ebony marble, was vast as a modern cathedral. The impression was of endless black and clear glass interwoven with stainless steel scaffolding and girders. And light, white light, both natural and artificial infused the whole area. The effect was awe-inspiring.

The security men behind the desk were immaculately turned out in short sleeve open neck grey shirts and black trousers.

Announcing himself, Jack was addressed by a balding guard in his mid forties whose stomach hung over the waistband of his trousers. "Who're you here to see, Mr. Purdoe?"

"I have an appointment with Mr. Walter Schumacher."

"Can I see your ID, sir?"

He couldn't show them anything with a photograph on it, so he brought out his wallet, filled with David's credit cards. Extracting the Visa card, Jack tried to ease some of his tension by breathing in deeply, as discreetly as possible. It was impossible and the longer the inspection went on the more Jack wanted to sigh, or yawn, or stretch his arms. It was like being tied into a straight jacket, watching the big man gaze first at Jack, and then back at the card. Eventually he looked up at Jack again. He had probably taken little more than three or four seconds glancing at the card; it had seemed like an hour. Please don't ask for anything with a photo, Jack thought.

"You from England, sir?" The security man was tapping a keyboard checking appointments on a computer monitor behind the desk.

"That's right." For God's sake don't ask for my passport.

"Where you staying?" The enquiry sounded no more than casually conversational.

"At the Waldorf."

"A fine hotel, sir." He paused and smiled politely, but didn't hand back the card. "Can I maybe see your passport?"

Was it Jack's imagination, or had the reception area gone deathly quiet. "I don't have it with me. It's with hotel reception. I should have retrieved it this morning and carried it with me." This was not going as well as Jack had thought it might. If he had hoped for a cursory check, he was finding himself increasingly disappointed. Still, he had no choice but to hold his ground and bluff it out if need be.

"Would you have any objections if I were to call the Waldorf and check they're holding your passport?" He was punching the numbers on his telephone as he spoke.

"None whatsoever."

"Waldorf? Give me reception, please." There was a brief pause. "Good morning. My name's Elmer Donovan, head of security at the American Union Insurance building. Do you have a Mr. David Purdoe staying with you at the moment? Room number?" He looked back at Jack enquiringly.

Caught off balance for a moment, Jack gave his own room number which the security guard repeated into the telephone. A moment later his confusion became absolute when the guard, his eyes narrowed to a slit, said to Jack, "Ain't no Mr. Purdoe staying in that room, sir. Only someone called Gregory." The enormity of his blunder hit Jack with the force of a baseball bat in the face and he felt himself flush red.

"Sorry," Jack said, groping affectedly in his jacket pocket. Extracting David Purdoe's room key, he held it up for the guard to see. The suite numbers varied by only one digit; his mistake was perfectly legitimate. The security guard nodded, apparently convinced, when the room number was confirmed by the hotel.

Despite the air conditioning, Jack could feel prickles of sweat on his scalp. Resisting the temptation to run his handkerchief over his head he forced himself to gaze again at the stupendous surroundings.

"If you'd like to come this way, sir." There was to be no turning back, and anyway, he'd been guilty of nothing except stating a false identity to these people, so far.

Leading the way, the big man accompanied Jack to the bank of elevators and stayed with him until they reached the thirtieth floor and Walter Schumacher's office where he deposited Jack and returned to his post.

Coming around from the back of his desk, Walter Schumacher approached Jack. The managing director of AUIG was a bull necked, stocky little man, with large feet, and hands like a builder's. His suntanned face was framed by a head of thick white hair and a neatly trimmed white beard. "Glad to make your acquaintance, Mr. Purdoe."

The older man had something of an old world courtesy about him, and Jack found himself wondering whether Schumacher could possibly have had any idea about the joint manoeuvrings of Hepton and the Bermuda branch of AUIG. Almost certainly not, Jack decided, and for an instant sensed a shade of regret that he might be risking humiliating an innocent gentleman. Just as quickly, Jack dismissed the idea. So what, he debated with himself, he was only out to take back some of what had been taken from him. If all was fair in love and war, this was most definitely war.

Motioning Jack to an armchair, Schumacher seated himself opposite, his massive interlocked fingers resting in his lap like a bunch of pink bananas. "Tell me something about yourself, Mr. Purdoe. Where have you come from? How does a man like yourself suddenly spring onto the insurance scene? Believe me, sir, I am fascinated."

This was it, the question whose reply Jack had rehearsed a thousand times and more. Jack had it all worked out; a CV spanning his education, professional qualifications, and ascent in the world of business. His reply was a masterpiece of smooth sales talk, a lecture that would take him at least thirty minutes to deliver. Schumacher would be left in no doubt of this young man's bona fides or ability. Jack would be ready to field any questions lobbed his way with consummate confidence. But it wasn't going to be that way.

Schumacher might want him to go through the motions of courting him, but Jack was going out on a limb to play the part of the reserved suitor. He was going for broke. "You've seen the accounts, Mr. Schumacher."

"They're on my desk." Schumacher inclined his head in the direction.

"You're aware that they've been certified by one of the largest firms of Chartered Accountants in the UK."

"I'm perfectly well aware of that, Mr. Purdoe."

"Then that, sir, is my résumé. All of it." Jack leaned forward, his elbows on his knees, his hands clasped together palm to palm, and stared Mr. Schumacher straight in the eye. "Now," Jack said emphatically, "are we in business, Mr. Schumacher, or are we not?"

Remaining absolutely still, Jack continued to gaze at Schumacher allowing himself not so much as the telltale flicker of an eyelid. Stare down your quarry. Don't move. Don't blink. They'll cave in in the end. Ten, eleven, twelve. Jack's eyes were starting to water slightly as he counted down the seconds to himself. Eighteen, nineteen, twenty. He wanted to sneak a little sigh. The position he was sitting in was uncomfortable, a crease in his trousers made a knot behind his knee. Twentyeight, twentynine, thirty.

This was absurd. Schumacher's expression hadn't changed. The man hadn't blinked in three quarters of a minute. Jack could feel himself about to collapse; his eyes were watering so much with discomfort, in another moment he would surely feel a tear roll down his face.

What a bloody stupid game it had been. Jack should have delivered the prepared speech not acted like an arrogant young fool. Schumacher frowned, he looked angry. All that planning and effort was gone to waste, Jack thought, as Schumacher suddenly leaned forward his right arm outstretched, "I'm not sure I like your cheek, Mr. Purdoe. But I think I like your style." Jack took the proffered hand. "I think perhaps we might do a little business together, at least I'll give it my due consideration." Schumacher grinned, "What do you intend to specialise in?"

"Kidnap and ransom."

"Intriguing. Properly handled it could be a lucrative source of revenue. Come, David," Schumacher got up and placed a hand paternally on Jack's shoulder, "Let me introduce you to some of the boys. Then maybe we'll start to talk terms."

* * *

April 15, Thursday

The sun streamed through the window of the little office in the Strand illuminating the dust particles that floated in the air like hoards of aimless nomads.

In the next room Jack's staff, Bob Mansfield and Penny Jowett, experienced insurance people both in their thirties, worked steadily. Premium income was coming in and the business was growing. The company's account with Credit Lyonnaise in Liechtenstein, looked healthier by the day. With time and patience, Jack would soon have a substantial source of earnings to rely on. But Jack had no time, and as for patience, he was being torn apart by a restless agitation that threatened to leave him in emotional tatters.

Most of the kidnap and ransom that had come in to Goldleaf during the past weeks, had been transacted with European companies, either direct or through brokers, except for Italy where insurance against kidnap and ransom -- with that country's notable record on that front -- was illegal.

Jack had reinsured the European policies enacted with AUIG on an individual or group basis. The latter, known as treaty insurance, deals with policies en bloc in accounting transactions between the insurer and reinsurer. It is recognised in the industry that it is all too easy to avoid having to produce evidence of reinsurance policy contracts. Therefore, transactions are underwritten by the trust in which insurance companies place in each other.

It was under the latter heading that AUIG in Bermuda -- taking criminal advantage of accepted practice -- had managed through Luke Hepton to lodge their spurious twenty-two million dollar claim in the liquidation of Central Reinsurance thereby setting in train the events that had led to the present situation of an injunction and a bankruptcy order designed to nail Jack to the floor.

There would have to be two claims, Jack determined, ostensibly a joint kidnapping, involving payments of $6 million each. The claims would be lost amid the body of treaty insurance Jack would reinsure with AUIG.

Jack fingered the policy documents feeling the texture of the heavy paper as though it were fifty, Pound notes. The certificates were real enough; only the names of the insureds were a fiction, and it was unlikely Jack would be called upon to reveal those names. The whole purpose behind Jack's -- and AUIG's -- choice of kidnap and ransom was to minimize the possibility of detection of a fraud.

Three months, he thought. Before I slip in these claims. Hell, no. Can't wait that long.

Neither insurer nor insured publicise details of kidnap and ransom insurance. To do so would be to court disaster. Equally, discovering a fraudulent claim is notoriously difficult, handled with the greatest discretion and relying very much on the credo of the insurance industry, which is to act, "In the utmost good faith."

Two months, he'd wait. Never. He couldn't. He'd go mad.

So much for professional integrity, Jack mused grimly. He shuffled the papers on his desk until he'd found the completed claim documents, undated, and covering draft correspondence. He scanned them briefly. He'd already checked them a dozen times and knew they were in order. They, together with covering correspondence, would be posted to AUIG in New York with as little fuss as possible. To start faxing claims too soon would only be to invite scrutiny in a case where procedures took a given, often agonisingly slow, course.

One month. AUIG would never believe it. They'd throw them out.

Hell, would they even believe three months?

Slipping the letter and claim forms into their folder, Jack dropped the file into the top left drawer of his desk and locked it.

The arrangement with AUIG was for Jack to reinsure up to seventy-five percent of specific kidnap and ransom placed with Goldleaf. Hence, the two six million dollar claims would represent seventy-five percent of insurances of eight million each. Business had been sufficient to allow payments to

AUIG of the premiums represented by these and other policies. Although, had it not, it would have been difficult enough for AUIG to uncover the non-payment by Jack of such premiums; the same problem, had Hepton permitted it, which would have become manifest had there been any possibility of contesting the AUIG claim in the liquidation of Central.

Jack's immediate concern was the speed with which these claims were going to be submitted subsequent to the opening of his working relationship with the American insurance giant. Within days, Jack would be submitting correspondence to AUIG notifying them of a potential claim in respect of two policies whose numbers and dates he would quote. Shortly afterwards he would be advising AUIG that the claim had been settled and that Goldleaf would be obliged to receive two payments in the sums six million each in accordance with the enclosed claim documents. A month in all.

Would the claims attract attention? How could they not? Would they be contested? You could bet on it. But Jack would deal with that problem when it arose. Right now, David Purdoe and Charles Goldman, one of Jack's erstwhile partners were expecting him for lunch at Jamies in Kingsway. The prospect lifted Jack's spirits and made his mouth water.

One month. No longer. His mind was made up. Come hell or high water.

David and Charles were waiting for Jack in the downstairs restaurant seated at a corner table. The staff at Jamies were young, female and attractive. They all wore black blouses or jumpers with mini skirts and matching tights. No doubt the intention was to perk up the lunch hour of the establishment's overworked and overstressed professional clientele.

Shaking hands with the two men, Jack took his place opposite them. David was as ruddy cheeked and tousle haired as always.

Charles seemed to have lost some weight, and frowned as he gazed at Jack, "It's been months, Jack. Why haven't you been in touch?"

"I've had a lot occupying my time, Charles."

"So I understand. David's brought me up to date. We've tried calling your home, we've left messages..."

"I know, Charles," Jack interrupted him. "Let's decide what we want to eat, then we can talk.

All three men ordered the Crayfish, Avocado and Bacon Salad to start. To follow, Jack decided on the Chargrilled Fillet of Beef in brandy sauce, while David and Charles went for the Breast of Duck in mango chilli salsa. They complemented the meal with the House red. As ever, the food was delicious, and like boxers warming up before a bout, the three professionals avoided the main topic, concentrating on small talk until the coffee arrived. Then, as though breaking the ice for the first time, Charles said, "Jack, it's time we talked. I'm worried. You look dreadful. How much more pressure can you take? From what David tells me, you're so far out on a limb if you go any further the branch is going to break taking you with it to hell."

"Don't worry about me, Charles, I'll cope. I always do."

"Do you?" Charles looked unconvinced. "Where's Phyllida at the moment?"

"In the Paris flat."

"On her own?"

"She's got Harriette with her."

"You two shouldn't be apart. Not at a time like this, it's absurd. If ever a couple needed each other..." Then, turning to David, Charles said, "As for you, my friend. Your involvement in all this is courting professional suicide."

Looking down at the table, David said quietly, "They killed my fiancée. I'm seeing this through to the end."

"You won't bring her back that way, David."

"I know, Charles, I know."

There was a long silence which Charles eventually broke, "Very well gentlemen, have it your own way. Let me move on to more mundane items then. Jack, what have you done about addressing the accusations levelled at you by the DTI."

"Nothing so far."

"Nothing? Nothing since when? Your DTI interview of January twenty-fifth? That's practically criminal, Jack. We're talking three months for God's sake." Charles's voice was raised and he looked angry.

"All right, Charles," Jack sounded embarrassed and felt himself colouring. "Not nothing. But, okay, not enough. Anyway, you know that researches into allegations of this nature take months. They won't be expecting a reply for weeks yet."

"That's no excuse for letting this sort of matter ride. Jack, these are serious allegations the DTI have made."

"Look, I've had my people looking into a number of the allegations raised by the DTI. And I've copied you with Cuthbertson's letter to me. You can see how much research needs to be done before I can put together a definitive reply. They've been reporting back to me. But I've been abroad some of the time."

Charles sighed, "When you've finished with your international intrigues, has it occurred to you to concentrate some time on some of the other outstanding trivialities like contesting your bankruptcy and re-establishing your right to practice the profession of insolvency? I mean where are your priorities man?"

"There's only twenty-four hours in a day, Charles," Jack growled. "Anyway, I won't recover my licence to practice until the bankruptcy is annulled. David's working on applying to the High Court for the latter, but he needs information from me regarding inter company movements of cash; which," Jack's hands were raised in protest as Charles leaned forward to challenge him, "I'm working on right now."

"I'm aware of that. But Cuthbertson raised issues concerning your handling of one liquidation in particular, that of Storm Safe Ltd. Jack, for God's sake, that letter you showed me suggests you might have been complicit in defrauding creditors of twenty thousand Pounds in respect of your preliminary fees, monies ostensibly paid to you to have you look the other way when Edgar Ransom of Winter Warm Metal Windows took over the work in progress of Storm Safe."

"I know, I know."

"You know, you know. Jack, have you forgotten, there was also the question of the Aston Martin that went missing? And last, but very definitely not least, there was the minor matter of the Director's loan account that you had failed to chase up. According to Cuthbertson, Mr. Toby Piggott had borrowed some two hundred thousand from his own company and failed to repay it."

"It all comes back to me."

Charles Goldman cupped his chin in his hands and looked gravely at Jack. His eyes appeared tired and there was an air of indecision about him. "I'm glad, Jack," he said at last, "because the allegations contained in the letter Cuthbertson sent you comprise nothing more nor less than a catalogue of offences for which lesser mortals have faced prison. You read the newspapers, don't you?"

"What do you want me to do, Charles?" Charles was right of course. In his quest to seek retribution from AUIG, Jack had ignored much of what should have enjoyed the benefit of his undivided and urgent attention. The prospects of extracting millions of dollars from the American insurance company, it had to be admitted were minimal. The prospect of Jack facing a custodial sentence was a distinct probability.

"I want you to start behaving responsibly. You've got to get your priorities right. Start thinking about your family, Jack. What use will you be to them if you're locked away for years."

"I have to finish this, Charles. It's not just a question of revenge. They want my guts on a plate. Anyway, I'm in too far to get out now."

"Your mind's made up."

"I don't have any choice." The comment had a finality to it. For a moment Jack experienced a sense of misgiving. If he failed... He'd all but admitted to himself that his hopes of success were slight. God, Phyllida, Phyllida. He longed for her and the baby. He had to go on. And he had to win. There was no other way. "I'm sorry, Charles. I'll attend to the DTI letter as soon as I get the chance."

"Very well. I'm sorry, Jack," Charles said as he reached into the inside pocket of his jacket. David, who had made no comment during the exchange between the other two, frowned questioningly at Jack who merely shrugged in reply. "Since it's clear nothing is going to deter your obstinacy, I've been doing a little research myself." Charles unfolded a letter typed on unheaded paper and placed it on the table in front of Jack. At the top right hand side, it bore Jack's home address.

"What's this?"

Shaking his head as though addressing a recalcitrant schoolboy, Charles said, "A draft reply to Cuthbertson. It runs to fifteen pages."

"But how could you...?"

"I had my own staff do the research. Jack, you've got all the answers in that letter. All you need to do is check it and if you agree the contents, sign it."

"You devil, Charles. But why did you lead me along like that?"

"I wanted to be sure that you were absolutely certain in your own mind that you were committed to the lunatic course you're chasing before handing this to you." Charles shook his head as though doubting his own sanity.

"But all those allegations raised by Cuthbertson."

"All addressed."

"I can see you've been busy, Charles."

The letter was brief and to the point, its tone carried a note of surprise, even astonishment. Far from their client owing the company anything, it averred, Storm Safe, the company in liquidation, owed Mr. Toby Piggott considerable sums in respect of monies he had brought in to shore up the business when it's future had first started to look shaky. "Charles, this is fantastic. I'm off the hook. But why the hell didn't Piggott tell me this when I first met him? His company statement of affairs makes no mention of him being a creditor."

"I don't know, Jack. But it doesn't matter does it? Just get that letter off to the DTI as soon as you can."

Jack sighed, then reached out to shake Charles by the hand, "I don't know how to thank you Charles."

"I'll think of something, Jack. For now, try to get yourself sorted out, and Phyllida and the baby home again."

David Purdoe smiled broadly, "Things are looking up, Jack, they are definitely looking up."

"Not before time, David," Jack replied.

"Cognac, dear boys?" David enquired as he beckoned the waitress.

Both men nodded in assent and Jack reached for a cigar.

Sipping from the brandy glass, Charles said contemplatively, "The immediate priority now, Jack is to provide David with the information to have your bankruptcy annulled. Tell me which of your company records to look in, and I'll see if I can work something out for you.

Nodding to Charles, Jack felt better, more comfortable. The cognac was delicious, and the cigar tasted rich and dark.

The lunch had been a success and Jack felt easier as he entered his offices. Penny greeted Jack as he sat down at his desk. She was dressed in a grey two-piece suit, and her long reddish brown hair was drawn back and held with a ribbon behind her neck. She looked extremely pretty, and, Jack noticed she glanced at him in that sort of approving way she had whenever he wore a tie or suit she seemed to particularly like. Yes, things were definitely looking up. "Good afternoon, Mr. Purdoe."

"What?"

"I said, good afternoon, Mr. Purdoe."

"Oh, yes. Good afternoon, Penny," Jack replied good-humouredly. "Any calls for me?"

"Yes, there was one, a gentleman with a Chinese accent asking for Jack Gregory."

"My God," Jack intoned. "What did you tell him?"

"Well, what else could I tell him, Mr. Purdoe," Penny said smiling sweetly. "I told him I'd never heard of anyone by that name."

Chapter 23

May 24, Monday

The early morning sound of a milkman on his rounds floated up to the top floor bedroom of the tiny hotel in Paddington. Jack stirred in the sagging bed half consciously dragging at the inadequate blanket in an attempt to cover the bulk of his shoulder and gain some warmth.

The day after the revelation that the Chinese man had found the telephone number of the accommodation address in the Strand, Jack decided to spend as little time as possible at Highview. It was clearly too easy for him to be followed from there into town, or indeed anywhere. Expensive hotels were out of the question, not because Jack couldn't afford them, quite the contrary with business as brisk as it was, but because he wanted to pay cash. Anything other than cheque or plastic in even a mid-range hotel would risk attracting attention.

Although it was late May, at six a.m. the hotel room felt cold. Looking around him, Jack saw a large patch of running damp had lifted the faded floral wallpaper, which was peeled away in a diagonal line between wall and ceiling. Outside, it was raining steadily and the constant dripping of water down the hall reminded Jack that the roof leaked directly into the shared bathroom.

Whatever Charles Goldman had managed to achieve on Jack's behalf in regard to the DTI investigations, Jack was still in deep trouble. The matter of the disputed ten million judgement Hepton had secured against him was still to be settled, the bankruptcy had not been annulled and Jack was in the middle of an attempt to pull off a twelve million dollar fraud that could land him in prison for more years than he cared to consider.

Time was dragging where Jack wanted it to race, and racing where he wanted it to drag. The last five weeks had been employed with building Goldleaf's business and its credibility with AUIG while haranguing David Purdoe on just about every other front. Phyllida was still in Paris. And Jack had precious little he could offer by way of incentive to her to return. Their infrequent conversations alternated between politeness and hostility.

Rubbing the palm of his hand across the stubble of his beard, Jack dragged himself out of bed and into his dressing gown before collecting his sponge bag from the top of the ancient chest of drawers and making his way down the hall. The floorboards showing through the frayed carpet creaked with every step he took, and Jack anticipated a bath of at best, luke-warm water.

The face that regarded him in the bathroom mirror was haggard and drawn. His back and neck muscles ached from the stress of being continually on the alert to everything both in and out of the office, and the noise of drunks and partygoers that had interrupted his sleep throughout the night left him feeling hung over. He'd drunk too much last night anyway, far too much. He could do with a large whisky right now come to think of it. Hair of the dog; something to smooth away the troubles. Lessons in alcoholism, part one, he thought. What a way to start the day. If this was what it felt like to hit rock bottom the feeling was not to be recommended.

"Give up, man," Jack whispered. "Call it a day. Ride out the bankruptcy. Start afresh when you get your automatic discharge. They've won, and you know it." He paused.

"Balls," Jack spat out. "I'll see this through to the end."

Jack's conversation with himself was interrupted by a loud and impatient banging at the door, and a bellowing Scots accent snapped him back to earth, "Are y'going to be there a' day talking to yersell?"

"Sorry," Jack called back. "Give me five minutes."

It was always better in the office. There were things to occupy his every thinking moment and Jack was able to lose the sense of hopeless panic that tore at him in the early hours of the morning when he would twist and turn shivering in a cold sweat.

Just the same, this day as with all the days of the previous five weeks would drag by in an aura of dread expectation. Every time the telephone rang, Jack would start, wondering whether this time it was going to be his Oriental torturer.

The call, when it came, was not what Jack had been waiting for and it caught him totally unprepared. Though he should hardly have been surprised. The scam was under way. The claims had been lodged with AUIG days ago.

At three p.m. Penny buzzed him and Jack held his breath. "I have a call for you, David," she said. "It's from New York." He wondered for a moment whether to put it off, then realising the call would have to be taken sooner or later said, "Okay, Penny. Put Mr. Schumacher through."

"Good morning, David. Or should I say good afternoon, it must be about three p.m. your time."

"How are you, Walter? It's good to hear from you."

"I'm fine, David, just fine." Schumacher's tone carried an edge to it, as though at any second he might erupt.

"What can I do for you?" Jack's voice sounded weak and lacking in authority, he heard what sounded like a break in it. Christ, what a great way to open proceedings. Keep calm, he told himself. Jack nervously straightened his tie.

Schumacher's response was not what Jack anticipated, but should have.

"What the fuck is going on here?" Schumacher screamed. "Five weeks. Five mother-fucking weeks. I trusted you and your certified balance sheet. Two hundred million net worth? Chicken shit! Five lousy weeks business and you stick in a fucking claim for twelve million. Who d'you think your dealing with here, son? If this isn't on the level, David, and don't tell me it is, I'll have your balls. So you better start thinking family right now, son, because when I finish with you, there ain't gonna be no more babies. Am I coming across?"

"Loud and clear, Walter. But what's the problem?"

"Problem?" Schumacher's voice was piercing and Jack held the phone away from his ear.

"Yes, problem. Goldleaf is putting mountains of business your way."

"Not enough to cover this claim, not in a hundred years."

"Come on, Walter, don't give me that. You've probably laid off most of it with other insurance companies. The net cost to you after tax allowances will be minimal."

"So?" Walter's voice was still hostile, but an octave lower and noticeably softer.

"So! It's our first claim with you. You know as well as I do that insurance is based on actuarial statistics, the law of probability. It could be months, years before we lodge another claim of this or any other magnitude with AUIG."

"Too right. It'll be years. Never, if I have my way."

"Walter, don't tell me you're not going to take any more of our business."

There was a long silence. For a while Jack wondered whether Schumacher had let the line go dead and he was tempted to ask if the old man was still there. Pressing the receiver tight up against his ear, Jack thought he could discern the sound of Schumacher breathing and he resolved to wait.

At last the old man spoke, this time in soft and calculated tones, "All right, David. We'll do things your way. The claims will be processed in the usual manner, but I will personally supervise them every inch of the way. I shall nominate loss adjusters to interrogate police, negotiators, brokers, original underwriters and those responsible for effecting the insurances in the first place. Do I make myself clear?"

"I've got the picture, Walter. Now you listen to me," Jack said, letting his own voice start to rise. "You know damn well that kidnap and ransom can never be verified. Neither insurer nor insured would ever sanction it. Why the hell else do you think the premiums are so high? For God's sake, Walter, do I need to remind you?

"And talking about premiums, you weren't exactly slow about taking on the business I shunted your way," Jack shouted. "No one twisted your arm, my friend. There will be no interview with police or insurers. And as for the certified balance sheet, don't you dare impugn the integrity of Armstrong Graebner. They're one of the largest and most reputable firms of Chartered Accountants in the United Kingdom. If you're going to welsh on a payout..."

"Now wait a minute," Schumacher interrupted, "who said anything about welshing on a legitimate payment?"

"It should make a great press. Some of my friends on the Times..."

"The Times?"

"You heard me."

"Okay, David." Schumacher paused for thought again, and Jack gave him all the time he needed. "I'll give you one chance to convince me. Who handled the negotiations for payment to the kidnappers?"

"A man called, Oscar Nelhams. He's head of a consultancy called Crisis Management. They specialise in that sort of thing."

"Never heard of them."

"Precisely."

"If you ask me, this whole lousy deal stinks. Be in my office eight a.m. Thursday morning with this Nelhams. I'll give you both a half hour of my time. And David."

"Yes?"

"It'd better be good. Else it won't be me, it'll be the FBI on your ass. That's all."

The line went dead and Jack replaced the receiver, he was panting and his pulse was racing. He felt like a sponge that had been squeezed dry.

All bluff and bluster, he thought. Just bluff and bluster. He'd been on the telephone for a matter of minutes only; it felt as though he'd been talking for hours.

Penny poked her head around the door and looked sympathetically at Jack, "Drink, David?"

"Brilliant." He paused, thought about his knotted up stomach, "Better make it a tea, Penny."

Chapter 24

May 25, Tuesday

He'd insisted Phyllida call him Jean-Claude, or simply Jean. The auction had lasted for some three hours, but it seemed like no more than minutes. Standing next to him in the crowded room with people shifting left and right to better view the exhibits, Phyllida had picked up the excitement of the bidding from Jean-Claude. The thrill of anticipation he conveyed when they first spoke in the Tuilleries, had multiplied five-fold when he was faced with a situation that demanded his total commitment.

Phyllida had been right about him being an actor, his sense of theatre seemed to mesmerise those around him and, judging by the whispered comments of those nearby, he secured a number of pictures at incredible bargains. Presumably that theatricality would translate itself later into sales talk guaranteed to procure equally incredible prices or commissions for those same bargains.

Afterwards they walked along the Seine in the late afternoon sunshine watching boats and barges carrying animated groups of tourists moving up and down the river.

She had put Jack off a couple of weeks earlier. He'd wanted to come to Paris but his presence alone filled her with mixed anger and confusion. She wanted to be away from anything and everything that might remind her how tenuous their relationship remained. The weeks in Paris gradually wrought a change and she finally felt as though she were beginning to pull herself together again.

Sighing, she looked across the table at Jean-Claude. At the end of the auction, she'd felt as drained as if she'd been bidding herself. The walk was refreshing, and when he suggested a meal, it only took a moment's thought and a quick call to the babysitter to confirm she was free to stay with Harriette for another couple of hours, before Phyllida agreed.

Cilette's was situated in the Place du Tertre in Montmartre. Half the tables were inside the restaurant, the rest were laid out in an open courtyard at the rear interspersed by a greenhouse of climbing and potted plants. The owner, Monsieur Giraud, white haired, rotund and sixtyish, was clearly an old friend of Jean-Claude's and he immediately found them a spot in a secluded corner amid the greenery outside. A gentle breeze fanned the candle flame on their table, its flickering light in the approaching dusk reflecting on Jean-Claude's dark complexion giving him a mysterious aura.

Attending the auction seemed harmless enough, accepting an invitation to dine seemed equally so. Now that they were seated in this romantic setting, however, Phyllida felt a trace of guilt. But she felt good. In fact, not only had Phyllida's nerves become calmer recently, but Harriette had become less fretful, too.

Welcoming the return of some of her old poise, Phyllida had chosen to wear a blue check Louis Feraud jacket and skirt for the afternoon. Even with her face set against any possibility of a romance, it was nice to be in the company of an attractive and attentive man.

She decided on oysters, Jean-Claude chose moule mariniere and selected the wine. The owner served them.

It was not necessary to add much to Jean-Claude's conversation, she was content to sit and listen. He told her his father was French, his mother Portuguese and hence his colouring. He'd been brought up on his parents' farm in Normandy displaying a consummate disinterest in the life style. He'd first visited Paris at the age of twelve and been taken around the Louvre by a friend. From that time on he was hooked. Despite the protests of his parents Jean-Claude had left home at the earliest opportunity, and working his spare time and living on a starvation diet, had eventually secured an art degree at the Sorbonne. From there he talked his way into jobs, first in Sotheby's, London and later Sotheby's, New York. An attractive American widow, a Mrs. Madeleine Ellesworthy, had taken a shine to him and despite their age difference -- she was thirty years his senior -- had started an affair with him.

Cilette's became more crowded as the evening wore on. With darkness overtaking the dusk, discreetly positioned lights were turned on to supplement the candlelight. Their steaks arrived. Phyllida's well done, Jean-Claude's blue. Monsieur Giraud served everything with a flourish.

Already in his middle twenties, he went on, Jean-Claude's single-minded ambition precluded frivolous timewasting. Madelaine Ellesworthy was his first sexual encounter and not one he was likely to forget. Jean-Claude shot his cuffs and adjusted his cufflinks, an odd mannerism he used often before emphasising a point. Phyllida watched him, fascinated, and waited to learn the purpose of the gesture as it related to his story. When she first took off her clothes for him, Jean-Claude said, it had left him amazed. She'd had the body of a woman half her age. "Don't think this comes easy, my darling," she laughed, then went on to detail a regime of daily exercise she subjected herself to. Her sexual prowess and appetites more than matched her enthusiasm for aerobics and weight training and for a month Jean-Claude was treated to the sight of his mistress awaiting his return from work, naked and impatient for him in the bedroom of her luxury apartment.

Then, one day, almost in passing, she mentioned she was interested in finding someone with the experience and contacts to seek out and buy pictures for her outside the auction houses. She loved art, but the time taken up by her social round and charitable work left her little time to study catalogues and attend sales.

"Let me be your agent," he said. "Tell me what you want me to find, or leave me to my own judgements and I promise I will not disappoint you."

"But you have no experience of acting on your own, no contacts and if you give up your job, you'll have no money," she protested.

"Try me; just once, and I will fill your home with more masterpieces than you own right now. From my trades on your behalf I will make you richer than you are today. I promise, you will sack your stockbroker."

Mrs. Ellesworthy had stared at Jean-Claude long and hard, and then said softly, "I believe you might do just that, my sweet."

Today, Mrs. Ellesworthy was approaching ninety. As spry and alert as ever, she kept her original promise to him as Jean-Claude had kept his to her. In return, she had introduced him to her wealthy friends, many of them widows. He charmed them all in the first instance and then went on to impress them with his talent in the second. He became wealthy and he made them even wealthier.

Until ten years ago he never married. There had been neither the time nor the need, those of his patrons benefitting from the knowledge Jean-Claude had first gained at Mrs. Ellesworthy's eager tutelage more than fulfilling his carnal requirements. Engrossed in business, the possibility he might one day fall in love had never crossed his mind.

Then he found Dahlia. Of Spanish origin, she was tall and slender with long black hair and an olive complexion like his own. She was studying art and architecture and spent all her free time in the Louvre which was where first he met her. He'd never come across a woman like Dahlia before. As introverted and taciturn as he was dynamic and forceful, and as innocent as he was sophisticated, she was more beautiful to him than Titian's Venus. Her simple, naive approach to life was in stark contrast to the businesslike attitude of his American matrons in everything including their love lives. Dahlia's interests were as wide ranging as his own, from arts to science, and ballet to opera, and despite his years of experience, she could hold her own in any discussion of art with him.

Within six months of meeting Dahlia, Jean-Claude married her. She was twenty-five years his junior, it was his own situation in reverse. Six months later she bore his son, Thomas. Four months later they both died in a car crash on the Champs Elysee when a drunk driver collided with their taxi. Jean-Claude smiled as he spoke, as though the sixteen months had been a gift to rejoice in, not a loss to regret. And it was his smile that made Phyllida cry for him.

When Jean-Claude forced his attention back to the present and his gaze back to Phyllida, he was about to apologise for neglecting her and for monopolising the conversation with details of a past he never spoke about, when he saw her weeping. Reaching out across the table he put his hand on her's and said softly, "Enough of this, let me escort you back to your flat."

Chapter 25

May 26, Wednesday

Hurrying away from the hotel, Jack pulled up the collar of his raincoat to prevent his shirt and tie from getting soaked. Then he swore under his breath as a passing bus splashed through a puddle drenching the bottoms of his trousers. A moment earlier it had looked like remaining dry after a night of continual drizzle. It was a mistake not to have brought the umbrella, a still greater mistake not to have gone back for it. Not the first time Jack guessed the climate incorrectly.

Too bad, he was in a hurry to speak to Danny although not from the office telephone or his mobile phone. The call to Danny was too important to risk even a one in a hundred chance of it being overheard, or the call traced. Swinging open the door of the public call box the first thing Jack noticed was the overpowering smell of urine; the next thing he became aware of was the fact that the telephone had been ripped off at the bolts that were supposed to support it. Four boxes later, Jack found one that worked. Stepping inside he shook some of the water off his raincoat and then reached into his trouser pocket for a handkerchief to wipe the top of his head and his neck.

The telephone rang only once before Jack heard Danny's voice on the line, "Jacobovits."

"Danny!"

"Jack, my boy. Where are you? I've been trying to get hold of you. You're harder to find than a needle in a lokshen pudding."

Everything seemed so much better when he spoke to Danny, and Jack grinned. "Who does your cooking, Danny?"

"My wife, my life. He's so poetic at eight in the morning. When Miriam cooks she caters for an army. Listen, Jack, I need to speak to you. Mistry..."

"Danny, hang on a second. I need to speak to you, too, urgently. Can you meet me somewhere neutral?"

"How about the lounge of the Cumberland Hotel in Marble Arch?"

"Perfect. One other thing."

"I'm listening, Jack."

"The lunatic you talked about."

"Oscar Nelhams."

"Is he around?"

"I'll try him. I was supposed to introduce you to him weeks ago."

"I know, Danny, but I've been busy."

"So what else is new?"

"Bring him with you if you can. I need him, like yesterday."

The muted lighting in the Cumberland Hotel added to the sensation that Jack would be unobserved and safe to speak freely. He had taken to looking over his shoulder every time he stepped out of the office or hotel, frequently making detours and doubling back on his tracks in what appeared thus far to be the mistaken impression he was being followed.

The stress had become so intense that Jack was beginning to imagine he could see Hepton or the Oriental man either approaching or receding along every street. And although the pains in his chest seemed to be less frequent than before, when they did hit they served as a reminder that if he didn't wrap this whole thing up soon, there would be no need for his pursuers to chase him any longer, unless it was with a shovel and to a depth of approximately six feet.

Danny was sitting in a corner of the lounge, a pot of tea already on the table. He stood up and extended a hand as Jack approached, "How are you?" Then frowning, he added, "Don't tell me, I shouldn't ask. But really, Jack, look at you."

"I know, I know," he replied testily.

"You're going grey."

"Surprise me," Jack snapped. "Look, Danny..."

"And you've lost more hair."

"How can you tell?"

"There's one on the lapel of your coat."

"Jacobovits, you are a pain," Jack smiled and shoved the other man affectionately on the shoulder. "Now, how about pouring me some of that tea."

Twisting out of his raincoat, Jack draped it across the back of a free armchair, and seated himself opposite Danny.

"You said it was urgent, Jack."

"No, Danny, you shoot first. Just one thing though, did you get hold of Nelhams?"

"He'll be here shortly."

"You're beautiful."

"Try telling my wife."

"I would, but she's bigger than me."

"Right, young man, business." Danny paused and gazed at Jack for an instant, then his face broke into a huge grin, "The sites are all cleared."

Smiling back at Danny, Jack said, "Fantastic. The local fire officers?"

"Were going crazy, but I kept stalling and you're in the clear now. Any longer and you'd've become a celebrity in some areas. They've been threatening to go to the press."

"Very sensible," Jack nodded gravely. "I'd have done the same myself."

"Hmm," Danny muttered under his breath.

"What about the continuing security at the sites until Mistry completes?"

"It's arranged. But, Jack, I have to warn you, the bill for guarding the sites up to this point is going to be horrendous."

"I'm not sure I want to hear this."

"I've bargained and negotiated until I'm blue in the face."

"I don't doubt it for one moment."

"I've got eighty percent of the deal on credit. I knew you didn't have the funds available."

"How much, altogether?"

"Also, they've allowed us a fortnight further security without charge, if, Mistry can complete in that time. After that they charge at half rate for the next two weeks, then it's back to full billing."

"Danny, however did you manage that?"

"I promised them more work in the future if they were nice to me now."

"After all that, it seems churlish to ask how much. But, Danny, what is it all going to run up to?"

"Are you sitting comfortably?"

"Danny, for crying out loud."

"Two hundred thousand."

"What!" Jack exploded.

"Sorry, Jack. But in the end there were tyres scattered around a dozen sites. I didn't tell you because there seemed no point. You had enough on your plate."

Jack closed his eyes, and, leaning his head in his hands rubbed his temples with his fingertips. "There's still the balance of the cost of clearing the sites to find."

"Yes, but I thought you'd arranged to increase the bank borrowings to cover that. "

"I had, I had. Then Tony Trent told me he'd arranged with Malaysia Oil to have them pay half the two hundred and sixty thousand to clear the sites up front with balance on completion of the sale. The Midlands hauliers have had the first half."

"Are you telling me there's problems with the second instalment?"

"I don't know, Danny. I hope not, but with the time all this has taken, the interest accruals are certain to leave me with a massive shortfall to fund."

"God, Jack. Where are you going to find the extra cash?"

"The theory of the thing is why I wanted to meet Nelhams today. I need to go to New York immediately. I'll explain it when the man arrives."

"I can't wait to hear."

"By the way, Danny, you said the security people had allowed you eighty percent credit. What happened about the down payment? You said you didn't want to ask me for any money, so where did it come from?"

"Me."

"What!"

"You owe me forty `k', Jack"

"You put up your own money?"

"With that brain, Jack, you should be on Mastermind."

Jack sat staring at Danny for several seconds. He felt his eyes become moist and he clenched his teeth to prevent him making a fool of himself in public. When he spoke, his voice croaked, "I could hug you, Danny."

"Well, you'd better not, Jack," Danny replied. "Nelhams just arrived and he might get the wrong impression."

At five feet ten, the man was about three inches shorter than Jack. He was lean as a whippet with a weatherbeaten face and a permanent suntan. His light brown hair was cut slightly longer than an old fashioned short back and sides, and that, together with his ramrod posture suggested a man with a military background.

"Jack, I'd like you to meet Oscar Nelhams," Danny looked as proud as if he were introducing his own offspring as he continued, ostensibly for Jack's benefit, to recount Nelhams's CV. "Ex-army, ex-SAS, ex-mercenary. He fought in the Falklands, and also Malaysia, Namibia you name it. And he's got experience in negotiating kidnap and ransom."

Jack took Nelhams's right hand in his own and found himself staring into the bluest eyes he had ever seen. Something about Nelhams's gaze, like the twin barrels of a shotgun aimed at Jack from beneath the fringe of the man's eyebrows bored into his head as though Nelhams was sizing up his quarry. The man's grip was uncompromisingly firm as if hinting at a power held in constant check, though when he spoke it was with a cultured accent spoken in a tone so gentle as to be barely audible.

The three men sat down to tea, Jack and Danny in their formal suits lounging against the soft leather of the armchairs, Nelhams, by contrast, in casual brown check shirt and corduroys and highly polished Timberland climbing boots, sitting bolt upright as he drank from the cup Danny poured.

This isn't what I want, Jack thought, this man's born and bred to kill. I want someone who can convince Walter Schumacher that twelve million dollars should be paid to Goldleaf in a kidnap and ransom case. I need help from a negotiator not a necrophiliac. "Has Danny given you an outline of why we're here Mr. Nelhams?"

Nelhams replaced the cup on the table as gingerly as if it were an unexploded bomb. Clearly, old habits died hard. "Why don't you give me an outline of why we're here, Jack."

Somehow there was nothing amiable about Nelhams's use of the familiar. Jack explained the background of events to date, noting as he did so that Nelhams had a tendency to sit facing him squarely while he talked, as if to ensure that every aspect of what Jack had to say would be absorbed by him in its entirety.

"So you see, Oscar," Jack concluded, "I need a man to front my company, Crisis Management."

"I see, and how long has your company been in existence?"

"About eight years, but it's been dormant throughout. I registered the name, among several others, thinking it might be useful one day, although I had no idea at the time in what way.

"Won't Schumacher conduct company searches and find that it's never traded?"

"He may, but that's not my problem, I'm neither a director nor a shareholder."

"And I am?"

"No."

"Well who is?"

"The original subscribers of convenience. The same people will be the directors and shareholders of dozens of other companies they set up for the express purpose of their being sold, off the shelf, as it were. Nothing can be traced back to them, including documents I had them sign eight years ago giving me sole rights of attorney in the matter of share transfers and operation of bank accounts."

"But you said I'm supposed to be a director of this company. Searches won't show that up. Surely Schumacher will smell a rat."

"Secrecy is the essence of kidnap and ransom, and Schumacher is well aware of that. A director of a company is anyone who holds themself out to be a director, one with the power to make executive decisions on behalf of the company, to sign cheques and so on. It's of no importance that you're not registered with the Registrar of Companies as a director of this company; if anything it's probably an advantage."

"Very neat. But that still leaves the question, how do you, or rather how do I, get around the non existence of accounts if Schumacher asks?"

"You'll tell him that you operate as a sole trader and as such you need not lodge accounts with the Registrar."

"In that case why have a limited company at all? Surely it's just begging for unwanted enquiry?"

"Not at all. In the first place, you registered Crisis Management eight years ago to stop anyone else from taking the name. Second, the existence of Crisis Management for eight years will suggest you've been in business for all of that time. You won't need accounts to prove anything else. That's all Schumacher needs to know."

The corner of Nelhams's mouth curled up slightly in what Jack took to be the man's concession to a smile, "I understand. One more thing."

"Well?"

"Why me?

"Danny says you've had experience in kidnap and ransom."

"Minimal."

"That's all I'll need."

"But you must know many others who have a far wider knowledge than I."

"Of course, I do. But they know me don't they, and everyone else in the insurance fraternity. I could hardly demand their absolute discretion, and even if I could, what right would I have to ask them to jeopardise their careers and risk prison?"

"You're expecting me to chance prison though?"

"That's only one of the two risks involved."

"I see. You mean I might still be able to secure employment with an insurance company. After I come out of prison that is."

Suddenly Jack found himself warming to Nelhams, and he smiled, "That's about the size of it, Oscar."

"Anything else I should know? Anything else you need me for? I'm still not certain that any bright spark couldn't do this job just as well as I."

"Most aren't as used to taking calculated risks as you are; and yes there will be something else."

"I had a feeling there might be."

"If Schumacher pays out now, someone must eventually make the link for him between David Purdoe and Jack Gregory. They might pick it up in New York or from contact with their Bermuda branch. Time will tell, of course it could arise through Luke Hepton."

"The liquidator Danny told me about?"

"Right. Or via the Chinese man if he's close enough to me. It's only a matter of time before he knows I'm operating from that accommodation address in the Strand. It's been weeks, so far. From now, it could be days, maybe hours."

"What happens when Schumacher makes the connection?"

"I get a visit from the FBI if I'm in America, or the boys in blue if I'm here. I should think Her Majesty's Government would be only too pleased to hand over a felon for trial in the US; particularly one who's lifted twelve million dollars for himself."

"Tell me, why did you use David Purdoe's name at all? Isn't that just adding to the problems?"

"I needed someone I could trust. Before I formulated the whole plan in my mind I decided I wanted it to be a lawyer. By the time I knew what I was about, David made it clear he was willing to go out on a limb on this one."

"Why?"

"Because Hepton had his fiancée murdered in Bermuda."

"Nasty business."

"She had information that could have helped me, and at the same time interfered with Hepton and AUIG's fraudulent grab of my funds."

"Very well, what do you propose?" Nelhams turned away for a moment to grasp the fresh cup of tea Danny had poured him. He drank it then faced Jack again.

"I've got to have something on AUIG. It's my only hedge. Without it I'm dead, maybe literally the way things are going."

"What did you have in mind?"

"I need absolute proof that their twenty-two million claim in the liquidation of Central Reinsurance was a sham."

"And you don't anticipate getting much in the way of helpful replies to your enquiries from the liquidator of the company."

"My only hope is to get documentary evidence from the offices of AUIG in Bermuda. If I could show discrepancies in dates or invoice numbers between that paperwork AUIG was issuing in the normal course of business and the false invoices submitted with their proof of debt before the meeting of creditors of Central, I'd have them."

"And of course you can't simply walk into their offices and demand things."

"Of course not," Jack sighed. "That's where you come in."

"You want me to break in?"

"Break in; walk in; trick your way in. I'm employing you to get me what I want anyway you can."

"You'll need to accompany me. I wouldn't know what documents to look for without you there."

"I'll be there."

"Risking prison with me."

"We might get adjoining cells." Jack shrugged.

"Is that supposed to be compensation, Jack, or an added hazard to be covered by an appropriate charge?" Again the hint of a grin played about the corner of Nelhams's mouth.

Jack decided he was definitely beginning to take to Oscar. "Okay, I suppose we'd better talk fees, Oscar. What's all this going to cost?"

"I'll quote you separate charge out rates for each undertaking, the trip to New York, and that to Bermuda."

"Danny said you were reasonable."

Nelhams nodded, "For the round trip to see Schumacher, if we're successful, four thousand a day plus expenses, if we fail, eight hundred a day plus expenses."

Suddenly Nelhams's wit didn't seem quite so levitating, "God in heaven, Oscar; how much?"

"What does an insolvency practitioner charge, Jack?"

"How many creditors have you faced baying for your blood? How many split second case decisions have you been forced to make that could result in your personal financial ruin if they go awry?"

"How many prisons have you been in?"

"Touché," Jack shook his head in resignation. "Eight hundred it is."

"You're not optimistic then?"

"I'm always positive, Oscar, but I'm also a realist. It's the best strategy, you don't suffer so many disappointments that way."

"Don't you want to know what my fees for breaking and entering AUIG's premises will be?"

"I can hardly wait to hear."

"Half the fees I quoted for New York."

"Why so generous, Oscar?"

"Because we'll only be attempting to pilfer paper, not to defraud twelve million. Also, I offer quantity discounts where several days work is involved." Another flicker of a smile.

"Count yourself hired."

"When do we start?"

"Right now. We catch the Virgin flight at 14.00 hours arriving Kennedy 16.40 local time. We see Schumacher at eight a.m. tomorrow. That's right," Jack said to Nelhams's unspoken enquiry, "Thursday."

"How do you know you can get tickets for this afternoon."

Reaching into his inside pocket, Jack extracted a travel agent's envelope and waved it under his chin like a fan, "Shouldn't be a problem."

"How did you know I'd fit the bill?"

"I have infinite faith in Danny's judgement." Turning to Danny, Jack said, "Before we dash off, Danny, I've told David Purdoe to issue contracts to Mistry. He says if Mistry's solicitors are quick off the mark there's no reason why we shouldn't exchange within a few days. Things are definitely improving." Getting to his feet, Jack stretched and reached for his coat.

"Jack, before you go, there's something maybe you should know," There was a hint of concern in Danny's voice. "I don't want to put a damper on this morning's dealings, but I don't want you to get too optimistic just yet."

"Perish the thought, Danny. What's the problem?"

"Mistry has been spending a lot of money on petrol sites over the last few months."

"I'm delighted to hear it. He's obviously a wealthy man."

"He owns a lot of garages, Jack, but they're all mortgaged up to the hilt. He thinks he might be a bit short on our deal."

"God no," Jack groaned. Then he reconsidered, "The hell, we'll negotiate a price. I'm not going to let this one fall out of bed for the sake of a couple of thousand pounds. How short is he Danny?"

"A quarter of a million pounds."

Chapter 26

May 26, Wednesday

"When're we going to see some money, Luke?"

"Soon, soon. I told you guys everythin's under control." Seated behind his desk, Hepton faced his two partners. Karl Mallett, fiftyish, grey haired and tall as Hepton; and Clay Dixon, in his thirties, with a moon shaped face and a small upturned nose that was almost lost beneath heavy black framed spectacles which only partially disguised a cast in his right eye.

Hepton thought about the ten million dollars he'd taken in fees and expenses from the liquidation of Central Reinsurance and resisted the temptation to smirk. He would pay it into the account of Hepton Mallett Dixon when he was good and ready. For now it was squatting comfortably where the other two couldn't find it, earning Hepton a tidy sum in interest.

Mallett spoke again, a deep voice, powerful, commanding, "How much are the Chinaman's fees going to be? You said he didn't come cheap."

"You don't mind him none. I ain't paid him a cent so far."

"I said, how much, Luke?"

He hesitated, whether to tell them the truth or not. They'd have to know eventually. "Four million so far."

Leaning forward, his elbows on his knees, Mallett said, "You're telling us you've built up an account of four million with this unknown?"

"He ain't unknown to me."

"Jack Gregory could've been taken out tidily for a fraction of that amount."

"Guys, guys. We don't want him taken out. We just want him frightened off."

"Why don't you want him taken out, Luke?" Dixon had a high-pitched voice. The question was put politely.

"We don't want anythin' to look too obvious. We are a firm of professionals. We are attorneys at law, not the M-a-f-i-a." He spoke each letter separately through a broad grin. "We gonna haul in over twenty, maybe thirty million on this deal. And it's all gonna be legit. If ah can, I gonna discredit the good Mr. Gregory. Ah got plans for him. We need the guy alive. Don't want him gettin' any sympathy, now do we? Don't want to risk anyone lookin' in this direction neither."

Mallett and Dixon looked at each other, apparently unconvinced.

"Our direction, Luke, or yours?" said Mallett.

"I think it's time we got someone else working on this," Dixon was polishing his glasses, thoughtfully. "I say we call in Dimitriou. Get him and his boys on Gregory's case." Mallett nodded in agreement. "Let's wrap this thing up now, nice and clean." Dixon replaced his spectacles and made them comfortable on is nose. "It's getting too complicated and way too expensive."

It was the last thing he wanted. Start bringing in contacts from the other two, and Luke Hepton would soon start losing control of the operation with all its added perks.

"Not long now, fellahs," he said. "The Chinaman's carryin' a pack of fifty-two aces. Gregory ain't gonna be no trouble."

"Don't get too clever, Luke." Mallett's voice was soft and persuading. "And don't forget you're outvoted here, too. I want an update, and I want it soon."

Chapter 27

May 27, Thursday

From the moment the plane touched down at Kennedy the previous afternoon, and with every step he took after disembarking, Jack's nerves became more raw. They say there's nothing like a hanging in the morning to concentrate the mind, he mused. Certainly, he seemed to perceive everything however mundane, with a crystal clarity. His mind was racing, deliberating strategies and weighing odds as though his life depended on it, which, he grimly acknowledged, it probably did. Was this visit going to be an avenging triumph for him he wondered, or a formal execution?

Although Jack carried ID from David Purdoe in case it was needed, nonetheless he had no option but to book into the Waldorf in his own name without the cover of David in the next room. Nelhams would pick up the tab so there would be no need for Jack to tender cash.

At seven fifty-five a.m., Jack and Nelhams, accompanied by the heavily built head of security, were soaring through concrete and steel to their planned interview with Walter Schumacher, chairman of AUIG.

Oscar Nelhams had occupied himself throughout the transatlantic flight reading through reams of documents he carried in a black leather attaché. There had hardly been a word of conversation between the two men. Looking at the other man in the few moments before they reached their destination, Jack tried to judge what was going through Nelhams's mind. If the man was nervous, he betrayed nothing in his demeanor, the cobalt eyes staring impassively and apparently unseeingly ahead.

There had been no concessions to business convention either, Nelhams wore denim jeans and leather jacket over a blue check shirt. The Timberland boots were honed, as before, to a ceramic glaze. The man was an unknown quantity, Jack's faith in him being based entirely on Danny Jacobovits's recommendation and his own first impressions. Twelve million dollars worth of trust, and only one chance to get it right. Trying to nail Schumacher was going to be like trying to hit a moving target in the dark, a target that was likely to shoot back.

Expecting to be shown into Schumacher's private office as before, Jack was surprised when Donovan ushered them into a boardroom the size of an aircraft hangar.

Seated at one end of the vast conference table was Walter Schumacher. He faced Jack and Nelhams as they entered the room with a face that was as grey and as animated as a slab of granite. Seeing Schumacher served to demonstrate to Jack the measure of the hostility he was up against.

Unfortunately, Schumacher was not alone. If Jack was expecting a one-to-one confrontation, he was sadly mistaken. Seated around the table were twelve people whom Schumacher introduced as AUIG's directors. They were all men, in their forties and fifties with that universal smooth complexioned suntanned look that seems to distinguish the very wealthy from the rest of the world. On separate chairs, and to one side of Schumacher sat a couple of pretty girls Jack assumed to be secretaries. They rested with dictation pads to the ready, pencils poised.

Think positively, Jack said to himself as he took one of the pair of seats reserved for himself and Nelhams at the bottom end of the table; and then looking at the battery ranged before him, like the broadsides of the cannon of two men-o-war, he thought, I must be raving mad. Picking up the pencil on the note pad in front of him, Jack absently scribbled 'David Purdoe' and then inclined the paper slightly towards Nelhams. One slip from the latter, one mention of the name Gregory... Nelhams blinked once only -- it was enough.

"Shall we begin?" Schumacher sat with his fingers interlocked on the table in front of him, it was eight-o two a.m. and the only sound was the muffled hum of the air conditioning.

"Good morning, gentlemen, my name is David Purdoe and I am the chairman and managing director of Goldleaf Insurance Ltd. This is Oscar Nelhams, principal of Crisis Management Ltd., the consultants I have used in negotiating a settlement in the kidnap and ransom claim I presume is to be the subject of this morning's conference." Nelhams nodded at the gathering but said nothing. "You wanted to see me Walt... Mr. Schumacher."

"Damn right I did," The conference hadn't even commenced and Schumacher's face was already flushed with fury. "Before I pay out a cent on this damn claim you're going to have to do a lot of convincing to me and my board. You don't hand me less than five weeks premiums and then slap in a twelve million dollar claim."

"Oh, but we do, Mr. Schumacher," Oscar Nelhams soft spoken voice seemed to cut through the atmosphere like a shard of glass and all eyes turned to him.

"Mr. Purdoe is under no obligation to divulge anything in regard to the facts of the case. Your acceptance of Goldleaf as a business partner, and the taking of premiums from that company are more than sufficient. I don't need to remind any of you of the need for absolute secrecy in the matter of kidnap and ransom." Nelhams smiled broadly, but his eyes remained impassive. "Our presence here today is no more than a courtesy; a gesture of good faith." There were murmurs from around the table, one or two of the directors seemingly embarrassed by the proceedings.

Schumacher remained unmoved by Nelhams's confident opener, "Who the hell is Crisis Management, anyway? I've never heard of you, not in forty years in the business. Our searches of your UK Companies Registry shows a name registered, and nothing else. Annual returns with nothing except `company dormant', and no accounts lodged in eight years. How do we know you're anything more than a name?"

"The name Crisis Management, which indicates the profession, was registered to prevent any one else from using it," Nelhams said, repeating the information Jack had given him. "I trade as a firm, not a limited company, and as such I have no need to register accounts; not even my name appears on the register of directors or shareholders. My incognito is preserved intact."

As though reading the minds of those present, Nelhams went on, "This can hardly be a ruse. You will appreciate, gentlemen, the company was not incorporated eight years ago in anticipation of this morning's conference."

"So you're an expert on kidnap and ransom, are you, Mr. Nelhams?"

"Among other things, Mr. Schumacher."

"What's your background?"

"I was in the British army for twenty years, retiring some nine years ago having attained the rank of Major." Nelhams's voice was soft and the delivery confident. "I served some time in the SAS where I was given a grounding in kidnap and ransom from the standpoint of the hostage rather than the negotiator. The experience was to prove invaluable later on."

"How many people do you employ?"

"No comment."

"Where are your offices?"

"No comment."

"How do you run your operation? What are your heads of department?"

Jack glanced sideways out of the corner of his eye to see how Nelhams would handle the enquiry. What on earth could Nelhams possibly know about running an operation? How could Jack have allowed the two of them to come to this interview with so little preparation, even in view of the short time that had been available to them? It was amateurish, and Jack was for a moment embarrassed at his own naivety and lack of professionalism. This was one situation that would not be won through bluff and bluster.

Nelhams continued with hardly a pause. He might have been reading from a prepared script. "I establish an IMT, you know what I mean," he smiled confidentially, "an Incident Management Team, comprising, Manager, Security person and Legal department. Then there's a Specialist Consultant, a Representative from Corporate HQ when needed, and finally a Negotiator, that's me."

Jack's eyes opened wide and he had to stop himself from gaping. Nelhams was a solid gold K&R expert. But Schumacher was still not convinced and started firing questions with increasing rapidity at Nelhams, "What's the first thing you do when confronted with a case?"

"Assess the threat, determine whether it's genuine or hoax. Establish communications between IMT, my group, and CMC, that's the Crisis Management Committee set up by the corporate entity. We're talking corporate hostage here of course, not political, not hijacking, not bomb threat or product contamination."

The man's a genius, Jack thought. Danny Jacobovits I love you. And as though in answer on Danny's behalf Jack silently mouthed, "He loves me."

Schumacher was still far from convinced however and pressed on, "How do you know the kidnappers have the hostage they say they have?" Schumacher leaned forward, his elbows on the table, and dropped his voice to whisper, "They could be bluffing, or their guy might be dead? And don't tell me they can put the hostage next to a current newspaper. That's been done before with a corpse propped up for the snapshot."

If Jack expected Nelhams to show any signs of flagging he was mistaken. If anything he seemed to be getting more relaxed about the whole thing, "Ask the hostage for current information only he can supply. What was the last gift you bought your wife? Or, when did you last make love to her?"

There was a ripple of interest in the room, and Nelhams continued, "We had one case where the answer given was, three years ago. The captors were so sorry for the beautiful young wife, they offered to let the hostage go at once." At that the whole place erupted into laughter and there was a brief easing of tension.

Looking thoughtful, Schumacher said, "Okay, so you know a bit about K&R. But this is a big claim you've slapped on my table..."

"On the contrary, Mr. Schumacher, it's modest. Most of the smaller claims that gain the attention of the press will find them printing details without restriction. In the case of the really big claims, initial press blackouts are followed by pressure from corporations, governments and so on to prevent details from escaping and encouraging others to try their hands. Only a fraction of what gets paid out actually gets reported.

"An exception is the case of the Montoneros in Argentina who are publicly known to have extorted more than any other group on record. In the late 1970's alone, they demanded and got in excess of two hundred and forty million. Since then, there's been a pattern of extortion in South American countries. Colombia is notorious for K&R today. But then you know all this anyway, Mr. Schumacher."

It was quite a lecture but Jack wondered, had Nelhams overplayed his hand? Was he getting a little too cocky?

"Very competent, Mr. Nelhams," Schumacher was smiling, always a danger signal, Jack had found with people in his position. Now down to brass tacks. "This double claim you've negotiated on behalf of Goldleaf Insurance." He paused, "Political?"

"Industrial. I've already said it."

"Twelve million?"

"Sixteen million. Only seventy-five percent was laid off with AUIG."

"Eight million apiece. They must have been pretty important guys. What was the original asking price? I assume you bargained."

"There was little time available. These were key executives in a giant international corporation. One of the two was a diabetic, on insulin injections twice a day. The kidnappers soon realised they had a strong point in their favour and used it to their advantage."

Schumacher appeared to be softening slightly, some of the hostility was going out of his voice and Jack began to feel for the first time since they had entered the room that perhaps they might stand some chance of pulling it off. Then the chairman asked, "Which country were the insureds from?"

"Italy."

"Italy!" Schumacher's face had gone crimson. "For Chrissake, K&R insurance is illegal in Italy, and you're sitting there smiling like a fucking sphinx and telling me you've laid off a kidnap and ransom policy from Italy." Schumacher was punching the air with his forefinger, "You've been remarkably silent up to now, Mr. Purdoe. Maybe it's time we had some answers from you. What the hell are you doing taking K&R from Italy? It can't be done, as you well know. I'm looking forward to a great answer to this one before I throw you two imposters out."

It floored him for a second, completely floored him, and to cover up his total confusion, Jack looked around the room and smiled with the confidence of a benevolent dictator about to distribute charity to the starving. Saying the first thing that came into his head, Jack drew on a comment made by Nelhams a moment ago, "Of course the really large claims relate to K&R in South American countries."

"Which did you have in mind, Mr. Purdoe, Bolivia? Peru? And what the fuck does that have to do with Italy?"

"Colombia," Jack said, and then instantly regretted it. What might he be committing Nelhams to, and would the latter have the answers to whatever Jack might have dumped him in? Probably better to keep on talking, "Italian companies needing cover seek it from insurance companies in other European countries, France, Germany, Switzerland. There's nothing the Italian government can do to stop it."

"And which country did your original underwriter come from?"

"No comment," interrupted Nelhams. "We're getting close enough as it is."

"Don't let him tell me 'no comment,'" Schumacher bellowed at Jack. "When I agreed to do business with you it was on the understanding that one hundred percent of your reinsurance was placed with AUIG."

"And so it is," Jack replied.

"In that case you're not telling me you took on reinsurance from another underwriter before reinsuring with AUIG?"

"No, I'm not. Mr. Nelhams is only trying to protect the position by being discreet."

"Discreet?" Schumacher was beginning to look as if he'd shortly need the attentions of a doctor. "We're talking twelve million dollars of discretion here, Mr. Purdoe. Do you mind telling your fucking stooge here what this game is all about?"

Turning to Nelhams, Jack said, "It's all right, Oscar; they're entitled to know we're the original underwriters." Nelhams nodded noncommittally in reply.

Schumacher was dragging at his white beard as though he wanted to pull it out by the roots, "All right, gentlemen, let me ask you another question. You say Mr. Nelhams had to negotiate with kidnappers in Colombia. I suppose, next thing, you're going to tell me he speaks Spanish?" Schumacher turned to Nelhams as he addressed the question to Jack.

"Of course," said Nelhams.

Of course, thought, Jack. Schumacher would be an unlikely candidate to speak Spanish. How many Americans of Schumacher's generation spoke anything but English? Spanish was widely spoken in the southern States today. But, come to think of it, how many Americans in New York of todays...

One of the directors, a man with a dark complexion and shiny black hair abruptly broke in to the conversation with a comment addressed to Nelhams that left Jack aghast, "Lleva usted mucho tiempo en este negocio?" he asked.

There was a desperate moment of silence in the room as Nelhams leaned forward as if to hear the better. He looked very taken aback, but to Jack's astonishment replied slowly, "Ocho anos"

Back came another question from the same man, "En que capacidad trabaja usted en su negocio?"

Another pause, then Nelhams said, "Yo soy el director."

The director was speaking more quickly now, "Que talentos le hace falta en su trabajo?"

Nelhams was grinning, the man actually looked amused, "Mucha paciencia y un sentido de humor y poder lablar Espanol."

The dark complexioned man laughed, and Schumacher scowled, "What the hell was all that about?"

Retaining his sense of urbanity, Jack said, "Yes, Oscar, what was that all about?"

Still grinning, Nelhams replied, "The gentleman asked me, how long I've been in this business, what is my position within my own firm and, what are the talents needed for my profession."

Is that all? Jack thought, trying to conceal a sigh of relief, "And you replied?"

"I said, I've been in business eight years and I am the director of my own firm." Then gazing around the room as though to ensure he had everybody's undivided attention, Nelhams added,

"As for the talents that are required in my profession, I told the gentleman, one needs, a lot of patience, a sense of humour," here Nelhams paused again for effect, then quite suddenly he went on.

"And the ability to speak fluent Spanish."

There was an outburst of laughter, and nudging Jack, Nelhams got to his feet to bid his goodbye. "Always leave 'em wanting more," he hissed. "They can call for their encores after we've gone, if they want." Jack followed him obediently as Nelhams walked towards the top of the table.

"Where do you think you two are going?" Schumacher exclaimed as they both approached him "I'm not done with you yet. I still haven't seen evidence that any abduction has taken place. I've not been shown proof of life, nor proof of demands submitted. How do I know anything was ever paid out? I want facts, figures, details."

Nelhams had reached Schumacher's side, and he now smiled down at him, "I'm sure you wouldn't want to compromise our clients, Mr. Schumacher, nor undertake the risk, if you'll pardon the pun, of prolonged court action with its attendant publicity. That is unless you're proposing to question the honesty of Mr. Greg...Mr. Purdoe. Come to think of it, I wonder how your shareholders would react to the knowledge that having taken Goldleaf on board, within five weeks of commencing business with them you had decided you didn't trust your original judgement when it came to meeting a claim.

"You've had all we have on offer today, sir. Goldleaf has acted in the utmost good faith and expects reciprocal treatment. We look forward to receiving settlement, and of course to conducting business with you in the future."

Grudgingly extending his hand to Nelhams and then to Jack, Schumacher muttered, "I'll need to discuss this with my claims department and directors. I'm not happy about any of it. Don't think this is the last you'll be hearing from me, Mr. Purdoe."

The sound of their own footsteps padding on the thick pile carpet resonated in Jack's ears like muffled drumbeats as he and Nelhams walked towards the door. Under his breath he whispered, "You were brilliant, Oscar." It was a virtuoso performance and more than he could have dared hope for. Only a few steps further and they would be out of the conference room and on their way out of the building. Nearly there, nearly there, Jack held his breath.

It seemed like an afterthought, but as Jack and Oscar reached the door, Schumacher suddenly called out, "By the way, something Nelhams said just reminded me. What was it now?" He stared thoughtfully at the ceiling. "Oh yeah, who's this man Jack Gregory?"

Jack stopped dead, his sight blurred over in shock and he turned around slowly, unseeingly, "I'm afraid I haven't the slightest idea."

"You, Nelhams?" Schumacher barked.

"Never heard of the man."

"Well, we'll see," said Schumacher. "We'll see."

Chapter 28

June 1, Tuesday

"Is this it then? Is this where the mighty Goldleaf Insurance operates from, just two crummy little rooms at an accommodation address?" The man, spoke with mixed sarcasm and surprise. "You know, David, Walter Schumacher is not a happy man."

"He made that clear enough at the meeting."

"Well what did you expect?"

"I don't know what I expected, to tell the truth." Jack paced the small office restlessly, "But I certainly didn't expect to be treated like some sort of half baked criminal when I came to America. I found your board meeting an uncalled for embarrassment. If Walter doesn't like paying out on legitimate claims, Mr. Peters, Walter shouldn't be in the insurance business. What's more, if you don't like our offices, you're not manacled to the floor; you're free to leave any time you wish. I didn't ask for this inspection."

Peters looked up from where he sat at Jack's desk, his eyes, under flat black eyebrows, narrowed into a hard and uncompromising challenge. "No, Mr. Purdoe, but you're getting it just the same." In his late thirties, Peters was cleanshaven with the healthy complexion of a regular golfer. He was also a big man, both taller and broader than Jack, with a clear penchant for gold. He wore large gold signet rings on the third and fourth fingers of his left hand together with a wrist chain, which looped around and through what looked like a gold Rolex. Clearly AUIG directors were more than adequately remunerated. "Is this everything I'm going to need?"

"It's all there, Mr Peters; documentation, correspondence, bank statements. The lot."

"It had better be," Peters' delivery was in the measured tones of one whose temper was contained on a short leash. As if to emphasise the fact, whenever he spoke he leaned forward slightly in an attitude that carried more crude menace than dignified professionalism about it. Now was not the time for arguments.

"You won't need me here so I'll leave you to it, I've a number of appointments. Back in an hour or two. Call Penny or Bob if you need help, coffee or copies," Jack said and, glancing for a moment at the pile of books and papers and computer printouts surrounding Peters, he left the offices before the director from AUIG had time to consider a reply.

It was mid morning, sunny and fresh with surprisingly little traffic on the road. The walk to Jamies in Kingsway took Jack about twelve minutes from the Strand, and when he got there he found Oscar Nelhams already seated downstairs at a discreetly placed corner table. Nodding at one of the waitresses. Jack mouthed, "More, please," and pointed to the coffee on the table.

"Been here long, Oscar?"

"About five minutes, the coffee's still hot. But not hot enough I suppose." Oscar smiled as Jack sat down, and the waitress, as if she had been expecting Jack's imminent arrival put a fresh pot on the table. "Is their man here yet?"

"Mr. Peters is nosing around in the office right now."

"Shouldn't you be there with him?"

"No, Oscar. The less I'm available, the less opportunity he gets to question me."

"Will they pay you out?"

"All the documentation's in order. Every last piece of paper. There's even a bank statement showing a sixteen million dollar payment. That should surprise them, at least it will if they thought I'd been bluffing up to now."

"Who's the payment to?"

"AUIG only get to find out if I'm absolutely pushed into a corner."

"Well?"

"It's to a large Italian outfit. Of course if questioned they'll refuse to be drawn on the subject, but if necessary I can prove they received it and when. Tony Trent organised it for me."

Oscar Nelhams rested his chin in his hands and raised his eyebrows, he looked impressed, "All right, Jack, let me ask you something. What happens if after all this, AUIG still refuse to pay you out?"

"I can threaten them with everything under the sun, official complaints, reports to Lloyds, going public and so on."

“And if that doesn’t work?”

Jack shrugged, “Short answer?”

“Short answer.”

“I’m buggered. Simple as that. The game’s all over.”

“Okay then, let me put something else to you.” Nelhams pinched his chin thoughtfully with his forefinger and thumb, “What happens if they do pay you twelve million on the claim and then find out at a later date they made a big, big mistake?”

“I’ve got problems.” Jack shifted his bulk uneasily in the chair.

“With the assistance of Interpol and our own boys in blue, you’ll have the FBI after you, you know.”

“I do know, Oscar.”

“They’re thorough and relentless, and you’ll very be easy to find. Should be a routine exercise for them, sort of thing they put their rookies on.”

“Thank you for the vote of confidence. David Purdoe already warned me. That’s why you’re here.”

“I’m listening.”

“Remember our first meeting…”

"Yes."

"I told you I'd need documentary evidence that AUIG's original claim against Central Reinsurance was a fabrication. It's my only insurance, if you'll pardon the pun. If I can get it, I can hold it over them. Without it..." Jack shook his head resignedly.

"Remind me, precisely how were you proposing to get this evidence?"

"The only way I can is by somehow arranging for someone to break into AUIG's offices in Bermuda."

"I remember, and that someone would be me?"

"Can you do it, Oscar?"

"I told you I'd need help."

"I'll see who I can find."

"You've got to be joking."

"You're right, I am."

"When do we leave?"

Reaching into his inside jacket pocket, Jack extracted two sets of airline tickets and dropped them on to the table in front of Nelhams. "Two days."

Back at the office, Peters was ready to leave. It had been his turn to pace the office impatiently awaiting Jack's return.

"Sorry if I kept you waiting," Jack said. "Did you find all you wanted?"

Glowering back at Jack, Peters muttered, "I'll let you know. I've got all the copies I need." He indicated his slim brown brief-case.

"Good. Well, keep in touch." Jack smiled congenially. Peters had raised no specific objections. There was nothing, as Jack saw it, that AUIG could do to deny him the payment now. What happened after that was another matter. As long as payment was made before the Chinaman got any closer. Jack started to feel better again.

Peters was at the door, "One other thing."

"Yes."

"Who is this man Jack Gregory we keep hearing about?"

Chapter 29

June 1, Tuesday

"Luke, I really don't like any of this. In fact I'm beginning to lose a little sleep."

"Whatsa problem now, Clay?"

"Same as before. We're not seeing any money. Luke, I'll tell you the truth, we are beginning to wonder whether you and the Chinaman are doing some sort of side deal."

"For Chrissake, you guys," Hepton sighed. There was nothing to do; he'd have to pay over some of the fees he'd taken.

"You wouldn't be holding out on us now, would you, Luke?" Mallett locked his gaze on Hepton's and held it there until the latter turned away in embarrassment.

"What do ah need to do to convince you two ah'm on the level?"

"Bring in Dimitriou," said Dixon. "Lose Gregory. Cut the crazy costs this Chinaman's chalking up and grab whatever you can from Central."

"Ah tell you what, I'll think about it. Gimme just a bit more time. God, you two's in such a helluva hurry. Believe you me we can clean up here, boys. Easy as harvestin' oranges."

Mallett regarded him sceptically, "So far, Luke, we've been relying on you for the harvesting, and we've yet to see so much as a pip. Just don't play any games with us, partner, else you might be the first to find out how the pips squeak."

Chapter 30

June 1, Tuesday

With Peters gone, Jack sat back at his desk and considered the situation. The smell of the man's aftershave lingered in the air and Jack wrinkled his nose in disgust. Whatever the directors of AUIG knew, or thought they knew about a man called Jack Gregory they'd not made known to him. Clearly they were getting close, were probably too close already. But so was Jack. It could only be a matter of days now before one of two things happened, either AUIG made payment to Jack, or else they discovered the ruse and the whole thing collapsed.

If the latter occurred, Jack would have no bargaining power whatsoever and the future didn't bear thinking about. Again the vision of a prison cell flitted across Jack's mind and he shuddered. There was still time to pull back, pull out, withdraw the claim made to AUIG. A mistake had been made, the Italian company had been able to retrieve the ransom money, Goldleaf had recovered their sixteen million. No need for AUIG to hand over twelve million to Goldleaf.

Sorry guys. Everything on hold. Apologies for the inconvenience. Still, no damage done eh? No need to call the Feds.

Sorry? Hell! Jack was on a roller coaster and there was no climbing off. Besides this was becoming too good to miss; it was more fun than raking in the millions he'd made with Central. He was a predator, a lion stalking a zebra. With each stage of the advance he was getting closer to the kill, the quarry was looking over its shoulder now, the whites of its eyes a statement of the fear in its heart. The old maverick was still on form.

Jack ran his hand over the strands of hair on his head and squeezed the bridge of his nose wearily with his forefinger and thumb. He had to keep thinking positively. There was no time for even the shadow of a doubt. The luxury of rest, win or lose, would come later.

Opening a couple of familiar, hand addressed brown envelopes extracted from the pile of correspondence requiring his attention, Jack glanced at the first of the notes, it was from Danny Jacobovits and dated the previous day, it read:

> Jack,
>
> Call me. Urgent. Mistry still short of funds. What do you want me to do? Security people want paying. I can't stall them much longer. Can't risk leaving the sites unattended.
>
> Danny.

"Bugger it!" Jack muttered under his breath, and pushing the chair back from the desk got to his feet idly shuffling through the rest of the mail as he did so. There was a third envelope in what looked like Charles Goldsmith's hand and Jack stuffed it into his pocket before calling out to Penny that he'd be gone for an hour or so again.

Despite the proximity of David Purdoe's office, Jack avoided it. Equally, he had issued instructions to all and sundry not to telephone him at the offices in the Strand under any circumstances, save the direst emergency. He was living in a hotel in Paddington, paying for everything in cash rather than risking being traced through cheque or card encashments and making all telephone calls to associates from public call boxes lest conversations be traced back to him at the accommodation address.

For all of the precautions he'd taken, Jack still felt that Hepton and the Oriental man were breathing down the inside of his shirt collar. Come to think of it, even the meetings he had had at Jamies were probably ill advised; too close to David's offices. But then perhaps the Strand was as well. And Tony Trent was just around the corner. Maybe he was just paranoid. And maybe he wasn't, he thought as he hurried to an inconspicuous call box in Charing Cross main line station.

Standing in a booth, Jack tore open the second envelope. The note inside was dated the previous day. Jack read as follows:

> Dear Boy,
>
> Contracts have been exchanged with Mr. Mistry. His solicitors have assured me their client will be in funds in time for completion, which is due to take place in a

few days. I have heard nothing further from them since exchange, and I am bound to say I am becoming seriously concerned.

Danny spoke to me a few days ago, he sounded frantic. I recall your mentioning your having committed Phyllida to the bank borrowings required to secure the sites. What is happening?

I must have your immediate instructions.

Bertrand Ffolkes, your trustee in bankruptcy, continues to press me for details of your whereabouts. He is threatening to seek your arrest and public examination for starters if you ignore him any longer.

I really think it will be in your best interest to make some sort of contact with him now. You can't avoid him forever. And, incidentally, he's threatening to sell Highview and the Paris flat if you won't cooperate with him. I appreciate the Trusts you have created for Harriette in regard to the properties, but it is all starting to look most unpleasant.

Again, your instructions please.

Truly,

David

"Bugger the man," Jack said aloud thinking of Ffolkes. "I'm running out of time. Too bloody bad, there's other priorities right now." Picking up the receiver, Jack stabbed at the buttons. A few moments later he heard Danny's voice.

"Hi, Danny," he said.

"Jack! At last. We've got major problems."

"I know, I know. I saw your note, and I got one from David Purdoe as well, so I'm up to date."

"Have you spoken to David yet?"

"No I wanted to talk to you first, Danny."

"All right, Mr. Magician, what are you going to conjure up this time? And don't forget, we're not playing, 'Find the Lady.' We need another quarter of a million out of Mistry."

Scratching his temple, Jack sighed and shook his head, "To tell you the truth, I'm running out of ideas on this one. If Mr. Mistry with his millions can't find another two fifty thou' I don't know what I'm supposed to do to produce it for him. What about your contacts, Danny?"

There was a long pause at the other end of the line; Jack could practically hear Danny's thought processes as he waited for a reply. Eventually Danny came back, he sounded pensive, "Well... I might be able to rustle him up another hundred thousand through some of my contacts. It'd be pushing it for time though, David's almost ready to complete." There was silence on the line again, save for the sound of Danny's breathing. Then he said, "Trouble is no one's going to want to lend without some sort of security and the sites are committed up to the hilt."

"Any ideas?"

Danny hesitated for several moments. Then he said thoughtfully, "As a matter of fact I do."

"Go on."

"What am I saying? Of course, I do. The man's a putz. Jack, we're selling the sites. All of them. The existing mortgages will be coming off when Mistry completes. You won't be making the profit you hoped for, but you will be discharging the outstanding borrowings, in full."

"I hear you. I think I'm ahead of you."

"If I can raise another hundred for Mistry, it can be advanced on completion, and the lender can take a charge over any one of the sites. They're all worth a hundred plus."

"Is a hundred thousand all you can raise? The sites are worth four million."

"Jack, if I had more time to get trading figures from Mistry. Remember, it's not just the capital value of the sites, but also the borrower's ability to service a loan."

"No matter, Danny. You've given me an idea. Young man, you are a genius."

"Well, if you insist on putting it that way, I'm a genius." Danny reflected for an instant, "Jack, why am I a genius?"

"Listen, Danny. If you can raise one hundred thousand pounds against the security of the sites, I'll complete the deal but that'll leave me short the balance of one hundred and fifty thousand on the deal."

"That's genius?"

"I'll then take a mortgage over the sites for that shortfall of one hundred and fifty thousand and give Mistry, say, three months to pay. If he fails, we put the sites back on the market, sell for whatever we can get, take out the hundred and fifty Mistry owes and pay him back what's left."

"Now that's genius."

"It was your idea, Danny."

"It was my idea?" Danny sounded doubtful. "Will you bring Tony Trent up to date on all this? Or shall I? I seem to recall he is the liquidator of the company. You're going to need his signature on one or two things."

"You'd better, Danny. I'm pressed for time."

"Jack, before you ring off, Miriam's doing chicken soup Friday night; and lokshen pudding. Why don't you come round."

"I'd love to Danny, but...no wait. I'd love to."

"Seven thirty?"

"It's a date. And Danny."

"Don't tell me."

"You're lovely."

"Who am I to argue with such perception?"

Jack rang off. Later he would drop Danny a note apologising for being unable to make it on Friday. Was he being overapprehensive? No matter. If Danny's phone was being tapped the listener would expect Jack to be enjoying a Sabbath evening meal at the end of the week, rather than planning to examine the records of a certain American insurance company in Bermuda.

The call to David Purdoe took less than ten minutes. If Danny could come up with his end of the bargain, David would have charge documents, contracts and correspondence prepared for Mr. Mistry to sign on completion allowing him three months to find the balance of the monies for the purchase of the petrol stations.

Despite David's protestations Jack had stubbornly sidestepped the issue of Bertrand Ffolkes, refusing to give it houseroom let alone priority over the matter of the sale to Mistry. Still, the matter clung to him like a vine and David was sounding increasingly agitated. Jack would not be able to avoid a confrontation with Ffolkes much longer.

Sighing with something approaching relief, none the less, at the end of his conversation with David, Jack replaced the receiver and tore open the third letter. As expected it was from Charles Goldman. He wrote:

> Dear Jack,
>
> I am writing pursuant to our recent meeting at Jamies when I outlined to you my progress in dealing with the DTI's various lines of enquiry.
>
> I am now delighted to report to you further in the question of the ten million judgement secured against you in the liquidation of Central Reinsurance.
>
> You hardly need me to remind you that this matter is the foundation of your immediate financial troubles. It is

the plank upon which your bankruptcy is based, and the source of your monetary strait jacket in the form of the Mareva injunction presently in force against you.

Even with your memory for financial detail, I doubt whether you could have recalled more than a fraction of the transactions, dozens of them quite small, that comprise the ten million in question.

Without going into great detail, suffice it to say, that I have personally been through the books and records of your various companies, all presently dormant, and can prove beyond any argument that all transfers of funds between them were perfectly legitimate. Copious schedules with supporting documentation have been prepared in evidence thereto. No doubt you will derive much pleasure perusing them in the fullness of time.

I am in the course of forwarding all details to David Purdoe so that he may immediately apply to have the ten million judgement against you set aside and thereafter arrange for your bankruptcy to be annulled and the Mareva injunction to be dismissed.

I have deliberately avoided troubling you with details of the attempts Mr. Bertrand Ffolkes has been making to effect contact with you. I understand David has been in touch with you in that respect. I shall, none the less, apprise Mr. Ffolkes of my findings in anticipation of David's next moves.

Bingo, Jack thought, sighing. And then said aloud, "BING-GO." He continued reading:

You will appreciate that your complex and frequently convoluted financial dealings have made this into a prolonged perquisition. I am therefore so very pleased to be in a position to impart this good news to you.

Please call when you get the opportunity, there are matters we need to discuss.

Yours truly,
Charles Goldman
cc David Purdoe

Charles's letter could not have reached David as yet, Jack would call him right away. Then a call to Charles with heartfelt thanks. The possibility that Jack's insolvency practitioner's licence might be restored, *must* be restored. Cuthbertson of the DTI could hardly refuse, no matter what ingenious overtures Hepton or his sidekick had originally contrived.

Then a call to Phyllida. Jack closed his eyes. Dear God, he thought, let me salvage the marriage if it's not too late.

Leaning back against the wall of the telephone booth, Jack breathed in deeply the petroleum fug of the London traffic. It smelled and tasted of country air.

Chapter 31

June 2, Wednesday

Natasha had taken Harriette for a walk in the Tuilleries, they would be gone for an hour or more.

In the kitchen of the apartment, a cup of steaming camomile at her elbow on the breakfast bar, Phyllida sat wrapped in a towelling robe, her damp hair twisted into a knot on her head, her skin still tingling from the hot shower. Sunlight flooded the flat, at one moment lifting her mood, and in the next the harshness of its glare seemingly reproaching her for her lack of loyalty.

When Jack called the night before he'd sounded ecstatic. Charles Goldman had confirmed that there was no reason why Jack should not have the bankruptcy annulled and his right to practice insolvency restored. The sale of the petrol stations still had to be completed, but that was now well advanced.

There was just one other matter, the business involving all those recent trips abroad that Jack didn't want to discuss over the phone. She should have felt as overjoyed as he; yet any mention by him of `matters' still outstanding made her limbs leaden with fear. Whether Jack wanted revenge, retribution or reinstatement of part or all of the millions fraudulently taken from him, she did not know; she did not want to know. He still insisted that the whole exercise was critical if their future security was to be assured. He was probably right.

Gazing through the kitchen window over the rooftops of Paris, Phyllida drank from the cup relishing the calming effects of the herbal drink: she simply wanted an end to it all.

Knowing Jean-Claude had been a help. In fact it had been a Godsend, the answer to a non-existent prayer. The last week had been a round of theatres, operas, expensive restaurants and laughter. She'd forgotten how good it was to laugh. Jack's outlook had always been serious, intense, committed to his business goals with little time for humor. Jean-Claude's gentle witticisms delivered in his deadpan manner made her shake with mirth. His art dealings left him with time for leisure and he used it to the full.

Of course it was wrong to make comparisons; it was Jack she loved after all. But the way Jean-Claude looked at her and treated her when they were together made her feel like a woman again, even if she was clear in her own mind that she was not about to make love to him. And, she could not help remembering the difficulty Jack had been experiencing sexually, however he tried to disguise it, and her own sense of feminine inadequacy, before she'd left for Paris.

Rubbing the towelling robe against the remaining moisture across her stomach and under her arms Phyllida was suddenly conscious that she was feeling very sexy. Looking down at the deep cleavage showing at the open collar of her heavy gown she was aware of her breasts beginning to tingle, becoming firmer, and she cupped them thoughtfully feeling their soft weight against the palms of her hands.

She thought about Jack, wished she were with him and, closing her eyes, squeezed her nipples gently making herself breath in sharply, she saw Jean-Claude's face and she frowned, annoyed with herself and snapped back to the present. In a few hours Jean-Claude would be calling for her. She was looking forward to La Boheme, it was one of Jack's favourite operas, as well as her own. It always made her cry. No matter how often she saw it La Boheme always had the same effect on her. Driving back to Highview from Covent Garden late at night she would rest her head on Jack's shoulder and let the arias float through her mind. Whatever the sadness of the opera, and however it seemed to reflect her own insecurities, Jack had always been there for her. But now Jack was otherwise occupied.

Perhaps Jean-Claude sensed it. Seated next to her now, in the back of the taxi on the way back to his hotel from the opera, Jean-Claude took her hand in his own. His palm, she noticed, was softer than Jack's and more slender, almost like a woman's. It was the first act of physical intimacy he had displayed in all the weeks since they had first spoken and the hesitancy of the gesture combined with the absolute respect he had shown her hitherto implied no suggestion of expectation or demand.

Smiling at him Phyllida realised she must have been crying, for Jean-Claude caressed her cheeks with his forefinger wiping away the dampness of her tears. In a simple act that left her shocked, Jean-Claude then kissed his own fingertip sucking her tears from it into his mouth. "Please," she whispered touching his hand. "You shouldn't."

"Do I offend you?" He looked troubled.

"No. No, of course not. It's just that..."

He looked at her concerned, kindly, "Forgive me. I was too forward, but you looked so unhappy, so..." he paused. "Triste."

The taxi was pulling up outside the Ritz and the liveried doorman reaching for the cab door. They alighted, Jean-Claude first, then Phyllida, with Jean-Claude extending his hand to help her out. Paris's best, the hotel, a superlative example of seventeenth century architecture situated at number 15 Place Vendome was exquisite and the views of the city by night, its better known buildings and landmarks illuminated, romantic and exciting. The more so for being viewed from this setting.

It was the first time Phyllida had been back to his hotel at the end of an evening. They would eat in his room; the cuisine was second to none, before he dropped her back at her apartment. The suite was magnificent, fit for royalty. But then so were all of the suites at the Ritz. Phyllida let her cashmere coat slip from her shoulders and draped it over a chaise. She was wearing an ankle length off the shoulder black dress that hugged her figure, accentuating her rounded hips, tiny waist and full bosom. She realised glancing down at the contours of her breasts that she should have worn a bra, the dress was really far too revealing.

Picking up the room service menu, Jean-Claude gestured Phyllida to join him. He had worn a dark suit for a change, with a white shirt and pale blue tie. He was immaculate and elegant, the combination of dark clothes and black hair framing an olive skin set against the white of his shirt making him look quite devastating. Curious how little she had been aware of his attraction when she was first intrigued by the way he folded his sandwich paper at the Tuilleries, when she first thought there was something menacing about him. Odd, how wrong initial impressions could be.

Looking over his shoulder at the selection of food on offer she realised she was not really hungry at all, "I'm not sure I want to eat right now, Jean-Claude."

"Eh bien! Perhaps a drink, coffee, tea. Maybe something alcoholic?" The subtle smell of his cologne mingled with something faintly sweet, something masculine became apparent to her and she moved away from him, blushing slightly. He glanced at her, amused, enquiring.

"It's, it's nothing," she stammered. And then, "A brandy would be nice." It sounded so lame. "And then, I'd better be getting back for Natasha."

The Remy Martin was soft and soothing, and Phyllida felt her earlier discomfiture fading. Sitting back in the huge Empire armchair she watched Jean-Claude, seated in its twin, as he toyed with his brandy glass. So elegant, she thought again, and such a gentle man.

"The opera was wonderful, n'est ce pas?"

"Wonderful."

"The leading lady and the leading man have a little something for each other I think." He waggled his open hand speculatively.

Phyllida glanced up at Jean-Claude, surprised, "How could you tell?"

"The look of love in his eyes, the way he caressed her breasts, touched her *derriere*." Jean-Claude demonstrated by tapping himself on the hip.

"On stage? You're joking," she gasped.

Staring back at her, his deep set brown eyes under the flat black brows a picture of seriousness. "Of course I am," he said gravely, and then burst out laughing.

For a moment Phyllida was totally taken aback, Jean-Claude's wry sense of humour left her constantly flustered and perplexed, "Monsieur de Riviere, you are teasing a helpless woman."

"Not so helpless I think," he wagged an admonitory finger at her.

He was beautiful. She must go before she regretted staying. Getting to her feet, Jean-Claude rose in response. "It's getting late. Natasha will be wondering..."

"Of course." Retrieving her coat, Jean-Claude wrapped it around her shoulders and then standing behind her, crossed his arms across her chest holding her tight to him for a moment. It made her feel secure, gave her a flash of affection for this man who had been so patient and considerate. She closed her eyes, moved away from him and breathed in deeply, "Sit down please, I want to talk to you, Jean-Claude."

He frowned slightly, concerned, but did as she asked, "Bien sur, cherie."

She resumed her seat, crossed her legs, her coat still about her shoulders and composed herself. She was still undecided, "Something happened in my life..." She hesitated, "Something I never talk about."

Jean-Claude looked at her intently, then smiled slightly as though in encouragement, but made no comment.

"When you confided in me about the the terrible loss of your wife and son..."

"Go on, ma chere," Jean-Claude murmered.

She closed her eyes and saw Tom again. So young, so full of life. Her throat tightened and she could feel her pulse throbbing in her ears. "When Tom died," she whispered, "I was four and a half months pregnant.

We'd wanted the baby so badly. Then the accident. The shock. I started contractions. There were complications. The doctors said I must give birth naturally. They would induce. Abort. For the next five hours I felt my baby struggle to survive inside me and there was nothing I could do to help her."

Tears were streaming down Phyllida's face, "Do you see Jean-Claude? I was helpless. I was helpless then and I'm helpless now. My husband. I can do nothing when he needs me. I failed them both."

"But no, Phyllida. You have not failed them. What more could you have done?"

Phyllida went on as if Jean-Claude hadn't spoken, "I made them bring me my stillborn child, Jean-Claude." She turned to face him, "It was a little girl. I held her in my arms, like this," she said, and cradled her arms as though she were holding a living baby. "I tried to imagine what it would have been like to have nursed her. I decided to call her Poppy. She was like a soft pink porcelain toy. I held her warm body against her mine until the hospital staff insisted on taking my baby away. They told me I screamed and screamed. Yes I screamed, at the emptiness in my womb. At the emptiness in my arms. At the emptiness in my life."

Phyllida's voice had risen until she was practically shouting. Now, hoarse, exhausted and spent with the revelation, she collapsed back against the chair. After a moment she sat up and stared straight at Jean-Claude. "So now you know. I could not tell my husband before. I could not talk to anyone about it. I felt inadequate. Confused." She sat staring ahead for a while, then turning back to Jean-Claude she said, "Thank you for being there for me, Jean-Claude. I feel better now. Better."

Standing up she stretched out a hand to Jean-Claude who, joining her, took it in his own. Phyllida looked up into his face, "Kiss me, Jean-Claude. And then take me home."

That expression of concentration on his face again, Jean-Claude hesitantly brought his face close to hers like a teenager about to experience his first moment of stolen love. When he brushed her lips with his Phyllida noticed he was trembling. But she wanted the kiss, wanted to press herself against him, wanted to taste the sweetness of his saliva, to feel the long slender hardness of him against her thigh. At last she was no longer trapped. By the memories, the trauma, the agony. She was breathing faster now, her breasts heaving, time to stop, but it was so good, so very good. A woman again. Just a few seconds longer. His hands on her back sent shivers up and down her spine and she offered no resistance when he gently slid down the zip of her dress and let it fall.

"Please," he murmured pushing her away from him. "Let me look at you." She watched as his gaze seemed to eat her up, travelling from her ankles to the soaking patch in her tiny briefs. She could see the vein in his neck pulsing as though he might explode at any moment and acknowledged her own impatience. As he stared at the flat tummy and the wide pendulous breasts she did something she had never done before, she put a hand on her hip and stood with her legs slightly splayed. "My God, Phyllida, you are animal."

She was tearing at his jacket, ripping the expensive shirt, dragging at his trousers, pulling him down onto the carpet, down on top of her. No time to take off the briefs, she dragged aside the crotch and taking the point of his cock in her hands, steered him into her. He was thin, narrow, slender, but oh so long. So gorgeously and deliciously long. Her body was in spasm, her hips rising and falling to meet his, faster and faster. More, more, more. It wasn't enough, she had to get everything out of her system until she was screaming. Her back curved up to him, his swollen tip expanding in her, bursting, spewing, shooting. She could feel the flicking of his come deep within her belly and she moaned again.

It was over. She had lost track of time. It was minutes, hours, years. He was spreadeagled on top of her, the lightness of him gently pressed against her for a moment, and then he was gently withdrawing, gently so she shouldn't feel used and abandoned. He settled himself next to her on the floor. "Je t'aime, Phyllida, je t'aime."

She kissed him gently on the eyes, "Moi aussi, cherie."

He paused for several seconds, "You know, I have to go away, Phyllida."

"What do you mean, go away?"

"Business. I did not want to spoil the evening," he shrugged sadly.

"How long, Jean-Claude?" Now she was confused.

"Six weeks, two months. An eternity. I shall try to cut it short. But I have obligations."

Suddenly she felt flat, empty. She wanted to cry, but knew she shouldn't. Who was she to cry for, Jean-Claude? Jack? Herself? "Of course, Jean-Claude." She got to her feet and selfconsciously pulled her dress over her nakedness, "Can you show me where the shower is? I really must get back now, Natasha you know..."

Jean-Claude waited until Phyllida was in the shower, then walking swiftly into the bedroom, he picked up the telephone and dialled a number. After a few moments it began to ring, and then a voice with a distinctly Oriental accent answered.

"Bonsoir, Kim," said, Jean-Claude.

"Bonsoir, Jean-Claude. Ca va?"

"Ca va bien, mon ami. Ca va tres bien."

Chapter 32

June 3, Thursday

It was after eight-thirty p.m. and Jack paced the tiny hotel room, restlessly. Hamilton, Bermuda had never seemed more inviting and Jack's mood during the flight had been euphoric despite Oscar Nelhams having counselled caution. Nelhams was right of course, but the temptation to relax just a bit, the desire to yield to an orgy of self-congratulation had been more than Jack could resist after so many months of hell and he had, wisely or not, indulged himself.

Now, left on his own while Nelhams reconnoitred AUIG's premises in town, Jack had time to come down to earth again. He was far from home and dry and knew it; indeed, without absolute and unarguable proof of the fraud committed against him by AUIG, Jack was in the mire up to his ears. Even if AUIG refused to pay out the twelve million dollar claim Jack had lodged, there was no arguing he had been party to an attempted massive deception.

It was like walking towards the light at the end of a dark tunnel only to find upon reaching it that the tunnel started all over again. Despite Charles' good news, Jack felt as despondent now as at any time since the nightmare had begun. Oscar Nelhams was a help. The man's irrepressible energy was a fillip in itself, but more than anything else, Jack wanted Phyllida and she was not to be found. He'd telephoned Paris before leaving for Bermuda, but there had been no answer from the flat. He wanted to call her right now, but demurred. If the line was tapped Jack wanted no possible leads to his present whereabouts. There was nothing to do but to sit tight drinking endless cups of coffee until Nelhams returned.

Reaching for the coffee pot, Jack was about to pour another when he heard a tapping at the door. He froze for a moment, then shrugging, went to the door and aggressively threw it wide. No one knew they were there, and if anyone did, there would be no running away.

Oscar Nelhams strode into the room. He was holding a slim black Gucci brief-case which he placed on the floor. With barely a glance at Jack, he tossed a small leather wallet on to the counterpane and sat down on the edge of the bed. "If you're pouring, Jack, I'm drinking."

Grinning, Jack handed Nelhams a coffee and then sat down opposite him in the room's solitary armchair and waited to hear what the man had to say. Nelhams took his time, savoring, it seemed, both the moment and the searing black liquid which he swallowed in great gulps oblivious to the damage it must have been inflicting on his throat.

Now, waiting for Nelhams to report on his findings for the day, Jack found himself irritable with impatience. "Well?" he thundered at last.

Unperturbed, Nelhams replaced the cup on the bedside table and then hoisted his legs up onto the bed where he crossed one over the other before leaning back against the headboard with his hands comfortably behind his neck. Fixing his gaze on Jack, he said, "We go tonight."

"What! Already?" Surely it was too soon. They'd been in Hamilton barely twenty-four hours. Nelhams couldn't possibly have the lie of the land in so little time; could he?

"Tonight."

He could, and it seemed, he had. Of all the fantasies Jack had harboured, visualised and enacted during the past months, this was the most unreal. Even as he considered it, the anticipation of the next few hours began to take on a dream like quality.

Jack stared at Nelhams without speaking. Words like, `break-in', `criminal', and, `scene of the crime', kept popping up in his mind. Nothing professional here, and nothing over which Jack had any control. He was entirely in the hands and at the command of this man; taking orders from others was an entirely novel experience. The prospect was worse than daunting, it was terrifying. Jack could hear the clang of steel doors reverberating in the back of his head and he unconsciously rubbed the palm of one hand against his shirt front.

"Nervous?" Nelhams must have read his thoughts.

"Beyond description," Jack smiled weakly. Even his voice sounded tremulous in his own ears.

"Good."

"Good? Why?"

"Because overconfidence usually leads to errors of judgement. Where we're going is uncharted territory for you, I need you to be keyed up; and above all I need you to do as you're told." Nelhams grinned.

"I'm entirely in your hands, Oscar. If you foul up..."

"Don't worry, I'll be gentle with you." Another of Nelhams's rare stabs at humour, it seemed as oddly incongruous as everything else about him.

"Hmm," Jack grunted noncommittally and reclined in the hardbacked armchair.

"I wouldn't get too comfortable if I were you."

"Why not?"

"Because I'm about to brief you, then we're going."

"Shoot," said Jack.

"Not literally, I hope," Nelhams muttered under his breath.

"Okay, here goes. We're not breaking in."

"What?"

"You heard."

"But I thought...."

"Well you thought wrong." Holding up his hand before Jack could protest further he continued. "It's too dicey. Too many ifs."

Jack rubbed his eyes with the heels of his hands, "Okay, so how do we get what I want from microfiches?"

"Do you remember, `The Colditz Story'?"

"The War film?"

"Yup."

"Well?"

"Remember how some of the British prisoners escaped?"

"Yes. They dressed up as German officers and walked out."

"Well, we're dressing up as AUIG executives and walking in."

"You're joking!" Nelhams said nothing. "Christ! You're not joking."

"See these?" Nelhams extracted two plastic cards from the small wallet on the bed. "Swipe cards. One each. They'll get us through the turnstiles at the reception and, hopefully into the microfiche room."

"Where the hell did you get those, Oscar?"

"Not difficult. I followed some of the AUIG staff after they left work to go for a drink. Their execs all seem to leave their ties on but take their jackets off to relax in the pub. Bit like sheep really. When no one was looking I slipped the cards from a couple of top pockets. They'll probably think they dropped them. Happens all the time."

"Oscar, before we go on, tell me something. How did you gain entry to the AUIG premises at all today if you didn't get these swipe cards until this evening?"

"Easy," Oscar grinned. "When you know how. I simply tailgated one of their execs through the turnstile. Made a couple of superfluous comments about the weather and shot off in a different direction once I was through."

Jack leaned forward and smiled, "Oscar, is there anything you can't do?"

Oscar pondered for moment, then gravely replied, "Flower arranging."

"I knew I shouldn't have asked," Jack said.

"Listen carefully, Jack. This is important. I wasn't able to check out the microfiche room, so I don't know whether we need to swipe to get out as well as in."

"Does that matter?"

"I should say it does," Oscar looked grim. "Swipe cards carry different priorities. For example, the cleaning staff can generally swipe out, as it were, till around 6.00 a.m. Execs, usually till 11.00 p.m. Directors, at least in this organisation, I found, till 4.00 a.m. It may seem arbitrary, but they have their reasons. It varies from one company to another."

"What happens if we overrun our time? Are we trapped?"

"No. The cards will still get us out. But as we use them, all hell will break loose. We'll have security on our tail like a herd of bull elephants."

"God!" said Jack, bleakly.

"Just don't waste time once we're in."

Getting up off the bed Oscar opened the brief-case and extracted a white shirt and lightweight business suit, which he started to climb into. "Come on, Jack, get changed. On the way I'll outline the rest of what I have in mind. I hope you're ready."

Taking a slow deep breath, Jack replied, "About as ready as I'm ever likely to be."

* * *

The air was chill and the night crystal clear. Both men in their expensive suits and sober ties looked like the executives they were supposed to be. Nelhams led the way from their hotel to the acquired Toyota Carina E parked outside. It felt good to be in the open; the hotel was small and claustrophobic and reminded Jack of his ghastly digs in Paddington. A far cry, he thought, from the so recently stolen lifestyle. Who could have predicted how quickly it could all disappear.

Climbing behind the steering wheel, Nelhams threw a second slender Gucci brief-case onto Jack's lap, tossing his own onto the back seat. "I think we'll look the part," was all he said. Then he turned the ignition key, the engine firing into life straightaway. The car had a new smell about it.

Before moving off, Nelhams looked at Jack, as though checking him out.

"Remember, there are no guarantees this'll work."

"It must though, Oscar."

They drove in silence for several minutes, then Nelhams said, "You're all clear on everything?"

"All clear." Jack glanced at his watch; it was midnight. He wondered where Phyllida was, what she was doing. Why hadn't she been at the flat when he'd called? Was Harriette alright? The bubs. He blinked his eyes as though wiping them clean of unwanted images and forced himself to concentrate.

"There it is," Nelhams whispered as though someone might be eavesdropping. He pointed out a nondescript three storey concrete and glass building about a quarter of a mile ahead. Trees dotted the pavement on both sides of the road, in too sparse and random a fashion to be described as an avenue.

Apparently the room which housed the microfiches Jack needed access to was in the basement of the building. Jack could feel his head throbbing in time with his pulse, and there was a tightening across his chest.

Not much further.

Security in the building, Nelhams had ascertained, comprised three teams of guards who worked in pairs on eight-hour rotas. They were stationed, along with several closed circuit TV screens, behind the centrally located reception desk, which was itself visible from the street through the plate glass frontage. Swipe card entry was effected through turnstiles to one side of the reception desk. Overall supervision was exercised through a central control room located in a back office on the first floor of the block. Surveillance was effective therefore on a twenty-four hour basis. The new shift would have come on a couple of hours ago, and they'd still be fresh. Was that a good thing? Jack wondered.

"By the way," Nelhams sounded casual, almost indifferent. If anyone asks, I'm Walter Schumacher junior."

"Christ Almighty, Oscar." Jack turned to face the man sitting next to him. "What about the accent?"

"Don't worry, I'll manage. I've spent a lot of time in the States."

"Who am I then? If anyone should ask."

"We'll say you're Colin Kervil, my assistant."

"But he is my assistant."

"Exactly. You shouldn't have any difficulty remembering the name.

Barely two hundred yards. Jack squinted, ground his teeth. This pantomime had to work, the hell with accommodating failure.

Chapter 33

June 3, Thursday

The barely audible hum of the air conditioning ran parallel to that of the traffic whose murmur was just discernible through the double-glazing of the office. Surveying the chaos on the smoked glass top of his vast desk, Hepton pressed the telephone to his ear. "Who is it, Mandy?"

"He says it's your agent, sir."

Hepton grunted under his breath and waved away his secretary. The girl, in her early twenties looked at Hepton, uncertainly, and then pulled at the front of her grey jacket, straightening it, patted nervously at the side of her short black hair, and finally shuffled her papers together before leaving the room. Hepton watched her leave, with growing impatience. "All right, Mandy, put him through."

A moment later Hepton heard the sound of the Chinese man, "Mr. Hepton?"

"Yeah, Kim. How's tricks?"

"Tricks, as you put it could be better."

"What'sa problem?"

"I think you know what the problem is, Mr. Hepton. But let me remind you anyway. You owe me considerable sums in respect of unpaid accounts."

Hepton sounded bored, "Yeah well, you ain't comin' up with the goods, son."

"I have more than come up with the goods, Mr. Hepton," the voice carried a trace of irritation. "Mr. Gregory has been made a bankrupt and the subject of a Mareva injunction, as was contracted between us. Furthermore he has been unable to move against you in the American courts, or those of Bermuda. Central Reinsurance is being bled dry of funds to cover the fees and expenses of its liquidator, Mr. Hepton."

"Well, that's my business, son, not yours."

"I think it is very much my business: let me say particularly when the eloquence with which you were able to persuade the Bermuda High Court to overturn the adverse decision of Central's Committee of Inspection in refusing you the liquidator's fees you had requested, was supported by me."

"You had nuthin' to do with it."

"On the contrary, who do you imagine helped get your nominee, Chief Justice Douglas Tandy, appointed?"

"You?"

"Me."

Hepton ran his teeth under the edge of a fingernail and thought about his secretary. Prissy little madam, always straightening her hair and her clothes, making sure her skirt didn't ride up too far when she sat down. Might be worth working on though. The shy ones usually turned out the best in the end, particularly if they were trying to keep it special for some guy.

Like that blonde bitch: Hepton grinned as he recalled it. Thought Luke Hepton didn't know she had a boyfriend stashed away. Pretended she liked him. Thought he didn't see her mouth curling in disgust. Still she liked him in the end didn't she, came real good. Gotta see her again some time. Had to hand it to Kim, he knew how to find'em.

"Crap! It was me who got him appointed, not you." He sounded uncertain. "Anyway, so what! Tandy couldn't argue with me. I had him all tied up in knots. He came over sweet an' gentle as a baby, said I was entitled to my proper fees and expenses."

"Douglas was fully briefed by me before you set foot in the court, Mr. Hepton."

"What?"

"I'm sorry to disillusion you, but the outcome of your so-called eloquence was a foregone conclusion, your appearance a formality."

"Bullshit! Tandy couldn't offer any arguments to the case I presented."

"Douglas is a dear friend, Mr. Hepton, a kindred spirit if you take my drift. We go back a long way. He was pleased to do me a small favor. You have taken all you want from Central, and considerably more than you need or indeed merit. Now it's my turn."

"Now you see here, Kim. Ah got others on Gregory's case, 'sides yourself."

The note of irritation returned to the Oriental's voice, "I was to have had complete discretion over this operation, Mr. Hepton. There were to be no others beyond myself and my own trained staff."

"Too bad if I'm offending you, boy, but ah need results."

"I have given you results."

"Not good enough though. You know damn well, Gregory is about to get his bankruptcy annulled, and the Mareva injunction withdrawn. Heck, he's practically got the filling stations sold. Next thing, he'll be gettin' his licence back to practice insolvency."

"You knew the tactics we adopted could be no more than a holding operation designed to stall Mr. Gregory for long enough to allow you to gain access through the Bermuda High Court to Central's funds. That object has been achieved."

"How do I know he won't start gunnin' for me when he's back in practice again?"

"Mr. Hepton, your actions have been underwritten by the Bermuda High court. What more do you want? Gregory has no funds to pursue you anyway. Even if he had, he has no case."

"You said you'd take care of his wife."

"His wife is taken care of. De Riviere has been most charmingly persuasive."

"Whaddya mean, she's been taken care of? It's all s'posed to have happened a long time ago. So Jean-Cleade screwed her. So what? All a friggin' waste of time an' effort. You fouled up, boy. Got your scheduling wrong; left it all too late. And now you're complainin' 'bout fees. I pay for results, my man. Not promises.

"And I bill for my efforts and expertise, Mr. Hepton. The results will follow in due course. Substantial time and energy were expended in planning Mrs.Gregory's affair de coeur. There are considerable charges accrued on your account."

"Gregory's gettin' himself back together again. The good lady was s'posed to demoralise him with her foolin' about." Hepton studied the backs of his fingers.

"So she will, if need be."

"How, and when?"

"Let me worry about that, Mr. Hepton. Mr. Gregory has not yet reached home base. He misses his wife. If he has any further plans, he will be unwilling to carry them out without her acquiesence. He has put her through too much already. Anything further, and she will think seriously about the future of her marriage."

Hepton stared at the ceiling, drummed his fingers on the desk, "What sorta plans you talkin' bout, Kim?"

"Mr. Gregory has gone to ground. A temporary disappearance, I shall locate him shortly. He may have other ideas in mind."

"What the hell're you talkin' about, he may have other ideas in mind? I pay you to know what's goin' on."

"On the contrary, Mr. Hepton. I am still awaiting payment."

"I want you to put him away."

"You want me to kill Mr. Gregory?"

"That's right."

"Unwise and unnecessary. A direct attack on Mr. Gregory would almost certainly bring you yourself directly to the attention of the authorities. It is well known that there is more than a simple lack of love between you both. My own activities of the past few months would almost certainly be linked with, and very likely attributed to you, if they are not already. Do you really want to take the credit for them?"

Hepton debated the issue with himself for a moment, then he said, "I think you're just buckin' the issue."

"I'm sorry, I really don't follow." The tone of the reply was one of surprise.

"I think you're gettin' soft on the guy."

"Flights of fancy Mr. Hepton. I don't allow personal feelings to impinge upon my assignments. Remember Osbert Standish, I had the utmost professional and personal respect for him, but I carried out your request. And in due course Osbert's successor, Tandy, gave you your fees, and issued the ten million dollar judgement against Mr. Gregory upon which we relied in securing his bankruptcy et al."

"Yeah, well that's all goin' out the window now. So when're you goin' to use the wife?"

"I will make use of her present attachment to Jean-Claude, if and when I think it appropriate. Not before."

"She your `ace in the hole.'?"

There was a moment's silence, then, "Oh, that. No, as a matter of fact I have other ideas if Mr. Gregory displays ambitions beyond his station."

"You seem very sure of yourself."

"I am, Mr. Hepton, I am."

"Well, ah ain't so sure of you, and this little talk's done nuthin' to change my mind. If you ask me, pal, your losing it."

The response was barely above a whisper, "My account, Mr. Hepton... I should really hate us to fall out over the question of money. And take my earnest advice, leave this operation in my sole charge as we agreed."

The phone went dead and Hepton stared at the door to his office, then muttered under his breath, "Ain't nobody tells Luke Hepton what to do." Dialling a number, he waited for a moment listening to the ringing tone, then a voice replied, "Dimitriou."

"Ah ain't gettin' nowhere with the Chinaman," Hepton rasped. "Find Gregory for me and tell me what he's up to."

Chapter 34

June 3, Thursday

10.00 p.m. "Ready, Colin?" Oscar had his hand on the car door handle ready to go. They were parked outside the AUIG building. "You look a bit pasty, my friend."

Jack closed his eyes, swallowed to quell the feeling of fear rising in his chest and breathed in slowly. "Let's do it," he said quietly.

Nelhams left the car doors unlocked and gave Jack the keys. No one would steal the vehicle outside this building, and they had to be clear for a quick getaway if one were needed.

The two men walked briskly towards the plate glass front doors and Nelhams pressed the call button. "Who is it?" The voice was loud and deep.

"Walter Schumacher junior and my assistant Colin Kervil. We're down from the States, working late and I need access to the microfiche room. We were in earlier on, didn't get all we needed."

"Your card?"

Nelhams waved the swipe in front of the CCTV for the security man to see.

"Well," he sounded hesitant. "I s'pose it's okay. Come on in."

The door buzzed and the two men strode in purposefully.

Even seated, it was clear the security guards were big men. Jack guessed they'd be around two hundred and fifty pounds. In their early forties, one was dark haired, the other fair. They both wore guns, Jack noticed. Legal in Bermuda, he wondered? Still, AUIG probably wrote their own legislation. On the desk in front of them were two long black nightsticks. Jack felt the hairs on the back of his neck rise.

Oscar smiled a tight little smile at the darker of the two still seated men as he walked towards the turnstile, "Thanks, Pete."

"How d'you know my name?" the other replied.

"Don't you remember? Earlier? We were chatting by the drinks machine upstairs. You weren't on duty."

"Oh, yeah. Yeah." The man sounded doubtful.

Without turning his head again, Oscar slid the card down the slot and pressed up against the turnstile. Nothing happened. The fairer of the two security men hoisted himself to his feet and said, "Gotta problem, sir?"

Jack could feel his guts turn to water, but Oscar was quite unperturbed. He turned to Jack and smiled, "Problems with my swipe, Colin. Probably only works on the internal doors. Sometimes happens. Let's try yours." This time the card worked and the two of them were through and on their way to the door at the back of the reception leading to the stairs down to the basement.

"Go on down, Jack. In case there's any trouble. I'll keep an ear open behind the door."

It felt cold and airless, like a dungeon. The atmosphere was damp, musty. Lest there should be any mistaking it, the door marked, `microfiche,' also had a vertical strip of wire reinforced glass down one side through which Jack could see rows and rows of shelving. He made a clenched fist salute with both hands. "Paradiso. If we live to tell the tale," he said under his breath.

Jack, swiping his card on the unit on the wall, was through the door in moments. To his immediate right was the microfiche reader and printer. Flipping on the light, he proceeded up and down each row of shelving. Accounting information was down one side of the room, correspondence and internal memoranda, down the other. Everything was delineated in years and months.

Central Reinsurance had been first placed into solvent liquidation by Jack in February of last year. The meeting of creditors where Jack and Tony Trent had lost control had taken place in November of the same year. AUIG's monster claim, all twenty-two million dollars worth of it had been among one of a short series of contrived invoices for a handful of related, but non-existent claims. The invoices were all dated July or September of that year. There were three for each month.

Despite the one-month gap between the invoice dates, the invoice numbers ran consecutively; surely a slip up. Probably no one ever anticipated the invoices would be scrutinised that closely.

In any event those for July were code numbered: Jul 5795, Jul 5796 and Jul 5797.

The September invoices were coded: Sep 5798, Sep 5799 and Sep 5800.

It was straightforward, the month followed by the invoice number. It was ludicrous to suppose that the company had raised no invoices whatsoever in the month of August last year. Finding the column and shelf for the same dates was no problem; they were all marked clearly. Reaching for the boxes containing the required microfiches, Jack carefully pulled out the two for July and September. Then, after a moment's pause, he dragged down the one for August as well.

Hurrying to the reader/printer with the boxes under his arm, Jack started to feed on to it the various microfiches. If he found what turned out to be true copies of the so-called invoices lodged against Central, he was sunk. As long as the copy invoices he found differed, either in content or code number, he was home and dry.

The operation took very little time, or so it seemed. Jack glanced at his watch; it was midnight. He should have checked it first before starting. How long had he been searching? He had no idea. There'd been no word from Nelhams; presumably all was well up top. Jack had gone through the whole of July, August and September. All the invoices for the three months ran consecutively and were numbered from 8000 up. There were no gaps in August. It was exactly what he'd hoped for, a con.

Excitement building up, he started up the printer. Then a thought struck him: `memoranda'. As soon as he'd finished gathering the invoice evidence he'd take a look at the correspondence section of the room. It was a long shot, but in his own investigations he'd more than once come across examples of directorial malpractice all carefully documented and retained on file. The arrogance of some people was beyond belief.

1.00 a.m. Jack had a tidy stack of papers ready to be carried out. I've got you you bastards, I've got you, he thought and moved on swiftly. The correspondence sections were just as clearly marked as the accounts section and were simply waiting for him to plunder. Jack started hauling out box after box. He'd been so absorbed he didn't hear the soft footfall behind him and nearly exploded out of his skin when a soft voice said, "They're getting shifty, Jack. Wondering what's keeping us. We'd better make tracks."

But Jack had already spun round with shock and grabbed a bunch of Nelhams's shirt in the fist of one hand, the other was drawn back ready to strike. Nelhams stared insolently at Jack, the intense blue eyes impassive, "You're starting to lose it, Jack. Pull yourself together man."

In a crazy release of pent up fury, Jack punched the air several times, then stood panting, his nostrils flared.

Looking at him more kindly, Nelhams said softly, "Come on, Jack. We've got to get out of here."

"But I'm getting all the evidence I need to show up these bastards for what they are. Give me another half hour, if I can't get hold of anything else I'll call it a night."

"And if you can? You stay here 'til morning? Half an hour; that's it." Nelhams loped off, clearly irritated, and left Jack to the boxes of memoranda.

Jack checked forward seven months. AUIG had waited until September of last year to lodge their claim, two months before the November meeting of creditors he'd been forced to call for Central. It was a fair bet AUIG and Hepton would have been debating the issue around about that time.

Jack paused for an instant and checked the time, it was 2.15 a.m. Just a few minutes more.

Reading everything he could find, Jack discovered nothing of any value in September. He went back to August, looking at internal and external memos, correspondence, notes left on file, anything. Still no result. The minutes were still ticking away, but Nelhams had not returned. July was the same, as was June. Nothing, nothing, nothing.

It was now 3.10 a.m.

They couldn't have been planning as early as February, it wasn't possible, Jack had only just put the company into solvent liquidation at that time. That left, March, April or May. He decided to start at the other end and pulled out the March file taking it over to the reader, by now frantically running through the records, scanning, skip reading, and jumping back and forth, days and weeks at a time. If not March, then April, the search was becoming disordered, haphazard. Nelhams would be hauling him out by his neck at any second.

3.30 a.m. Maybe it would be better to get out now while he was ahead. The invoices would suffice. Jack stared down at the microfiche reader and held his breath as the door to the room opened and Nelhams hurried in. Jack had finally found what he wanted. It was all there in memos passing between J.Hepton of Hepton Mallet Dixon and at least six different names at AUIG Bermuda. Unbelievable, the whole thing had been conceived as early as March last year. It was too good to be true. Incontrovertible evidence. No matter whether it would ever be admissible in a court of law. It was here, and he was taking it.

"We've got big problems, Jack, they're both talking about coming down. If we move now, and I mean right now, we might just squeeze past them. I've given you more than enough time."

"But I've found what I want, Oscar. It's all on record. I can't go yet."

"You have to, Jack. That's an order." Nelhams had taken hold of Jack's sleeve and was trying to drag him towards the door.

Putting his hand on Nelhams's wrist, Jack deliberately twisted it off his sleeve, and speaking through clenched teeth, rasped, "Well, Corporal's disobeying orders, Major. I'm not leaving until I've got everything. Do whatever you have to with those two."

For a second Nelhams glared at him, then he seemed to relent, "Have it your own way, Jack. I'll go on keeping a lookout. But don't blame me if this all goes sour."

Stacking the records in the order he wanted them, Jack started printing again. He was working frantically as the minutes ticked away. Nelhams came back from time to time to look over his shoulder, but made no further comment; the perspiration on his face was statement enough. Another ten minutes and it was done. Everything he needed was in a tidy little stack.

3.59 a.m. Nelhams was back, "Let's go, Jack, for the love of Christ."

"I've just got to return these boxes to their shelves."

"Leave the boxes, Jack. For God's sake, we're out of time."

"If I leave this lot lying around they'll know we've been here."

"Jack, they'll know someone's been here snooping anyway. Leave the boxes and papers scattered all over the place. They'll never know who was looking for what. It'll create a diversion. By the time they find nothing's actually missing, we'll be well away and they won't know what this was all about. They might even think it was some sort of industrial vandalism."

"I'll be two minutes."

"Follow me when you're ready, Jack." Nelhams scratched his head. "I'll try to think up some sort of diversion, play it by ear. Just be ready for anything."

4.00 a.m. Cursing under his breath, Nelhams raced back upstairs, his rubber-soled shoes squeaking angrily as he went. Jack scattered papers and files haphazardly about the floor, turned off the printer and raced for the door. All he had to do now was to get out. He'd been so pre-occupied the consequences of failure had not even crossed his mind. Now with the prospect of imminent discovery, he began hyperventilating. His back and chest were running with sweat, and the papers he carried were becoming soaked in his hands as he tried to jam them into the brief-case. How could he have been such a bloody fool? The invoices would have been enough. He'd rue the day...

Sliding his swipe card in the attachment on the wall as Nelhams had, two minutes ago, Jack's head was lanced by the ear splitting howl of the alarm system as it went off.

Stopping himself from going completely over the top, Jack took several deep breaths, then chased after Nelhams up the stairs, taking them three at a time. He found him crouching at the top surveying the reception area.

"There's four of them, Jack."

"How come?"

"They're just changing shifts."

"Bugger it. I'd forgotten."

"Seems there's quite a lot you forgot, Jack."

"What are we going to do?"

"Hit them before they hit us."

"How?"

"On a count of two we race out." Nelhams, talking fast, edged the door open a crack and pointed. "Look, they're on their way to meet us now. Hit whichever one you reach first, then vault the turnstile and start the car. I'll follow."

"But!"

"No buts, man. One, two. GO! GO! GO!"

They were on the reception area. The place was awash with sound, sirens wailing like air raid warnings. Bodies moving around, blue uniforms, brawny arms. A herd of guards.

A fist hammered Jack's jaw and he reeled back, regained his balance and hit out blindly. Felt his fist connect with flesh and bone. Heard a man grunt in pain.

To his right a guard was falling, Nelhams stepping gracefully out of the way. Night sticks flailing, one glanced off Jack's shoulder and he ducked to avoid another.

They'd never get out. How long before reinforcements arrived. Outnumbered, outgunned. All for some extra papers. The brief-case! Christ! He'd dropped it. Forgotton it. Saw it to his left. Kicked it like a football towards the turnstiles. Watched it skitter along the floor, under the turnstiles towards the plate glass doors.

Two guards down.

Jack saw the fairer of the two original security men swing his nightstick back and bring it in a low sweeping arc towards Oscar's stomach. It happened in slow motion, the weapon connecting and Nelhams folding over, coughing a spray of blood. Nelhams on his knees, looking up at Jack imploringly. God in heaven. He was bellowing at Jack through the blood, "Run man. Get to the car."

Only one other guard unoccupied, the man turning his attention to Nelhams, then back to Jack. Reaching for his gun. A moment to decide. Jack ran for the turnstiles and vaulted them. Slipped, picked up and dashed for the door grabbing the brief-case before exiting. Outside, a wash of fresh air. Running to the car. Frantically searching for the keys Nelhams had given him.

Hauling open the door, Jack slid behind the wheel, started the engine. And waited.

He heard the explosion. A gun going off. God! no. Not Oscar. Jack made to open the car door. No way he was going to leave the other man. He was mad to have listened to him. Got to get back.

The plate glass doors swung open and Oscar appeared, staggering towards the car, his front covered in blood. Jack leaned over and pushed open the front passenger door and Nelhams practically fell into the vehicle. "Drive," he ordered in a voice that was icy calm."

* * *

June 4, Friday

As the plane lifted off, Jack relaxed a little and smiled, "Making some progress at last."

"You did all right, Jack." Nelhams was rubbing his chest again, "But you're an insubordinate bastard."

"Needs must sometimes, Oscar. You're pretty argumentative yourself at times. How ever did you survive in there?"

"I've dealt with worse."

"Worse? How could it have been worse?"

"Only one shot was fired," Oscar smiled.

"What do you normally expect then, a hail of bullets?"

"No, of course not. But I was lucky. None of them was martial arts trained. I am," he said simply.

"So I saw, Oscar. Tell me how's the chest? Come to think of it, how's the rest of you?"

"I'm not sure," Nelhams undid several of the buttons of his shirt and pulled it open revealing a swathe of purple-black bruising. "I think our friend may have broken a number of ribs when we clashed. Probably why I was starting to get short tempered with you at the time. I'll get this bound up when we get home."

Chapter 35

June 7, Monday

Jack's adrenalin had given out at about the time he and Nelhams had arrived at Bermuda airport. He'd barely made it to the aircraft, and, once on it, apart from the brief conversation he had with Nelhams at the start of the flight, had slept for the entire journey. It wasn't enough, he felt like a shredded rag and his shoulder throbbed painfully where the nightstick had struck it, a month's sleep would have been nearer the mark.

If Nelhams was in a bad way, he didn't show it. The punishment he'd taken would have wiped out a lesser man. Nothing had been left unfinished. Nelhams even remembered to retrieve the second brief-case from the back seat of the borrowed car before returning the vehicle to the showroom from whence it had come.

British Airways flight 232 from Bermuda touched down at London Heathrow, Monday morning spot at its scheduled arrival time of 6.50 a.m. Oscar Nelhams took himself off to hospital as soon as he cleared customs. And Jack, despite his weariness, had gone to the office; there was a lot of catching up to do.

All of that day was spent dealing with the mountain of correspondence that accumulated during his brief absence. It was absurd, he had intended to retire from the reinsurance business but work was flooding in. The two staff, Penny Jowett and Bob Mansfield, could barely cope; more people would have to be employed.

In Jack's absence David Purdoe had prepared application to have Luke Hepton's ten million judgement against him set aside, and subsequent to that would seek the annulment of Jack's bankruptcy and the lifting of the Mareva injunction. Charles Goldman had written to the DTI; there would be no reason to withhold his insolvency practitioner's licence any longer. He should have been feeling elated, instead he felt empty.

He'd called Phyllida countless times in the last few days and never once found her in the Paris flat. Of course she was okay, she'd left messages with Mrs. Llewellyn at Highview to say everything was fine and she was sorry she missed Jack's calls and she knew he wouldn't want her phoning him in London, wherever he happened to be. Mrs. Llewellyn told Jack that Mrs. Gregory sounded happier than she had for months, so Mr. Gregory shouldn't worry his head. Mrs. Gregory would be coming home just as soon as she felt really able to cope again.

Months, Jack thought. She'd been away for over three months. Was it his fault? Phyllida's fears? Her anger? For the umpteenth time he asked himself, should he have dropped the idea of some sort of reprisal? At the outset Phyllida backed him all the way, although she later questioned his judgement. Would he have survived anyway, physically, spiritually, if he'd let everything go once they'd sunk their teeth into him? Luke Hepton? AUIG? The Chinese man?

He had the evidence he needed to get them all off his back. Even if AUIG refused to pay out on the insurance claim, they wouldn't be in a position to hound him any longer. For the sake of security, he forwarded copies of all the documents, invoices and memoranda to both David Purdoe and Tony Trent. It all sounded wonderful, and it all felt like failure. He was like a hollow oak, solid on the outside, rotting emptiness inside.

The old man's face that stared out from the bathroom mirror that morning had horrified him. Vanity wasn't the problem, premature aging was. His face was twisted with tension and tiredness. The sparse hair had become even thinner; the loss of what little remained at the peak of his forehead changing the whole aspect of his face. And it was greying. Greying? God it was going white. He wondered whether Phyllida and Harriette would even recognise him. And yet faced with the same problems, even with the benefit of hindsight, he could see no other way he could have dealt with matters.

Jack shrugged off his despondency. Monday, he thought. Weary and jet lagged, a lot was supposed to happen before the day was out. The separate threads that represented months of planning were finally coming together, yet in a totally unplanned way, and he would need all his energy and attention to see things through. Contact from America was due later in the afternoon. AUIG would honour the twelve million he claimed, or not. He pondered it for a moment. There was no reason why they should not pay, and no way that he seriously believed they would. If nothing else their excuses not to shell out would make an interesting news story.

Then there was the question of Mr. Mistry, and the garage sites. God knows what the interest accruals on the loans would be by now. Would Mistry's offer still be enough to cover the mortgages plus the extra borrowings? Impossible. The man was light on funds already. Danny was tied up preparing an auction out of town for the last two days and had only been able to reassure Jack in hurried telephone conversations him that the hundred thousand required to cover Mistry's shortfall would be there on time. On time? After several delays David Purdoe had set today as the final date for completion. There would be no more postponements. Even if Danny were successful, there was still the question of the costs for laying on security at each site? Jack sighed, the once hoped for surplus had long sinced diminished to no more than a prayed for break even situation.

The more he dwelt on it, the more anxious he became. The worries had a domino effect, one disaster linking itself to another. He wondered about Phyllida; if she knew Jack had pledged her credit to part of the borrowings. It didn't bear thinking about. He closed his eyes and ran his hand across his scalp. If he didn't call a halt he'd have a nervous breakdown himself. "Bollocks," he muttered. There were no ifs or buts; they absolutely had to complete today.

Penny came into the room. In Jack's absence, she ran things. Come to think of it, in his presence she largely ran things as well. Already experienced in the field of insurance and reinsurance, Penny Jowett learned more quickly and was generally better organised than any staff he had ever employed. A hard taskmaster, Jack placed total trust in her abilities and judgement. As well as everything else she always looked so smart and unruffled. Today, she was wearing black slacks and a high neck emerald green blouse with Victorian balloon type sleeves. She stood over his desk, looking at him dubiously. "Are you all right, David?"

David? Christ, that was another thing. The prospect of his convincing a court that he'd not really been acting illegally in using a false name to take on a company directorship -- while still an undischarged bankrupt -- for the purposes of perpetrating a fraud flashed across Jack's mind. One more detail to worry about. Too bloody bad if it happens, he thought, trying yet again to shake off the mood.

"I'm fine, Penny. Why?"

"Just that you don't look too good."

"Jet lagged."

"If you say so. By the way, there's a pile of phone calls to get back. That Chinese sounding man called several times last week. Told me if I happened to speak to someone by the name of Jack Gregory, to say that Kim would be in touch with him on Monday with the solution. Mean anything to you?"

Jack felt the blood drain from his face and neck. Today or never, he thought. He glanced first at his watch; it was midday, then up at Penny again. Her reddish brown hair hung loose about her face, making the expression of concern that furrowed her brow very like that of a child. He must be getting old.

"It means Penny that I only have a few hours to complete a couple of important deals and settle one or two long-standing debts."

"Do you think they'll go through all right?"

"Oh, bound to Penny. Bound to."

The phone rang on Jack's desk, "Call for you, David," said Bob from the next room. "Wouldn't give a name."

"Hello uh, David?"

Jack recognised Tony Trent's voice immediately. He drummed his fingers on the desk, what the hell. "How are you?"

"Fine. How was the trip?"

"Oh, you know, all business. You've seen some of the documentation."

"It's all beautifully presented, seems to cover every detail."

"I'm glad you like it. How about today?"

"All set to complete. I've seen your solicitor. Fingers crossed the buyer finds all the funds."

"I'm relying on the little man in Hampstead to help us."

"Of course. I'm sure he won't let you down."

"Please God," Jack said, thinking of Danny. "Call you later."

He'd hardly replaced the receiver when Bob rang through again, "Another mystery caller, David."

Danny Jacobovits came on the line, he sounded as uncertain as Tony Trent, "Mr. Purdoe?"

"Good morning." There was only one question, "Have you found the extra funds for our buyer."

There was a brief pause, then Danny said quietly, "Not yet." Then he added more positively, "But I'm working on it."

Furious, Jack shouted back, "Working on it? God, man it's nearly twelve thirty and we're supposed to be completing today." Stopping for a moment to collect his thoughts, Jack came back, his tone more conciliatory, "Very well, my friend. You keep working on it, but hear this: unless the banker's draft is delivered to the solicitor's before the banks close this afternoon, I'm pulling out of the deal and putting the goods back on the market."

"But you can't."

"Watch me."

"But this is the best buyer we've had."

"I haven't seen anyone buying anything so far. All hot air. I think he's bluffing, probably hopes we'll bring the price down a bit."

"Maybe."

His jaw set, brows knit in an angry latticework, Jack said, "I'll give him until four o'clock. If he walks into the solicitor's one minute after that I'll have him kicked out, draft or no draft." Without waiting for Danny's reply, Jack slammed down the receiver.

The office was as oppressive as his hotel was. Jack had to get out into the fresh air. Telling the other two he'd be back shortly, he grabbed his mobile phone and made his way to the foyer of the building where he called David Purdoe. They agreed to meet at Jamies.

Squinting in the early afternoon sun, Jack strode up Kingsway. It was mid summer and the traffic was comparatively light. Being outside the constriction of four walls felt like freedom and he breathed in deeply. It was too early for Schumacher to be calling from America. Tony Trent had long since overseen the exchange of contracts for the sale, if it actually happened today. Increasingly unlikely. There was little to do but wait.

David Purdoe was sitting in their usual corner when Jack arrived. The solicitor looked concerned. "All this cloak and dagger, Jack, all this cloak and dagger. I just hope it's not in vain." He shoved the teapot to Jack's side of the table.

"Not half as much as I hope, David. I keep thinking about the way I've involved Phyllida in all this." Nodding at the waitress, Jack ordered two rounds of wholemeal buttered toast for himself. David wasn't hungry.

"Do you want to see the completion statement, Jack? I've bought a copy with me."

"Not yet. Show me later, if it happens. I'm getting superstitious."

"You know Danny's managed to raise an extra hundred and fifty thousand for Mistry?"

"What! An extra hundred and fifty thousand pounds? I spoke to him only a few minutes ago and he said he was still trying to raise a hundred for Mistry. What the hell's he playing at?"

"Putting off completion time and again has resulted in further interest charges, Jack, and a lot more on the security bill. Danny's been organising the whole thing for you. He's re-negotiated the offer with Mistry -- don't ask me how -- to cover part of the added interest charges and raised some cash against the sites towards the running security costs. Tony Trent's been a party to everything of course. As liquidator he's had to be. Don't forget there's still the additional one hundred and thirty-two thousand to be paid over at completion by Tony to cover half the costs of tyre clearance. Didn't you know all of this?"

"Well, I thought I did. I know about the hundred and thirty-two, but the rest is all new to me. And I bawled out Danny just now. God, I wish I'd known everything."

Jack's order arrived at the same time as his mobile started to bleep. Putting the phone to his ear, he chewed of a large piece of toast. Danny came on the line, he sounded ill at ease. "We've got problems."

"Surprise me."

"I'm meeting a blank wall."

"Totally?"

"I can get so far, bits here and there, then no further."

"Why didn't you tell me about the extra money you managed to raise?"

"What was the point? If the deal's a flop, what should I do claim credit for a failure? Anyway, we're still no better off, I'm still trying to find another hundred thousand."

"Danny, earlier on, I was a bit, well you know..."

"Forget it. You're under a lot of pressure."

"You said problems, what else is there?"

"I've had reports from my people that there's been new dumping of tires at five of the sites that aren't covered by security."

Jack closed his eyes, "I don't believe it. What a bloody farce. Does Mistry know?"

"Not yet. Although it'd make no difference anyway. If we got completion today, Mistry could arrange his own security if he needed it. Which of course he wouldn't, no one's after his guts."

Resting his chin in his hand, Jack stared balefully across the restaurant, a couple of tables had become occupied and there was a murmur of conversation, "So we're finally buggered. We really have lost. All that effort for nothing."

Danny said nothing in reply. David reached forward and touched Jack's arm as though to reassure him.

Looking back at David, Jack shrugged hopelessly, "So bloody near. Danny, haven't you managed to find Mistry any further funds at all?"

"As I said, bits only. I can probably fix another sixty thousand, but that's all. I wasn't going to worsen the agony. We're probably only forty short. I mean fancy losing a four million pound deal for a pathetic forty grand." Danny was silent for a moment. Then he breathed, "Wait a minute though. I'm forgetting, if I take my fee out of the completion statement; one percent of around four million is forty thousand. We'd have enough."

Jack waited several seconds before speaking again, then he said softly, "Danny, what do I say? That means I'd owe you eighty thousand pounds."

"The hell, I'm not doing it for you. This is all for Phyllida."

Feeling his spirits lift fractionally, Jack smiled, "You bastard. Listen, I meant what I said about that deadline; we have to stop somewhere. You've got less than two hours. I want David to call me by four this afternoon and tell me he's got a draft to cover everything. Let's see if Mistry really can complete his part." Jack pressed `end' on the mobile.

David was looking at him ruefully, "Would you really put the sites back on the market, Jack?"

"Absolutely," Jack said cramming the last of the toast into his mouth. "What choice would I have? Mistry's been messing us around for months. Either he can or he can't, and either he will or he won't, complete. We'll all know before the day's out."

David smoothed back his thick black hair, "What about AUIG, Jack? All those plans, the struggle you've had, the risks you've taken."

"I'll know about that today as well. Their man turned our place over before I went off to Bermuda again."

"Was he impressed?"

"I don't think so."

"Will they pay out?"

"God knows."

"Gut feeling?"

"Based on twenty years experience in accountancy and business? I'd say doubtful."

Gazing around the restaurant which was now filling up, David spotted someone he knew, nodded at them and turned his attention back to Jack, sighing, "What a position to be in. You could end up losing everything, dear boy."

"I thought I'd already lost everything. From now on, I only stand to gain." Jack looked grim, "Got to be positive, David. Unless I lose Phyllida, too."

"Perish the thought, dear boy. Perish the thought."

Pushing back his chair, Jack stood up, "Look, I'd better get back. If Schumacher calls early, I want to be there for him."

Twenty minutes later, Jack was in the office again. The toast had been a help, but he was still desperately weary. He'd barely been at his desk five minutes when the call came through. It was 3.00 p.m. local time, 10.00 a.m. in New York. Penny buzzed, "Mr. Schumacher for you, David."

Psyching himself up for what he knew in his heart would be the last time, he straightened his tie, took a deep breath and, shaking off his fatigue, sat up straight, "All right, Penny. Put him through."

"David?" Schumacher's voice rasped down the line, he didn't sound in the most charitable of moods.

"Walter. How are you?" Fighting to keep the tremor out of his voice, Jack made himself sound as calm as he could.

"Little better for having to deal with you, my friend." What the hell did that mean? "I've been looking at this twin kidnap and ransom claim of yours. I can tell you Phil Peters was not impressed with what he found at your place."

"Oh? What was his problem?" Jack leaned forward on the desk his eyes drooping wearily in reaction to Schumacher's opening assault, despite his efforts to combat the exhaustion in his system.

"The problem wasn't his, David, it is yours. Since when did a two hundred million dollar outfit operate with only two staff in two rooms, and at an accommodation address for Chrissake?"

Jack kept his voice soft his manner supremely confident. "No Walter, that's not my problem at all, it's yours."

"I don't think I like your tone, David. If you really are David Purdoe. I've been hearing some odd things about someone called Jack..."

Now! Jack thought. Now's the time to counter attack. "Cut the crap," he roared at Schumacher with his last dregs of energy. "Get to the point, man. Is Goldleaf Insurance getting paid its twelve million dollar claim, or do I go legal and public."

His voice echoing in his own head, Jack sat silently awaiting Schumacher's reply, his hands trembling, his chest heaving.

"I don't trust you, David. Maybe it's your smart English accent. Maybe it's just intuition, but I've been around a few years and I got an odd sensation about this one." Jack debated whether to hang up on Schumacher, and go home to sleep. Instead, he sat, elbows on the desk, dumbly listening to the transatlantic monologue as it unfolded.

"The board's given a great deal of thought to the claim. Sure it looks kosher on the outside, even the paperwork Phil went through at your place checks out. I can't argue that, but something here keeps nagging at me, and I've decided I'm not paying out twelve million bucks of AUIG's money on something I don't like the look of."

If Jack had been less dead, if he had not felt on the point of physical collapse, he'd have told Schumacher where to put his money. But it wasn't like that. Jack shrank back into his leather chair like a recalcitrant schoolboy. Whatever AUIG Bermuda had perpetrated against him with the connivance of Luke Hepton, had nothing directly to do with Walter Schumacher. The game was at an end, Jack was at an end, and he listened quietly as Schumacher rounded off his speech.

"You've put in twin claims for six million each," Schumacher sounded angry. "Frankly, David, it stinks, so I've decided I'm not going to give you the benefit of more than one claim. The diabetic's the one I'm buying this time. I'll need a lot more convincing before I pay out on the second. Don't get me wrong, I've got the additional six mil' ready and waiting. Show me why I should believe you and I will. In the meantime I'm arranging an electronic frequency transfer to your UK account."

"Thank you, Walter."

"Oh, and David. I really do want you to convince me, you hear? Because if I find you've been misbehaving, it won't just be the FBI you'll have on your tail."

"I hear you, Walter." Jack rang off, and sat back, totally drained. A squeezed out sponge. The time showed 4.05 p.m. He'd check out his banks in the UK and Liechtenstein in an hour, see if Walter had kept his word.

Four o'clock? Hell, it was deadline time, and no word from David Purdoe. Picking up the telephone, he dialled Danny's number. The auctioneer answered almost immediately.

"Danny. What's happening?"

"I've been trying to get hold of you for an hour. Your office said you were on a call and couldn't be interrupted. Mistry's on his way with the draft."

"All of it?"

"Bar my fee, yes."

"He's beyond the deadline, Danny. I said 4.00 p.m latest."

"So be a mensch, Jack, take his money."

Penny peeped around the door to Jack's office and whispered, "I've got someone on the other line who says he's you, David. He's got a Mr. Mistry with him, and he wants to know if he should accept a draft for four million and something pounds."

"Tell him yes, Penny. Tell him absolutely and positively, yes, yes, yes." Resisting, with the greatest difficulty, the temptation to stand up and cheer, Jack said to Danny, "It's done, Danny. The sites are finally sold." Then he sat quiet for a few seconds, minutes, he wasn't sure. He was swamped with relief, it was like witnessing a cancerous growth shrivel and die before his eyes.

"Are you still there, Jack?"

"Danny, I said no names. Godammit, who cares? Look, I wanted to say, I know I've been a bastard at times."

"At times? Jack, you've been a bastard all the time."

"I don't know how to thank you for all you've done my friend."

"Don't worry, I'll think of a way."

"You know something, you're beautiful."

"You know something? You could be right."

Penny looked in again and mouthed, "Urgent call," and Jack interrupted his conversation with Danny, said he'd call him Tuesday.

"Who is it, Penny."

"He says his name is Kim. He says he wants to speak to a Mr. Jack Gregory, and that that's you." She was looking puzzled as she spoke. "Do you have any idea what he's talking about?"

"I'll explain later. Put him on."

"Well, hello again, Mr. Gregory," the Chinese accent was unmistakeable. "It has been a long time since we spoke. You have really been quite ingenious, and most elusive, but I think I have calculated precisely what is happening.

"You have very nearly got away with a great deal of money, Mr. Gregory." There was a hint of something like admiration in the voice "Mr. Schumacher is most annoyed. He has had to give very swift instructions to withhold that six million EFT you were awaiting. Such a pity, all so cleverly contrived, and all so nearly successful. You must be feeling very disappointed."

Jack said nothing, there was nothing to say. Everything was out in the open now. Let the little man finish his speech, then Jack would pick up the car and drive back to Highview. He'd checked out of the Paddington hotel that morning vowing to return home in the evening no matter what the outcome of the day's events. Jack could hear the laugh, that familiar sinister echo, mocking, arrogant, triumphant, and then the line went dead and with it Jack's brief euphoria of a few moments ago.

Should Jack call the bank? It was after 5.00 p.m. He tried Barclays. Too late, the branch was closed. Was it worth trying the Liechtenstein bank? They were on the Continent, an hour ahead. Extracting his Casio digital diary, Jack turned it on and selected `tel'. Then he punched in `Wey', and `search,' and the name `Weyden, Georg Van Der', appeared on the little screen. One last try before calling it a day.

The telephone seemed to ring for an age. It was Van Der Weyden's private line and the man had probably left for the evening. Jack had started to reach forward to replace the receiver when he heard Van Der Weyden's voice. He sounded as though he was out of breath. "Georg? Is that you?"

"David?"

"Good to hear your voice. I thought I'd missed you."

"I don't usually work late on a Monday. How's life in the insurance world? Busy I presume, the account has been very active in the months since we first set it up."

"It's been a hectic period. Georg, I wonder if you could do me a favor."

"If I can."

"Can you get into the account? I've been awaiting a large settlement."

"Is this the twelve million dollars you mentioned to me?"

"Right."

"It's very late, I may not be able to find out at this time. Wait a moment."

"Oh, but Georg..." Jack said, but the manager was gone.

While Jack waited for him, Penny came in again, "I've got the man called Kim on the line."

"Tell him I've gone home."

"And Walter Schumacher called."

"If he calls back, I've gone home as well."

Van Der Weyden came back, "No, luck I'm afraid, Jack. Nothing of that magnitude."

"Damn," Jack sighed. "Damn, damn, damn." All too bloody late.

Penny looked in once more, "A Mr. Luke Hepton. He sounds very angry."

"Christ!" Jack pinched the bridge of his nose. This meant trouble. He debated whether to take the call. Still, he had the bargaining power he wanted. "I'm putting you on hold for one second, Georg," Jack said, and stabbed the `hold' button on the telephone.

"Put him through, Penny."

Luke Hepton's voice came on the line, it was soft and serpentine. "So, Mr. David, Jack Gregory, Purdoe, we gotcha at last. You been real smart, but not quite smart enough. I told you not to mess with the big boys, little man. We told Schumacher to stop the EFT. Now you got nuthin'."

He laughed, a rasping sound like a file hacking against metal. "Y'all fouled up, son. Better luck next time. 'Cept, they ain't gonna be a next time." The tone dropped to a whisper. "We gonna keep an eye on you from now on. Got lotsa plans for you," he hissed. "Gonna have the Feds start extradition proceedings if need be." He hung up.

Resting his forehead in his hand, Jack swallowed; his throat was so dry it felt as though he were swallowing pine cones, and his pulse was racing again. God, he wanted out of this mess more than practically anything else in his life right now.

He waited until he felt calm enough to talk once more, then he opened the line to Liechtenstein again, "All right, Georg, sorry about the delay. Thank you for checking that out." Then as an after thought, he added, "Georg, you said, nothing of that magnitude? Did I hear you correctly?"

"That's right. There was an EFT from American Union Insurance Group in New York for six million dollars though. But that's not what you were asking me about, was it?"

"No, Georg, it's not what I was expecting at all, but it'll more than do."

"I'm delighted."

"Do you know when it came through?"

"I should think, about forty-five minutes ago."

"I'd been led to believe the instruction to put through the EFT had been countermanded in New York. It must have just squeezed by. Thanks again, Georg." Jack replaced the receiver and called Penny in.

Penny sat opposite Jack and crossed one leg over the other, placed her hands in her lap, and waited to hear what he had to say. Jack felt as if he'd just shed twenty years. Beaten at their own game, he thought, and closed his eyes briefly to savour the moment. His exhaustion gave way to mixed feelings of disbelief and ecstasy and he sat staring at Penny, grinning. Wanting to laugh, to shout, it's over. Over at last. He needed to collect his thoughts; there were one or two calls to be made, but first, "Penny."

She stared levelly at Jack, "May I ask something?"

"Fire away."

"Who is David Purdoe?"

"David Purdoe is my solicitor."

"And who then is Jack Gregory?"

"I am, Penny." Jack held up his hand before Penny could ask another question. "Wait a moment. Let me ask you something. How would you feel about running your own insurance company?"

She frowned, uncertain whether or not Jack was playing games with her, "I'd like it very much"

"Could you do it?"

"Of course. I've been running this business for months."

"How would you feel about buying Goldleaf from me?"

"Who are you?"

"I told you, I'm Jack Gregory, and this is my show."

"How much?" she stared back at him insolently.

"Seventy-five percent of super profits, assessed by an independent accountant and spread over a three year period."

Without pausing she said, "I'll give you twenty-five percent over five years, and you can retain forty-nine percent of your shares."

"Cheeky blighter," Jack said, smiling hugely, and extended his hand to her, "You'll do. I'll get the real David Purdoe to draw up the papers this week."

A moment later, Jack had his housekeeper on the line, "Mrs. Llewellyn? I'll be coming home this evening. Sorry it's such short notice."

"No matter, Mr. Gregory. It'll be lovely to 'ave you back. Maybe you can persuade Mrs. Gregory to come back home now as well. Anyway, I'll 'ave a hot meal waiting, and a large nail thing, or whatever it is you call that drink of yours."

Chapter 36

June 8, Tuesday

The curtains billowed slightly from the gentle breeze that filtered through the partially opened windows. On the ceiling, the light from the full moon made an open hand of white rays whose fingers moved in time with the undulating drapes. Jack lay on his back unable to sleep staring at the changing patterns over-head.

Next to him, Phyllida slept on her side, her face to him, the sound of her breathing soft and even. Her hair, red and gold in the moonlight, was fanned about the pillow. He was almost overwhelmed when they'd arrived home that afternoon. Dressed in a simple brown Dior jacket and pleated skirt, her hair loose and wild, Phyllida looked ravishing. She'd seemed pleased to see Jack, confident in herself yet somehow distant, or distracted all at the same time. He wasn't sure what it was about her he could discern, but he had his suspicions.

He shifted his posture slightly, but Phyllida remained undisturbed. The smell of her skin mingled with slight traces of the perfume she wore reminded Jack how badly he had missed her. Thank God she and the baby were safe where he could keep an eye on them. If anything had happened to them while they were alone in Paris, it would have been his own stupid arrogant fault.

Mr. and Mrs. Llewellyn had been waiting in tears to greet Phyllida and the baby. She'd prepared a banquet fit for royalty which Jack had consumed hungrily and Phyllida had picked at bravely. She simply wasn't hungry.

The baby asleep, they turned in early. In the knowledge that his impotence was a thing of the past, Jack wanted to hold Phyllida to him, to make love to her, to devour her. It was his moment of triumph after all and he wanted this to be his way of sharing it. But she demurred, said she was tired at the end of a long day and he let it go. There was still tomorrow and tomorrow and tomorrow. The nightmare was over, his judgement had been vindicated; it had been a test of his strength and ingenuity and he had won and managed to take back a little of what had been taken from them.

And then, before they'd gone to sleep she'd told him. She'd told him everything about what had followed Tom's death. About the contractions, about the abortion and about Poppy. She'd talked for over an hour, and the more she talked, the more he knew how much he loved her. She missed him, she said. She had let him down. She loved him more than she could ever say and never wanted to be separated from him again. She clung to him and he watched over her, caressed her cheek, stroked her hair. He reminded her they both had Harriette and she reminded him they had each other. Gradually she calmed down and drifted off to sleep.

And now, he should feel better in himself than he was. Stretching his folded arms behind his neck, he yawned and shifted his broad shoulders into a more comfortable position. He was tired, but restless. Glancing at the watch on his wrist he saw it was half past three. If he didn't drop off soon, he'd be past trying.

Still thinking about Phyllida's terrible loss and its effect on her, Jack slipped finally into an uneasy sleep. Once, he thought he partly woke to see a light showing under the bedroom door and along the vertical edge between it and the jamb, making a large letter `L', but it was just the same old worry dream he had before and he refused to let it drag him from the security of his delicious slumber.

Jack was disturbed by something in his sleep and shifted his position in bed. But it came again, like a scream. He pulled the blanket over his head and hunched his shoulders to shield himself against the dream. But the sound was still there. And yet again he seemed to hear it, just like a scream. Or an animal cry of anguish. He couldn't shut it out. Still weary. Desperately tired. Need to sleep. His eyes opened to the white glare of daylight shining throught the sheet over his head. He was surrounded by a cacophony of sound. Noise everywhere. Thudding, banging.

"Phyl?" he growled. "What's going on?" Receiving no reply, he frowned. Irritated. Levelling the back of his wrist with his line of vision he saw it was 10.00 a.m. He blinked away the sleep and sat up in bed, slouched forward. Something going on. He rubbed his eyes and shook his head to focus his mind on what he was hearing. What the hell was he hearing? And where was Phyllida?

Harriette. Jack held his breath. Please God, not Harriette. His bones and flesh were ice. He knew. Before he tore off the blankets. He knew. Before he raced from the room. He knew. Stomach fluttering, heartbeat going crazy. He knew.

From the baby's bedroom Jack could hear Phyllida screaming and the sound knifed into his head like a million razor blades. He wanted to run towards it, but the shock froze him to the spot. Then he was moving towards the door, but in a trance. At least he was trying to move towards the door, but Phyllida's screams were like a wall he couldn't penetrate. It was as if he were being physically punched backwards. His feet were welded to the ground, the soft pile of the carpet like a bed of nails boring into his soles. Vision unclear, brain not working properly, he was on the landing, the bannister drifting past him. Mrs. Llewellyn downstairs calling something he couldn't make out.

At the door to Harriette's room Jack witnessed his wife looking like a robot stamping her feet, one two, one two. Fixedly running her hands through her hair. Her movements jerky, machine like, dragging at her nightdress, running her hands through her hair again and clawing at the nightdress, which was fast tearing to shreds at her shoulders and breasts.

His bottom lip spouting blood where he'd bitten through it, Jack was crying, screaming, shrieking before he reached his wife. Falling to his knees he wrapped his arms around her thighs crushing his head against the flat of her stomach.

His chest in spasm, he was retching, hiccoughing, choking, "I'm sorry, Phyllida, I'm sorry. It's my fault, I know it's all my fault. What are we going to do, for God's sake what are we going to do? I can't stand it. I can't live without her, Phyl, I can't live without her. God, my baby, my baby!"

There was no need to read the note left on the tiny mattress, the empty cot said it all.

* * *

Detective Chief Inspector Gantry and his team were at the house for hours. In his late forties and with a soft spoken manner, Gantry asked repeatedly why Jack had not advised the police of his suspicions in regard to the events of the past months, and Jack replied alternately through his rage and his tears in a slurred and heavily sedated voice that there would have been no point. There was nothing to report and nothing to investigate.

Now Jack sat in the kitchen staring blankly ahead. The last comment he had made in response to the DCI's observations about the situation they faced was that there was little the police could tell him about kidnap and ransom he didn't already know. After that he'd let the tranquillisers do their job, allowing himself to lapse into an isolated silence.

Sitting next to her husband, her shoulder leaning against his, her similarly drugged mind a torment of conflicting emotions, the one thing of which Phyllida felt absolutely certain, the one idea she had to cling to, was that her baby would be returned unharmed only if they kept their heads and did as they were directed by the police, the kidnap and ransom team who had been summoned, and the kidnapper, their torturer.

She wanted Jack's comfort, wanted to hold him and have him hold her; but she was angry, furious. This should never have happened. It was his fault. What had possessed him to imagine he could win in this no win situation? They held all the trumps, Hepton and the Oriental man, they had done from the start. When Luke Hepton had been appointed liquidator of Central Reinsurance, Jack should have accepted defeat and come home as he originally planned to be with his family. His earnings from the insolvency practice would have been more than sufficient for the most ambitious of men. Central had been a challenge, no more. Jack had said it himself often enough: it wasn't the money he was interested in.

The fight back had been a challenge, too, one that Jack just could not resist. So he'd duped them out of six million dollars. So bloody what! Phyllida rested her head in her hands and closed her eyes, and so they had taken her baby.

Where was Harriette? Who was holding her? Were they being kind to her? Where had they told her she was being taken? Was she crying for her mummy? Had her nappies been changed? Had she been fed? Was she hungry? Would they know what to offer her to eat? She was off her milk at the moment, had a craving for fresh orange juice. And she was hungry all day. Phyllida planned to cook her a lamb chop with mashed potato, carrots and mushy peas, her favourite just now. Would they even begin to understand her baby's talk? All the mispronounced and half spoken words with bits left out everywhere.

Harriette's face was there all the time, laughing, crying, concentrating the way she did, her brows knit, when she was trying to make herself understood. Phyllida couldn't bear it, she was going mad. Physically exhausted with emotion and weary from the sedatives, her mind was still needle sharp and there was no escaping the torment, every second was like that first moment she'd discovered the baby was missing. The shock hit her again and again like the blows from a ramrod smashing into her chest. She was screaming and raging inside. Her cheeks hurt from crying. Looking up she saw Jack's unshaven face gazing at her, haunted, sunken and for a moment she hated him.

"I know it's my fault," he said. "I'm beyond insanity. Don't despise me, Phyllida."

Before Phyllida could reply, DCI Gantry came into the kitchen accompanied by an intense looking young man with puffy tired eyes and a pasty complexion suggestive of long hours worked under conditions of extreme pressure. The latter was introduced as Edwin Parr, senior negotiator with Risk Assessors Ltd. of Mayfair. The two men sat down opposite the desperate parents. Gantry, tall and slim with an almost aristocratic bearing and careworn face that betrayed the stresses of years in his profession; Parr, a shortish man who would not stand out in a crowd, an individual whose casual sports jacket and open neck shirt belied the business like approach he adopted.

For the next three hours Parr drained the couple of every morsel of information he could extract from them. Utterly persistent, he pushed them through every barrier of exhaustion, until, apparently done, he sat back and folded his arms and contemplated the wall beyond Jack and Phyllida's back.

Gantry listened without interruption to the whole interrogation. Once or twice he frowned and leaned forward as though about to intervene on behalf of the distracted parents, to plead with Parr to let them be, if only to give them pause for rest, but each time he thought better of it and left the younger man to his remorseless probing. And now he waited for Parr to say his piece.

"Well, Edwin?" Gantry asked pensively. "What do you think?"

"How blunt do you want me to be?" Parr said to Phyllida and Jack.

Extending his hand onto the table, his palm uppermost, Jack looked at Phyllida, the black craters of his eyes pleading with her, and she, slowly, with apparent reluctance moved her hand over his until their palms touched, and then clasped tightly, their grip making a double fist, she, suddenly turning to face her husband leaving go his hand and throwing her arms about his neck and clinging to him as though he too might be dragged from her.

Eventually she turned back to Parr, staring first at him and then unseeing at the cold cup of tea before her. There was silence in the room as though an announcement of some moment was imminent. Finally she said, "Tell me everything, I can't bear not to know."

Rubbing his chin speculatively with one hand, Parr said, "It's not good. Kidnapping of babies and very young children is something very much different from the abduction of adults. Children need special care and attention. To take them often implies that the kidnappers are after either of the following," Parr counted out the examples on his fingers, "First: Particularly callous and uncaring. If some sort of revenge is the motive, don't expect the child to survive. I'm sorry, but there may well be some element of retribution in this case. But whether it's Hepton's or that of this Chinese man, I don't know.

"Second: They may be desperate for the immediate response that taking infants is likely to engender in parents. Expect vast ransom demands. They'll almost certainly ask for the return of the six million you tricked AUIG out of and then seek much more if they think they can get it.

"Finally: I think the second alternative may be the most likely although it carries a strong element of the first."

Parr had been addressing Phyllida and Jack exclusively, his steel grey eyes flicking from one to the other apparently taking in their every physical response to his monologue as though assessing how much he could say, how far he could go. Now he turned his attention to include DCI Gantry.

"From what you both tell me, this is not just about money, despite the huge sums involved. I think what we're looking at here is a personal battle of wills. Mr. Gregory has refused to lie down or be cowed into submission. I'll tell you, in all truth, they have actually won, at least, that's how they should perceive it. But they don't. Nothing less than complete capitulation is what they want. Ergo, they see themselves as the losers in this. They've lost face. They want revenge and their money back. This case is special, we're looking at both alternatives one and two I'm afraid."

He paused for a long moment, and then faced Phyllida and Jack squarely before delivering his final salvo. "You've asked for the truth, I'll give it to you. I'm very sorry, but I do not think Harriette will be returned alive."

At the mention of Harriette's name in this context, Phyllida screamed like a scalded cat. She shook her head as though refusing to believe what she heard, and banged her fists uselessly on the table. The truth was more than she could bear. Like Jack's truth months ago, she hadn't really wanted to hear it, not like this. She wanted to hear that everything would be alright, that Mr. Parr would spell out the risks and costs and then get her baby back. She clung to Jack's hand, her nails digging into the back of it unaware that she had drawn blood.

Gantry said nothing; for all his experience and his debonair demeanour, he looked embarrassed. Perhaps deducing that his presence at that moment was not called for he excused himself on the grounds that he needed to ask the Llewellyns some questions.

Parr, studied Phyllida as though calculating whether to go on or not. In the event, he said nothing further.

Eventually Jack spoke, his voice old and cracked, "I hear what you say, Mr. Parr, but there's been no word. You could be wrong. There might still be a ransom demand in due course."

"There might," Parr agreed. "But somehow, I think not." He addressed Jack softly as if Phyllida might hear, although she was sitting as close to him as Jack was. "Did DCI Gantry show you this?" He held up a piece of paper.

"Wasn't that left in the baby's cot?" Jack looked quizzically at Phyllida who shrugged with an air of hopelessness. "I gave it to Gantry when he arrived," she whispered. "I couldn't bear to look at it."

"Do you know what it says?" Parr enquired of them both as he straightened out the note on the table. They shook their heads and then both read the note that Parr had turned around for them to see. It ran:

Jack and Phyl would like to kill
The man who took their daughter.
But is it real or is it bluff,
And will they have the strength enough,
To help prevent her slaughter?
Ancient Mariner

Jack turned the note over in his hand. "Why's the note written in red ink? Was the bastard hoping to make more of an impact than he already has?"

Edwin Parr looked down for a moment avoiding Jack's scrutiny. Then, staring Jack straight in the face, he said softly, "I'm afraid, sir, it's not written in ink."

"NOOOOOOOOO!" Phyllida howled and grabbed Jack's hand, holding to her breast. "I can't bear it, I just can't bear it anymore. Make it go away, Jack. Please, darling, make it all go away."

"I see," Jack's tone was conversational, as though Phyllida weren't there. "He's toying with us. No matter what we're asked for or promised, the Chinaman's murdered Harriette already. He's like a cat playing with a mouse before killing it.

"Well, I'm going to kill this mutherfucker," he said softly. "I know where his boat is parked, and I'm going to kill him. Then I'm going for Hepton."

"Think what you're saying, Mr Gregory." Parr was speaking in quiet measured tones. "We don't know anything for certain. We'll still need to do DNA tests... You could jeopardise this whole operation. And if Gantry hears what you just said...."

"You do what you have to do, Mr Parr," Jack stared at Parr and raised his forefinger, "but don't even think about getting in my way. As for Gantry," Jack leaned forward towards Parr and spoke through a clenched jaw, "if he finds out what I have in mind, I shall know who to look for, shan't I."

Parr shrugged, "Very well, Mr Gregory. Have it your own way. But be it on your own foolish head."

As if seeking final affirmation, Jack looked at his wife, at her wild and unkempt hair, her swollen eyes and collapsed cheeks. He watched her as her lips drew back revealing her teeth in an animal snarl as she spat out,

"Do it then! Just do it! Find them and kill the fucking bastards."

Chapter 37

June 11, Friday

"Thanks for helping, Oscar. I appreciate it." Jack was slouched in an armchair in the cramped and ill-lit bedroom of a small hotel not far from the one that he and Oscar Nelhams had used when they gained entry to the premises of AUIG in Hamilton, Bermuda. There was no air conditioning and despite the open window the lack of any breeze meant that the place was sweltering. While Jack continually mopped his neck and scalp with a handkerchief, Nelhams, sitting on the edge of the bed opposite him, his elbows resting easily on his knees, looked the picture of cool urbanity. The bandage that bound his chest was clearly visible at the vee of his open neck casual shirt.

Forcing the exhaustion from his system, Jack dragged himself into an upright position, his hands gripping the sides of the chair, "Did you get the things I asked for?"

"Yes, I've got what you wanted. White Toyota parked outside the hotel with a couple of spare cans of petrol in the trunk. Keys." Nelhams reached into the top pocket of his shirt and extracted the car keys, which he handed to Jack. "Outboard motorboat tied where you asked in the harbour.

"Details of the Mariner so far as I could glean them from crew members," he went on. "There's a crew of about a dozen. Most luxury yacht crews get Saturday nights off to go ashore, if they're not needed by the owner. They mostly go in to Hamilton looking for girls, but there'll always be one or two left behind minding the shop." He passed over a sketch plan of the boat drawn on a sheet of crumpled A4, and Jack took it from him, casting an expert eye over it as he did so.

Nelhams reached behind the bed and produced a black Samsonite brief-case, which he rested on his knees. Clicking the twin locks outwards with his thumbs he lifted the lid and extracted one white and two brown medicine bottles. He gingerly deposited the brown bottles on the bedside table. The white one he waved to indicate it was different to the other two, and muttering, "Mickey Finn," placed it separately.

Next he withdrew two pairs of hancuffs. "Rigid, UK standard police issue," he advised Jack. "Slap them over a wrist and they click shut automatically. None better. Hope two pairs will be sufficient, they're all I could get hold of in the time. Keys," he said, holding up two pairs and laying them next to the cuffs on the bed.

Finally, Oscar extracted a leather shoulder holster and three menacing looking handguns and placed them on the bed. "Know how to use one of these?"

"Nope."

Oscar looked at Jack, wide eyed, "You mean to tell me I've brought along three semi-automatic weapons for you to choose from and you've never used one before."

"That's about the size of it," Jack said, sitting back and belligerently folding his arms across his chest

Shaking his head in resignation, Oscar said, "All right, Jack. I have to say again, this is absolute folly." Holding his hand up before Jack could interject, Oscar went on, "Okay, have it your own way. Take your pick."

Three black guns. Jack selected the nearest, read the inscription, Walther P99. Not heavy, he noted. Fitted the palm of the hand neatly. Oscar Nelhams picked one of the two remaining guns and nodded at Jack, "I'm holding a Sig Sauer 220. Swiss made. Very compact. Favored by undercover units and the SAS."

"Your crowd."

"Ex crowd."

"Okay," Jack nodded.

"The Walther you're holding is the latest James Bond. All three guns work much the same way. Sig Sauer carries a magazine of 12 or 13, 9 millimeter parebellum bullets, the Walther about the same. Load less than the max to reduce the chance of jamming. Walther has a wide ejection port. See?" Nelhams indicated a gap along the top of the gun. "Also lessens the possibility of jamming."

"What's parebellum?" Jack asked.

"God in heaven, Jack. Parabellum refers to copper jacketed lead bullets. The copper has a kinetic effect on entering the body, spreading itself around, the lead carries on until it's stopped by bone. Or not, as the case may be."

"Jesus," Jack breathed.

"You asked. We're playing for real here, Jack." Oscar paused then went on, describing how to slam in the magazine to the hand grip, how to decock and how to fire the gun. He didn't look at all happy. "Make your choice."

"Which would you choose?"

"I like this one," he said referring to the Sig Sauer. "It's a mass produced gun, but it does the job."

"Jams, you say."

"They all can. Sometimes."

"The other gun?" Jack glanced at the third gun on the bed.

"Heckler and Koch, HK 40. First class combat weapon. Every one is hand finished. Carries fifteen rounds."

"I'll stick with this one," Jack held up the Walther. "I like the wide ejection port."

Nelhams shrugged, "It's your choice."

"By the way. How noisy are these things?"

"They all have a distinctive signature, particularly at close quarters. Outside, and from a distance, it depends on wind direction. Might sound like a sharp crack and no more."

"Okay," Jack sighed. "That'll do me. What else?"

"I've kept an eye on the boat for the last three nights and I've made some discreet enquiries of the locals and also one or two crew members who frequent a particular bar in the harbour area nearby. I've also chased up my contacts in the States in regard to a couple of other things."

"Go on."

"The Chinese man comes ashore most nights around 11.30 p.m. He's taken in a stretch-limo to a private casino in the heart of Hamilton. The place is small, expensive and caters only to a very select clientele. He is brought back to the quayside on the dot of 4.00 a.m. every morning. Our Oriental gentleman is very much a creature of habit and routine."

"Does he go alone?"

"No. Your friend Hepton goes with him."

Jack nodded, "That all?"

"No. There's a girl with Hepton, a tall blonde, very striking."

Slumping back in the armchair, Jack stretched out his legs, "Damn! That complicates things."

"My contacts tell me her boyfriend, one David Sanderson, is a high flyer on the New York Times, I understand it's unlikely he knows she's here. Her name is Suzanne Olsen and she's of Scandinavian extraction. She models. You know, Vogue, Harpers, that sort of thing. What she's doing with Hepton is a mystery, but I should think he's got something on her. Either him, or the Chinese man. Whatever. I was surprised that Hepton was on board at all, I understand he owes our Chinese friend considerable sums of money. It's pretty common knowledge. I presume the girl is the draw. Hepton, it seems, is somewhat taken with her.

"I probably shouldn't ask, but what are you up to, Jack?"

"You shouldn't ask."

Nelhams sighed, but persevered, "When you asked me to get you nitric and sulphuric acid," he inclined his head towards the bottles on the bedside table, "I thought straightaway, nitro-cellulose."

Jack glanced half enquiringly in the other man's direction.

"Gun cotton," Nelhams explained.

"You were right, flash paper, as I've been told."

"Who're you planning to blow up? As if I couldn't guess. And with what?"

There was a long silence. Jack studied the backs of his nails then said, "It's probably better if I don't go into it."

Nelhams sighed again and, getting off the bed, went over to a chest of drawers on top of which was a bottle of White Horse and some glasses. "Drink?" he asked, pouring himself a liberal slug.

Jack shook his head, then changed his mind, "Okay."

Handing Jack a whisky, Nelhams said, "You can't have flown into Bermuda with a suitcase-full of explosives, Jack, so just what are you up to? The Mickey Finn in the case is enough to knock out a horse for a week. For God's sake remember to use it sparingly. A few drops are all that'll be required to keep a large man sleeping for twelve hours or more." Nelhams studied Jack for several seconds. He was frowning and looked agitated. "Well, Jack, tell me something about what's happening."

"Let's call it an experiment in simple creativity." Jack took a long draw on the tumbler and paused as the spirit burnt a line into the pit of his stomach. He felt the force of Nelhams's piercing blue eyes boring into his head but he ignored it.

"You know, you could easily get yourself killed."

Too right, Jack thought. Still Danny Jacobovits's friend, Richard Cane, of Cane Demolition and Controlled Explosives had been most helpful. Trust Danny to come up with the right man at the right time. Just as long as Jack got it 'all right on the night'. There'd be no time for dress rehearsals.

"If anyone knows anything about explosives, I do."

For a moment a feeling beyond fatigue swept over Jack. He was a thousand years old, shrivelled, broken, crushed. His eyeballs weighed like ballbearings in their sockets, his joints were seized, his muscles shot with pain. Then he thought about his daughter, saw the face he tried to banish from his thoughts, heard her laughter, felt her breath against his cheek and her heart against his own when she cuddled him, and he was strong again. He was raging, his fists clenched.

"They've taken Harriette." He shouldn't have said it, shouldn't have brought it all back. He wanted to be clear headed, not burning with hate. His own voice sounded distant and he dimly heard but did not discern Nelhams's astonished reply.

"Before you do anything crazy," Nelhams urged him softly, "remember, I really do have experience negotiating in kidnap and ransom situations."

"They've killed her. My little girl."

"You can never be certain. Killing hardly ever..."

"Believe me, I'm certain," Jack interrupted. "This is a personal thing. It's not just the money."

Nelhams poured Jack a fresh whisky and then sat down again, and sipped speculatively at his own, "Whatever you have in mind, I can't be a party to murder, Jack. No matter what my personal feelings may be in this."

"I'm not asking you to. I'm doing this alone." Jack tossed back the glass gulping the drink in one and went over to the chest of drawers for another. Resuming his seat, he said, "You've done all I needed. I'll do the rest." He hesitated then added, "There is one thing though. I don't want anything to happen to the girl you mentioned. The model. I'm moving tomorrow night, Saturday. Can you stop her going back to the boat when the other two return?"

Placing his tumbler on the floor in front of him, Nelhams ran his fingers through his hair and rubbed his temples with the tips of his fingers. "Possibly," he smiled slightly.

"Forget possiblies, Oscar. It has to be definite. I don't want anything to happen to her. So far as I'm aware she hasn't any part in this."

"I'll think of some pretext to get her boyfriend over from New York. I'll have him waiting for her on the quay."

"What if he won't come?"

"He will. Leave it to me. And if he won't," Nelhams saw that Jack was about to protest yet again, "I'll think of something else."

"I'll leave it to you. But even if you have to push her into the harbour, don't let her get back on the boat with the others. Do I make myself clear?"

"Yes, Jack, I understand. Only too well."

"Stop them all from getting back on the boat if you have to, and if you must, but once I've started there'll be no way I can reverse what's going to happen."

"I'll make absolutely certain the girl is safe." Nelhams rubbed his chin thoughtfully, then added softly, "But I will say it again, I cannot, and will not be a party to murder. Once I've done my part with the girl, you are on your own. And I mean, entirely on your own. Our professional relationship comes to an end at that time, and you won't see or hear from me again."

"So be it," Jack sighed. "So be it."

* * *

June 12, Saturday

10.00 a.m. Jack stirred on the bed and then rolled over and sat up abruptly. He'd had a bad night and his temples throbbed. It had taken him until after 3.00 a.m. to drop off in the cloying humidity of the room, and when he had, his sleep was restless and troubled. Dragging the sheet aside he threw his legs over the side of the bed and sat with his head in his hands for several minutes. With Nelhams gone, Jack felt as isolated as a deepsea diver whose lifelines have been cut.

Working on autopilot, Jack opened his brief-case and extracted a jug which he filled with water from the tap at the hand basin in the tiny adjoining en suite shower room. He then plugged in a small element at a point close to the floor and dropped it into the jug to boil the water. In a matter of moments the smell of instant coffee permeated the room and Jack was busy.

From his case he now took metal cooking tongs, two metal bowls, a small hammer, six light bulbs, three light bulb sockets attached to lengths of wire flex, and a quantity of cotton wool. Checking in the case, he picked up two alarm clocks and held them to his ears to ensure they were both in working order. Satisfied, he returned them to the case, placing them next to a pair of batteries.

In a glance, he took in the other items in the case, pliers, further wiring, a spare element and some elastic bands together with a trio of four-foot lengths of strong cord all of which were looped into slipknots. He'd also brought a quantity of Mars bars to sustain him if he started to flag once things were under way.

Apart from the bed and bedside table, an armchair, wardrobe and the chest of drawers, the tiny room contained no other furniture. Working in the cramped surroundings, Jack boiled a second jug of water. Waiting for the water to start bubbling, he carefully unscrewed the tops of each of the two medicine bottles on the bedside table and, putting a large wad of cotton wool into the first of the two bowls, soaked it in a mixture of the two acids.

Saturday morning. When he was ready there'd be hours to kill. Reluctant to set foot outside any more than necessary, Jack would eat in the hotel restaurant, if the poky little room could be called that. No chance of a smoke here though, far too dangerous.

He drank more of the instant coffee, involuntarily curling his lip in distaste, and then using the tongs he slowly lifted the soaking cotton wool from the acid filled bowl and placed it into the jug of boiling water. After letting it stew for ten minutes he extracted the cotton wool from that jug and placed it into the second bowl where he left it to dry out. He then repeated the process with second and third wads of cotton wool.

Next Jack turned his attention to the light bulbs. It was necessary to break two of them without damaging the filaments. He slotted the first bulb into its socket letting the length of wire flex hang free. He'd brought six lights in case he made a mess of it. Remembering that bulbs had a habit of exploding when they were smashed, he wrapped one in a pillow case taken from his bed, and rested it on the floor before tapping it with the hammer. But he'd hit it too hard, and when he examined it the filament was wrecked. The second one went the same way. But he was luckier with the third and fourth whose filaments remained undamaged. That left two spare, maybe he should have brought more with him.

The cotton wool dry, Jack made a flat pad of the first wad and laid it on the bed. It was about the size of two open palms. He then placed the first of the broken bulbs on the surface of the cotton leaving the flex trailing behind it. Now came the hard part, and Jack, shoving his hands underneath the cotton wool brought them carefully together over the top of the bulb enclosing the filament without damaging it. In order to hold the whole thing in place, Jack took one of the elastic bands from his case and pulled it around the white pad doubling it as he did so. When he finished, the thing looked like a bandaged finger trailing wires. He repeated the process again without damaging the second exposed filament and was pleased that he still had the two extra bulbs in reserve. Not that there would be a second chance.

That was it, he thought, and neatly packed the two items in his brief-case. Then he glanced down at his hands. Cane, the explosives man, hadn't said anything about wearing gloves, but Jack noticed his palms were pink and itching from the acid. Probably been in too much of a hurry, he thought and washed his hands letting the cold water run over them for a long time.

No need to get dressed yet, Jack decided as he wandered around in his boxer shorts, but time for a shower and shave. Chucking the shorts on the bed he started the shower. Once he was soaped from head to foot he stood under the freezing jets, letting the water stream down his upturned face. Then he flopped back on the bed and slept.

When he awoke it was dark and for an instant he was disorientated, forgetting where he was. Then it all came back to him in a rush and as he thought about his daughter it was all he could do to stop himself crying aloud in anguish. Setting his jaw he denied himself the luxury of bereavement and brought his mind back to the present.

Christ, he thought, and checked his watch. It was 11.00 p.m., he must have been sleeping for hours. He was now tight for time. Swinging off the bed he grabbed one of the chocolate bars from his case and chewed through half of it before depositing what was left of it on the side table.

Then he slid into a pair of cream colour slacks, pulled on matching silk socks and slipped his feet into a pair of white and brown loafers. Next, a white shirt with a brown and cream patterned silk tie, which he left loose at the neck for the time being while he concentrated on fixing in place the shoulder holster Oscar had provided. Then he slipped the loaded Walther into its leather home.

Hoping he'd covered everything he hesitated for a moment, then remembered. Taking the two pairs if cuffs he hung them from the back of his trouser belt, securing them with their spring clips.

Finally he slipped a hip flask of whisky, laced with the Mickey Finn, Oscar provided, into his inside jacket pocket.

He was set. Quickly ducking into the bathroom, Jack damped his hair down on top of his skull and at the sides of his head and combed it back. A quick check in the mirror showed his eyes were still full of sleep, but otherwise he looked okay. Draping the lightweight brown sports jacket over his shoulders he picked up the brief-case, snapped it shut and left the room.

Now or never, he thought grimly as he chased downstairs towards the street. Now or never.

* * *

June 12, Saturday

It was midnight and something had clearly gone wrong. Pulling the car over to the curb by the harbour, Jack could see the stretch-limo Nelhams referred to; it should have left a half an hour ago. Outside the vehicle, the Chinese man and Hepton appeared to be involved in a heated discussion.

The girl didn't seem to be with them although Jack surmised she might have been in the vehicle already.

Winding down the car window, Jack strained to hear what was being said, but could only discern the Oriental making comments about not being prepared to wait any longer. Hepton countered with something about not being satisfied. It made no sense and Jack, frowning with anxiety at the altered timing and routine, could do no more than hang on in the hope that their regular schedule would be resumed. Eventually, the Chinese man throwing his hands up in what appeared to be a gesture of exasperation, climbed into the black limousine followed by Hepton and they drove off.

Deciding he would give it fifteen minutes before moving, Jack leaned back, the bulge of the gun digging into his chest, and prepared to wait, and then he noticed a folded scrap of paper he hadn't noticed before on the front passenger seat. He flipped the paper open with his thumb and saw it was a scribbled note:

Girl taken care of. Coast clear. Take care. O.N.

Crushing the paper in the palm of his hand, Jack breathed in relief. "Thanks, Oscar," he muttered.

The best way to avoid drawing attention to yourself is to go about what you're doing as if it's the most natural thing in the world. Don't look furtive, it only invites scrutiny. There were a number of people in the harbour area, no matter what the time of night. Climbing out of the car with the brief-case in hand, Jack opened the trunk and retrieved the two flat cans of petrol before locking the vehicle and, with one can in each hand and the brief-case under his arm, made for the spot on the quayside. If anyone had noticed him, Jack was unaware of it.

The boat was tied up where Jack had directed. Making two trips up and down the ladder, he was able to take first his case and then the two petrol cans with him. The outboard motor started first time. Untying the small boat, Jack steered it into the bay towards where the Mariner was moored. The water was flat calm and the slight breeze in the air, cooled Jack sufficiently for the sweat that had threatened to drench his back spoiling his appearance, to stop spreading.

Looking at the boat's outline illuminated in the light of the full moon, Jack was struck by the utter beauty of her. Built by Oceanco and designed by Gerhard Gilgenast, in profile she looked like a white arrowhead. At nearly fifty metres long, she'd normally carry a crew of ten or eleven. It would accommodate a similar number of guests in five sumptuous staterooms and would have cost the Oriental man in the region of ten million dollars. She would be equipped with every conceivable communications device from direct dial satellite telephone to fax machines, telex and radio telephone. Her twin 2000hp engines would propel her at a majestic fourteen knots.

Compared to Jack's boat, the Phyllida, designed by Feadship and built by Van Lent, with both guest accommodation and also crew of six, the Mariner was a monster. Seemed a pity to contemplate what Jack had in mind for her. But then, remembering everything that had transpired in the months since, culminating in the abduction of his daughter, Jack's face became taut with fury.

Approaching the stern of the Mariner, Jack tightened his tie, ran his fingers over his hair smoothing it into place and straightened his jacket. Then as two faces appeared over the rail, Jack cut the outboard motor and smiled up at the crewmembers. In snow white tee shirts, they both looked to be mid-thirty, one of them with gingery hair and pock marked skin, the other long faced, possibly Japanese was smooth shaven with shiny black hair. They appeared nonplussed by Jack's arrival and glanced at each other in surprise.

"The name's Hugh Kavanagh," Jack said, imbuing his tone with the finest of upper crust English accents. "I've a delivery for you." He held the brief-case aloft.

The two men stared back as though they'd not heard a word Jack said. Then the ginger-haired one spoke, his eyebrows raised in astonishment, "At this time of the night? You must be joking."

"No, actually I'm from Coutts bank in London, I'm charged with the task of delivering these papers urgently. They are expected. I know it's late, but I've been unable to get here earlier."

"The owner said nothing about any delivery."

"Oh, these are not for the owner, they're for a Mister Luke Hepton, the US attorney presently a guest of the owner. If you'd care to call him..."

"He's not aboard."

"Well the owner then."

"He's not aboard either."

"Well, Mister Hepton's colleague, Ms Suzanne Olsen," Jack ventured."

"She left hours ago."

Sighing with relief at the confirmation of Nelhams's note, Jack ploughed on, "I do need to leave these."

"Well, you can hand them up to us."

"I'm supposed to hand them over personally."

"I already told you..."

"I know, I know." Jack hesitated. "I suppose if I could be allowed to deposit the papers in Mr. Heptons quarters I should have fulfilled my brief."

The two crew looked at each other for a moment, and Jack held his breath. Eventually, shrugging in resignation the same one said, "Okay. I suppose it won't matter. Come aboard." The man pressed a button and the passarelle started its noiseless descent. Jack, using one of the oars, manoeuvred his boat towards it. Once there he tied up and climbed onto the lowered platform. Another press of the button and Jack started to ascend, brief-case in hand.

He was in a state of ice cold calm, every detail of his surroundings being magnified into crystal clarity. The minute scratches on the boat's hull, missed by crewmembers responsible for maintenance, the smell of the sea, the gentle touch of breeze that disturbed his clothes. He could even make out the sounds from the shore -- the hum of traffic, people talking, laughing, Latin music from some unknown source -- as though it were around and on top of him.

The crewmembers were both slightly taller than Jack, and evidently in good condition judging by the muscles bursting through their flimsy tee shirts. As they appraised him, Jack was aware that no matter how odd his sudden appearance, he looked and sounded convincingly well to do. Who else but a wealthy Englishman and a banker to boot would be crazy enough to turn up in the middle of a bay at half past midnight in a jacket and tie. The Japanese man bowed and said, "I think if you have a card you should perhaps leave it."

"Of course, no problem at all," Jack beamed as he undid his jacket apparently reaching into his inside pocket. The Walther fitted comfortingly into Jack's palm and he let his hand rest there for an instant before swinging it out and waving the point of the barrel under the noses of the two unsuspecting men.

The eyes of the Japanese man opened wide with fear and his lips parted slightly as if he were about to speak, but he remained mute with fear. His companion regarded Jack with mixed puzzlement and contempt, "You are of course joking."

"Unfortunately not, gentlemen." Jack pointed the gun directly at the throat of the ginger-haired one, holding it about two inches from his larynx. "Now if we agree to behave properly, we can all save ourselves a great deal of time and mess." His comments echoed in his head like the words of an actor addressing a monologue to an empty auditorium. Realising that if he let his concentration lapse for even an instant he would lose credibility, he fixed his mind on the faces of the crew.

Fishing to the back of his belt Jack extracted the first of the hand cuffs and tossed it to the ginger-haired one, "Slip these onto your friend's wrists, behind his back."

"What if I won't?" The man defied Jack who, unprepared for this challenge, and aware he must under no circumstances lose his advantage, brought the gun away from the man's neck and, pointing it into the air, squeezed the trigger. The report was deafening and nearly knocked Jack off his feet with shock. If there were anyone else on board this would surely bring them running.

"Move!" Jack roared. "Or I'll blow your fucking throat apart first, then his."

Shocked, the man clasped his hand to his neck as if he'd been shot and then pulled it away. Without another word he cuffed the Japanese man's hands behind him, the latter now gibbering unintelligibly, his face streaming with tears.

"Now you," Jack commanded, and the ginger-haired man obediently turned his back to him allowing Jack to slap the second set of cuffs over his wrists, securely behind his back.

Jack checked his watch, it was 1.00 a.m. "And now gentlemen, I think it's time for me to extended a little hospitality to you in my admittedly somewhat more modest accommodation." Jack inclined his head towards the motorboat he arrived in.

He was met by silence as the two men glanced at each other, uncomprehendingly.

"I want you both in that," Jack bellowed. "Now!"

"The passarelle?"

"The ladder." Exertion would add to the force of the Mickey Finn.

"But how will we climb down the ladder with our hands behind our backs?" The man's pocked marked skin had become blotchier about his cheeks and forehead, presumably brought on by his own fear.

"Carefully," Jack snapped, and watched as first the pock marked man, then the Japanese man made their way awkwardly down the ladder to where Jack's boat was bobbing.

It had taken about forty minutes for Jack to ensure they were both secured in his small craft from the time he'd first made his appearance on board. They'd both accepted the whisky with puzzled gratitude and were now unconscious. Hopefully, if Jack hadn't killed them, they'd sleep for some fourteen hours. Then he muttered to himself, "And now we go to work."

* * *

Without taking the time to check numbers, a quick glance had confirmed that the gas cylinders were located in a cupboard towards the stern of the main deck. They would be collected shortly. He had to move fast, it was now 2.15 a.m. It had taken two trips up and down the passarelle to bring the petrol cans on board and double check one of the two sleeping sailors who appeared to be stirring. He was now down in the engine room, one of the fuel containers stashed in a corner, the other still on the main deck.

Kneeling down, Jack flipped open the catches of the Samsonite and, laying it flat on the floor, lifted the lid. First he extracted one of the light bulbs wrapped in gun cotton. Opening the hatch to the bilges he considered secreting the bulb in it, but then decided against it. The space in the engine room was sufficiently confined for his purposes and he simply laid the padded bulb on the floor and extended the wires in a swallow's tail behind it.

Next he took an alarm clock, one of the batteries and some lengths of wire from the brief-case. Setting the large square battery upright on the floor he twisted the exposed end of one of the measures of wire flex around one of its terminals before attaching the other exposed end, in a simple knot, to one of the wires trailing from the light bulb. He now had a single straight connection between the battery and the bulb, but not a complete circuit.

With a second length of flex in hand Jack made a connection between the second of the two wires running from the light bulb and the hour hand of the alarm clock whose glass face he had earlier removed. Continuing with great care so not to damage it Jack ran a length of wiring from the minute hand of the alarm clock straight to the battery, though without yet attaching it to the other terminal. Once hooked up to that terminal a complete circuit would be made: battery to light bulb, light bulb to hour hand of clock, minute hand of clock back to battery.

Although the two alarm clocks had run down, Jack would neither wind them nor make the final connection of the last of the wiring to the second terminal of the battery until he was ready to flee the boat. At that time he would set each of the clocks to 11.30, allowing thirty minutes before the two hands met at twelve finally completing the circuit and the job in hand.

Pausing for a moment Jack checked his watch: it was 2.45 a.m. Time seemed to be running away. He had just forty-five minutes to complete the job and get free of the boat if he were to allow himself a full half-hour before everything went up. For a moment his pulse raced at the thought of his failing to execute the task properly or in time, but he dismissed the idea.

Satisfied that he had set up the first of his timers, Jack ran back up the stairs to the main deck where he dropped his brief-case before making his way towards the stern. Usually a boat of this size could be expected to carry three or four cylinders of Calor gas. When Jack opened the cupboard door again he was confronted with eight cylinders and he whistled softly between his teeth.

The cylinders were waist high and weighed thirty-two kilograms each. Hefting two at a time and carrying them like a child across his arms, Jack chased back down to the engine room with two, and then two more. Despite the air-conditioning onboard, Jack began to perspire heavily, his shirt and the legs of his trousers stuck to him.

The journey from the stern of the main deck down a flight to the lower deck and then forward to the prow with two and then two more gas cylinders took longer than anticipated because of the distance involved and because it was necessary to go through several doors from one part of the crew's quarters to another before he got as far forward as the could go. Another storage room, little more than a walk-in cupboard was where he left the next four cylinders, propped against the wall.

3.00 a.m. Thirty minutes to go. Racing back to the main deck where he left his Samsonite, Jack retrieved both it and the final can of fuel, then dashed back down and forward through the crew's quarters to where the second set of four cylinders had been deposited. Taking the stairs too quickly he slipped and fell heavily twisting his knee and ankle. Groaning with the pain, he realised he was losing precious time as he inspected the damage. The fall was bad enough to have caused a break, but for once fate didn't conspire against him. He was breathing heavily though, and his heart, hammering from the exertion, only served to intensify his increasing tension.

Because his hands were wringing with perspiration he fumbled the second set of connections, cursing under his breath when, in his haste, he nearly tore off one of the clock hands.

Nearly there. It was now 3.35 a.m. He was already short of time, overrunning his calculated agenda. He should have been off the boat five minutes ago. If the Oriental kept to his schedule, he would be back on the quay in twenty-five minutes. Jack still had to set the two timers, motor back to shore leaving the two unconscious sailors to sleep it off and, ideally be clear of the quay in the little time left. Now a seeming impossibility.

Jack's limbs were leaden and he remembered he'd hardly eaten. Grabbing another Mars bar, he chewed as he worked on, completing the second set of connections. Then he picked up the alarm clock and checked his own watch. It was 3.48 a.m. He had to rethink it. If the Chinese man came back on time, he would get back on the boat by about 4.15 a.m latest. If Jack set the clock too far forward, the man might have time to discover the device and either disconnect it, or otherwise abandon ship. Too soon, and the device might explode before he and Hepton were on board.

3.50 a.m. Jack made his decision and set the clock at five minutes past eleven and hooked up the trailing wire to the second battery terminal completing the circuit. The two hands would cross in fifty-five minutes when they met on the twelve by which time it would be 4.45 a.m., thus allowing a forty-five minute overrun on an evening that had already started half an hour late. If the Chinese man got back at the usual time, ten minutes hence, Jack was done for.

He paused for a moment, undecided again, wondered whether he should reset the clock. The Oriental was set in his ways, a creature of habit; he would want to return at the usual hour. Hepton would want to stay on, gamble a little longer, make up for the time lost by their late start. They would argue, his host would make an allowance. Rubbing his temples with the fingers and thumb of one hand in a torment of indecision, Jack finally wound on the minute hand of the clock by five minutes. Then, shaking his head, he put it back to the original position of five past eleven.

The upset schedule was making guesswork, which had been difficult before, now quite impossible. Everything would go up at 4.45 a.m., as long as they weren't on the quay already. Jack wouldn't change his mind again. This time he was committed.

3.55 a.m. Christ, he had to move. Grabbing the petrol can, Jack unscrewed the top and swilled out the contents letting petrol splash over the Calor gas cylinders and throughout the interior of the cupboard and over the floor and walls, with the remainder poured into the cabin behind him. Then he carefully unscrewed one of the valves at the top of a cylinder. With a long sigh gas started to escape. Repeating the action with the other three cylinders it was clear that the whole of the crew's quarters on the lower deck would soon be thick with fumes.

In the tight area, the mixed aroma of fuel and gas was immediately overpowering and Jack, his eyes watering, nose and mouth full of the smell and metallic taste of it, realised he was now inhabiting a live time bomb, and he dashed back up onto the main deck, where he peered towards the shore to see if he could spot the black limo. Seeing nothing, he tore down to the engine room for the final preparations. It was now 4.02 a.m. If they were back, they'd see him leaving the boat and smell a rat. Too late to stop now or change direction, Jack hooked up the clock, hands slippery and shaking, setting it at seventeen minutes past eleven. It would go in forty-three minutes, at 4.45 a.m, the same time as the clock in the crew's quarters.

Finally splashing petrol all around as before and opening the valves at the head of each cylinder, Jack stuffed the remaining loose measures of wire flex into the Samsonite and thought about a fast departure. Gradually beginning to recognise the pain that was knifing through his ankle, Jack limped tortuously up the steps.

In the open, he paused for only an instant, his chest heaving, his breath now coming in sobs. 4.10 a.m. Allow five minutes to be well away from the boat, and ten minutes to get to shore. He'd be there at 4.25 a.m, just five minutes before he guessed, and hoped, Hepton and the Mariner's owner would be returning. That is, if they weren't already in the tender heading for the boat. Then another fifteen minutes before the thing blew. Bloody ridiculous, it simply wouldn't happen that way. Too many things to go wrong, too many assumptions made. All a futile effort.

The jolt that passed through Jack's body was like a ten thousand volt electric shock. The man was every bit of six feet six inches tall with the chest and shoulders of a bull elephant. He was naked from the waist up to his pink shaven head. The tiny sleep filled eyes that stared at Jack were watery blue, the pupils pin points of madness. In his left hand he carried a three-foot length of metal with a forked flattened tip like a crow bar.

His accent was Continental, Austrian or German. "What are you doing?" The whispered enquiry through clenched teeth was polite. "What game do you play?"

Jack dropped the brief-case and his hand went to the gun at his shoulder in the same instant as the sailor raised the crow bar above his head. The action was so swift, Jack had little time to counter, his responses slowed by hunger, exhaustion and pain. Dredging some sort of reaction from his collapsing frame Jack swung lazily to one side bringing the gun up as he did so. A squeeze of the trigger and the Walther blasted as the lump of iron descended with a whistling noise just missing the top of Jack's head and knocking the gun from his grasp. It skittered over the side of the boat and plopped harmlessly in the sea. Jack was defenceless against the giant.

The iron bar was raised a second time, and again Jack was able to anticipate its trajectory, swinging languorously the other way. He screamed, the inside of his skull exploding in a cascade of white and red stars as the metal tore into his face at the side of his nose, smashing it and his cheek bone. Spitting blood, Jack lurched against the cabin wall and slipped to one knee. Through the haze of blood he saw the man's arm was raised again and with the knowledge of his own imminent death, Jack swung his fist hard into the man's gut. The sailor grunted and the instant of hesitation gave Jack the chance to drag himself to his feet.

Putting the whole of his weight behind the blow, Jack buried his knuckles in the man's solar plexus a second time hearing him grunt once more as the iron bar crashed down across Jack's spine. Jack screamed again and straightened up in agony as the man, under the force of Jack's blow, began to bend at the waist like a great tree toppling. As the shaven head slumped level with Jack's waist, he drew his knee up hard under it as though he were kicking a football, catching the man full in the face.

The sound of bone crunching told Jack he'd inflicted much the same damage on the sailor as he'd suffered himself a moment before. As the sailor lurched beneath him, through vision that was blurring into unconsciousness, Jack now brought the heel of his hand down on the back of the sailor's neck with the last of the force he could muster, and the man slid onto the deck where he lay like a sack of coal.

He'd been unconscious, for how long he had no idea, but when he came to, Jack was lying next to the fallen crewman. Jack's face and head were cupped in palms of fire, his back swollen and cricked as though it were broken. Afraid to look at the time, he hauled himself unsteadily to his feet. Tempted to leave the man where he lay, Jack reminded himself his targets had been and still were Hepton and the Oriental.

Taking in the bulk of the insensate individual on the deck, Jack became aware of the enormity of his task. It was impossible to guess at the sailor's weight, but it was probably in the region of two hundred and seventy-five pounds. Lifting him off the deck would be a virtual impossibility, even if Jack were in a fit state.

Grabbing the man under the armpits, Jack knelt next to him and concentrated the whole of his being on what he had in mind, at the same time ignoring the body that shrieked its pain at him. Straightening his leg, he shoved it under the man's torso, then bent it at the knee lifting him into the same position across his thigh. He then forced his shoulder under the sailor, his arm up and around the man's waist, and tried to get to his feet. It was near impossible. There'd be little time left, there might be no time left at all, and Jack with a weight lifter's roar of defiance forced himself into a standing position. The ankle threatening to give way beneath him, he then shuffled towards the side of the boat where he manoeuvred the sailor until he was draped over the edge, feet first.

His eyes were smarting with the tears of his agony, his mouth and cheek dripped blood onto his shirt, and his face was swelling up like a balloon. Jack eased the man further and further over the side, until, hanging on to his wrists with what strength he had left, Jack finally let him drop towards the motor-boat. The clump that followed suggested he had not fallen in the water, and when Jack looked over the rail he saw that the sailor had crashed face down against the other two, one of his arms trailing in the sea.

Resisting the temptation to check the time, Jack retrieved his jacket from the saloon, picked up the Samsonite and climbed down into the motor-boat. Its engine kicked into life at the third attempt, and Jack let go the mooring and chugged away from the Mariner towards the shore. The cool breeze was reviving.

The first two crewmen were breathing evenly, the third was beginning to move and twitch slightly as though he might regain consciousness at any moment, and Jack, fumbling in the brief-case, fished out the white medicine bottle, forced the sailor's mouth open and let several drops of Micky Finn settle on his tongue. In a second his breathing had become as regular as the others and Jack concentrated on steering back to the quayside.

The three sailors were still unconscious when Jack tied up. He unlocked their handcuffs and left them. When he staggered on to the quay, Jack saw no sign of anyone in the vicinity and he quickly made for the car. Once behind the wheel he felt deathly cold, his sweat-soaked clothes felt like a clammy shroud, and his jaw began shaking and his teeth chattered with shock.

Starting the engine, Jack put the car's heater on full. Time to glance at the time. It was 4.28 a.m. In the rear view mirror Jack saw the nose of the black limo come into the harbour area, and he shifted the gear into drive, moved away from the harbour area and cruised back to his hotel. Best not to be seen anywhere near the quay. Police might be doing their rounds at any time too.

There was no one at the hotel's tiny lobby to see the state he was in and Jack limped to his room where he deposited the brief-case on the chest of drawers and fell onto the bed. Lifting his wrist he checked the time. It was 4.45 a.m. The yacht should have blown by now, but there was no sound of explosion.

There was a partial view of the bay from his hotel window; part of the stern of the Mariner was visible from Jack's vantage point. He dragged himself off the bed and stared out at the first signs of dawn all the same.

4.50 a.m. Nothing. The timing couldn't be that far out. Even a cheap alarm clock wouldn't lose five minutes in an hour. They'd discovered it. He'd never leave the island alive. All wasted effort.

The sudden sound was numbing. Awe-inspiring. Beyond anything he'd ever heard, seen or imagined. KAKA, KAKA BOOOOM, it hiccupped as a mountain range of flame illuminated the pink-grey sunrise.

Chapter 38

June 13, Sunday

Jack dozed fitfully on the flight back, hardly even aware of a refuelling stop, and now sat in the Jaguar in Heathrow's long term car park, his head resting against the steering wheel, his body clammy cold and shaking with shock. Having effected the best he could with his appearance using bandages and plasters he'd made it onto the aircraft with his heart in his mouth. There were police everywhere in the airport, looking for what, they probably didn't know. The three sailors should still have been unconscious when Jack's flight took off, apparently sleeping off a massive binge and in the case of one of them, what would look like the effects of a fight ashore, Jack hoped.

And now he was practically home, having achieved nothing. Everything was futility. He hadn't risked any contact with home since he'd left.

Slipping into the Jaguar at the airport and catching sight of his face in the rear view mirror he was aghast at what he saw. The makeshift plaster and bandages had worked their way off during the flight and he'd not bothered to replace them. No wonder he received some odd looks. The right side of his face was puffed up like a football the colour of plum topped with a jagged vertical streak of black clotted blood. His lips were likewise swollen and his right eye, which was almost closed, showed crimson through the slit where there should have been white. Several of his teeth felt loose.

Leaning back he winced as he became aware of the bruises across his spine where he'd been struck with the crowbar. He smiled wryly as it occurred to him his ankle was holding up well. Everything hurt. If he moved so much as a finger he suffered agony somewhere in his body. He needed to sleep, a thousand years wouldn't be enough. Turning the key in the ignition he heard the car's big engine fire into life first time, the familiar ringing tone followed by a roar as Jack caressed the accelerator.

The drive home took no more than forty minutes. As he entered the drive he was struck by the beauty of the summer colours in the approaching twilight. A rabbit ran across his path, lolloping into the trees to his left. He should have called from the car to say he was on his way, but he didn't want to hear Phyllida's grief over the phone. The plane had come in at eleven a.m. and he'd cleared customs a little after noon.

The car crunched on the gravel and he brought it to a halt in front of the big house. Climbing out of the vehicle he was aware he was sick with fatigue. The car door swung shut with a clunk, and Jack dragged his feet through the pebbles on the drive making slowly for his own front door while fumbling with his keychain for his doorkey.

His mind was slipping into torpor and he was unaware of the door in front of him being opened, although he walked through it and found himself in the hall. Out of focus he saw Mrs. Llewellyn at the back of the hallway. She was grinning, or perhaps leering at him. He wasn't sure, but he wasn't thinking clearly.

Gliding elegantly past Mrs. Llewellyn and towards Jack was a tall lovely woman dressed in a coral blouse and navy slacks. Her thick hair hung loose to her shoulders and she too was smiling, although her smile became suddenly a look of concern as her brow creased with worry. She was saying something to him, but Jack could not discern the words.

In his dream a small child in a red and blue dress came running towards him, her arms outstretched. She cried, "Dada, Dada," and then questioningly as she stared up at the ruined face, "Dada?"

And as the trance overtook him, its cruel perjury a retribution for his arrogant and misguided behaviour, he dropped to his knees and felt the chubby arms tighten around his neck, heard the delicious tinkle of baby laughter, felt the sweet breath in his face, sensed the tiny heartbeat against his own.

Until they had taken Harriette, he hadn't cried since he was a boy. Now he was sobbing, his shoulders heaving, his face running with his tears. Phyllida was crying too as she knelt next to him and Harriette, hugging them both. "Jack, Jack, for God's sake darling, your face. What's happened to your face?"

But her words were slipping into the far reaches of his awareness. He was too tired to answer, too tired to listen, too tired to move.

Epilogue

June 16, Wednesday

Mr. Llewellyn had hauled him up into his bedroom. Jack, awakened in the middle of the afternoon three days later, had had to take a long hard look around his room before it had sunk in that his homecoming had not been a fantasy. Sitting in a corner close to the window, her hair tied in a bow in the nape of her neck, a pile of knitting in her lap, needles clicking busily, was the same lovely lady he'd seen when he'd entered the house on Sunday evening. She wore a white polo neck sweater and black culottes. She was no fantasy.

Still lying on his back, Jack touched his face gingerly. The movement sent a stream of pain cascading down his spine and between his shoulder blades. He grunted under his breath. The nose and cheek were where he'd left them, and whilst some of the swelling had diminished and there was no immediate pain, he would need hospital treatment to set the bones.

Seeing his movement Phyllida glanced over at her husband, "How are you feeling, darling?"

"Apart from the bumps, no words could describe it right now. Home! Need I say more?"

"The face?" She looked worried.

"It'll do," he said tentatively exploring the area around his right eye. "I nearly didn't make it off the boat, you know. It was pretty tight."

"Do you want to tell me about it?"

"Later, when I've got myself together."

"Doctor wouldn't let me disturb you," she said, putting down her knitting and coming over to the bed. "But I'll drive you to the hospital as soon as you're ready. Take a shower and come downstairs. I've got something that might interest you."

"Phyllida!" Jack sat up in bed, wincing at the pain that racked his body. "Harriette's home. How? When?" He closed his eyes, "And... and, Phyllida I have to tell you something." He swallowed hard and stared, half vacantly, ahead. Then he turned to his wife and began, "I've...." He looked down for a moment, unable to face her. Then he started again, his voice barely a whisper, "I've killed two men." He took a deep breath, and this time he looked at her, full on, "You know who; Hepton and the Chinese man."

"Shush, my love." She put a finger to her lips.

"But, Phyl, don't you see?" His words were distorted through the puffy lips.

"Shower first, then we'll talk."

"I've done some lunatic, crazy, things."

"Haven't we all," she sighed, and left Jack by himself.

Ensuring the water didn't touch his bruised and broken face, Jack stood under the steaming jets for half an hour before donning a soft towelling robe and joining Phyllida in the drawing room. God, it felt good to be home. How long, he wondered before the police started knocking at the door.

He sat back slowly in the armchair feeling it support him as he came to rest his injured spine against it. Phyllida, looking grave, sat on the pouffe at his feet, her arms around her knees. On the coffee table next to him was a faxed copy of a newspaper extract, a parcel the size of a wine bottle, and by the side of it two whisky tumblers. From the kitchen chatting animatedly to Mrs. Llewellyn, came the singsong of his daughter's voice.

A moment later, Harriette came waddling into the sitting room pushing a green plastic toy lawnmower. It made a series of clickety clicking noises and blew a stream of bubbles all over the place. She looked at Jack and gave him a cheeky grin. Then she stopped what she was doing and came to stand in front of her father whom she scrutinised for several seconds as if to reassure herself it was really him. With a shriek of pleasure she turned her attention back to the toy, and Jack in turn felt his heart lurch with the love of her. From inside the kitchen Jack could hear Mrs. Llewellyn calling Harriette back and exhorting her not to make a mess with the soap bubbles all over her nice clean house.

"Okay, Phyl, let's hear the worst," said Jack. "And the best. First Harriette. When was she returned?"

"Jack, she was brought back, and left outside the front door in a pushchair, well and happy, on Sunday morning."

"What!"

"That's right."

Calculating in his head the time since the explosion, Jack said, "But that's impossible. I was certain Harriette was dead. I went out there to kill those, scum. I did kill them. In that case," he wondered aloud, "who can have given the order to return her?"

"Think about it, Jack" Phyllida replied.

Rubbing his temples, Jack, his voice rising said, "God in heaven, have I killed two men or not?"

"Not exactly, darling."

"What do you mean, Phyl, for crying out loud; this is no time for jokes."

"I'm not joking. Listen, on Monday, the day after you got back, I got a call from a Mr. Nelhams. He kindly faxed through an extract from a Bermuda newspaper of the same day." Phyllida nodded towards the fax on the coffee table.

"He must still be out there," Jack muttered. "Tell me about the paper."

"It referred to the early morning blowing up of the Mariner, a sixty metre luxury yacht belonging to an Oriental financier."

"Is that all? What about casualties?"

"There were none, apparently; apart from three sailors, found rather the worse for wear, in a motor boat in the harbour." Phyllida raised her eyebrows quizzically at her husband as though expecting an explanation.

"But I saw the black limo arrive back at the harbour at 4.30 a.m."

Ignoring the remark Phyllida went on, "In a separate but related article it was reported that a US attorney, a Mr. Luke Hepton, believed to be a guest of the owner of the Mariner was found murdered outside Hamilton. Earlier the two men had been seen quarrelling furiously. Witnesses said they'd heard, money, and something about a missing man called Dimitriou being mentioned. Hepton's body was discovered in a gutter with the back of his head sliced open."

"Wow!" Jack paused, "The bastard's actually dead then, and I'm not involved. So, that means I only killed the one then. The Chinaman. God, I'm still in big trouble."

"Possibly."

"What do you mean possibly? I told you, I saw his car coming back to the harbour."

"Did you actually see him getting out of it?" Phyllida asked.

"No, but..."

"Well, I don't know about any car, but I think you should look at this." Phyllida reached into the open top of the parcel and handed Jack a typed note.

"What the hell is this?" Jack asked, holding the piece of paper aloft. "And when did that parcel arrive?"

"It was delivered yesterday. It was post-marked Monday of this week."

Casting an eye over the typed note, Jack muttered, "Good God! It's from him. The Chinaman's not dead after all. I am completely free." He threw his arms outwards in a gesture of triumph ignoring the pain in his back. "I don't believe it, Phyl, I'm actually in the clear." Jack put his head in his hands; it was the end of the nightmare and the sensation was a shuddering thrill. He was being bathed in champagne, showered in brandy, wrapped in alpaca. The feeling was heaven; it was paradise; it was practically aphrodisiac.

"Jack," Phyllida looked at her husband speculatively, then went on as he glanced up. "Maybe I'm missing the point, but can you tell me something now? Why, after everything that's happened, was Harriette brought home?"

"Because she wasn't the target, Phyl. I was. Don't you see? She was a bargaining chip, nothing more. With Hepton dead, the Chinaman no longer had a patron. Remember, our friend is a professional; he kills for money, not thrills. And, judging by what I've seen of Hepton, he must have owed money to him."

"And so, my sweet, you really are totally in the clear." Reaching towards him, Phyllida brushed her husband's bruised and lumpy lips ever so lightly with her own.

"But there's still the police over here to deal with," he said.

"The police were here for hours on Monday waiting for your return."

"Oh, Christ," he groaned.

"I wouldn't worry. There've been no contacts from Bermudian police from what I could gather. No formal complaints from any Eastern gentlemen about a boat being blown up."

"Hardly surprising."

"And Harriette is home. As far as our police are concerned, apart from a few loose ends, they said they consider the matter effectively closed."

"Wonderful," he sighed. Then a thought occurred to him, "With Hepton dead, I wonder who'll take over as liquidator of Central?"

"Business, Jack? Now?"

"Don't worry," he smiled. "It'll wait." Jack pursed his lips thoughtfully, "At least, until tomorrow. I'll talk to David Purdoe. There's a good chance we could recover some more of the missing millions"

"Really?"

"Truly. No one's going to appoint another Hepton. I've got the evidence to throw out AUIG's ridiculous claim...." He stopped talking and smiled.

"The old buccaneer," murmured Phyllida.

"You're right about old," Jack said ruefully. And hardly a buccaneer, he thought. More, a very tired, very foolish middle-aged businessman.

They sat unspeaking for several moments. Then, Phyllida broke the silence. "Jack?" She asked.

He looked enquiringly at his wife.

"Can I ask you something?"

"Go ahead."

"Was it a very big bang?"

Jack's mouth slowly hinged open in mock horror. "Phyllida!" He remonstrated sternly.

"Well! Was it?" She'd got up, was standing in front of him with her head on one side, her hands on her hips like a little girl.

He hesitated for several seconds; then, beginning to grin as far as his face would allow, he said simply, "Atomic."

"Really?" She sat down again.

"It was like Krakatoa. The volume was unreal. My ears hurt with the noise. It sounded as if the whole of Hamilton was going up. They must have heard it in Paris, Moscow and New York." He sat quietly for a while. "I was deranged."

"Yes."

"We got Harriette back," he said hesitantly.

"Yes."

"When I left here last week he knew I'd never stop. Never. The Chinaman." Jack sat idly for a time staring at nothing in particular, tapping his thumbnail against his teeth. "I'm a professional man," he said at last, as though the knowledge had just struck him. He spread his hands out in wonderment, "I blew up a boat." Jack stared at his wife as if he might find an answer in her eyes to an unspoken question.

"You were both obsessed. He was calculating. You were insane." Phyllida gazed back at her husband, a grin playing about the corners of her mouth, "I love you, Jack Gregory."

"I might have failed. Botched everything. Then what?"

"Why push your luck, darling? You won. Don't question it."

Jack leaned forward and peered into the package and frowned at his wife, "Hey, what's in the parcel anyway?"

Getting up off the pouffe, Phyllida reached in to the top of the package and withdrew a bottle of Johnnie Walker, black label, which she placed ceremoniously on the coffee table behind the two whisky glasses.

"A bottle of whisky?" Jack asked, his attention diverted for a long moment by the bubbles his daughter was spreading all over the room. He gazed at the little one as though she was a gift from Heaven, then looked back at his wife again.

Phyllida, a thoughtful look on her face, reached into the brown paper and pulled a second bottle slowly from the open top of the parcel and placed it next to the whisky bottle. This time the label read, Drambuie.

Jack grinned up at her uncertainly, "Oh, I get it. But no, surely not. It can't really be." He glanced again at the note that had accompanied the parcel. "It's utterly bizarre. I mean, the man's mad. Have you read this?"

Without answering him, Phyllida extracted the last item from the package, a six-inch length of metal, and laid it on the table, too. It was pointed at one end with a flattened round head at the other. And it was red brown with corrosion.

"It's not possible," he sounded incredulous, glanced down at the bottles on display, the rusty nail in front of them and then back at the paper in his hand again. "A murderer with a sense of humour?" Jack shook his head as he indicated the contents of the note to his wife. "It's hysterical. He's called it a day, as I just said, but in rhyme, for God's sake."

Phyllida said, "Well let's be serious for a moment, shall we, darling? I really think a couple of drinks are called for. After all, your Chinese friend has offered you a toast. Wouldn't you agree? Of course, you would," she answered for him. "Shall I do the honours?"

And as Phyllida, a broad smile on her face, poured a couple of the silky smooth cocktails for them both, Jack, in his own Nirvana, read once more from the note that had been delivered with the bottles as though to satisfy himself beyond all doubt, reciting softly:

"It was an ancient Mariner,
And he stopped more than three.
By thy short thin hair and glittering eye,
Now thou hast scuppered me.
With sloping masts and dipping prow,
As one pursued with yell and blow
Still trod the shadow of his foe,
And forward bent his head,
The ship held fast, loud roared the blast,
And homeward aye he sped.
I went like one that hath been stunned,
And was of sense forlorn:
A sadder and a wiser man,
I rose the morrow morn."
With humble apologies to Samuel Taylor Coleridge:
The Ancient Mariner

PS. Not what I originally envisaged.

Raising their glasses they clinked them together.

"To my wife," said Jack, angling his head in a show of affectionate deference.

"To my husband," she replied, grinning mischievously. Then she paused for a second, a slight frown creasing her brow, and Jack had a moment of misgiving as he wondered what next to expect from this intriguing lady.

"Now," she said firmly, a twinkle in her eye, "While I drive you to the hospital, perhaps you can tell me the rest of the details, sweetheart."

Printed in the United Kingdom
by Lightning Source UK Ltd.
111446UKS00003B/46-99

9 781425 906641